**MacAllister . . .**
**Such a Beautiful Hellcat. . . .**

"I'm going for a walk on the beach, Wild Honey. Get to bed." He realized that, more than anything else, he wanted to crawl between the covers with her, feeling the warmth of her nestled softly in his arms. . . .

"Where does MacAllister go?" she demanded hotly.

"I told you. Down to the beach." His voice was more intense than he would have liked.

"Among the Seminoles, my people," she told him, "we cast aside those warriors who will not look upon a woman and share a chikkee with her."

Her eyes looked into his. With a sound that was more closely a groan and a plea, he brought her to him, crushing his mouth against hers, tasting her, feeling her lips yield to his. When he broke away he saw the flush in her cheeks, the way her lips were parted, lifting once again for his kiss.

"What is this when you put your mouth to mine?"

"A kiss, damn you. A kiss. A show of affection, of liking you!"

"I think I like white men's ways. Kiss again, damn you," she mimicked him, lifting her face to his. . . .

**Books by Fern Michaels**

The Delta Ladies
Wild Honey
Without Warning

Published by POCKET BOOKS

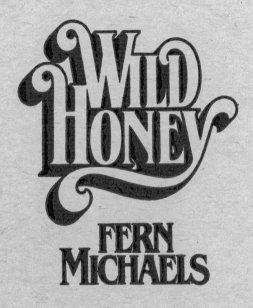

# WILD HONEY

## FERN MICHAELS

PUBLISHED BY POCKET BOOKS NEW YORK

Distributed in Canada by PaperJacks Ltd., a Licensee
of the trademarks of Simon & Schuster, a division of
Gulf+Western Corporation.

Another *Original* publication of POCKET BOOKS

POCKET BOOKS, a Simon & Schuster division of
GULF & WESTERN CORPORATION
1230 Avenue of the Americas, New York, N.Y. 10020
In Canada distributed by PaperJacks Ltd.,
330 Steelcase Road, Markham, Ontario.

ISBN: 0-671-42207-3

First Pocket Books printing November, 1982

10 9 8 7 6 5 4 3 2 1

POCKET and colophon are trademarks of Simon & Schuster.

Printed in Canada

# Prologue

## Alabama—1818

In the deep green forest the late afternoon sunlight slanted downward, piercing the early summer foliage to illuminate the fertile mossy earth. The pungent fragrance of new grasses, still wet with the recent blessing of rain, was light and perfumed, and the tender green shoots were cool and soft underfoot. Tall trees, sycamore, pine and ash, with trunks broader than a man, reached skyward, their lowest branches forming a roof, over a small, grassy clearing.

A bone-handled deer knife found its mark with an accuracy born of long practice. The red-skinned boy grinned, his black eyes filled with mischief. He folded his youthful, muscular arms across his lean chest. "Match my target, brother."

Sloan MacAllister eyed the quivering knife and whooped with laughter. "I'll do better than match it. I'll knock it right off its mark and replace it with mine. Stand back now and watch a true test of skill! When are you going to get it through your head, Osceola, that I am every bit as good as you are? The Indian blood that runs in your veins makes no difference. If only you'd admit the truth," he mocked, "you have white blood also." Not waiting for the usual angry denial whenever he teased his step-brother about his heritage, Sloan's knife sailed through the air and unseated the protruding knife, finding its own mark in the same spot.

"See!" he crowed in delight. "I told you I could topple your knife. Now what have you got to say?"

Osceola flashed a wide smile. "The wind changed;

1

any fool can see that. When will *you* learn?" A long stream of Muskogee words rolled off the Indian lad's tongue. Sloan frowned as he tried to keep up with the rapid-fire epithets.

"Speak English, damn you. The next time you call me a horse's ass will be the last time." Osceola laughed as he sprinted away, daring his brother to chase and track him through the woods in the day's fading light.

Sloan ran in pursuit, his lean, stripling muscles carrying him swiftly and almost soundlessly through the woods circling the perimeter of his father's farm. As he had been taught by his adopted brother, he attempted to pick up some sign, some clue, to the direction Osceola had taken. His piercing gray eyes, sharp and deliberate as a wolf's, strained into the umbrella of dark shadows. The tall, rangy youth brought all his senses into play just as Osceola had taught him. The eye could only see so far; the ear could only strain so hard; but the slightest breeze could carry the scent if the hunter was aware. He moved agilely to flatten himself against a gnarled hickory, and concentrated, savoring the thick woodsy scents around him, the tangy, pungent flavor of the Southern pine, the ripeness of the moss at his feet. And something else. Osceola's body scent; the oil he used to slick down his braids, something the Indian boy had recently started doing. Sloan's nose wrinkled in delighted anticipation as he crouched low. Pacing slowly, cautiously, he stalked Osceola, all senses alert. "Got you!" he shouted with victory as he seized his brother from behind. "I win!"

Osceola shook loose, refusing to allow Sloan to see his dismay. "How? What gave me away?"

"Simple. That grease you plaster on your hair. If it weren't for that grease, I never would have found you. You would have won, brother," Sloan told him honestly.

Osceola punched Sloan's shoulder with good-natured affection, but as he turned away, Sloan caught a fleeting expression of sorrow dimming his smile. Osceola walked abruptly into the sunlight, bare arms hanging loosely at his sides. His black hair shone like the blue hues of a raven's wing. His skin, deeper, more bronze now that summer was upon them, blended into the deerhide vest he wore. Many long nights their mother had sat stitching varicolored beads and intricate patterns onto the tanned hide. As he had been so often lately, Sloan was again aware of the differences between himself and Osceola. Where last year they had been the same height, now Sloan was a head taller than his red-skinned brother. His own hair was the color of newly mown wheat, brilliant and soft, capturing the sunlight and reflecting its brightness. Osceola's was thick and coarse, straight as a fence post and blacker than night. Since the beginning of last winter Osceola had allowed his hair to grow and had abandoned trousers and shirts for breeches of deerskin. They had been together since the age of seven, and until recently Sloan had been unaware of the contrasts between himself and his brother. Of late, other children at the schoolhouse had begun to torment Osceola, calling him names. Battle after battle erupted between the brothers and the other children until the local minister visited the MacAllister farm suggesting that Billy, Osceola's given name, should not return to school but rather be tutored at home.

"I have to speak to you, brother, seriously," Osceola said, his face portraying all the melancholy Sloan had perceived in him.

The pain on his brother's face made Sloan's stomach rumble and squeezed his heart up to his throat. He had known it was coming, this talk, and he dreaded it. He could already feel a sense of loss, the absence of his brother. But it was time. In Indian tradition Osceola had counted his age at fourteen summers, a few months older than Sloan, and manhood lurked on the horizon. Soon, time would call a halt to these games they played, to the sharing and the camaraderie. But it was time. "Do you want to talk here or go back to the house?"

"One place is as good as another. It is time for me to leave here, my brother. Time for me to go to my mother's people. I must take my place among them; it is my destiny. I am not a farmer and I never will be a farmer. This world belongs to you, Sloan, never to me." His black eyes looked so sad, and Sloan felt his breath catch in his chest. "I thought to leave here in two days' time, brother." His words fell with deadly weight.

"I should have known. For weeks now your eyes have been on the eastern sky. The day you made those braids I knew you were planning this. Have you told our mother?" Some desperate hope flickered in Sloan and was immediately extinguished. Osceola's mother, a Muskogee Indian herself, would understand her son's need to take his place as a man among his own people.

Osceola's expression stiffened, forcing himself to relinquish the securities and ties of his youth. He liked it when Sloan referred to Polly as "our mother" even though Polly was actually Sloan's step-mother. "Our mother understands. She will grieve, but knows it is my destiny. She has taught you our ways. Tell me, brother, that you're happy for me and wish me well."

There was pleading in the Indian's eyes—needing Sloan's understanding, and only half expecting to receive it. His decision had been made and his fate was written in the stars. There could never be a life for him in the adult white world. There were too many prejudices, too much hatred for the red man. Perhaps if his hair wasn't quite so black or his skin quite so dusky . . . no, those were the wishes of a child, wanting to change what could not be changed. He was Osceola, son of Polly Copinger, Muskogee Indian. Somewhere, deep within him, was a burning need to belong, to make his mark in the world. Although his own blood father was a white trader and in the one room schoolhouse he was known as Billy Powell, his outward appearance pronounced him an Indian, and only among Indians would he find true acceptance. Bearing a white man's name was useless if you also bore the stamp of a red man on your face. True belonging could only be found among the Indians where he would find a welcome despite the fact he was also the son of a white man. Here, among whites, he would forever be known as a half-breed, always on the outside looking in. Even Polly knew this and understood, reluctantly blessing Osceola's decision.

"But I'm not happy," Sloan bellowed belligerently. "I'm selfish. I don't want to lose my brother. Pa can hardly leave his bed to sit by the fire and may not last through the winter. We're both needed here! Don't you think you owe him something?" he added hotly.

Osceola's eyes left his brother's face, his gaze dropping to the spongy earth beneath his feet. "I am Muskogee."

"Hell you are! You're just as much white as you are Indian!" Sloan raged through his own torment. "Christ, even our mother tells you that she has white blood herself. What about that Scotsman, James McQueen, who was your great-grandfather? And I suppose you're going to tell me that your grandmother wasn't married to a half-breed named Copinger. That was our mother's name before she married your father, William Powell, and now her name is MacAllister since she married *my* father! We are brothers through their marriage. Step-brothers!"

"I am Muskogee." The statement was flat, devoid of emotion. Only his black eyes conveyed the seriousness of his statement. "You forget, brother, my people believe a man to be a member of his *mother's* clan, and home is where the women of his clan live. The mixture of white and Indian blood is not significant. Our mother has always told me that I am Muskogee because she is Muskogee. She is Muskogee because her mother, who married the old white man many moons ago, was Muskogee. She has told me that my blood is Muskogee for more moons than there are leaves on a great tree."

The two boys fell silent for what seemed to them an

eternity. There was more than friendship between them; there was a sharing of roots, the security of a family, a love of brother for brother.

At last Osceola spoke and his words were softer than the autumn breeze filtering through the tree tops. "You are the one who is needed here, Sloan. You will never lose me, brother. If the day ever comes when you need me, you will only have to mention our mother's name, or my own, and my people will be your people. No, Sloan, we will never lose each other."

"Our mother. What of her?"

"I entrust her to you, my brother. She loves you as she loves me. I know you will be good to her. There is no other way for me. Tell me you understand."

Sloan saw in Osceola's eyes the look of a man. He heard the voice of a man. "I understand," he said solemnly, wondering where he drew the strength to give his much loved brother his blessing to leave. "I will be here for our mother. For the both of us."

They embraced, no embarrassment flawing the deep love they felt one for the other. And when the moon slid from its protective cloud curtain, there was a moistness glistening in the Indian's eyes while a lone, shameless tear coursed down the white boy's cheek. Arms wrapped around slim shoulders, the two youths left the woods in silence.

Occasionally a letter would arrive, obviously posted months after it had been written and routed through New Orleans. From time to time a hunting or scouting party of Muskogee would arrive at the MacAllister farm, making their camp fire just outside the barn yard. They would bring Polly news of her son from his new home among the Seminoles deep in the Florida frontier. With stoic grace she would accept gifts of warm leather slippers and handwoven blankets which Osceola had sent her while she listened eagerly to news of her son.

Since the death of his father, Sloan knew that Polly

often entertained thoughts of leaving the farm to join
Osceola in Florida, but she was suffering from rheuma-
tism and the journey was impossible. It was also
unthinkable for her to leave the son who worked the
farm to provide for her. Sloan had come softly into her
heart and dwelled there as tenderly as the son she had
birthed.

The year Sloan turned nineteen Polly died of what
Sloan called loneliness. He buried her quietly and sold
the farm for a dazzling amount of money, half of which
he sent to Osceola. He was not surprised that the young
Indian did not return for the burial. While Polly's
physical body died, her spirit lived on. Osceola grieved,
of that Sloan was certain. One day a lone Indian rider
rode into the farm with a singed feather which he
extended reverently to Sloan. This alone bore out to
the young man the depth of Osceola's grief. No words
were needed.

Carefully, Sloan placed the feather among his important papers and then wrapped them in an oilskin
packet.

It was time for a new life. He had kept his promise to
his brother to care for their mother. This life was over.
It was time to move on.

He didn't look back, nor did he send a farewell to
Osceola. He would never say good-bye to his brother.
They would meet again.

## Alabama

## 1823

The cabin rested on the side of a gently sloping hill,
its roof rising unexpectedly out of the landscape like a
ground hog poking its head out of its burrow. There
was a fire in the hearth and Mama bent over the round
iron pot, stirring their evening meal. Savannah liked
this time of day best of all. Soon it would be dark and

Papa would be coming in from the field, freshly washed from the water basin and strong brown soap Mama kept for him on the front porch. He'd sweep into the room, filling it with his bulk, and grab her into his arms while he kissed Mama.

Savannah was practicing her letters on the small chalkboard, carefully copying from the sample alphabet Mama had drawn for her. The kitchen was thick with the good smell of freshly baked bread and rabbit stew, and Savannah's stomach rumbled expectantly. Wiping her little hands on the blue apron Mama insisted she wear while doing her lessons, Savannah watched out the window, wishing for darkness and Papa's arrival.

Perhaps after supper Papa would play his fiddle and make Mama smile and tap her foot while she rocked near the fireplace doing the mending. Already Mama had shown Savannah several simple stitches and the child was becoming quite proficient on her sampler.

"You shouldn't be daydreaming, child," Mama chided gently. "Soon winter will come and the daylight hours will be short. A child needs bright daylight to see to her lessons if she doesn't want to need spectacles when she's grown."

Savannah giggled as she imagined herself balancing spectacles on her pert little nose. "Papa will be coming in soon. May I set the table for supper?"

Mama laughed. "You're only trying to find some way out of finishing your lesson." She glanced toward the window, the slanting light falling on her face lighting her gray eyes and golden hair. "Does seem as though the day is in a hurry to leave us. All right, wash your hands and do the table. You're six years old now and that's time enough to learn what it takes to keep a house. Won't be too long before you have a home of your own, I expect."

Caroline James looked at her young daughter, her soft glance almost a touch. How pretty Savannah was, and so bright and intelligent. She often wondered if she and Alfred had made the right decision to leave Mobile to eke out an existence on this meager farm in the middle of nowhere. If they'd stayed in the city and Alfred had continued with his position in his father's store, Savannah would be wearing the prettiest frocks and going to school with other children her age. It was important, she knew, for a child to have companionship, something she herself hadn't been able to provide. Since giving birth to Savannah, none of her pregnancies had gone past the fourth month. "Be careful with the platters," Caroline cautioned as she watched the little girl carry the china to the table.

"Yes, Mama. I know, it was a wedding gift to you and Papa. Will I have a wedding and will I get pretty things for my house?"

"Of course you will. Only you mustn't forget that there are many things more important than pretty things. Someday you'll meet someone you'll love just as much as I love your Papa, that's the most important of all."

"Couldn't you love Papa if we had stayed in Mobile instead of coming out here to the farm? Do I remember Mobile?"

"I don't know, Savannah. That's something only you can tell. You were about three and a half when we came out to the farm. Do you remember Grandma and Grandpa James?" Something in Caroline's voice was sad and regretful.

"I remember the letters we get sometimes and their pictures we keep in the Bible right under the picture of you and Papa when you were married."

"But you don't remember them and how much they loved you? Well," Caroline sighed, "that will soon be remedied. Grandma wrote that they'll be coming to see us this Spring."

"Sometimes I think I remember them. But mostly I remember a scary man in a dark coat who was angry. The man hollered at you, Mama, and made you cry."

The child would remember that, Caroline told herself mournfully. How could she not? It had been a terrible scene. Thomas was cruel and sadistic and actually threatened Alfred's life. Poor gentle Alfred, quite ineffectual against his brother-in-law's rage. Thomas had been the primary reason for their leaving Mobile. His interference and hostility was making their lives impossible. She was sure his generosity toward Caroline and little Savannah had been contrived to make Alfred appear a failure in being a provider for his family. Not that she hadn't defended Alfred or Thomas one to the other. But his possessiveness of her was becoming a constant thorn in her marriage. When Alfred said he wanted to try his hand at farming and gave her a choice of going home to Thomas or going with him, Caroline had realized there was no contest. She loved Alfred, his gentleness, his loving nature. Her place was with her husband because that's where she wanted most to be. Thomas had never forgiven her.

Caroline glanced out the window again. The sun was almost set; Alfred should be coming up the path now, a broad grin on his face, satisfied with the day's accomplishments. The farm was going well, and this year they expected to turn a profit. Alfred was even talking about a trip into Mobile sometime near Christmas.

Savannah hummed to herself while she placed the flatware beside each plate when a sound outside the cabin made her silent. She turned quizzically to look toward the door. She hadn't heard Papa come up the path whistling one of the tunes he liked to play on the fiddle. Something, some inner sense, made the hairs prickle on the back of her neck.

Suddenly, the door was thrown open; Savannah saw Mama jump out of her rocker, her hand clutching her throat. The sudden draft of air made the flames in the hearth leap higher and brighter; the bright gingham curtains Mama hung at the windows whipped backward as if they, too, wanted to escape from the horrors that had burst through the door.

The light fell on three Indians dressed in buckskin, their features contorted into frightening grimaces. Low, guttural sounds filled the small kitchen as they spoke to one another, their black, fathomless eyes scurrying like mice around the room. Caroline seemed to gain possession of herself and stood tall, facing them, her hand falling onto Savannah's head as the child buried herself in her mother's skirts.

"What do you want? Go! Leave us!" Savannah heard the authority in her mother's voice, but her eyes were squeezed shut and she dare not look up to see the fiercesome intruders' reaction.

There was another low grunt and her mother was torn away from her shrieking. Hands captured her, holding her, mindless of her kicking and scratching and cries for her mother. The child saw Caroline back across the room, nearing the hearth. The terror in her mother's eyes was communicated to the child. Caroline looked toward the window, a prayer in her eyes that Alfred would come whistling up the path.

"Food, you want food," she croaked in a quivering voice, making motions of eating by bringing an imaginary spoon to her mouth. Her hand reached for the cauldron of boiling stew, the handle of the serving ladle gripped in her fingers. Again, her eyes traveled to the window looking for her husband.

The Indian closest to her seemed to understand this gesture. A cruel, monstrous grin split his face, accompanied by thick, indistinguishable words. In his hand he was holding a chain and cross, the last of the daylight capturing the metal and glancing off it. Caroline nearly swooned; she felt the floor coming up to meet her. Alfred's chain and cross . . . Alfred wouldn't be coming up the path for supper!

The Indian holding the chain closed the distance between himself and Caroline, cornering her between himself and the fireplace. The savage holding Savannah suddenly lunged forward, his treetrunk arm tightening

around the child's middle in a rib crushing vise, making
her gasp painfully, stilling her struggles to run to her
mother's side.

The third Indian, acting on Caroline's distraction,
circled around the table, coming up behind her. But not
quickly enough. In a last act of desperation, her hand,
gripping the ladle, whipped forward, carrying with it
boiling stew which she deliberately threw at his eyes.

A horrible sound echoed and bounced off the walls
as the man clutched his face, doubling over in excruciating pain. The cabin seemed to fill with sound. The
Indian's screams of pain, Caroline's shrieks of terror
and Savannah's throat-tearing cries for her mother.

Savannah was still screaming for Mama when she was
carried outside into the twilight. Mama was lying very
still near the hearth, a bright red ribbon of blood
around her throat. Nearly paralyzed with terror, Savannah was very still, allowing herself to be put atop a
horse, knowing only in the very deepest recesses of her
mind that one of the Indians had climbed up behind
her, holding her in front of him while they rode. Wide,
staring eyes filled the little girl's face as they rode
through the barn yard. The chickens clucked and the
pigs snorted expectantly for their evening slops.

"Papa, Papa," her lips soundlessly whispered as she
recognized a shapeless form heaped near the path. He
was still, so still. Why hadn't he come to help her? To
help Mama? So still.

It seemed forever before the Indian holding her
kneed his pony into action. By this time the man Mama
had thrown the stew at had come out of the cabin, a
cloth tied around his head, covering one eye. He
carried Papa's shotgun from over the mantle and
Mama's bedspread stuffed with household items. The
third Indian had already loaded his pony with food
from the larder and was wiping his mouth in satisfaction
the way Papa sometimes did after eating supper.

Savannah's eyes focused on the cabin, seeing the

light inside become brighter and brighter. Within moments, flames spread to the roof and out the door. Even at her tender age she knew that all that had been was no more. The night seemed to swallow her as she felt the pony move forward, away from Mama and Papa, away . . . away. . . .

# Chapter One

### Galveston—1836

Just off the eastern coast of Texas, placed precariously in the volatile waters of the Gulf of Mexico, the island named Galveston rested in the last light of a setting sun. The month of November was ritually a wet season, and this year was no exception. The winding streets leading from the docks to the soft rise of land on which the main town sat were knee-deep in mud. Several well-traveled thoroughfares were paved with stone, making progress easier, but not the far end of Santabel Boulevard where Annemarie Duval's house was located.

The sky from the south was blackening with the threat of still another rainstorm as Sloan MacAllister picked his way over the high spots from the stables to Annemarie's front door. It would be a relief to sit in front of her fire and warm his icy toes and sample her private store of cognac before going up the long, winding staircase with Beaunell to the warmth of her bed and the heat of her clinging arms. It had been at least two years since he'd seen her, but he knew from the blacksmith, in whose care he'd left Redeemer, that Beaunell Gentry was still in Annemarie's employ.

Puddle jumping his way to the three-storied mansion's front steps, he paused a moment to shake the last remaining droplets from the shoulders of his topcoat and to rake a hand through his thick, light hair, smoothing it into respectability before replacing his wide-brimmed Stetson.

Almost before his hand was lifted from the door it

was opened by a huge negress in a dark dress and white cap and apron.

"Mastah Sloan!" Aunt Jenny cried in surprise. "I nevah did think these old eyes would see your likes agin'. C'mon in, Miss Annemarie's gonna fall down at the sight of you."

Sloan found himself captured in Aunt Jenny's plump arms and squeezed against her massive bosom. "You come at jest the right time, Mastah Sloan. Miss Annemarie is in the parlor and that handsome face of yours is jest what she needs to brighten her day!"

As Aunt Jenny helped him off with his topcoat, her pleasure in seeing him was evident in her dancing black eyes and wide, toothy smile. "Law's sake, if'n you ain't a sight fer sore eyes. Mus' be about two years since Miss Annemarie last throwed your hide outa here. An' if that's a question I sees in your eyes, yes indeedy, Miss Beaunell's still waitin' and a pinin' for you. Lawd, ain't she gonna be glad to have y'all in her bed agin! I always did say you was a right fine lookin' man. Fer a white man, that is," she qualified.

"Aunt Jenny, you never change. Still don't think I'm good enough for you. C'mon, Aunt Jenny," he teased, giving her a salacious wink, "when are you going to take me to that back room of yours and teach me what a woman likes?"

Jenny's laughter resounded through the hallway, her double chins quivering with glee. "G'wan with you! If I ever took you up on that offer, you'd scramble outa here like a dog what's had his tail singed."

"Aunt Jenny! What's going on out here . . . Sloan!" Annemarie Duval stood frozen in the doorway for an instant, long enough for Sloan to see that the two years which had passed since he'd last seen her had left no visible trace. Her white skin, contrasted against her ebony hair, was still luminescent, and her remarkably blue eyes were wide and sparkling with a youth that was no longer hers. She was and always would be, he decided, a beautiful woman, and he regretted, not for the first time, that Annemarie insisted that their relationship remain platonic instead of finding ground on a deeper, more intimate, level.

"Sloan, how wonderful to see you. I can't believe it. But," Annemarie smiled, "I should have known it was you. You're the only one Aunt Jenny crows over. Come in, come in and sit down. We have so much to talk about. Or," she said, winking devilishly, "would you rather visit Beaunell now and talk later?"

"Only if later means you instead of Beaunell. No," he said, not waiting for a response from his beautiful hostess, "I want to have a drink and talk. You can fill me in on what's been going on during my absence. You're the only one I can depend on to give me straight facts." He settled himself on a deep crimson love seat, and fumbled in his breast pocket for a cigar. "Do you mind?" he asked, indicating the cigar.

"Not if it's a good one. Wine, whiskey?"

"Whiskey will be fine. Join me, Annemarie, I don't like drinking alone."

Her long, slender hands poured the whiskey from a crystal decanter. Annemarie sat down across from Sloan and smiled warmly. "I've missed you, Sloan. I miss those long talks we used to have, the long dinners with you falling asleep on this very sofa. Your letters told me how well you were doing in Europe. Did your luck run out, is that why you've come back to the States?" A slender brow lifted in askance, her ruby lips parted to reveal white teeth.

Sloan spread his hands and smiled. Annemarie could always be counted upon to be direct to the point. "You're a good friend, Annemarie. I wanted to see you. I wanted to see Beaunell. I've been gone a long time, too long, I think." He paused a moment, then frowned, and blurted out with more honesty, "I have this gut feeling that something's wrong. I've been in Europe, Russia to be exact. Brought back the most wonderful piece of horseflesh. Name's Redeemer."

Sloan's pride and pleasure in his acquired animal was evident by his broad grin.

"A horse!" Annemarie scoffed. "Why didn't you bring back a wife and give up your wild, whoring life. It's time you settled down, Sloan. One of these days you're going to wake up old and no sweet young thing is going to take a second look at you. Then what will you do?"

"Take Redeemer and ride into the sunset, I expect," Sloan shrugged. "Just a man and his horse. Someone will take pity on me. You'd never cast me out to drift alone, would you?"

"Only if you gave me the bill of sale for your horse. Redeemer, you call him? You obviously set great store by him. What's he like?"

"He's no thoroughbred, that's for sure. He's a little bit of everything, I suspect. I bought him from a Cossack who stole him from some gypsies, or at least that's what he'd have me believe. Annemarie, you've got to see him to believe it. Biggest damn horse I ever laid eyes on. If I were to guess, I'd say he's a mutt breed of Arabian, Russian Cosar and plough horse. A great beast with great heart. Won't let anyone else ride him but me."

"Sloan, you make him sound like a Crusader's destrier."

"In a lot of ways, he is," Sloan told her, beaming with pride.

"It's settled then. I would definitely demand ownership of this Redeemer to look after you in your old age," Annemarie laughed, a quiet, ladylike sound.

"Cold as ever. You always were a shrewd businesswoman. You must be worth a fortune by now."

Annemarie shrugged. "I have a high overhead." Languidly, she waved her hand to call his attention to the lavish furnishings.

Sloan followed her gesture. She kept her establishment in top order, he had to give her that. Like

Annemarie, it was tasteful and expensive. Only the best whiskey and wine were served, and he knew for an absolute fact that she paid her girls well, and when their youth was diminished and they could no longer catch a man's eye, she either pensioned them off or found suitable husbands for them. It was a full-time occupation, according to Annemarie.

In all things, she was a lady of breeding and quality. Born in Atlanta of good family, she married a blue-blooded aristocrat from New Orleans. Childless, bored and definitely out of love with her husband, she became infatuated with a Creole gambler from the low country for whom she gave up everything. She traveled with her lover for several years, learning about the seamier side of life, accepting the fact that she had become a scandal to her family, and was totally ostracized by them. When her lover had met his end at the heated end of a poor loser's pistol, she had taken everything she owned and set up business here in Galveston. With barely enough to set up shop, so to speak, she managed to open her establishment and keep it running productively. The secret, she claimed, was turning people away at the door. Demand for something not readily available always drove the price up. Her taffeta petticoats rustled softly, as she crossed the turkey-red Oriental carpet to sit beside him on the love seat. Her expression underwent a subtle change, and Sloan knew from long association that what she was going to tell him next was serious business.

"Sloan; unfortunately, it would seem, none of my letters ever reached you. In fact, several were returned to me. I know that if you had received them you would have returned home before this. I hope your adventures proved to be profitable, because I have a feeling you're going to need every cent you can lay hands on. Tell me, Sloan, how long has it been since you've been in touch with Osceola?" Annemarie's voice was too intense. Her aquamarine eyes seemed accusing.

At the mention of his brother's name Sloan felt his

stomach muscles tighten. Several years ago, in a particularly nostalgic mood, he had confided his relationship with the Indian to Annemarie. "I docked only hours ago and spent most of that time at the blacksmith's. Then I came straight here. I've heard nothing from my brother for years now."

The last he had heard from Osceola was that he had found a place for himself among the Seminoles in Florida, becoming a member of the nation in full standing because of his marriage to a Seminole widow woman. Some mention had been made at that time that Osceola also hired himself out as a scout to army regiments who were developing forts in the Florida wilderness for the purpose of mapping and charting the area. Sloan also construed from the message that Osceola had decided it was in his own best interest to conceal his affiliations with the white race. The missives were signed in a hastily scrawled B.P., signifying Osceola's given name of Billy Powell. As far as Sloan knew, only himself and Annemarie knew of the Indian's beginnings.

Seeing Sloan's distress, Annemarie's tone softened, filling with compassion. "Your brother and his people are in a great deal of difficulty. All the Seminole nation is. I've tried to help, surreptitiously of course, but it isn't easy. I did it out of my friendship for you, but," she shrugged, "I'm afraid it isn't nearly enough."

"Trouble? What kind of trouble? There's always been bad air between the Seminoles and the United States Government, but nothing the Indians couldn't handle. Since that last disaster they call the Seminole War ended nearly twenty years ago, I had assumed things were under control. Now what kind of trouble?" he barked, almost rearing up from his place beside her.

The aquamarine eyes went momentarily blank. How could he not know? "The newspapers are full of the conflict between the Seminoles and President Andrew Jackson's determination to drive them out of their homelands. For the most part, the general consensus is sympathetic with Jackson, but there's always an acid tongued reporter who dissembles to the Indian plight. I know it's contrived and only for drama, something like the rumblings of the Northern abolitionists, but you know the saying, 'where there's smoke, there's fire.'"

"What kind of smoke?" he demanded impatiently, his broad shoulders hunched, his muscles rigid, ready for action at the word that Osceola was in trouble and might need him.

"They're starving, Sloan. Literally starving. I thought you would have heard something. Somehow gotten your hands on an American newspaper."

"Well, goddamn it, I didn't know! How can they be starving? That's supposed to be rich, fertile land . . . a paradise, grazing land, fishing . . ."

Placing a quieting hand on Sloan's arm, Annemarie said quietly, "Calm down, Sloan. I see I'd better start at the beginning." Taking a deep breath, she began. "The entire drama seems to have begun several years ago, although nothing ever seemed to be reported to the general public. There's a battle on for the Florida territories. Six or seven months after you left for Europe I began reading the first accounts of the Indian situation in the newspapers. When I first learned of the situation, as I've already told you, I managed to send a little help to your brother through a courier. I knew it was something you would have wanted me to do. In fact, I sent it in your name. It was risky, and to this day, I've no idea if the gifts I've sent have ever been received by Osceola. Because of our friendship, I watch the newspapers for the smallest mention of the Seminoles."

"If it's money Osceola needs, then he has it! I was successful in Europe, Annemarie. Especially in Russia. I was offered a chance to buy into some European bank stocks in payment for a gambling debt. It was a lucky break. Right now, I'm sitting pretty and I'm in a position to help. Osceola's problems are over. I'll leave for Florida first thing in the morning."

"Your money is useless. In my opinion the only thing that can help the Indians now is a miracle."

"To hell with miracles, Annemarie, tell me what the hell happened when I was gone. I want to know everything!" he said bitterly.

Sloan grimaced as he once again settled himself beside her, feeling somewhat comforted by the touch of her hand on his arm.

"The Seminoles are on the run, Sloan. They're being forced off their reservation by government land grabbers. They can't farm, they can't hunt and how can they fish when it's forbidden? They receive government rations that are barely adequate and, at best, hardly edible. They break away, go to the swamps and try to eke out a meager existence."

"They can't do that," Sloan pounded his heavy fist into the other palm. "Where do they expect the Indians to go? Where do they want them to live?"

"There's something about them being relocated with the Creeks out in Alabama."

Sloan's face froze into granite lines. "That's impossible. You may not know this, but there's a lot of bad feelings between the Creeks and Seminoles. My brother's people would never consent to that! Who's responsible for that stupid idea?" he asked derisively.

"None other than President Andrew Jackson himself. Bad blood you say? Then that would explain why a contingent of Creek warriors have offered their services to the United States Army. One reporter even accused the government of sanctioning piracy. You see, Sloan, it's understood that enlisted volunteers are entitled to bounty, the spoils, so to speak. Reports have been published that land, cattle and even the blacks who live among the Indians have been taken captive and forced back into slavery."

Annemarie allowed Sloan time to digest this information before continuing. "President Jackson replaced General Scott with Richard Call several months ago and installed him as governor of the Florida territory.

Now, he's combined his civil post with that of commanding a field army. He started a fighting force of over a thousand men, according to reports. Something went wrong with his strategy and his forces dissolved before they could reach the battlefield."

"Battlefield!" Alarm rang in Sloan's voice.

"Are you going to rant and rave, or do you want to hear the rest? The Congress learned how foolish it is to enlist volunteers for only a three-month period, so they've raised it now to twelve months. Governor Call then increased his fighting strength with volunteers from Georgia, Alabama and Tennessee, and succeeded in recruiting Creeks also. Everybody wants anything they can get, all at the expense of the Seminoles. Even the Creeks in Alabama signed a contract to furnish men for service until the Seminoles can be conquered."

Sloan's agitation was evident but he waited for her to continue, to bring him up to date. He was mortified that he hadn't been available to help his brother's people when they most needed it. And the whole time he'd been carousing around Europe having the time of his life.

"Last summer Governor Call's troops fell ill," Annemarie told him. "The Seminoles took the opportunity to store what provisions they could muster somewhere near the Withlacoochee River. Call's driving ambition was to devastate the villages along the river and lay claim to the plunder."

"Well, did he?" Sloan thundered. "Did he succeed?"

"No, he didn't. When he got to the cove, the log villages were empty. In a rage he burned everything to the ground. But he did succeed in one respect. The Indians are now on the run with no place to go, and what little food they had is now gone. They're starving and it's going to be a hard winter for them. No crops, no harvest. But the Seminoles are still resisting and that's something. Several of the letters I sent you contained newspaper clippings. I felt they could say all this much better than I ever could. If you had received them, you would have seen Osceola's name continually mentioned. It would seem that your brother has made a name for himself as a warrior among his people. They refer to him as a chief."

Sloan's mind raced. Twenty years since he had last seen Osceola. What must he be thinking and feeling now? What kind of man had he become to have made his way to the position of chief? Did he feel that Sloan had abandoned him? Sloan hoped not. The bond between them was too strong. "I hadn't the slightest idea that Osceola had become so influential among the Seminoles to be appointed a chief."

"According to accounts," Annemarie volunteered, "this status is fairly recent. There was a small biography concerning him in a New Orleans paper. Apparently, your brother's intimate knowledge of the United States Army, earned while he hired out as a scout, has served him well. I would also gather that he has kept it his secret that he's well versed in the English language. I read something about him using an interpreter named Abraham."

Sloan smiled. "That fox. It would be just like him to pretend ignorance of English. No one is going to pull the wool over his eyes by trying to trick him into something he doesn't fully understand. He probably gets great enjoyment out of watching them try. I can imagine he's thought to be quite wise and cunning among his people."

Annemarie tapped her tooth with her fingernail. "Hmmm. Yes, it would seem to fit. There was something about Osceola attending a treaty meeting as a bystander. Apparently, the army interpreter was translating exactly what he had been told, but there was some behind the scenes conversation between Governor Call and General Scott that contradicted what the Indians were being told. It's said that Osceola rose up and claimed treachery. Another chief attending the

council praised your brother, calling him wise and
brave, and evidently welcomed him into the Seminole
hierarchy of leaders."

"Will you be able to help the Seminoles, Sloan?"
Annemarie asked anxiously.

"Of course," Sloan replied with more confidence
than he felt.

"Then you should know that the man who replaced
Call is a major general with a mixed reputation. His
name is Thomas Sidney Jessup. It's said that Jessup is a
card playing man and likes to play for high stakes."

Steely gray eyes took on a hard sheen as he stared at
Annemarie. "Does he now?" His voice was suddenly
lazy as his mind raced. A poker playing general who
wanted to do Osceola and his people in. Not, by God,
while he had any say in the matter. "I don't suppose
you would happen to know where this Jessup is quartered about now, would you, Annemarie?"

"Indeed, I would. Try New Orleans. The Floridas
are too uncivilized for his tastes." Suddenly, Annemarie's face portrayed her concern. "Sloan, you aren't
thinking of doing anything foolish, are you? I mean,
smuggling foodstuffs into Osceola is one thing, but to
become actively involved is quite another. It's . . . it's
treason!"

"I've been skidding along by the seat of my pants for
some time now, Anne, and I don't suppose now is the
time to worry about it. I've been lucky with my
investments, and I've been lucky at the card table. The
friends and connections I made in Europe were very
helpful with both. There's no reason for me to believe
that my luck is going to run out."

"You're very confident," Annemarie told him. Her
voice was quiet and solemn, betraying her doubts and
fears for this young, virile man who, on more than one
occasion, had proved himself her friend. But then,
Sloan MacAllister had been born confident. He had
proven this when she was having difficulties with old

enemies of the lover for whom she had left her husband and family.

When word broke that Phillipe had met his end in a crooked game leaving Annemarie a healthy stake, the scurves began crawling out of the woodwork. Shortly after opening this establishment in Galveston she discovered her problems weren't nearly over. Sully Birdson, a menacing, evil man, claimed that he held gambling markers belonging to Phillipe which totaled to a huge amount of money. Birdson would content himself with Annemarie's business. If it hadn't been for Sloan, she would have been left with nothing, walking the streets to make a living. Mistakenly, Birdson underestimated young MacAllister's sense of justice, as well as his expertise with a pistol. One foggy night, Birdson expected to dispense with the interfering MacAllister once and for all by ambushing him as he was leaving Annemarie's house. But it was Birdson who died, with a surprised expression on his ugly face.

A spark shot upward in the fireplace and caught Sloan's attention. He stared into the orange flames, eyes narrowed, elbows on knees. How quickly he had decided to aid Osceola in his struggle against the United States Government. It wasn't until Annemarie uttered the word "treason" that he realized the full implications of helping the Seminole. Treason. It wasn't a pretty word. But neither were starvation, or injustice, or landgrabbing, or slavery pretty words. For years Sloan had known that the Seminole gave sanctuary to runaway slaves, and somewhere in the midst of this political genocide grew this ugly issue. It wasn't very difficult to see that the dispersion or annihilation of the Seminole would profit the government and those men who had the most to gain by declaring themselves patriots. If labeling himself a patriot meant he must sit by and watch the extermination of a people, then he preferred treason. There were ways, he knew, to petition Washington, to speak out publicly in favor of the Seminoles, to grease palms and influence the influential. But all that took time, too much time, and there was no guarantee of success, none at all. He only had to think of the support and organization of the Northern abolitionists and their fervor to abrogate slavery to realize how ineffective this course of action would be. And in the meantime Osceola's people would die, victims of government and greed. Osceola's chances for even a small victory would be slim, but at least there would be honor in trying. And Sloan was determined to give Osceola that chance.

Annemarie watched Sloan slump back against the love seat, raising his arms and running his hands through his golden hair. There was an expression of resolution about his mouth. So, he had decided. Osceola would soon be hearing from his brother.

"You're tired, Sloan. Would you like to go upstairs? I have a spare room where you can be alone—sleep. Or are you more inclined to forget your troubles in Beaunell's company?"

A slow smile appeared and Sloan winked at her. "What do you think?"

"I should have known," she laughed, glad to see that he was restored to himself. If Sloan had rejected the offer of Beaunell's company, Annemarie would have been gravely concerned.

He stood, pulling himself to full height, which seemed to dwarf Annemarie's sitting room. "Do you think Aunt Jenny would see to having my clothes laundered? If I'm going to New Orleans I'll have to spruce up a bit."

"I can tell by your sheepish expression that you've already made arrangements to have everything sent up from the ship to be delivered directly into Aunt Jenny's capable hands. Everything will be ready for your trip to New Orleans so you can pretend to be a gentleman acceptable to General Jessup's society."

"That transparent, am I?"

"To me, anyway. I saw the wheels turning in your head when I mentioned the man and his penchant for cards. For now, I think there's someone upstairs who finds you more than acceptable. Even the score for Osceola, Sloan, and tonight is on the house."

Annemarie was speaking of Beaunell, he knew. "Don't get up, Annemarie. I know the way."

Sloan loped up the stairs in search of Beaunell. He deliberately thrust all thoughts of Osceola and the past conversation with Annemarie from his mind. Tonight was his. Tomorrow and every day after would be devoted to helping his brother. He needed this evening. It had been a long time since he'd lain in a woman's arms.

At the top of the stairs he headed toward the guest bathroom, as Annemarie called it. No man, no matter who he was, dared to set foot in one of her beds with one of her girls until he was scrubbed down either by Aunt Jenny or some other house servant. Aunt Jenny always saved her special attentions for Sloan. He groaned as he saw the wicked anticipation in Jenny's eyes. He also remembered her less than gentle touch. No soft washcloth for Jenny. She much preferred a stiff, bristly brush that he knew in his gut Annemarie used to curry her horse.

"Now you just shed all them there clothes and hop in this tub. Ize gonna scrub you till you sparkle. Miz Beaunell is goin' to get the cleanest, ugliest man in this here house."

Sloan obeyed. He always obeyed Aunt Jenny. He also sat very still. "Yo' is goin' brush them there teeth, ain't you, Mastah Sloan? Yo' is goin' shine like a beacon in the night for Miz Beaunell. Miz Beaunell got herself a fancy wrapper all the way from New York."

"It's not her fancy wrapper I'm interested in, Aunt Jenny."

"I know that and you know that, but Miz Beaunell don't know that. She's been prettying herself up ever since she found out you wuz here. You're just like all men, you want soft, silky skin and bones." Sloan felt the brush dig deeper into his back but remained still. He knew better than to speak when Jenny was off and talking up a storm. "Now, you take me; look at all this fat on me. More for old Ezekial to love, I say. We do make those mattress ropes shake. He never go away unhappy." Sloan nodded fretfully as the brush worked its way down his chest.

"You are some kind of woman, Aunt Jenny," he said fervently. "I know you make Ezekial happy. He brags about you all over Galveston."

"He does, does he? And what might he say, Mister Sloan?"

Oh, Christ, now he had gone and done it. "Well, only good things of course."

"What kind of good things?" Jenny persisted. The brush was below his navel now and swirling the suds into a tent of lather.

"About how warm and soft you are. How pretty you are. Why, he said he wouldn't trade you for all the girls in Annemarie's," he added desperately.

Jenny forgot the brush for a minute. "Tell me somemore lies, Mister Sloan. I jest love it when you lie. Here, you can finish your private parts yourself."

Sloan heaved a sigh of relief that he was certain could be heard all the way downstairs. "Hell, Jenny, a man's got to tell the truth when he's talking about a woman and how good she is in bed. Ezekial says you're the best and that's good enough for me."

"You ever have a hankerin' for me?" Jenny asked curiously.

"You're too good for me. Annemarie would have my hide and you know it." Jesus, he was sweating like a pig in summer, and the water was just tepid. He had to get out of here and find Beaunell. This was no time to get caught up with Jenny and her views on men.

Hopping out of the tub, he draped a towel around himself and made tracks for the hallway, calling over his shoulder, "I need my clothes by morning, Jenny. I'm heading for New Orleans at first light."

Jenny nodded, her wide chocolate eyes on the slim hard body beneath the bath sheet. Sloan felt as though he was being chewed alive. He had a feeling he would be if he didn't get out of the bathroom. "I'll settle with you later, Jenny."

He hurried down the carpeted hall, eager to escape Aunt Jenny's clutches, and skidded to an unmanly stop as he approached Beaunell's door. What had Aunt Jenny told him—something about a wrapper all the way from New York? Probably all laces and froufrous, and it would take him an hour to get to the soft, silky skin beneath.

Taking a deep breath, he knocked softly and entered the room without ceremony. Beaunell had lusty appetites, almost as hungry as his own, and she never stood on formality where he was concerned.

She turned to face him, pretending to be startled by his entrance. He knew better. Beaunell had a talent for knowing everything just as soon as it happened. Little vixen, he thought smugly, I can almost smell the lust radiating from her body. The stage was set, he was flattered to see, for his pleasure. The lamp behind her glowed softly, outlining her slim, lithe body beneath the most outrageously red wrapper he had ever seen. Gauzelike, it just skimmed her body, accentuating her shining dark hair and ivory skin. She hadn't changed since the last time he'd seen her. Her small, perfect breasts were thrust upward. Her legs, nicely turned and slightly voluptuous, were exposed between the folds of her wrapper as she stood perched on feathered slippers with incredibly high heels. But it was her smile that entranced him, holding him captive under its spell. She was tiny in stature, but experience had taught him she was a veritable tornado once she found her way between the sheets. A long moment was spent allowing him to drink in the sight of her before she flung herself into his arms, squealing a joyous greeting.

His hands found her breasts, her hips, holding her against him, crushing her mouth with his own. The last thing he remembered saying before Beaunell revealed her full beauty to him was what a lovely dressing gown she wore.

"Sloan," she whispered throatily, allowing his name to fill the room, her being. "Why did you wait so long before you came back to me? I knew you'd come back. I always knew it."

Her perfume engulfed him, setting his pulse racing in a sensuous throbbing that was echoed in his loins. She was beautiful, this little desirable sweetmeat. He wanted to lose himself in her, drink her in. He nuzzled the soft skin at the base of her throat and delighted in hearing her gasp her pleasure. His hands covered her breasts, found her tapering waist, caressed her flaring womanly hips. Every remembered curve and crevice filled him with renewed hunger for her.

She yielded beneath his touch, welcoming him, needing him as desperately as he needed her. Her hands found the smooth muscles of his back, the lean, taut lines of his haunches, arousing him to great heights with her fingers and lips. Sloan MacAllister was an enigma to Beaunell Gentry. She was jealous of the friendship he shared with her employer. Why couldn't Sloan take her into his confidence the way he had taken Annemarie? But it was always to *her* bed that Sloan would finally come, hungry and needing, making love to her as no other man ever had. He knew every pressure point, every caress. She loved the way his hands took possession of her, the way his lips found her most sensitive areas, the strength of him and the weight of him between her thighs.

He was a considerate lover, and there was never a need to pretend satisfaction when she was with him. No other man, not one in hundreds, could leave her panting and breathless and always wanting more. No other man could give her more.

With the perception known only to a practicing

whore, she knew this man appreciated and savored a woman. When Sloan MacAllister made love to a woman, it became art, a deliberate and intense pleasure that left her pulse pounding and blood racing.

She loved it when he crushed her in his arms, holding her prisoner, touching and kissing her, demanding to be loved in return. When she was in his arms this way, she could forget all her jealousies and grievances, and just love him. For the moment Sloan was hers and that was all that mattered.

Sloan pulled her atop of him, demanding she seek her own pleasure, helping, thrusting while she rode him in a wild rhythm in which ecstasy was its own reward. Her thighs gripped his haunches, applying and releasing pressure. Her body was sacrifice to his touch, her breasts, her hips, the place where their bodies met and became one. Sloan's eyes locked with Beaunell's, watching her, enjoying her passion, reveling in it.

Tremor after tremor seized her body. Bold, shameless eyes gazed into his. At last, body arching, head thrown back, she groaned with relief that she had captured the sensual gratification she had been chasing.

Slowly, deliberately, Sloan seized her by her firm, white buttocks and rolled her over, following her with his body, keeping himself deep between her soft, gripping thighs. He buried himself in her, taking his pleasure of her, moving in slow, unhurried thrusts. Imperceptibly, his movements quickened, making her gasp, pulling his name from her lips in a deep, contented groan.

Beaunell drew in her breath and writhed sensuously beneath him, meeting each thrust with one of her own. Her body glistened with a veil of perspiration and she reached up to grasp handfuls of his golden lion's mane. She cried out in a voice that was more animal than human, "Love me, Sloan, love me!"

He reached beneath her, lifting her tight, white bottom, savagely bringing her to him.

Their lust for each other blazed and their bodies sought to quench its devouring flames.

They slept, Sloan with his head nestled between Beaunell's soft, full breasts. Twice during the night he woke to stifle the pleas of desire whispered in his ear. At first light he was about to slip from the warm bed when Beaunell pulled him backward. He groaned inwardly. She was insatiable, among other things.

Long, silken strands of hair fell over Beaunell's cheeks as she leaned toward Sloan. Her heavily fringed sapphire eyes were tear-filled, purposely so. "Sloan, take me with you to New Orleans. It's time I thought about leaving this place. I can arrange it with Anne-marie."

Sloan was startled. And here he had thought all she wanted was another go-round on the sheets. If there was one thing he didn't need now, it was Beaunell trailing him all over New Orleans. He realized he had to be careful, not make his denial seem an outright rejection. Gently, he cupped her delicate oval face in both hands. Hell, what was one more lie. "There's nothing I would like better than to take you with me, little chicken, but I can't. I have Indian business to take care of. Now, you wouldn't want one of those savages to get their hands on your lily white body, would you?" At her blank look he posed another question, "Or would you?"

"I'm not a fool, Sloan. New Orleans is civilized. I hardly think I would be attacked by savages in your apartments. You're wealthy now. Aunt Jenny told me all about your time in Europe and how you're into the banking business. You have your own ship now. You can afford to take care of me and buy me the finery I like. Why can't you be as good to me as I've been to you?"

Sloan felt an itch start between his shoulder blades. Why did women always have an ulterior motive? Why couldn't women just accept what they had and let it go at that? Why did they always want to get married and settle down? Beaunell was right about one thing, she was no fool. And he would have to be very careful when he answered. "Look, Beau," he said tenderly, "I'm not the marrying kind. If I was," he added hastily, "you can be sure you would be my first choice. Would you be prepared to hang up all this finery, give up this glamorous life, give up meeting all the rich, fancy men who come in here and give you presents and perfume? No girl in her right mind would want to part with all of this." He hoped he sounded convincing. She was thinking. He didn't know if that was good or bad.

"That doesn't make any sense, Sloan. You're wealthy now; why would I have to give up the finery? You could buy me presents. I know I'm not a very good cook, but I could learn or you could hire servants."

Sloan heard a whining threat in her voice. Goddamn women, they were never satisfied. You bought them a horse and the next thing they wanted a carriage. You took them to bed, enjoyed each other's passions and they demanded marriage. He conveniently ignored the fact that he had taken to Beaunell's bed many times over a five-year period of time. A fact of which she quickly reminded him.

"Honey, I would like to stay and argue with you, but I can't. I really do have pressing business in New Orleans. I can't even promise when I'll be back." Without another word he was off the bed and dressing.

"Damn you, Sloan, is there someone else? Are you ever going to marry me?"

"No, there is no other woman in my life. You know how I feel about marriage." Hell, he could do worse than Beaunell. But he had to be realistic. If he ever did marry her, she would probably kill him by the end of the first year. A smirk of pleasure played around his mouth as he flexed his muscles. He wondered what they would put on his grave marker. Died in his bed? Died smiling?

He didn't like the sudden, calculating look in Beau's

eyes. She was up to something, planning something that was going to blow an ill wind in his direction. "Tell you what, Beau. Here's two hundred dollars. You buy yourself whatever pleases you, and when I get back, we'll do this town up right. I've been thinking of setting you up in an apartment," he added rashly as he slipped into his jacket. The calculating look was rapidly turning murderous. He swallowed hard as he measured the steps to the door. Thank God Aunt Jenny had hung his clean clothes on the hook outside the door sometime in the wee hours of the morning. The rest of his baggage should be waiting near the front door. Breakfast suddenly seemed like a poor idea.

"Damn you to hell, you bastard! Set me up in an apartment!" Beaunell shrieked, in outrage. "But you won't marry me, is that it? I'm not good enough to marry, is that it? Well, let me tell you a few things. You were nothing but a clod farmer with dirt between your toes when you first came here. You didn't know the first thing about making love to a woman. I taught you everything you know. You had the fastest, clumsiest hands of any man who ever crossed Annemarie's doorstep. You're a bastard. You led me to believe that when you got back we would get married. Why did you lie to me?" she continued to shriek.

Sloan shrugged as he inched closer to the door. "It seemed like the thing to say at the time," he defended honestly.

"Get out of here," Beaunell screeched. "Now!"

A look of disgust washed over Sloan's face as he exited the room in a near frenzy. A tear or two would have made it all believable. Not that he could blame her. He *was* a rotter. A bastard. He deftly added another hundred to the amount on the dresser. By noontime Beau would hardly remember his name as she tripped from store to store in search of the finery she loved. Love, bah! Marriage? Never!

# Chapter Two

Sloan MacAllister took in the remembered sights and sounds of his favorite city. New Orleans. Colorful, bewitching, wicked New Orleans. Street vendors hawked their wares on busy corners, their voices lifting in a lilting patois that was somewhere between French and English. It belonged only to this magical city set between the blue-green waters of the Gulf of Mexico and the murky, gray fog over Lake Ponchartrain. Even the air was different here—perfumed with the flowers of a thousand gardens and smoky cook fires wisping up the chimneys.

It felt good to be back here. He felt alive and eager, as he contrived a means to make contact with Brevet Major General Thomas Sidney Jessup. If he was lucky, and he usually was, he would be sitting across a poker table from the general this very evening. He intended to become quite good friends with the general by making sure Jessup would go home with a considerable chunk of his bankroll. Experience told him that beating a man hands down at poker never encouraged his friendship.

He cut a fine figure as he strolled along Saint Mark's Place. Aunt Jenny had worked wonders pressing his European tailored suits and had laundered his shirts to an elegant whiteness. The diamond stickpin in his silver-gray cravat and sapphire pinky ring were exactly correct. They spoke money, not too loudly, but loud enough to hint at a healthy bankroll, all of which would

find a new home in Jessup's hip pocket. But first things
first.

At the top of the list was registering at a respectable
hotel and having his baggage brought up from the
docks. Secondly, accommodations must be found for
Redeemer, and last, but not least, he would inquire,
discreetly, of course, the whereabouts of Jessup and see
to it that he was included in the general's next game of
chance.

This last, he expected, would be quite simple. Any
man with a known appetite for poker was always eager
to prove himself against a professional gambler. For the
time being, that was exactly how MacAllister intended
to present himself.


General Thomas Sidney Jessup, in full uniform, sat
in the library of his rented house on Magnolia Street,
looking approvingly across his massive desk into the gilt
mirror on the far side of the book-lined room. He
deliberately lifted the corners of his mouth into what
passed for a smile. He liked to think of this as his pose
for his Presidential portrait. Other military men had
made it to the country's capitol, why not himself?

Jessup was as American as apple pie or, in the
analogy he preferred, the Winchester rifle. An American, that's what he was. Staunch, upstanding, fighting
for the right of good over evil. He had insisted that his
rented house be in the American side of the city rather
than in the glamorous French Quarter where some of
the wealthiest and most influential people in New
Orleans resided. An all-American. And now, at last, he
had the opporunity to be of some real value to his
country. To say nothing of the advances it could mean
in his own career and his future political ambitions.

Before he'd taken over command of the Florida
forces from that procrastinating fool, Richard Call,
who had botched things with the Seminoles so badly,
Jessup had been transfered from one Indian War to
another. A flare-up among the Creeks in Alabama the

previous spring had produced a near panic in Washington, fear rising that the Seminoles and the Creeks would forego the hostilities between them to reinforce one another. Accordingly, commanders in the Creek country were ordered to seal off the routes from Alabama to Florida.

It had been early May when Jessup had been sent to take command against the recalcitrant Creeks, but he had hardly had his tent pitched when Winfield Scott arrived from Florida to supersede him and steal his thunder as senior officer. Even now, Jessup's face drew down in a scowl at the reminiscence. He had finally been given the opportunity to prove himself only to find a fool like Scott standing in his way!

Scott, with his usual fetish for details, was using Georgia as a staging area where he was trying to assemble enough men and material to crush the Creeks. He offhandedly ordered Jessup to pass on into Alabama to assume command of the Alabama troops and to be prepared to later join in a converging movement against the Indians.

Join, indeed! Jessup glowered at his own reflection in the mirror. It should have been *his* command, *his* glory! Victory would have assured him favor with the President and his cabinet, and it was no mean feat to bask beneath the favorable eye of Andrew Jackson.

Bitterly, Jessup recalled how he had followed Scott's orders, to the point of making contact with the Alabaman militia.

Once taking command, he made sure those Alabama hillbillies knew they were under orders from a first-rate military man. With an iron hand he had moved his troops into the field and began operations without notifying Scott.

Scott sent a letter by Indian runner through hostile territory and it reached its destination the next day. ". . . I desire that you stop all offensive movements on the part of the Alabamans until the Georgians are ready to act!"

Jessup later claimed that he had not kept Scott informed because of the press of responsibilities; he had not averaged three hours sleep out of twenty-four in two weeks. But in his written response to Scott he excused himself by claiming he had acted because the situation demanded it. "I have none of that courage," he wrote in his best hand, "that would allow me to remain inactive when women and children are daily falling beneath the blows of the savage."

This, Scott knew, was an excuse. He was well aware of Jessup's hatred for the Indians, having heard somewhere that Jessup's only sister was murdered in a massacre and his six-year-old niece had never been found. A personal tragedy, but the battlefield was no place for a man with prejudices that clouded his duty. With this knowledge and with private suspicions that Jessup was trying to take full credit for subduing the Creeks, Scott fired off another letter. "Who gave you the authority to roam at pleasure through the Creek nation?"

When Jessup read the latest letter the blood pounded between his ears. The audacity of the man! Commander or not, Jessup was determined to take this opportunity to prove his military strategy and strike a heavy blow against the Indians. He hated the red man with zealous fervor. All red men.

Jessup had fifteen hundred Indian warriors with him, Creeks fighting Creeks as usual, who would defect if he hesitated and waited as Scott had ordered; he also had to keep moving to retain the Alabama militiamen. He decided to advance, in spite of Scott's order and, by doing so, he secured a good many prisoners.

A second order came from Scott. Not daring to disobey again, Jessup halted his force and hurried off to Fort Mitchell to confront Scott. Unable to locate his commander, he wrote another message smoothly stating his belief that if Scott would make his move the war could be won before the next night. Realizing Scott's suspicions, Jessup added that he was not ambitious of the honors of Indian warfare and merely felt he could prevent the escape of the enemy, suggesting that if Scott were to attack from a frontal position the honor would belong to him.

"Again that addlepated malingerer failed," Jessup swore beneath his breath, conscious of the aide-de-camp stationed outside the library door. Reflexively, his fist smashed down on the desk. "We could have had them! We could have annihilated them all!"

In red-faced fury he shuffled through the papers lining his desk top. With a thin-lipped grin, he recalled the stir his letter to the editor of the *Washington Globe* had created. Francis Blair was a political crony of President Jackson's, and Jessup knew the Commander in Chief would be apprised of its contents. He had accused Scott of delaying the battle that would have terminated the war and saved the government hoards of cold, hard cash. He painted himself in the most favorable light, claiming that the success of his progress was terminated by orders from Scott—progress that would have tranquilized the entire American frontier.

"Eight days," Jessup chortled, "only eight days and Scott was ordered to transfer command of the Creek country to me!" It had been a stroke of genius to write to Washington. And Scott, ignorant of the letter, had believed Jessup had acted in good faith. At least until he was recalled to Washington where he learned of Jessup's letter to Blair. His gorge rose and he called the letter a treacherous instrument that had stabbed him in the dark.

Jessup laughed aloud. From that moment the war between Scott and Jessup was on, but Jessup emerged clearly as the victor.

"And that pompous fool calls me shifty," Jessup sneered once again into the mirror, admiring his steady, intelligent eyes and prominent square jaw emphasized by prematurely white hair. "Whatever name he puts to me, I'm the man Washington judged most able to run the Florida War!"

The aide-de-camp standing just outside the library door shifted uneasily from one foot to the other. The general was alone in the library, he knew, and it always sent chills up his spine to hear the officer laugh so uproariously to himself.

Sloan ordered whiskey neat and gulped it down. He ordered another and carried it to a small table in the lounge of the hotel. Damn, it had been three days since he'd arrived in New Orleans. Three days of letting everyone know he had a more than adequate bankroll and would be willing to part with it in a poker game. If he didn't receive an invitation from Jessup soon he would have to take other measures. According to the hotel desk clerk, General Jessup hosted a high-stakes poker game every Friday evening. This was Friday. A new man in town with money was always invited, or so said the desk clerk. Sloan was just about to grab the man by the scuff of the neck and demand his twenty dollars back when a messenger came up to him and handed him a sealed envelope. Sloan tipped him and noted the smirk on the desk clerk's face.

Sloan read the terse invitation. If he cared to attend, he was invited to Brevet Major General Jessup's home for a game of cards. Refreshments, cigars and chips would be provided. Game to begin promptly at eight o'clock. There was no mention of how many others would play or what the stakes would be.

Sloan smiled. There were few situations in poker that could surprise him. There were few tricks he couldn't sniff out. He had learned at the hand of a proficient teacher, Annemarie. The lady had taught him all she had learned during her years with Phillipe, one of the most successful Mississippi gamblers. Sloan had sharpened his abilities on some of the best cardsharps in Europe. After being fleeced on numerous occasions, he quickly realized an honest game of poker was a rarity.

Knowing that a smart man always played by existing rules, Sloan had taken to do a bit of fleecing himself.

Bathed, shaved and dressed in a carefully chosen somber suit and subdued burgundy brocade waistcoat, Sloan made his way down the magnolia-lined street. Promptly at eight, he dropped the knocker against a heavy brass plate. The door was opened by a slim negro youth dressed in white livery. He reached for Sloan's hat and then ushered him into the library.

A balding, white-haired man in uniform walked toward him and extended his hand. Sloan disliked him on sight. Shifty was the description that popped into Sloan's mind, after noting the beady, snake eyes, deep wrinkles and a severe slash for a mouth.

"General Thomas Jessup," the man introduced himself in a rasping authoritative voice. "And you are Sloan MacAllister, I presume."

Leading him to a round table arranged in front of a fireplace, Jessup made the introductions. "Our leading banker, Mr. Calvin Willer, on his left Mr. Nathaniel Devereau, cotton broker and owner of one of the largest plantations in Louisiana. Here, on my right is Major Henry Cooper." Obviously, Jessup was, among other things, a social climber, given to surrounding himself with wealthy, influential people. "Gentlemen, Mr. Sloan MacAllister. You've recently returned from Europe, if my sources are correct."

"Correct," he admitted, watching a slow, serpentine smile widen the general's thin mouth.

"And I trust you've brought some of that European money home with you? We always like fresh money, MacAllister. Can't guarantee you're going to leave with it. We play for money and blood."

Sloan grinned, acknowledging the general's statement. "It's the only way to play." His eyes went to Major Cooper who was dangling a gold watch fob in his right hand. Sloan wondered where a man like Cooper would get the money to sit in a high-stakes poker game. His insignia said he was a cavalry man. Why would

Jessup allow a common horse soldier to sit in on one of his games unless, of course, it was rigged to the general's advantage.

It was Jessup who assigned the positions at the table, and it was Jessup who motioned for Cooper to sit directly across from him. Sloan immediately picked up the odd arrangement of furniture in the room. Either Jessup was a very vain man or the many mirrors had other functions. Small tables with assorted bric-a-brac cluttered the room. He wondered vaguely if there was a Mrs. Brevet General. Not likely, the room was a horror. Tall brass vases that were shiny as mirrors sat on both ends of the marble fireplace. They held nothing. They were also out of place.

Sloan sat down and bought his chips; all his senses alert to pick up the slightest irregularity.

"Jacks or better," Jessup said as he waited for the others to buy their chips. The going stake seemed to be a thousand dollars. Sloan anteed up and took possession of the small stack of chips. The military must be paying well these days, or else he was getting a bonus for Indian scalps, Sloan thought sourly.

Within minutes, a fog of thick gray smoke circled toward the ceiling. Sloan played clumsily, deliberately losing to Jessup. He enjoyed the greed in the beady eyes as the general used both hands to pull his chips toward him. In true green-horn style he lost three games, won a small hand and lost three more. There was no small talk as the men slid cards to the middle of the table. He noticed that when Jessup was ready to bluff he clamped his cigar between his front teeth. Cooper sucked on the spit he allowed to accumulate in his mouth and then spit it out into the spittoon at his feet. They were a team, there was no doubt about it. Not that he cared.

He was here to ingratiate himself, to be seen in the general's company, to be accepted and hopefully somehow, to pick up some vital information. It would be good for Jessup's ego to blather around that he had milked a professional gambler. He, in turn, would say that the military man was just too good for him and come back to lose another thousand.

Jessup was a cheat. An obvious cheat. Sloan would stake his life that the Friday night card game would become a Monday and Wednesday night game as long as his money held out. They were amateurs, the lot of them, hardly worth the trouble and effort. His attention wandered as the men made their bids. Between the two brass vases on the mantle stood a portrait of a beautiful blonde woman. Too young to be Jessup's wife. He wondered who she was.

He had lost another hand, to Jessup's delight.

"What do you say to some refreshments and a stroll outside. The room is smoky. Cooper, open the windows and serve the whiskey. Bad night, MacAllister," he said slyly, turning his attention to Sloan.

"It happens that way sometimes," Sloan said nonchalantly. "I've been in Europe too long. You gentlemen are perhaps a little too good for me."

"Come now, MacAllister, are you telling us that we have those European gamblers beat to hell and back? Why, we're nothing but country bumpkins when it comes to cards. Hell, man, this is just a friendly little game. We do like our cards. Matter of fact, we play on Mondays sometimes when military business is slow. Would you care to join us and maybe win back some of your losses this coming week?" His voice was oily, unctuous, and grated on Sloan's nerves.

"If it's an invitation, I'd be more than glad to join you." He pretended not to see the amused looks on the other men's faces. "Tell me, General, who is the lovely woman who adorns your mantle? Your wife?"

"My sister," Jessup replied curtly. "Are we all ready for some air?" As an afterthought, he turned to Sloan. "Caroline was murdered in Alabama by marauding Indians."

As the men strolled the grounds in the brisk chill of late evening, Sloan tried to draw Major Henry Cooper out concerning the Seminoles. "What's the military's next move? Do the poor bastards have a chance against your forces?"

Major Cooper laughed, "Hardly, at least not with General Jessup in command. There's no organization among the Seminoles. They're spread all over Florida, which, I admit, makes it difficult for us, but it also puts them at a disadvantage. They work as independent groups instead of a single force. And each separate group seems to have its own chief. Actually, the army is only dealing with the chiefs who are in the vicinity of our established forts. Although, to their credit, they do seem to appoint intelligent leaders to speak for their people. In the St. Augustine area on the eastern coast, there's Phillip. *King* Phillip, if you would," Cooper said laughing. "Now, he's a wily old fox. We know he's at the center of the uprisings we're having in that area. Coacoochee is his son, a warrior; we'd love to get our hands on that troublemaker."

Sloan allowed the major to talk, inserting his own opinions of the Seminoles, listening intently for Osceola's name to enter the conversation.

"On the west coast," Cooper informed him, "where we've been most successful in establishing forts, there's an old man called Arpeika. Some say he's a medicine man, whatever the hell that is. He's got to be the oldest man alive. And a pain in the ass he is. We're hoping to have more luck with another thlacko, that means chief in Seminole, by the way," Cooper told Sloan, wanting him to believe he was conversant in the language.

Sloan drew deeply on his cheroot, casually exhaling the fragrant smoke, his heart beating expectantly for the sound of his brother's name. "Who is this Indian? Have I seen his name in the papers?"

"More than likely. Some of the correspondents seem to think he cuts a romantic figure. His name is Osceola. Young, quite presentable, by Indian standards of course. About your age, I'd say. In my opinion, this Osceola is going to be the man of the hour. He seems to command a good deal of respect among his people because the old man Arpeika has more or less taken him under his wing and sanctioned him. Wish we knew more about this Osceola; perhaps it would be useful in convincing him to move out of the territory and take his scruffy lot with him." Cooper spit into the bushes. "I'll tell you one thing; if anyone can move those savages out of Florida, it'll be General Jessup. Never saw a man who hates Indians more than the general. Mark my words, MacAllister, if the general has anything to say about it, the Seminoles are an extinct people."

At midnight the game ended with Sloan the clear loser to the tune of fifteen hundred dollars. Twelve hundred found its way to Jessup's pocket with the remaining three hundred sitting neatly in Major Cooper's pocket. Not bad for an evening's work. Arrangements were made for the following Monday. The game to be played again at Jessup's house.

"Good meeting you," Jessup held out his hand. Sloan fought the urge to belt the man right between his eyes. Instead, he smiled and made inane remarks about recouping his money come Monday.

"Cooper, find that blasted dog and walk him outside till he does what he's supposed to do." To Sloan, he added, "Damn fool dog is so fat he can barely walk. If you don't walk him on a lead, he sits down and goes to sleep. I should have him shot and put out of his misery like those goddamn Seminoles."

Sloan attended six more fleecings, six more poker games at the general's home. He was forced to admit to himself that he would never learn anything from Jessup concerning future strategy against the Seminoles. The man was quite professional and staunch when it came to military information.

This would be Sloan's last chance to gather any crumb of information. Jessup should be at home this evening since it was Tuesday and between poker sessions. Sloan grinned in the darkness. He imagined that every time Jessup clapped eyes on him he was trying to decide just how much more of a seemingly endless bankroll he could gouge out of MacAllister in future games.

Nestling the bottle of aged plum brandy under his arm, Sloan pounded the door knocker.

General Jessup himself answered the door and was more than a little surprised to see Sloan standing in the stream of light shedding through the doorway. "Mac-Allister, what brings you here?" His keen, shifting gaze fell to the brandy bottle.

"I came to say good-bye and to offer this excellent brandy in thanks for your hospitality."

Dismay was written on the general's face. "You're leaving? Come in, come in. We'll have a drink together." Turning quickly, to hide his disappointment, the general led the way into the library. He had taken this golden goose for a hefty sum, and there was more for the taking, he was certain of it. He almost snorted in disgust at the title Sloan had bestowed on himself—professional gambler. If the good-looking man was a "professional," then he himself was Andrew Jackson.

MacAllister watched with amusement as Jessup poured a stingy amount of the plum brandy into a large snifter. His own was filled a full inch higher.

After the first glass of brandy, Jessup declared it a too sweet drink and brought out a bottle of his favorite rotgut whiskey, known in the cavalry as horse liniment. Sloan sipped cautiously and watched Jessup down glass after glass. Once he saw the glassy, marble eyes start to twitch, he started to ask what he hoped were leading questions concerning the Indians.

"It's obvious there is little sympathy for the Seminoles in the Floridas," Sloan said quietly, conversationally. "I've been following the newspaper accounts, and only once in a great while is anything mentioned about the Indian side of the argument."

"They're goddamned savages is what they are," Jessup growled, slurring his words. "They should be slaughtered the day they pop out of their dog mother's womb!"

A sudden surge of rage made Sloan's fingers clench the glass in a white-knuckled grip. The pig! As if he knew anything about Indian women or the loving, gentle-natured mothers they were. He struggled to contain his temper and pretended to be sympathetic with the general's feelings.

"They *should* be slaughtered, the way they slaughtered my sister. Murdered her, you know. Her and her husband. I told Caroline not to follow that stupid bastard into Indian country. But would she listen to me? No. And she paid for it with her life. She had a daughter. A little girl who looked just like Caroline. The child, Savannah, was never found. Damn dirty Indians killed my baby sister. If it's the last thing I ever do, I'll annihilate those red-skinned savages." He drank greedily and poured his tumbler half full. His small round eyes were closing sleepily.

This wasn't enough, MacAllister told himself. If Jessup fell asleep, all hope would be lost of learning anything of his military plans in Florida. Having witnessed the general's excitement when he spoke of his sister Caroline and her young daughter, he persisted in keeping the subject open. "Are you speaking, sir, as a soldier or a man whose sister and child were . . ."

"Say it! Say they were slaughtered. Massacred. And my niece never found. Those savages are responsible for that and they'll pay. As long as there's breath in my body, they'll pay. The Bible teaches: An eye for an eye! They'll pay. I'll see to it!"

"How?" Sloan asked bluntly.

"By the most expedient method, of course," the general told him. "Divide and conquer. The Seminoles are in for a rough winter. We've seen to that. They'll starve for certain unless they throw themselves on my mercy." Sloan noted wryly that Jessup considered it *his* mercy that would or would not save the Seminoles. The audacity of the man!

"Also," Jessup continued, "I've asked Washington to deploy more troops into the area. They'll be outnumbered three to one before we're done. Naturally, it's President Jackson's hope the Seminole will surrender and join the Creek nation. I hope for this myself. Get them all in one place, I say, and it'll be my pleasure to massacre them!" He took a deep swallow from his glass.

"General, you speak of divide and conquer. How do you plan to achieve this?" Sloan's tone was casual, yet it held enough of a challenge to force Jessup's answer.

The general leaned forward, elbows on knees, the snifter balanced in his hands. "How long do you think the Indians will follow their chiefs if they're starving and sick? When they watch their children dying before their eyes, they'll come to their senses. Another thing, I've more or less given my sanction for any whites in the territory to claim any property, livestock and slaves they feel were stolen from them by the Seminoles. And to claim it by any method that seems appropriate at the time."

Sloan understood. Open season on the Seminole had been declared. White farmers in the area might find it tempting to acquire a new cow or slaves under full protection of the law. All they had to do to receive this protection was to kill a few Seminoles in the process. Bitter gall rose into Sloan's throat and he had to choke it down. If he had had any doubts about sacrificing his patriotism to help Osceola, they were gone. Jessup's policies were those of the United States and they disgusted him, totally repelled him. After a long moment, he spoke. "Major Cooper told me of a Seminole called Osceola. From what the major said, I'd count this Osceola to be a man of extraordinary strength and wisdom."

"Bah! Cooper believes that rot those newspaper correspondents sell papers with. . . . Osceola is no different from any other redskin. He's weak and stupid, and from what I hear, he's as used to a full belly as any other man. As a matter of fact, I might use this Osceola to convince the Seminoles under him to move out of the Florida territory. If one group leaves, you understand, the rest will follow like sheep."

Sloan put his glass to his lips to hide the smirk he knew was forming there. Jessup had quite a surprise coming to him if he thought Osceola would give up so readily. "When do you leave for Florida, General? I may find myself back in New Orleans before too long to try to win back some of my losings. You will give me an opportunity, won't you?"

"I'll be leaving for Florida shortly. When I've strengthened my forces. Yes," he brightened, "I'd be glad to give you a chance to recoup your losses. I'll be here another few weeks, at any rate. There are supplies being sent down from Washington, and I must be here to receive them. Then I'll be off to a place in central Florida called Silver Springs. We intend to try another treaty with the Seminoles. I expect I'll be meeting this upstart, this Osceola, face to face."

This was all Sloan needed to know. Osceola would be somewhere in the Silver Springs area. Annemarie had said the newspapers reported he was somewhere on the Withlacoochee River. With the general's information he could pinpoint the area where he could find his brother. Testing his luck again, Sloan pressed for more information. "What do you think this treaty will accomplish?"

For an instant it appeared the general was about to answer his question. Then, drawing himself into military attention, "A good soldier never reveals his strategy. Never!"

Sloan's mouth gaped as he watched Jessup's position falter. Jessup attempted to straighten himself, failed miserably and slid from his chair onto the floor. MacAllister grinned. He'd once seen a girl in Annemarie's, named Rowena, do exactly the same thing. It had taken them nearly three days to drive the liquor out of her. Damn rotgut whiskey. It would be days before he got the taste out of his mouth.

Standing over the general's prone figure, MacAllister was tempted to at least lift the man back onto his chair. On second thought, he decided, a night on the cold, hard floor would do the man some good. Get him used to the rigors he'd be facing in Florida. The general considered the frontiers of Florida to be too uncivilized and preferred the comforts of his home in New Orleans whenever possible. His lame excuse was that messages from Washington were more quickly relayed to New Orleans than to the wilds of the southernmost territory.

Sloan was almost to the door when he turned. He'd be damned if he would leave a good fourteen-year-old brandy for that swine. Corking the bottle tightly, he carried it in the crook of his arm and left the house.

The following morning after breakfast Sloan read the latest newspaper, his teeth clenched tightly. His meal lay forgotten, congealing in bacon grease. One large fist pounded the table, setting the cream pitcher dancing. Jessup's words of last night were coming true. Seminoles were reported to be stealing chickens, cattle and anything else they could get in their hands. The farmers were organizing with army troops to recover their goods, or if that was impossible, retribution. Retribution, Sloan scoffed. Retribution in the form of slaves, most likely. A good slave was worth six cows many times over. Open season on the Seminole had been declared. All in the name of justice when, in reality, it was greed. Greed. A greedy government that wanted to give white settlers an incentive to remain in the Florida territory.

And who wouldn't be tempted to steal—when they were starving, and watching their children die of hunger? Any man would—white, red, black *or* yellow. His anger threatened to choke him. By God, he wasn't going to waste another minute. He tossed a few bills on the table and stormed out of the hotel dining room.

Two hours later he was watching the last sack of corn being weighed and hauled into the hold of his ship, the *Polly Copinger*. He'd named the ship in honor of the only mother he'd ever known. She was a sturdy vessel, sporting twin masts and a high, proud bow. Her origin was Portugal, and she was well caulked and ready to sail the blue waters of the Gulf. You're going home, *Polly*, he said silently. To Florida. Sail swiftly and steadily. Your people need you.

The pack mules were readied at the smithy to be taken aboard ship. Several goats were also standing in wait, used for the tranquilizing effect they had on horses and mules at sea.

By the time he signed out of the hotel and paid his bill, the stores for Osceola would be stowed. They could sail on the next tide.

"Three hours to high water, Laddie."

The voice belonged to Captain Enwright Culpepper, a salty old man who could spit whiskey and reef a sail at the same time. A Scotsman, he was spare with his words, but Sloan had come to depend upon his friendship and expertise at the helm.

"We're ready and waiting, Captain. I hope none of the crew decided New Orleans was more alluring than shipping out. This isn't the time to go about trying to round up a crew." Sloan scowled.

"Not to worry, Laddie. These men have drunk all they can hold and fornicated till their family jewels have about shrunk to the size of grapes. Aye, they're a ready bunch. Have you decided where we're putting in when we get to the Floridas?"

Sloan laughed at Culpepper's colorful descriptions. "A place on the west coast. Cedar Key. There's a good harbor there on the leeward side of the islands, according to those charts in your cabin. The *Polly* needs a draft of one-and-a-half fathoms, isn't that right?"

"Aye, Laddie. And where to from there? That's wilderness if I'm not mistaken." Culpepper shifted his weight from his game leg to the other. He was almost sixty, salty as the sea and twice as deep. After nine months of close living with the man, MacAllister still knew little about him except that he could be counted upon to follow orders and captain the *Polly* with a loving hand.

"From there I go ashore with the pack mules and what supplies they'll carry. The remainder will be stored in the hold until I send for it." Captain Culpepper didn't press for more information. If his employer wanted to disclose his plans, he could wait for that time. For now, last minute preparations must be made for the *Polly's* voyage.

When the last streaks of daylight threw their golden hues across the sky, the *Polly* left her berth in New Orleans and headed into the dusk over the Gulf's warm, blue waters. Dressed in buckskins and soft deerhide boots covering his legs to his knees, Sloan felt fourteen years old again. He was ready to face anything that would be required of him. Ready to face the consequences of love and brotherly devotion.

# Chapter Three

Sloan's knees clamped tightly against his mount's flanks. He was certain he was being followed. The fine golden hairs at the back of his neck stood at attention, his pulses throbbed, his senses alerted to danger. Before embarking on this trip into Seminole country, he had calculated the odds against arriving at Osceola's camp undiscovered by Jessup's forces. Relying on his knowledge of deep forests and spurred by the needs of his brother's people, he chanced it.

Beneath him, Redeemer sensed his master's tension. He raised his massive black head, ears pricked forward, waiting for the instant when Sloan would spur him and give him rein to run. But no signal came. Instead, Sloan kept a tight seat, handling the reins gently yet with anticipation.

The mid-afternoon sun streamed through the trees, falling in dappled shadows, never really penetrating the darkness beneath the hovering branches of scrub pine and ash. The flesh of Redeemer's splendid curving neck quivered. He had heard it also.

Sloan smiled. Soon now, very soon, he would make contact with the Indian who so expertly imitated the call of the owl. His skin prickled as he heard the rustling of undergrowth. Redeemer's pace had slowed, but Sloan knew he could have kept his animal at a steady canter and still would have found it difficult to elude these hidden pursuers. Seminoles were renowned for their stamina on a long run. They would have kept pace with him, and only when Redeemer tired would they have closed in for the attack. He reined in the animal, holding him back, allowing himself to become a sitting target for the advance of the red men.

A footfall, a rustle, a war whoop and Sloan was surrounded by braves whose austere features were streaked with yellow and red war paint. Redeemer reared, blowing and snorting in defense, pawing the air, as his powerful hind legs tore the turf.

Sloan's knees gripped Redeemer's flanks, forcing the beast to remain still, keeping his seat on the saddle. His broad shoulders and straight back made an easy target for a Seminole lance, and he bridled the animal to turn about to face them.

From high atop Redeemer's back Sloan cautiously turned his head to survey his pursuers. His broad-brimmed hat cast a shadow over his face, and with a jaunty thumb he pushed it back on his head, revealing his steady gaze and firm jaw. He understood the Indian's uncanny ability to read a man's face and to know his mind. He wished he felt the composure that he fought to portray. Redeemer snorted, a soft, blowing sound. Not even daring to make a move to quiet his mount, he remained still and apprehensive.

The circle of warriors closed around him, reaching up with strong hands and powerful arms. He offered no resistance, allowing them to tumble him to the ground, waiting until they stood back to look down at him. Their expressions were inscrutable, showing only the dignity that was the stamp of Indian visage. Sloan noticed the feathers in their headdresses were fresh, signifying a recent and successful hunting expedition. But the leather pouches used to hold dried grain, hung at their necks, were limp and empty, confirming for Sloan the reports of their poverty. Dried corn was the Indian staple, used to fortify them during long days away from home. Yet, there was something about these braves in their bright leggings and feathered turbans that hinted at a controlled elation. He couldn't believe that capturing him was reason enough for their mood. More likely, they had participated in a very recent raid upon the cavalry and were successful.

The Indians remained still, lances pointed at Sloan's breast, as they examined their quarry. The initial gesture would have to come from Sloan. Watching them intently, and careful to make no quick motion that would seal his death, he rose to a half sitting position, balancing himself on his elbows. He tried smiling toward the warrior who stood closest to him. He looked into the impenetrable darkness of the man's eyes, judging him, being judged. He opened his mouth to speak, struggling to recall the language of his brother. "I travel through the land of my brother, Osceola. I seek shade from his trees and drink from his springs. I sleep beneath his moon. Your leader is my brother."

The tall brave standing closest to him made a motion with his lance, its red-dyed feathers dancing in the sun. The warrior scowled and his eyes, if possible, darkened. Distrust and hatred were apparent in the man's look, and Sloan realized that hearing a white man speak in their tongue was not a novel experience. Too often they had been betrayed by government representatives in their own language.

Feeling the distinct disadvantage of his position there on the mossy earth, Sloan made a move to get to his feet. Without ceremony he was pushed backward and held down by two braves. This time Sloan noticed how thin the men were, the flesh of their bodies stretched over sinewy muscles and high cheek bones. Pity was an emotion that MacAllister was unfamiliar with, but there was pity in him for these brave people of his brother.

Forcing his mouth to work, he wet his lips and spoke, "The mules carry food for the Seminole. It is my gift to my brother." He kept his gaze steady, looking directly at the young man before him.

"He speaks our tongue; he asks for our chief," one brave exclaimed, a young man who wore but one feather in his turban.

The tall warrior growled, an unintelligible sound. Then he broke into angry speech, glaring at each of his men, his authority unquestionable. "Many white men speak our tongue. All white men lie." With incredible swiftness, he grabbed Sloan's buckskin shirtfront and hauled him to his feet.

"I am not other white men. I do not lie. Osceola is my brother." His words were slow, heavy with meaning. He faced the tall warrior, his head high, his eyes steady.

The circle of braves mumbled amongst themselves, keeping their voices low, muttering their puzzlement over this man who claimed to be their War Chief's brother. Sloan heard them address the tall warrior, "Mico, we must bring this white face to our thlacko. If he has such a brother, he will tell us."

Mico's face darkened with rage. "Do you take this dog's word over mine? Do you think I would not know if our thlacko had such a brother?" He sneered, showing his hatred of all the white race.

Sloan remained still, waiting to be addressed and questioned, but the opportunity never arose. Mico turned his back and signaled for his men to follow, bringing the white interloper with them.

MacAllister was dragged to his feet. His belt and holster were taken from him as was his hat. In the manner of all hostages his boots were pulled from his feet and he was divested of his shirt. Naked, except for his buckskin breeches, his hands were bound behind his back and a loop of leather thong strung around his neck. Like a dog on a leash, he was pulled and shoved into his place among the ranks of warriors.

Sloan's eyes fell on Redeemer who stood, pawing the ground. Chancing a low whistle, he commanded the giant black beast to follow. Knowing that to a Seminole a horse was a prize above and beyond a king's ransom,

Sloan assured himself that Redeemer wouldn't be left behind. The pack mules might find their way into a Seminole cookfire, but not Redeemer.

The tallest warrior, Mico, gestured toward the animal, ordering it to be taken. The man's eyes perused the quivering horse flesh lovingly, no doubt thinking that as leader of this raid Redeemer would become his booty. When the young brave approached the beast, Redeemer reared up, pawing the damp forest air. His eyes blazed, his nostrils flared, blowing and snorting. In spite of his situation, Sloan smiled. Redeemer would fight and threaten, refusing to allow anyone save Sloan himself to handle him.

Three other braves stopped in front of Redeemer, their arms flailing, carefully avoiding the sharp hooves that could knock them senseless. They made soft hawing noises, seeking to calm this horse who reared and whinnied and whose eyes spoke rebellion rather than terror. Sloan whistled softly, and Redeemer quieted immediately, the muscles in his chest heaving with excitement. Bobbing his great head, the black animal fell into step behind his master. Sloan saw the amazement on his captors' faces, and he listened to their low mutters of appreciation for so glorious a beast.

Pack mules in tow, the small party traveled eastward through dense forest and over marshy ground. Considering the pace the Indians were forcing on him, Sloan figured the camp must be nearby, reason enough for these warriors to be so menacing. Inadvertently, he had come very close to their camp. It was little wonder that Mico and his band were so hostile. Allowing a stranger to travel so closely said little for their vigilance as scouts and sentrys.

Thick branches of long-needled Southern pines scratched Sloan's bare chest. Insects fed on his perspiring skin. The harsh forest floor with its nettles and sharp twigs stung his bare feet. Yet he kept pace with Mico, following the moccasined Indian step for step,

stride for stride. It had been too long since he had run
alongside Osceola, but he remembered the rigors of
those runs. He controlled his breaths, exhaling and
inhaling in long measures. He concentrated only on the
feel of ground covered by his long strides, blocking out
all pain and exhaustion. The terrain was flat with little
rise or fall to break his pacing. He wouldn't falter; he
couldn't. To do so would bring disgrace upon himself
and, more importantly, his brother. The leather thong
around his neck was tugged harshly, nearly knocking
him off balance. Mico had changed direction. Several
hundred yards later the village became visible through
the trees.

The low lying thatch and bark structures were built
on low stilts, and emitted aromas from cook fires
through the smoke hole in their roofs. Children played
their games, and women went about their business of
preparing food and other household duties. The camp
was quiet and serene, and yet the activity around the
cook fires created an air of celebration. Sloan suspected
that he had been correct in assuming there had been a
successful raid upon the blue-shirted soldiers. Sacks of
grain, bearing government stamps, were stacked beneath a roofed structure without walls. Army blankets
were heaped in a pile as were assorted foodstuffs and
cookware. From the way the spoils were assembled,
Sloan knew it had been a fairly recent undertaking and
that the village had not yet had the opportunity to
divide the plunder.

Mico entered the camp—the returning warrior victorious. It was the children who noticed first. They ran
and clustered around the captive, pointing and calling
to one another, catching the notice of the women.
Other men gathered around Mico and his braves, their
eyes raking over MacAllister, measuring his strength
and seeking his weaknesses.

Sloan stood tall, squaring his broad shoulders. Behind him, he heard Redeemer whinny as a brave threw
a blanket over the animal's head and another brave

quickly hobbled his front legs with a double loop of rawhide. Sloan was pushed roughly toward the center of the camp—the area around which the huts and long houses had been built.

Mico stood proudly, arms crossed over his chest, as he retold the capture of the white dog who had dared to enter Seminole territory. Sloan noticed how Mico avoided telling how close to camp the interloper had been found and how the tall warrior avoided his eyes as he told his tale. The young brave who had dared to question Mico out in the forest was also quiet. Sloan knew that to speak aloud and protest his capture by repeating that Osceola was his brother would make Mico his enemy for life. Better to keep his counsel until Osceola could come to his rescue.

Quickly, Sloan perused the encampment, seeking his brother. He sighted a longhouse, larger than the others, off to his right. Outside the entrance was the shield and lance of the War Chief, but to his dismay, the standard of yellow and red feathers, usually set into the roof announcing the thlacko was in residence, was absent. A low rumble of apprehension stirred in the pit of his stomach.

The rest of the camp gathered around. Black faces, runaway slaves who had found sanctuary with the Seminoles, were present. There were young people who, from their coloration and features, shared a heredity of both Indian and black, descendants of runaway slaves generations ago. Children, half naked, curiosity widening their dark eyes, darted between the legs of the adults. The women, long black hair pulled back from their handsome faces and brightly colored skirts swishing, pressed forward, amusement lifting the corners of their mouths and dancing in their eyes. The rumblings in MacAllister's gut increased. He could almost see the women wet their lips in anticipation. He knew it was considered unmanly for a hostage to be tormented by the men. That task was left to the women. And as fierce and ferocious as the men were in battle, so were the women when faced with the opportunity to vent their rages upon an enemy of their people.

Mico spoke, his voice barely concealing his contempt. "The women are greedy for their enjoyment. It is not every day a white dog is brought to them for their amusement."

Sloan's stomach lurched, his eyes flew to the hut bearing the banner of the thlacko. "Osceola is not in camp on this day," Mico smiled, his thin lips lifting over his teeth like a badger's. "And when the women are through with you, there will be little left to recognize." His eyes dared Sloan to contradict him, to plead with him. Instead, Mico found himself staring into Sloan's defiant flinty glare.

An ominous buzz trebled through the camp. The men and children had withdrawn to a respectful distance. The women came closer, huddling around their prey. Several held long sticks and willow branches, and some had scoured the ground for small rocks and stones. Suddenly, a commotion erupted in the ranks. A feminine voice, shrill with authority, demanded to be brought forward. At another time the voice might have been light and melodious, but now it was shrieking, aggressive, clamoring for attention and demanding obedience. "The dog is mine!" it repeated.

From out of the flurry of activity stepped a tall woman. Her long streaming hair was flaxen and shone against her honey-colored skin. Her eyes, deep and green as the forest itself, blazed with arrogance, as full, sensuous lips parted in a derisive smile over perfect white teeth. It was the face of an angel beneath the mask of a savage. Slender, lithe and graceful, she circled MacAllister, testing the length of the serpentine whip she trailed on the dry ground. Curls of dust eddied around her feet, and the slanted rays of the setting sun glanced off her smooth skin. Bright bands of color danced as her skirt swirled about her slim legs.

Her open necked blouse strained across her proud breasts. She was a vision; she was a nightmare.

Her intensity was almost tangible as she moved in his direction. A hush seemed to fall over the spectators, and Sloan stared dazedly at the brilliant haired wraith who was stalking him.

He watched with fascination as she wound the trailing leather over her hand. Wordlessly, almost expressionless except for the fires burning in her eyes, she jabbed the whip's handle into his gut, pushing him backward nearly off balance. Quickly, he stepped back, grappling for balance. With his hands tied behind his back it was a difficult maneuver, but one he was determined to accomplish. The last thing MacAllister wanted was to be curling in the dust looking up at this she-demon.

Again she jabbed; and again he moved backward, more easily this time since he had expected the thrust. Back and back she maneuvered him until he was standing in the center of the clearing.

She began to move about him, swaying slightly, crooning an obscure chant, her voice low and throaty, the syllables unintelligible. His eyes followed her—first to the right, then to the left. Her movements were hypnotizing, having the effect of a snake charmer's flute. Somewhere in his head was a great roaring, a portent of danger. Suddenly, she sprang toward him, spraying spittle at his face—a display of utter contempt.

With a crack, the whip snapped the air, its tasseled tip beating the dust mere inches from his bare feet. Sloan forced himself to remain still, fighting the reflex to leap away from the expected blow. The girl stood before him, their gazes locked. The whip flicked again, this time around his ankles, sending a rush of pain up his legs. It flicked again, at mid calf and again at his knees. The pain was intense, even through his buckskin breeches. The she-devil raised her arm to strike again, and he flinched before the blow fell. The braided snake found its mark at mid thigh, nearly rocking him off his feet.

As the women giggled and the men jeered, pure unadulterated terror coursed through Sloan as he visualized where the whip would strike next. Instead the creature lashed out again and again, striping his shoulders and chest. He could feel the heat of pain as the welts rose on his flesh. Still he stood, freezing his face into a display of indifference. The brother of the thlacko must not disgrace himself by crying like a child at punishment from a woman.

A querulous voice overrode the others, its strident quality clamoring to be heard. "Chala! Chala!" it addressed the light-haired demoness. "You overstep your bounds!" the voice complained. It belonged to an older woman who broke through the circle of spectators. Her clothing was somber, dipped in berry juice until its normally bright colors were dulled to a mottled brown. Her hair, streaked with gray, was tied at the back of her head and clubbed short. The absence of beads or ornamentation on her body marked her as a widow, as did the smudges of ashes rubbed into her face and the backs of her hands. In a flash, Sloan remembered Polly, Osceola's mother, grinding still warm ashes into her own pretty face after witnessing Jeb MacAllister's death. For the rest of her life she had dressed in the drab, unornamented garb of a warrior's widow, sacrificing her love of bangles and beads.

"The white-eyes is mine!" Chala protested. "Stupid woman, open your eyes and look! His skin is white, as is mine. And his hair is golden as the sun, as is mine. What better reason?"

"The reason of a widow," the woman stated loudly. "Did I not lose my protector beneath white-eyes' thunder stick? I will step out of my half death into the world of the living for this one reason. I will take my revenge on this enemy of my husband and my people!" As she cried the words, she beat her formidable breast with both fists, her sleeves falling away from her arms and revealing hard muscled forearms and the calloused working hands of the Indian woman. Quick as a fox, the woman reached for the whip.

With lightning reflexes the girl known as Chala backed away. "Do not force me to assert rights," she hissed. "I have claimed this dog for myself. I would not like to fight you for him." Her tone was venomous; her eyes spewed fire.

Sloan sensed the unease of the crowd. An Indian girl would never speak to an older woman with anything but respect, but the woman's position as a widow left her without standing in the tribe. Without a husband or a son to support and protect her, she was a virtual non-entity.

"Fight me you will," the woman threatened. "By your own words you declare yourself not a member of this tribe."

The woman's words seemed to ignite a spark of wild fury in Chala. Her eyes darkened, her grip on the whip tightened. "Step no further, Yahi, the half-dead have no rights," she warned.

Unheeding, the woman lurched for her, screaming a cry of vented rage. Immediately, the focus of the crowd swung to the grappling women. Men cried out and children squealed. But it was the women who stood by silently—watching, waiting.

Chala's skirt became a whirl of color as the two women rolled and wrestled on the ground. Teeth bared, hair flying, she pit her weight and strength against the older woman who was of brute proportions. Grunts and cries erupted from the opponents, each tossing and turning to gain the topmost position. Sloan heard the renting of cloth and saw the shoulder of Chala's blouse part from her body. In the wake of the fabric was the clawing and scratchings left by Yahi's nails. Like the cobra and the mongoose, they tumbled, clawing and tearing, each fighting for supremacy. Chala's skin glistened with sweat as she strained to overturn Yahi who had pinned her back to the ground with the sheer force of her weight. Panting, groaning with determination, Chala scrambled atop the widow, holding her down by pushing her forearm across the woman's throat. Breasts heaving, breathing rapid, she claimed victory for herself. "Know when you have been beaten, Yahi. Or would you have me snatch you baldheaded?" she threatened, plunging her free hand into the woman's hair and yanking it viciously.

Hesitantly, and with a great lack of grace, Yahi relaxed and ceased her struggles. A long moment later, Chala lifted herself from atop the woman's prone body and stood tall and proud. "Is there any among you who would deny me my right?" she challenged. Hearing no argument, she bent to retrieve her whip. When she lifted her arm to strike, she put the full force of her weight behind the blows. With a shriek that could only have come from a wild cat, she snapped the whip over Sloan's shoulders, lashing him again and again until his legs dissolved beneath him and he rolled in the dust, plagued by the fury of the lash and the cries of the woman.

The howls and jeers of the crowd became a roar in MacAllister's ears. The twilight sky darkened to a blackness, and the stars that shone through the breaks in the trees were sparks in his head. He turned his body in on itself, exposing only his back to the bite of the whip. Suddenly, he realized that the lash had failed to fall, and through pain dulled senses, the camp had fallen silent.

The orange flames of the ever-burning camp fire in the center of the clearing were shooting toward the sky. In the silence, the song of the crickets could be heard blending with the hoots of the owl. A tingle of expectation buzzed through the gathering as they stood in respectful silence. Only a child, with the innocence of the young, dared to breathe his name. "Thlacko!"

MacAllister lifted his head and saw through the dim a prominent figure standing near the edge of the clearing. His erect bearing and feathered turban lent him a certain majesty. Slender, with the corded body of the natural athlete, he stood with easy grace as his flashing eyes read the scene before him. His gaze fell on Chala, who stood with head high and eyes level.

"And so, Chala, I have heard that you caught yourself a wild dog. Is this why you have helped yourself to the lash which once hung on the wall of my chikkee?"

"Dogs must be trained, my chief. I did not disgrace your lash." She glanced at the prone figure of Mac-Allister and back at Osceola. "From the look of him I would say I have brought honor to your weapon."

Osceola glanced down at Sloan and back at Chala. "And to bring this honor to my lash was it necessary for you to be unkind to our sister, Yahi, who honors her husband by walking among the half-dead?"

Chala's serpentine green eyes lowered in shame.

"My scouts ran out to greet me and share the news of my camp," Osceola explained.

Chala raised her head brazenly, shaking back her wealth of shimmering hair. "It was my right!" she said defiantly. "See him. His skin is white; his hair is yellow. As he is like me, so it was my right!"

"And so is your heart Seminole. Was this your right to defy the wishes of Yahi who is your elder? To invade her world of the half-dead and come to physical blows?"

Instantly contrite, Chala hung her head, grateful for the curtain of hair that covered her shame. "I yield to you, my chief," she murmured. "But I would have you know that I would have fought your bravest warrior for the joy of beating a white dog!"

"A dog who claims to be our thlacko's brother," chirped the youngest brave, who had brought Sloan in from the forest.

Osceola's chiseled features hardened as his eyes found the prone figure sprawled on the ground near Chala's feet. He frowned and quickly handed his lance to a scout beside him. He covered the distance between himself and Chala's victim in three long strides, and his people stepped backward, allowing their thlacko to move forward unhindered.

Chala saw the haunted expression on Osceola's face, and unable to understand the shadows of ghosts in his eyes, felt the stirrings of dread grow in her belly. Standing her ground, hoping against hope, she turned on the young brave. "You are mad! The sun never rose on the day when our thlacko would call a white man his brother!"

Osceola stood for a long moment over Sloan, staring with disbelief into his dust-streaked face. Dropping to his knees, he reached his hand to touch the thick, sun-gilded hair, his fingers tracing the strong, square jaw. Gently, he cupped Sloan's face and turned it toward him. The face of the boy was still stamped on the man's features.

A terrible searing pain tightened Osceola's chest. A knowledge of all that was lost between them for so many years swelled in his heart, climbing up his throat and he released it in a soundless cry. This man, closer to him than any other could be, had come when the need was the greatest.

Slowly, Sloan opened his eyes to stare into his brother's face. Though no blood was shared between them, their hearts still beat in a shared rhythm. Though no words were spoken, each knew the soul of the other. Sloan longed to take Osceola into his embrace, to feel again, after these long years, the unity between them. Too weak, too helpless, to do more than initiate the gesture, he fell backward into the dust, only his steady gaze holding on to the boy who was now a man and a chief of his people.

Osceola bent closer, lifting Sloan's shoulders to take him into his arms. Quietly, in a whisper that was choked with grief and rife with hope, he uttered the words that healed the soul and bridged the past, "My mother's son, my brother."

Through his pain, Sloan gripped Osceola's shoulder,

his voice hardly more than a gasp. "My brother." Joy
sparked between them, two men who were in more
ways true brothers than if they had sprung from the
same womb. The years which had separated them now
brought them together.

Osceola looked up at Chala, Sloan still held in his
arms. "Indeed the sun has risen on such a day," he
spoke in low, vibrant tones. Every ear in the village was
intent on the words of their thlacko. "My brother will
reside with me in my chikkee. He will sleep at my side.
And you, Chala, will be quick to undo the damage you
have done to this man whose heart is never far from my
own."

A gasp went out from the crowd. In simple, loving
terms Osceola, War Chief of the Seminoles, had placed
this white man beneath his own protection and equal to
himself.

Tears glazed the cheeks of the women and the men
stood at respectful attention. Even the children were
silent, stilled, by the awesome emotions they had just
witnessed.

Osceola rose to his feet, muttering instructions for
Sloan to be brought into his chikkee. Several braves
moved forward, quick to do their chief's bidding,
honored by the opportunity to care for the man he
called brother.

Before following Sloan into his chikkee, Osceola
turned once again to the astonished Chala. "I trust my
brother has shown himself to be a man of courage."
Immediately, voices called out, elaborating on the
courage of the man who had stood the test of Chala's
whip without a whimper.

"I have you to thank for allowing my brother to
display his bravery, Chala."

Although the chief's words were said with humor,
her face reddened. The thlacko was showing her forgiveness, and his piercing black eyes were compelling
her to open her heart. She knew what she must do.

Slowly, she walked to where the widow Yahi was

watching. In a voice loud enough for all to hear, she
humbled herself. "I ask you to come with me to help
the brother of our thlacko."

Yahi's eyes lowered, but when she lifted them again,
it was to look directly at this golden-haired girl who had
lived so long among her people. She gazed at Chala
with gratitude. To nurse the brother of the thlacko was
a great honor. It would be a great service to the chief,
and would reinstate her in the tribe as a member of
Osceola's household.

Yahi's glance searched the clutch of women who had
gathered around to bear witness to Chala's humiliation.
Her eyes fell on Ina and Che-cho-ter, Osceola's wives.
Seeing each of them nod their heads in affirmation, she
once again faced Chala. With great dignity Yahi pulled
herself to full height and began to bark orders to bring
her ointments and medicines.

The chikkee of Osceola was filled with the pungent
aroma of ointments and salves. The cook fire, which
was the focal point of every Seminole household,
burned slowly as Yahi stirred and chanted over a
miniature cauldron of herbs and roots which were to
become a dressing for MacAllister's wounds.

Chala wiped the dust from Sloan's face and body
with a sweet scented lotion made from flower petals
and animal fats. Her face was pinched into a scowl, and
he felt her abhorrence of him as she touched his flesh.
The hatred he saw in her eyes made him want to recoil
from her even more than when she had held the whip.

The chikkee was larger than usual for a Seminole
dwelling, denoting Osceola's privilege and station.
Sloan estimated it was nearly twenty feet square and
thoroughly chinked with mud to keep out the wind and
rain. The roof was thatched with the necessary smoke
hole directly over the fire. The chief sat on his rug near
the back of the chikkee while the two women hovered
nearby serving him food and drink. It was not surpris-
ing to Sloan that his brother did not sit close to him

exchanging news of the years that had passed between them. That would come later. For now, Osceola was allowing Sloan the privacy to have his wounds tended. The chief sat on his animal skins near the back of the chikkee thoughtfully watching as the women ministered to his brother's wounds.

As Yahi knelt down beside her patient, Chala followed her instructions to tend the pot of simmering herbs. "That is Ina and Che-cho-ter, wives of our thlacko," Yahi explained when she noticed Sloan's curious glance. Her tone was solicitous and respectful as was due the brother of her chief. Also, there was an air of gratitude about her, no doubt because this white-eyes was instrumental in having her services called upon and installing her in the most notable household in the village.

The younger squaw handed Osceola a cup and their hands touched. Sloan saw them look into each other's eyes and witnessed the love and tenderness they shared.

"That is Che-cho-ter, our thlacko's second wife," Yahi commented as she swabbed MacAllister's shoulders.

"In your tongue she is known as Morning Dew," Chala interjected, not wishing to be outdone by Yahi. "Often I hear our chief call her by that name," she confessed, intending for Yahi and Sloan, both, to know that she was on intimate terms with Osceola's household.

"Che-cho-ter's father was a runaway slave," Yahi continued, disregarding Chala's inference of intimacy. "Her mother was a Seminole of Micanopy's people."

Sloan glanced toward Che-cho-ter again, noting her exceptional beauty and her dusky skin. It was evident that Osceola was devoted to her. Unfamiliar with polygamy, Sloan directed his attention toward Ina, who was much older than Osceola.

Again sharing his thought, Yahi explained, "Ina was the daughter of a famous warrior. She and our thlacko have shared the same chikkee for many summers. Our chief was very young and without a home or people. It is the way of the Seminole to be received by the woman's people. Ina was a widow, like myself, when Osceola took her under his protection. He fished for her and hunted for her and built her a chikkee."

There was a sadness about Yahi when she spoke of the chikkee. No doubt she was thinking of her own which had to be burned to the ground along with all her other possessions at the death of her husband.

"Gifts were exchanged with Ina's brother-in-law, and she became Osceola's woman. Her people became his people. Now Ina is like a mother to our thlacko and Che-cho-ter and like a grandmother to their three daughters. There is no jealousy, only respect and much love. Ina is blessed by the spirits of the forest," Yahi sighed.

"And what of your people?" Sloan asked curiously of Chala who was holding the small cauldron of steaming brew nearby, ready for Yahi's use. Yahi's medicines were working their magic and the pain was seeping from his body. But there was no doubt that Chala had nearly whipped him within an inch of his life.

The girl lifted her head, her delicate chin jutted arrogantly. "The Seminoles are my people," she retorted. Her agitated movements splattered the scalding liquid over onto MacAllister's bare belly. When he gasped, she taunted him. "Your skin is not as thick as you would have us believe, white-eyes."

Something in this girl's haughty, aristocratic bearing haunted Sloan. He had seen her face before. Somewhere. Or had it only been a dream? The sudden recognition faded, and he could think no more about it. Yahi had pressed a cup to his lips and sleep was quick in coming, diffusing the edges of his misery into welcome oblivion.

For the next two days Sloan slept, being awakened only for meals and Yahi's brew, then succumbing again to the healing power of sleep. On the third day he awakened feeling considerably better, and insisted upon doing for himself rather than to succumb to the women's attentions. His personal belongings were brought to him, and after a good wash he proceeded to shave, catching Yahi's attention by stropping the razor against the thick leather strap. With unabashed curiosity, she watched Sloan scrape the whiskers from his face and chin. For the most part Indian men had no need to shave. An occasional grooming with the blade of a knife was all that was ever necessary.

After attending to his grooming, Sloan felt he looked himself again although the lash-induced welts on his skin were still tight and burned. He watched the women silently leave the chikkee to allow Osceola and his brother privacy.

Seated on a rug not far from the central fire, the two men looked warmly into one another's eyes, finding there the friendship and camaraderie so familiar to their relationship. Sloan allowed his brother to speak first.

"It has been many summers since last my eyes looked upon you. We were boys and now we are men, and yet I can see the joy in my heart echoed in your eyes." Osceola spoke in the Seminole tongue, encouraging Sloan to do the same.

"It has been too long and the years have taken us on separate trails." Sloan's understanding of the Seminole language did not aid his use of it after all these years. The syllables and flowery phrases came awkwardly to his lips. "Have you forgotten the use of English?" he asked Osceola.

Osceola laughed. "No more than I have forgotten my brother, Sloan," he stated in perfect English. "There are very few people who know of my knowledge of English. I find it's an asset to use Abraham, our interpreter, when dealing with the military officials. Some things are better understood when heard the second time. It's most enlightening to hear what's said about oneself when the others think you cannot understand."

Sloan laughed. "You wily old fox. Well, it's not going to be easy for me to remember my Seminole vocabulary, but I'll try if you insist."

"Only when there are others present. I know whom I can trust; leave it to me to decide when we will speak in your tongue."

"Agreed. You aren't ashamed of the MacAllister name, are you, brother?"

"Ashamed, never. But giving an enemy a clue to your past gives him an advantage in deciding your future. Some of my heritage has been known and too accurately."

A quiet moment passed and Sloan spoke. "I had no idea of the troubles you were having until I returned from Europe several months ago. My first inclination was to come directly to you, but then I decided to hang around to see what information I could pick up from government sources. Things look bad for the Seminole, brother. Washington insists on emigrating your people into Arkansas territory and assimilating you among the Creeks."

"Creeks!" Osceola spit the word. "I will resist with the last breath in my body. 'The Creek nation will open their arms to the Seminole' we have been told. Bah! Surely, they will open their arms and accept us, *as slaves*. Also, I fear for our black brothers who have run away from cruel masters. They live beside us and many have their own villages. For this we Seminoles are condemned. We regard the blacks as our brethren and allies. In the past, before times were so hard, many of us purchased black slaves from the white men. The blacks would work and repay the price of their freedom. The Creeks have often raided Seminole settlements seeking slaves. Bah!" he spit again. "The only sentiment we Seminole feel for the Creek is contempt!"

"There are stories of Seminoles raiding white settlements here in Florida," Sloan stated.

Osceola's indignation was almost palatable. "There is no denying it. The Treaty of 1823 denied the Seminole our cultivated fields and good hunting grounds. We were placed in a wilderness unsuitable for farming or hunting. Because of this we have been left with the wretched choice of starving within our prescribed limits, or roaming among the whites to search for subsistence. Between the Seminole and the greedy land grabbing white settlers there is an unceasing contest for survival. It is not right. None of it is right. Tell me what you have heard, brother, spare me nothing."

Sloan hesitated, not knowing where to begin. Finally, after taking a deep breath, he said, "Washington pretends to have lofty motives. They recognize that the Seminole can't continue to live this way. To relieve this situation, they propose moving the Seminole nation west, as you said, among the Creeks. Also, there has been a change of command. General Thomas Sidney Jessup has been assigned to the Florida territory. I've met the man; he's dangerous. He bears a contempt for the red man and seeks to further his career in the military, especially if it is at Seminole expense."

Osceola's chin sunk into his chest, his shoulders hunched with weariness. His voice, when he spoke, was barely audible, his words meant only for Sloan's ears. "Do you remember when we were boys, that day we chased each other through the forest, and I told you that I must go to meet my destiny?"

"I will never forget the day you left the farm. There was a great emptiness."

"Yes, here within me also," the Indian brought his fist to his heart. "Perhaps if I had known what destiny I was chasing, I would have stayed with you. Life has put on my shoulders great responsibility. I am thlacko, leader, chief. I am thirty-three summers and already I bear the sorrows of an old man."

Sloan listened silently, knowing that Osceola had an enormous need to bare his soul and share at least a small part of his burden with his brother.

"I had no desire to be a leader among my people. I was content to live among them, to hunt their land and fish their streams. But war has come and with it confusion. I was considered a man of honor. I had the respect of the other men and a place near the council fire. It was all a man could want. When we, as a people, saw we were in danger of losing our home, many became bewildered. Which way to turn? What to do? Should we risk all and protest or should we meekly accede to the wants of the whites? Fear for our children beclouded some men's minds. The uncertainty of the future caused chaos. But not for me, brother. Not for me. In my mind there was never a question of my beliefs. I have lived among the whites. I know too well their prejudices and fears and hatreds. I have seen firsthand how they treat their slaves. I know what it would mean to leave here to join the Creeks in Arkansas. No, in my mind, there was never a doubt. The Seminole must stand and fight for what is rightly theirs. A man known to us as Arpeika saw this determination in my heart. He is an old medicine man and also a great warrior. Fearing there would be none to come after him who would uphold his beliefs, he raised me up in the eyes of the people. I became a chief by Arpeika's design, not my own."

"This, then is the destiny you chose when we were boys," Sloan told him.

"My destiny and my damnation. As always, in times of war, confused minds listen to the strong voice. It is not always the voice which speaks the wisest or the greatest truth. But it is a voice, and the timid and bewildered will follow it."

"My brother's voice is only one among many," Sloan comforted.

"Yes, one voice among many. Although not as many as you would think. There are those among us who believe the Seminole should join the Creeks. They are dazzled by the promises of the army to give us cattle and grain and money. But if we join the Creeks, we become their slaves and all that we own will become theirs." Osceola laughed, a hard, bitter sound. "We are a small nation, brother. For the most part, we are broken into three main groups. King Phillip and his followers are north of here along the eastern coast just outside of St. Augustine. Phillip is a fierce fighter and as cunning as a fox. His voice rises with Arpeika's and my own. I am here with Arpeika. This village is the smaller of the two. We had to separate from Arpeika's settlement because it is easier to feed smaller groups of people than one large camp."

Moving aside a reed mat near his foot, Osceola exposed the dirt floor of the chikkee. Scratching with his finger, he drew a rough map. "We are here, along the banks of the Withlacoochee River that runs from central Florida to the Gulf. Arpeika is here," he pointed to a spot centrally located. "Here, in the east is King Phillip. South and west is the village of Coa Hadjo. These are the main camps; there are many other small groups between these points I have shown you. For the most part, the blacks have formed villages of their own. Most of them lie along the banks of the Withlacoochee with only a few further south closer to Coa Hadjo. We are scattered, we all scratch the forest for our living, but we are all Seminoles."

Sloan watched as Osceola raised his head, his black eyes burned with fervor and outrage at the injustices committed against his people. "Our numbers are few," he said with strength and confidence, "but the white soldiers will feel the power of every man, woman and child before we see the end of this. We will speak more about this tomorrow. For now, I can see you need your rest."

It was true; Sloan was exhausted, yet he was exhilarated being here with his brother. A thought occurred to him. "I brought pack mules with me, carrying foodstuffs and necessities for your people. Also, I want to see Redeemer."

"We thank you for the supplies. They will bring a momentary respite from hunger. Right now, that is our most pertinent problem. As for that magnificent animal who carried you into Florida, Mico has seen to him. My bravest warrior will look after him through the night. Redeemer, did you call him? It's fitting then. The old wise ones in our village have said that the beast's spirit represents the aggressive determination of our people. Your Redeemer is fast on his way to becoming a legend among the Seminole. Come, we will walk out together to see this prize of yours."

Sloan smiled. Redeemer was worthy of Indian legend, he was certain. "That horse has traveled across the ocean with me from Russia. Supposedly, he was bred for a Russian Tsar. We've seen a lot of the world together. I'm only glad he didn't have to witness what one little honey-colored girl could do to his master. He might get the idea he could take advantage of me himself." Sloan followed Osceola outside the chikkee.

Reverting to the Indian tongue and wordlessly encouraging Sloan to do likewise, Osceola remarked on Sloan's wounds. "As the victim of an unfair flogging, you are entitled to restitution," he told his brother.

Chala, who was sitting crosslegged near the thlacko's chikkee, directed her attention to the two men. She heard Osceola's statement and glared with undisguised hatred at the white man who had been the cause of her humiliation before the entire village. This stranger would be well within his rights under Seminole law to return the public beating threefold. Silently, she waited for his reply.

"I'm no woman beater, brother. There are other ways to bring the girl to heel."

Chala jumped to her feet. The movement caught Sloan's attention. She spat at him venomously. "I am not a coward, or a creeping she-dog, wary of a man's foot. Beat me if you will and see for yourself that the bite of the lash is little more than the bite of the flea!"

Osceola looked at Chala, the authority in his glance silencing her. Sloan, on the other hand, was amused by her display of belligerence. "Don't tempt me, little one," his smile was a raw mockery that grated her self-esteem and riled her contempt.

Forgetting this man's relationship to her chief, Chala retaliated, "You are not a man to be tempted by any woman. You forget, it is you who bears the stripes from *my* lash." Her words were a satisfied hiss.

Still, the mockery did not leave Sloan's smile. Her words were insignificant, tossed off like the complaints of a child. She stood before him, daring him to defend himself, to make some move to deny her accusations. Her bright hair was tossed back from her face, her eyes blazed with scorn and defiance.

Never taking his eyes from her, Sloan spoke to Osceola. "I will demand my restitution." He spoke slowly, quietly, waiting for the reaction on her face. "Give Chala to me."

Her indrawn breath was a harsh rasp. In the name of all of the Spirits in the forest, she had never expected this. Her fingers curled into talons, she flew at the tall, golden-haired man like a screech owl in the night. The sounds that escaped her lips were savage, echoing in his ears. Her movements were swift and deadly. She buffetted against him, reaching for his face, intent on scratching out his eyes.

Sloan was swift, his reflexes quick and certain. He held her off, grabbing her by the shoulders and wrestling her away from him. Chala's feet kicked out, high and wild, aiming for the vulnerable flesh between his legs. Kicking and thrashing, she continued her attack, heedless of the harsh orders of her chief to cease and desist. She flew at Sloan again, hating him, wishing him dead, knowing only that she wanted to kill him, kill herself before she would ever belong to a white man.

One of her wild kicks caught Sloan high on the thigh, wickedly close to her target. Anger boiled in him as he shook himself free of her. Her strength amazed him; her unleashed fury astounded him. She flung herself again, locking her arms around his shoulders, reaching for his hair to yank it unceremoniously from his scalp.

With all her untamed rage, she wrestled him to the ground, rolling with him in the dust, impervious to the hands of her thlacko, who was unsuccessful in his attempts to pull her off. Sloan's hands discovered her wealth of long hair and he mercilessly pulled, drawing her head back in a neck breaking hold. Still, her legs thrashed wildly, aiming for dead center and seeking to render him helpless.

The advantage of his weight and height enabled Sloan to overturn her, pressing her back into the dust and holding her fast with his superior strength. She writhed beneath him, still flailing, breasts heaving against his chest. He accomplished drawing her arms up over her head, stretching her out beneath him, quelling her frantic actions. Suddenly, she was still, looking up at him from beneath lowered lids. Her incongruously dark lashes cast elongated shadows on her cheeks. Her skin was flushed pink beneath the honey tones, and her lips parted in a soundless cry.

Sloan filled himself with the sight of her. Beneath her savagery was an undeniable beauty that stirred his senses and quickened his pulse, and he knew he wanted her. As he had never wanted another woman.

Seeming to read his thoughts, Chala mocked him with her eyes and beckoned him with a slow, sensual smile that made a roaring in his ears and was repeated in his loins. "I claim my restitution," Sloan said loudly to Osceola, never taking his eyes from Chala. "I want this woman for my own."

"I would sooner give my brother a water moccasin than burden him with a woman such as this," Osceola smiled, understanding the attraction Chala held for Sloan. "However, if it is your wish, the girl is yours."

Hearing the dreaded words of her thlacko, Chala knew defeat. Her heart raced like a rabbit and her stomach fluttered in dread. The deed was done. The years with the Seminoles had taught her obedience even if they had not stifled her defiance and independence. It was decreed; she belonged to this golden-haired giant whom she could never hope to overpower. Even as she realized her defeat, something alien and unknown stirred within her, and quickened her breath and flushed her cheeks. Something that left her feeling cold and alone when Sloan lifted his body from hers and pulled her to her feet. She heard him mutter something concerning his horse to the thlacko and both men moved away from her. She felt discarded and repudiated. As Sloan walked off with Osceola, her eyes burned into his back. Whatever else this man would do to her, Chala was determined that he would never ignore her.

# Chapter Four

Celebration was in the air. The thlacko's brother had come to share his chikkee and the War Chief smiled. Children's voices were raised to a higher, more gleeful note; women bustled about tending their fires, preparing the food that had been divided from the supplies the thlacko's white brother had brought to them.

The aroma of fresh Koonti bread, made from the flour of the briar root, filled the air, reminding Sloan of his boyhood when Polly would sing her tri-note songs and prepare supper for her men.

Everywhere he looked happy smiles lit the people's faces; the thlacko was smiling, so should they. Happy faces, save one, the girl called Chala. If ever Mac-Allister saw a murderous expression, it was hers. Even Beaunell in her worst humor couldn't approach Chala's rage. Sloan made a mental note not to turn his back on this hellcat. This one was a tiger, and even Osceola with his stern warnings and even tempered words would have little effect on Chala's vengeance. Sloan remembered too well the joy she took in wielding the whip, and the strength in her brown arms and slender legs. There was no doubt in his mind that given half a chance she would cheerfully kill him and worry about the wrath of Osceola later.

"Your eyes follow our Chala," Osceola noted standing beside him. His handsome face smiled knowingly. "I have seen other men's eyes watch that one."

Sloan shrugged. "She's a hellion. It's beyond my imagination how you and your people put up with her.

And where in the hell did you get her? She's no Indian, not with that hair and skin.''

Osceola gazed fondly at Chala. "She came to us by chance of fate. Chala was found wandering in the forests, protected by the Spirits who guard the children. At the time she was merely six or seven summers. A scout found her and brought her here to us, to live among our people and make them her own. This she has done. The hearts of the Seminoles are soft for the little ones. Would it were so with the whites. Perhaps there would be an end to war.''

"All whites don't crave war. All whites are not alike just as all Indians are not alike," Sloan told him gravely.

"What you say is true, brother. Tell me, do your eyes follow Wild Honey and smile upon her?" Osceola translated Chala's name into English.

"Wild Honey." Sloan rolled the name around his tongue a few times. "I like my life as it is. Up till now it's been fairly uncluttered, and I have no desire to set up a chikkee with your Chala. However, I was serious about your giving her to me.''

Creases of puzzlement formed over the warrior chief's brow. "If you have no desire to make a chikkee with Chala, then why do you burden yourself with such an obvious . . ." he sighed wearily. "I must be honest with you. I am giving you no prize, my brother. Once you take her from my chikkee she cannot be returned. Ina and Che-cho-ter have been waiting for the day when some fool tries to tame Chala. My women rule my chikkee. They would refuse to take her back. I, myself, would consider my duty as her chief finished. No amount of pleading will change my mind," Osceola added hastily, watching for Sloan's reaction.

"That bad, is she? I thought as much. Well, I'll soon change all of that.''

An expression of amused pity crossed the Indian's face. "Perhaps we should sign something in the way of the white man. No return," he said adamantly.

"Agreed. But I'll soon mend her ways and have her rubbing against my knee like our mother's old cat."

Osceola laughed uproariously. His brother was soon going to discover that Chala, like Polly's old cat, had claws. There was no need to tell him of the young girl's screeching and caterwauling that made everyone in the camp run for cover. No need to tell him of the frenzied hours the women of his own chikkee suffered at her hands. Or of Chala's lack of expertise at the cook fire or the stingy way she had with soap and water when laundering clothes. He would soon see for himself. And then it would be too late—for Sloan. Osceola decided he wanted it written, treatied, the way the government men did it.

Sloan joined in the laughter, knowing it was at his own expense. "You will see, brother. That little hellcat will soon be obeying my every command. She'll know who is the master."

"And will you make her a slave? I think not, my mother's son. I think not, Look, your slave approaches with your dinner. She has cooked it for you herself," he said gleefully, anticipating Sloan tasting the thick mess in the bowl.

Che-cho-ter respectfully came to where they were sitting and handed her husband his meal. Sloan's eyes followed Chala as she walked in Che-cho-ter's wake, her head thrown back proudly, flaxen hair tumbling over her shoulders and swaying in a gentle rhythm which echoed the swinging of her hips. When he accepted his dinner from her, he was quick to notice the difference between his meal and Osceola's. Not only in appearance but definitely in aroma. He was also quick to notice his brother's amused expression.

Cautiously, Sloan sampled his dinner. He managed to swallow by sheer willpower alone. Rising from his position beside Osceola, he gripped the bowl in his hand and walked toward Chala. All conversation in the village seemed to stop. Everyone was watching, waiting, and it was not to their disappointment when Sloan

said harshly, "Come with me!" Chala cowered backward, not liking the authoritative expression on the
man's face. Her lips drew back, showing perfect white
teeth.

"NO!"

"You're going to behave yourself and do as I say. I
won't tolerate your vindictiveness or this slop you call
food. Now, get over here and follow me!" His voice
thundered through the clearing, seeming to bounce off
the overhead clouds and fill the twilight.

"No!" Chala cried desperately. "The thlacko was
making a joke when he gave me to you; I don't have to
go anywhere with you! Her eyes blazed fire and she
advanced toward him, brazenly staring up into his face,
allowing him to see her hatred.

Sloan's outstretched arm froze in midair. His mouth
opened in astonishment. In his rage he had spoken
English rather than Seminole. And *she had understood
him!* Gathering his wits, he menaced, "So, the little
hellcat is conversant in English, is she? From this
moment on you will speak English to me. Each time
you revert to Seminole, I'll have you whipped before
the entire village. When I tell you something, I tell you
once! If you don't obey, I'll turn you over my knee and
spank you. And don't pretend not to understand me!"
Not waiting for a screeching reply, he reached for her
arm and dragged her across the encampment to where
Redeemer stood waiting for his evening portion of
oats. Sloan held out the bowl Chala had served him to
the animal who sniffed, whinnied and reared back.

"This meal isn't fit for my horse! You're a disgrace to
Osceola and a disgrace to me. It's clear now I made a
poor bargain with my brother. He wanted to be rid of
you so badly, he'd do anything, to have you taken off
his hands. You will cook for me again, Chala. And this
time it'd better be edible."

"You lie!" Chala hissed in slightly accented English.
"My chief made no poor bargain with you. You lie
through your teeth, like all white men. Osceola is my

father, and he treats me as his own child. You lie!" she spat.

The bowl he held clattered to the ground, spilling its unappetizing contents near his feet. His hands seized her shoulders, capturing her in an unrelenting vise. "I never lie!" he told her, his face so close to hers she could feel his breath on her cheek. "If you were so wonderful, why was my brother so eager to be rid of you?"

"Because . . . because you brought him food for our people, and he was obligated to repay you." Her voice held a tremor she desperately hoped was unnoticed.

"I would have been satisfied with a simple thank you. After all, he is my brother. He gave you to me because you humiliated me and your chief with your barbaric behavior. You behave like a savage, and you are unworthy of the Seminoles. It's time someone taught you to behave like a lady. If that's possible!" Each of his sentences was punctuated by a ruthless shaking of her shoulders till Chala thought her neck would snap.

*"Halpatter,"* she sneered derisively, slipping back into the Seminole tongue.

"What did you say?" he shook her savagely. "What did I tell you about speaking English!"

"Alligator! Alligator! That's what you are. A smiling lizard, teeth ready to snap and grind and devour! There is no English word to tell you how much I hate you!" She faced him, eyes blazing, her breath coming in great heaves, daring him to strike her as would be his right by Seminole rule. No woman ever spoke to a man thus; even the lowest man was above a woman's scorn.

"Snake, toad, weasel!" she shrieked. "You will not speak to me in such a manner. Regardless of what Osceola says, you will not take me from this village, from my people. I belong here. And you will not make me into a lady. And," she threatened defiantly, "I will not cook your food. Starve!"

Sloan's actions were quick and sure. His hands slid

from her shoulders, pinning her arms behind her back, anticipating the blow she would have cracked to his face. "We can do this the easy way or we can do it your way. Which is it to be?"

At the sight of her stony resolve, he grimaced. "That does it, woman. I'm going to tether you. And I want silence too, Chala. One more word out of you and I'll gag you!"

Chala's eyes widened. She could feel the amused glances of the village upon her! Tethered! Gagged! She'd be damned, the target of everyone's jokes, easy prey for the women's scorn. Shame vanished, replaced by a blind fury. Before Sloan knew what was happening, Chala's foot swung out and up. Sloan doubled over as she brought her clenched fists down hard on the back of his neck. Without a moment lost she thrust both hands out and pushed, standing over him when he toppled like a sapling before the wind. A hoarse cry of pain escaped him. Chala crouched low, her arms held straight in front of her to ward off any retaliation. Seeing him helpless, she stood, shouting to him in the Seminole language, daring him to stand up and fight her.

Damn. Damn. Did he live under some black Indian curse, leaving him fair game for this honey-haired savage. Warily, he struggled to his knees, aware of the deep burning in his groin. Willing himself to his feet, Sloan and Chala circled and stalked one another. The people of the village stood silently watching. From their expressions, Sloan couldn't know if they were waiting for him to beat Chala to an inch of her life or for him to go running into the woods yelping like a whipped dog.

Without warning, Sloan dropped lower to the ground, reaching a long arm toward Chala's ankle. A lightning bolt seemed to rip through his wrist as she punched down hard. To his credit, he hung onto the girl's slim ankle, dragging her to the ground. It took more strength than he anticipated to hold her prone beneath him. In some obscure way, he was enjoying her struggles, feeling her writhe beneath him, powerless.

Imprisoning her hands in one of his, he found the loop of rawhide around her neck on which various beads and trinkets were strung. Slipping it over her head, he swung his body around, straddling her, feeling her fists beating against his back and haunches. Oblivious to the pelting, he hurriedly and deftly secured the rawhide around her ankles, successfully tethering her like a runaway colt. Seizing her arms once again, he dragged her to her feet.

Shrill, venomous shrieks ripped through the cool night air. Furiously, he ripped the sleeve from her wide necked blouse, rending the fabric, leaving her shoulder and the side of her breast exposed for all to see. Wadding the material into a ball, he then stuffed it into her open, complaining mouth. Silence relieved his ears. Suddenly, loud clapping and laughing resounded. The thlacko's brother had won; Chala had received her justice.

And just what had he won? Sloan thought frustratedly. One look into Osceola's laughing, smirking face told him. Not much except perhaps a chikkee full of trouble. With Osceola's "no return" policy it appeared as though he was stuck with a girl who could almost kill with her eyes. Deciding to make the best of a bad situation, he wrapped his arm around her slim waist and hefted her onto his hip. Carrying her, squirming in protest, he set her down near the fire where she had prepared the mess she had served him for dinner. "Now cook," he said, pushing her to her duties. She stumbled, the tether around her legs affording her only inches of walking room. "You even *think* about removing that rag from your mouth, and I'll pull out each and every one of your teeth!"

In the dim glow from the numerous fires outside the chikkees, Chala's green eyes spewed flames. Tomorrow was another day when the thlacko's mighty brother would not gain the advantage again! She hoped.

The two brothers, sat long into the night, sometimes talking, sometimes enjoying the easy camaraderie they had formed in their youth. The sky above was black, lit by a spattering of stars and a slice of yellow moon. The night had brought a coolness and freshness to the air, and the fire crackling before them provided a welcome warmth.

From time to time Sloan's eyes drifted to the pouting girl across the compound. She would not be permitted to enter the chikkee until she presented a decent, edible meal to MacAllister. She stirred the contents of the black, iron pot with a vindictiveness that neither surprised nor alarmed him. The blouse sleeve was clenched between her teeth. To remove it under pain of suffering further humiliation would be more than she could bear. He realized he was going to have to watch Chala closely and not expose his back to her.

Sloan turned back towards his brother, and noticed the yellow pallor of the chief's skin.

"Osceola, I see something that's eluded me before this minute."

"What do you see, my brother?"

"A sickness, not of the spirit but of the body. You look as though you've suffered. Tell me truthfully."

"It is no secret. This summer past the horse soldiers had an outbreak of the country fever. I and many of my people brought it into our chikkees. I have recovered, but at a great price to my physical stamina. It stays in my body, and from time to time it shouts to be released. Even now, I feel it between my shoulders, and in seven sleeps it will render me to my pallet."

"Malaria?"

Osceola shrugged. "Malaria, country fever. It is the same. When the sickness falls upon me, I am weakened. It is bad for my people to see their chief sweating and raving like a madman. Only white men rant and rave. The Indian is silent and suffering." A wry smile touched the corners of his mouth as he watched for Sloan's reaction.

Sloan said nothing in retort. He had no wish to be baited by his brother over white man versus red man. He was sick of public wars and tired of private ones that tore his guts apart.

"Tomorrow," Osceola told him, "we leave this camp. It is good you arrived when you did or you would have found me absent. It is time for me to seek out the medicine man, Arpeika. The whites call him Sam Jones. We travel to the Panasoffke Swamp near the Withlacoochee River at first sun. It is time to join with our black brothers. Loyal black brothers," he said defiantly, almost daring Sloan to disagree.

"I'm going with you. This is my fight too. I'm just sorry that it's taken me so long to get here. I ask your forgiveness."

"It is given." Again the wry smile tugged at the corners of the Indian's mouth. "You appear to have need of the medicine man yourself. Chala was heavy with her hand. You'll mend. A man needs to be beaten occasionally to remind him of the power he has over those weaker than himself. For a soft, white man you managed very well." There was pride in the Indian's tone. Sloan accepted the compliment, making no comment.

"What will the blacks do for you?" he inquired, changing the subject away from himself.

Osceola was thoughtful for a moment. It was important for Sloan to understand the prominence the blacks were playing in the present hostilities between the Seminoles and the United States Government. "Did you know, brother, that when the wild buffalo still roamed the open plain and when the white settlers came from across the sea to settle the northern states, the Spanish held this place of the Floridas?"

Sloan nodded, placing the time of which Osceola spoke as more than one hundred years before.

"At that time," the Indian continued, his voice deep and unhurried, "the Spanish governor opened Florida to runaway slaves from English plantations. Not out of sympathy for a race of people, but rather to plague the English for encroaching on Spanish territories. This Spanish governor armed the blacks and treated them as free men. It drew the slaves from the Carolinas in droves, all seeking freedom here in this land. Word spread of this land where a black man could be free. Many came into the western parts of Florida, as did the Creeks, who, as you know, are cousin to the Seminole. The tide of runaway slaves rolled in higher and higher, pledging service to the Seminole because in no other tribe are they so highly revered. The blacks live in separate villages and enjoy equal liberty with us. For sharing our land, the blacks pay us tribute with the products from their fields."

Sloan could understand why the blacks preferred to live among the Indian rather than among more "civilized" white owners. For the protection of the Seminole they paid a small tribute. No racial bars were ever raised against them, and intermarriage was common. Theirs was a mutual trust between the negro and Seminole in both war and council.

Osceola continued, "Among the blacks here are recent fugitives certain to be reclaimed by their masters if any white authority lays hands on them. But I fear as well for the blacks born among the Seminole who are the descendants of runaway slaves. The white man is greedy for the Florida land and the slaves to work that land. But the Seminole rightfully own this land, brother, and have sheltered the runaways and we will never give either of them up."

"You seem so certain of the black's loyalty," Sloan said somberly, testing his brother's faith in the negroes.

Osceola nodded. "I realize that all bands of our people cannot be controlled by me alone. But my lieutenants have been well trained and fight wisely. This man Jessup is said to have great numbers of troops. We're sadly outnumbered, but with small parties of our black and Indian warriors, it is possible to move quickly and harass small bodies of white soldiers. As you know, no alligator eats the whole calf; the *halpatter* rolls and churns to rip off pieces he can swallow. Eventually, the calf disappears."

Sloan looked doubtful. Was Osceola aware what a "great number" of troops meant? At best, his attacks would be those of a flea biting a dog.

Sloan listened as Osceola explained why the negroes would fight as warriors beside the Seminole. Not only could they accept discipline, but the forefathers of many of them had been fierce warriors in Africa. Most of the negroes were caught in a war they could not escape and fought bravely. Their race had more to lose; more to remember. Whether it was the overseer's lash at the plantation, or the wife sold at auction, or the raped sister; or the endless future of work in the fields until the slave was kicked aside to die. Fighting beside the Seminole might be a form of suicide, but at least the negroes were taking part in their own destiny, fighting for their rights as human beings. It was right, Sloan decided. It was good.

The camp fire burned low, the sapling logs hissing and flaring as they broke apart. Sloan raised his flinty gray eyes upward. The orange sliver of moon rode high in the sky toward its own destiny. A chill shivered up his spine. Nearly twenty years ago he had heard his brother tell him he was leaving the MacAllister farm to search out *his* destiny. Now, looking at the man Osceola had become, Sloan wondered where that destiny would take the young boy who had taught him to hunt and fish Indian fashion. Clouds darkened his vision, or was it the mercy of the gods who hid the future from the sight of mortal man?

It was time for sleep. Yet, Osceola sat warming himself near the diminishing fire. When he made no move to add more logs, Sloan reached for several logs and tossed them into the smoldering embers. They caught flame, sparks spewing. "My stomach rumbles. I believe it's time for my meal." Not wishing to shout to Chala, he rose from his crosslegged position and sauntered to where she waited. He helped himself to a generous portion of what appeared to be watery gruel like Polly used to make when the boys were sick. Cautiously, he sampled the new fare. The only difference he could discern between the original dish and this was the texture. It tasted the same. He grimaced, spat to show his displeasure and then tried it again. He felt as though his innards were turning in on themselves, but he had to eat; there was no choice.

"Tomorrow, you'll do better or you'll cook in that pot along with this concoction. You can spit out that gag for now, but one word from you and back in it goes. The village is sleeping, and my brother feels a fever coming upon him. Do you understand me?"

The girl nodded, watching him warily as she took the fabric from between her teeth. Sloan felt a moment of pity for the wretched beauty as she attempted to wet her lips and mouth.

"You will sleep now. Your chief tells me that tomorrow at sunup we leave for Panasoffke Swamp. We'll pretend that today never happened and start afresh. Go to sleep." His tone was not unkind when he spoke, looking deeply into the dark green eyes that could appear as black as night in the firelight. She did not speak but turned in the direction of Osceola's chikkee.

Sloan returned to his brother near the fire. "I think I'll sleep under the stars tonight. I'll wake at first light to help ready the pack mules and supplies for the trip."

"Sloan." It was part declaration, part question, part command. Sloan waited expectantly. Osceola rarely called him by his given name and for some reason the hairs on the back of his neck bristled. "If I seem preoccupied since your arrival, it is because I am deeply worried about my people. I cannot know how much more suffering they can carry. I want you to know that save for the births of my children, the day of your arrival will remain always with me. When I needed you, you came, without my having to ask. You are truly our mother's son." Osceola extended his hand for the white man's salutation of greeting. It was Osceola's tribute to Sloan and to his boyhood with Jeb MacAllister.

Sloan accepted the handshake soberly. When Osceola withdrew his hand, Sloan quickly embraced him. "And you are truly more my brother than if the same blood coursed in our veins. I see your Che-cho-ter has placed a blanket for me near the chikkee. Good night, Osceola, sleep well."

Chala stood silently in the darkness watching the exchange between her chief and the white man called Sloan. She frowned as she saw Osceola offer his hand. What a foolish custom. But a smile touched her face when she watched the man with the golden hair embrace his brother. For a moment she forgot her humiliation and anger. A warm feeling settled over her until she remembered the predicament she was in. Her eyes narrowed as she saw MacAllister pick up his blanket and spread it further away from the chikkee. Her own folded blanket hung over her arm. She no longer belonged in Osceola's chikkee. Wherever this man went she would be forced to go. The moment he settled himself she approached his blanket. Without a word, she unfolded hers and lay down, careful to stay as far away from his side as she could. She must keep telling herself she belonged to this man. At least for the present.

Sloan lay a long time waiting for the girl to explain her presence near him. Instead, he heard light, even breathing. It was a trick. She probably had a knife hidden in her moccasin, and as soon as he was asleep, his blood would run in the dust. He lay quietly for what seemed hours, his nerves strung as tautly as bow strings. It wasn't that he was afraid to die, just that he didn't want his death to be at the hands of a young girl. There was no honor in that kind of death.

Deliberately, he pretended a few loud, raucous

snores. He moved slightly, pretending restlessness and settled again. Now. She would make her move now! He counted to two hundred. Another snore, followed by a slight gnashing of teeth. Then a sound caught his ear. She was crying!

This was not the way Beaunell cried; it was soft, heartbrokenly soft and the sound tore at his heart. If it were Beaunell, he would perhaps give her money for a new pair of slippers and offer her his handkerchief. Beaunell would blow her nose lustily, kiss him wetly on the mouth and everything would be fine. He felt at a loss with the strange, heart-rending whimpering.

Without stopping to think, he rolled over onto his side and gathered Chala close. Gently, he brushed her wild hair from her brow and from her wet cheeks. He murmured soft, soothing words. Eventually, she settled into the crook of his arm, making a nest for herself. He liked the feel of her beside him. She fit perfectly against him. Soon, she was asleep. Sloan lay a few moments longer, savoring the feel and womanly scent of her. Stirrings of desire rushed through him. He knew he could take her here and now. He also knew she would fight him. But he had never taken a woman against her will, and he wouldn't start now. There would be other times, other places, when the moment would be the same. He was certain of it.

The last thought that entered his mind before he drifted into dreamless sleep, still holding Chala's warm body against him, was that now he had a serious responsibility. He now had a woman to protect and support. A feisty, she-lion of a woman who would not give him a moment's peace. Damn Osceola's generosity.

In the darkness of his chikkee, Osceola lay down beside his young wife, Che-cho-ter. In the white man's tongue, she was Morning Dew, a fitting name for her beauty. Her dusky skin was smooth, fresh, like the petal of a hibiscus in the first light of day. Her eyes were soft, loving, filling with admiration and burning passions whenever she looked at her husband. She was graceful, tender, and she was his, completely, without reservation. And to his greatest delight, this woman who was worthy of so much more was his friend.

Even in sleep she turned to him, caressing his cheek with her hand, settling her head upon his shoulder, reminding him that once she had told him it was her favorite place to be. In his arms her world was secure and held meaning.

Nearby, behind the colorful blanket hanging from the rafters, their three daughters slept. He could hear their quiet, restful breathing. A good sound, he had discovered so long ago, when their first daughter was born. What else did a man need from life, he questioned, finding sleep elusive. A warm, loving woman in his arms, his children fed and sleeping nearby. This was life and only this.

How then, he wondered, had he become responsible for the lives of so many people when simplicity and peace were all he wanted from his life?

As he turned his head to breathe the fragrance of Che-cho-ter's hair, he thought back to the day two years ago, an eternity ago, when his service to his people became clear. He had been becoming more involved with the politics of his tribe and, on several occasions, had had the opportunity to declare his views before the ritual council fires. Osceola's thoughts spun backward, recalling to mind each detail of that day when the destiny he had chased as a boy had reached out to seize him.

Under Arpeika's tutelage, he had taken great care with his dress for the visit with the chiefs and elders of his tribe to discuss the worsening situation growing between the United States Government and the Seminoles. His knee-length dress-frock bore intricate patterns of geometric design, each symbolic of a legend from his heritage and patiently embroidered by Che-cho-ter. Slim, fitted leggings ended in soft, doeskin moccasins that silenced his movements across the trail. Even now, laying here beside Che-cho-ter, he could smell the forest as it had been on that day. He had run ahead of his people to scout the area, and had positioned himself in a hickory tree where he could observe the military fort and at the same time watch the trail for the arrival of Arpeika and the other spokesmen for the Seminoles.

As the dawn slowly outlined Fort King, Osceola had watched, becoming aware of the distinctive smell of soldiers who were packed too many to a barrack. There had been an odor of woodsmoke, horses and stale cooking, and the aroma of baking bread.

Because of his past Osceola knew much more of the ways of the white man then either the soldiers or his fellow Seminoles suspected. He knew the whites' penchant for living according to the clock, and their compulsion for routine. The soldiers rose together, dressed alike, ate when ordered, and as the day progressed, they drilled obediently or labored in the sun until permitted to rest. At last tattoo, all but the sentries slept. Such was the routine, day after day.

To an Indian, this was strange behavior, but Osceola had learned the merits of such a routine from his step-father. Jeb MacAllister had taught him that soldiers who worked as a unit and fought on command presented a greater strength to their enemy. For the Seminoles to fight the white man, learning and obedience would be imperative.

Osceola had perched in the tree to watch the day begin at Fort King. On this dark morning, the forest had been ripe with the cool, wet aroma of greenery. The air was still and heavy. The quiet and silence had settled on the warrior's ears like a welcome friend. The only presence had been his own, except for a wolf, gaunt from hunger, whose howlings had been interrupted by the approach of day.

Dawn had whitened the eastern sky; a single bird screamed shrilly and was answered by another in the distance. In the tall, scrubby pines, squirrels had chattered at the form of the silent Indian who presented a threat to their lofty nests.

The thick foliage of the hickory had offered him cover and also gave an excellent view of the proceedings behind the stockades. He had watched and listened as the fort came to life. Before the sun would make a quarter arc in the sky, he would be joined by the most important chiefs in the Seminole nation. It was the day that would decide whether or not the Seminoles would make war against the white man.

He was to meet with Alligator and Arpeika and various of the other leaders opposed to the Florida Indian emigration into Arkansas. They had only recently received word that the Paynes Landing and Fort Gibson treaties for emigration had been ratified and proclaimed by the President. When word of this action had reached the Seminoles, they were stunned. Such a thing could not be. The Indian nation had not been consulted about moving! This was an unparalleled land grab.

The affairs of the Seminoles had been brought to crisis. Many starving bands were preying upon the cattle herds and provisions of the whites just to stay alive. The Treaty of 1823 had deprived the Seminoles of their cultivated fields and of a region of country fruitful with game. They had been placed in a wilderness that was unsuitable for farming or hunting, and people were dying.

And in answer to all this misery the government had demanded that the Seminoles move west and be assimilated into the Creek nation in Arkansas. This added insult to injury. The Creek were their enemy. There was unremitting bad blood between the two nations concerning the ownership of slaves. The runaway black slaves that the Seminoles had accepted into their nation had married and had children among the Indian. The Creeks had frequently raided Seminole villages, seeking slaves, oftentimes taking Indian as well as black man. The only sentiment the Seminoles felt for the Creeks was hatred. If the white man had his way, the Seminoles would become slaves to their enemies.

The sun had risen, and as he looked at the preparations taking place behind the stockades, Osceola heard the approach of many feet from a great distance away. His people had come to face the white-eyes and defy the terms of the treaty.

Within minutes he could see the feathered turbans of the warriors and the brightly banded skirts of the women who had come to bear witness and stand against the soldiers. When the head line was almost beneath the tree where he sat, Osceola lightly jumped to the ground, saluting Alligator and the old man Arpeika.

"I see the women have followed," he stated simply.

"Che-cho-ter follows with your daughters," Arpeika answered the question it would have been unseemly to ask.

His eyes searching, he finally saw her, leading their three little daughters along the trail. When she saw her husband, Che-cho-ter had smiled. "You have found me, my husband." Her voice was low, a pleasant thrum in his ears. He had not shared his chikkee with her for ten nights and he was hungry for her. The emotion was reflected in her eyes as she stood proudly before him. "We have dressed in our best so as not to bring shame upon you. Even little Lilka," she said, holding the baby out for him to approve.

Osceola had reached out and touched his youngest daughter, stroking the silken skin of her cheek. So like his Morning Dew was this youngest one. Even her quick smile and gentle features were her mother's. Turning his attention to eight-year-old Hola and five-year-old Mic-canna, he embraced them lovingly.

The more precocious of the two, Mic-canna had

asked, "Do we have to be very quiet as our mother told us?"

"Yes, little one. You must be very quiet and show the soldiers how well behaved Seminole children can be." He smiled, looking up into Che-cho-ter's face. Only she could read there the great weight he bore on his shoulders. Only she knew his agony at the thought of their people's blood being shed. Brave talk was for young boys; only men knew the meaning of death and separation.

"You must leave us, my husband. You must take your place among the leaders of our nation. We will be strong for you." Che-cho-ter had masked the emotion in her voice, and looked intently at her husband, hiding her fear and dread.

It was Thursday. Agent Wiley Thompson had convened the meeting at the agency within the stockade of Fort King. The Seminole chiefs had gathered within the building while lesser warriors crowded the porch or squeezed into the main room. The women sat beneath the trees surrounding the building, lending emotional support to their men. This was an important day for all Seminole women. Today would be the day the Seminole chiefs would decide whether to leave their homes for an unknown land and fall into slavery at the hands of the Creeks, or to make their stand against white authority. If war was declared, many of the women sitting beneath the shade trees in Fort King would become widows.

Agent Thompson, who represented the government, had addressed the gathering with a long speech, interpreted by Abraham, the negro. The tone of his message suggested that he considered the removal of the Indians all but accomplished.

Slim and tall, Abraham had delivered the speech to his friends, repeating Thompson's words in the language of the Seminole. "Your noble cousins to the west have invited the Seminoles to settle among them."

Groans and angry mutterings had filled the agency. Such behavior was a breach of Seminole etiquette and so rare that even Abraham had been astonished. The main cause for concern was the deep fear that the Creeks or white slave-catchers would claim the negroes who lived among them.

The conference fire in Fort King had burned brightly for many days as each *thlacko*, or chief, had had his say. Abraham, the negro interpreter, was present at each meeting as a trusted friend. He would represent them at the conferences with the white man.

Osceola had kept silent through most of these conferences, careful to keep his rage from erupting. At last, it was his turn to speak. Controlling his voice, he had addressed his leaders.

"Brothers, talk is good and helps to heal the wounds of betrayal. But now we must prepare for the worst. The Seminole is of this land. Our spirits walk the forests and fish the streams. Away from this land the Seminole does not exist. Our people must agree not to follow the dictates of the whites who want this land for their own. Our people must realize their blood may soak this earth. But we need to be united as a people, just as the white soldiers come together under their leaders."

"Some of our chiefs are willing to walk to the west," Alligator said, the deep lines in his face drawing his face down in a scowl. "Holata Emathla and his brother, Charley Emathla, believe it is good for the Seminole. Coa Hadjo first said he would not move, but now his mind is changing."

Osceola had stood, his slim, straight form outlined by the fire. "No! There is no good in it. To move is to become enslaved by the Creeks. Have we not seen the misery of slavery in the black faces who run from their masters to work beside the Seminole? We must turn their minds. We must also persuade Micanopy to stand firm. Micanopy, above all. He is a great chief and has

many warriors under him. Arpeika can influence him."
He turned toward the old medicine man who was
known by the whites as Sam Jones.

"So can anyone influence Micanopy," Arpeika had
observed wryly. The old man sat crosslegged, arms
folded against his breast. "We know of my kinsman's
weakness. Yet I believe Micanopy would die before
being driven from his home. He will stand when others
strengthen him."

"As we know, brother," Alligator had agreed. "But
words are not enough. The white warriors will try to
move us by force." There had been a note of regret and
resolution in his tone.

"If we must fight, we will fight!" Osceola had shouted. "And we should be ready to fight. We must save all
lead and buy kegs of powder. Every warrior must be
ready!" Voice shaking with emotion and fervor, he had
glanced around the camp fire, searching the faces of the
gathered chiefs. He saw sorrow and in some cases—
defeat.

So it was that Osceola had raised his voice, speaking
the hearts of his people, setting them on a course that
would mean victory at a terrible price or total defeat.
But his words were strong, his voice unquavering, and
in time of confusion and indecision his keenness and
self-assurance made his voice the one to be heard
and his heart the one to follow.

Arpeika, Osceola's mentor, had chosen his protege
well. In the soul of this young Seminole burned the love
of his people and the vigor of a mighty warrior. He
would see to it that Osceola would gain more and more
influence over the tribe and all the Seminole nation
would know him as chief.

Che-cho-ter moved in her sleep, bringing Osceola
back into the present. Sleep would elude him this night,
he knew. Wrapping his arm about his wife, he silently
thanked the Great One that his brother had come to his

aid. If this heaviness in his heart was prophetic, it would seem that Osceola, thlacko to the Seminole, was in the habit of leaving his women in his white brother's care.

Sloan woke as dawn crept close to the campsite, completely aware of where he was and his surroundings. The soft grays and purples of early light comforted him somehow. It hit him instantly that the warm presence of the girl was missing. Tentatively, he rolled onto his side to see where she was. To his left, talking agitatedly to Chala, was the handsome buck Mico who had led the scouting party which had brought him to the village. Comprehension dawned suddenly. Sloan imagined that he could feel deep hatred fan out from the brave's body. Chala's back was to him, so it was impossible to see her response, but he couldn't miss the heavy handed expressions the brave was using during his agitated conversation with Chala. Sloan decided not to interfere. This was something that must be settled by Chala herself. If she had been promised to Mico then Osceola would never have given him the girl, regardless of whether Sloan was his brother or not.

Chala's blanket lay folded neatly beside him. When he rose, he knew the girl would walk over, fold his blanket and place it on top of her own. For the second time it occurred to him that asking for the girl in a pique of anger had been a mistake.

A stray dog slinked past Sloan's legs, making him step sideways. He wondered vaguely how the scrawny animal had managed to survive the stew pot. It was a slat-ribbed dog with mangy fur and the saddest eyes Sloan had ever seen. He watched as the animal rubbed against Chala's bare brown leg. Absently, as if from long practice, the girl bent to scratch behind the dog's ears. Suddenly, she stiffened and then looked furtively over her shoulder at Sloan. He busied himself with tying the laces of his deerskin boots. When he looked up, Chala and the dog were gone. So, he grinned to himself, the little savage has a heart after all. The tears and the mangy dog were her release, her defense against things she couldn't control.

The fires burned low, the cook pots had simmered through the night. Each man was served his morning portion. Unable to eat Chala's contribution, Sloan made himself obvious near Osceola's chikkee. Without hesitation, Morning Dew ladled a large, generous portion of the fragrant stew into an earthenware bowl. She smiled in approval as Sloan wolfed down the food and held out his bowl for a refill. Within mouthfuls it was gone. Osceola's first wife, Ina, held out a slab of Koonti bread which Sloan ripped apart and savored to the last mouthful.

Osceola had not yet made his appearance. He inquired of Ina who shrugged elaborately, a sad look on her face. It clearly said it was not her place to comment on Osceola's absence.

Preparations for the move were underway. Yahi, the widow woman, was to stay behind to tend the chikkee. She accepted the order with pride, feeling needed once again in her old life. Within the hour all was in readiness. The last two things to be removed from the chikkee was Osceola's yellow and red standard, and the glowing, smoldering embers from the fire that were to be placed in a clay container which was affixed to a stick. At sundown, when they camped, the embers would need nothing more than pine straw to catch and flame, making the evening fire.

Small children capered to and fro, enjoying the thrill of early morning. It was amazing what warmth and a full stomach could do for a child's happiness. At that moment in time Sloan swore to himself that no matter what, he would do his best to make sure these children and all the people under Osceola's protection survived.

The cook pots seemed to the most important items of all, and Sloan watched the reverent way Osceola's women handled their precious possessions. Still, Osceola had not made an appearance. Chala was nowhere to be seen. The mongrel dog had long since disappeared.

Everything stood in readiness, waiting for Osceola to exit his chikkee and remove the yellow and red standard. Once it was removed, it meant the chief was not in residence. It was the last thing to be removed and the first thing to be hung upon making a new camp whether it was temporary or permanent.

Crisp, cold air made Sloan draw in his breath. He hadn't realized how chilly the morning was until he saw a cloudy vapor of his own breath. With the fires almost extinguished, he felt the chill creep into his boots and beneath the buckskin he wore. He knew from long practice that within the hour he'd be perspiring, and no doubt he'd remove the buckskin tunic. But Florida mornings were still cool in the winter, something to which he was slowly adjusting.

At last all was in readiness. Osceola's wives stood near the children awaiting the signal from their husband to begin the long walk to their destination in the Panasoffke Swamp. Their party was a small one: Osceola, his two wives, three daughters, Sloan, Chala and three warriors. Eleven, not counting the six pack mules and, of course, Redeemer. Sloan stood waiting for Osceola, Redeemer's bridle in hand.

"Give my brother any trouble, you cantankerous beast, and I'll see to it you find yourself in the same cook fires those mules are heading for, hear me?" Redeemer raised his head, the whites of his eyes showing, snorting vapors of clouds in the early morning.

When the chief exited his chikkee, he removed his standard with little ceremony. Quietly, he stood as the smoking pot of embers was affixed to a long stick. There was religious significance in bringing a fire from home to light the fires along the trail. It ensured safety, security and an uneventful night's rest.

"My brother will ride this unworthy beast I have

brought all the way from Russia," Sloan told him, eyeing the horse speculatively. Ordinarily, Redeemer never allowed anyone but himself to mount him.

As Osceola put his foot into the stirrup, Redeemer looked back at him over his massive black shoulder. Sloan pulled hard upon the reins, giving fair warning. Redeemer must have sensed the association between his master and this strange, dark man with feathers in his turban. Or perhaps he sensed the man was ill and he was needed to carry him. Osceola mounted with little difficulty; it had been years since he had ridden a horse because they were so scarce among the Seminole. Redeemer showed himself to be a gentleman. The others in the camp nodded their approval that their chief was able to ride the black stallion with such little effort. He was truly a great man in close company with the spirits of the forest. They had all witnessed the battle the animal had waged with anyone who had tried to approach him, save the white-eyes.

Osceola at the head, the small party followed single file behind Redeemer. Yahi's face was stoic, giving no hint of her feelings as her new family left the little village. Sloan was the last to fall into line. Suddenly, Chala was beside him. She refused to meet his eyes, aware of her tears during the night. It was one more humiliation she had to bear.

The day long trek was wearying. By sundown, it was apparent to Sloan that Osceola was more than a little ill. The medicine man, Arpeika, could help him if they had left in time. By noon of the following day they would set up their new camp and decide what they would do in order to survive Jessup and his men. It wounded Sloan to see the effect the trek was costing Osceola.

Ina and Morning Dew saw to their husband's comfort. His daughters stared at their father with dark, somber eyes. The littlest let her lower lip tremble when she clutched at her father's leg. Always before he would bend down, pick her up and whisper words that made her laugh in delight. This time he merely placed a tired, weary hand on her shiny black head. The child swayed back and forth, enjoying her father's gentle touch. With shaking hand, Osceola affixed his standard, and then with a deep sigh allowed Che-cho-ter to lead him to a pallet where he lay down heavily and seemed to drop instantly into a sleep.

The Indians began their preparation for building new fires and the evening meal. There was nothing for Sloan to do. The women wouldn't tolerate him standing around their fires; the children were content to play among themselves. The Indian braves stood in awe of him now that they were convinced he was their chief's brother.

Settling himself in a comfortable position against a sturdy Southern pine, Sloan watched Chala as she began to prepare his food. In a generous, forgiving gesture he had removed her tether for the long trek. He hoped it wasn't a mistake. She worked with an economy of motion and appeared to know what she was doing. If that was the case, Sloan wondered how the food could taste so awful. As he continued to stare at her, he became aware of the fact that she had combed her hair and pulled it behind her ears. Her profile shone in the light of the cook fire. She was a beautiful young woman. Something teased at his mind, niggled away at him as he watched her make the Koonti bread. Certainly, there was no likeness to Annemarie or Beaunell, but she reminded him of someone he knew. Perhaps someone he had seen, some brief acquaintance in Europe. Whatever, it would come to him sooner or later. He had a good memory for faces and rarely forgot names and places. He would remember. What he did remember now was the desire that rose in him while Chala slept in his arms and how he had to force himself to resist temptation. He closed his eyes and slept, knowing the girl would wake him when the food was ready. He was tired, he admitted to himself. The journey and ever-increasing worries had left him drained.

Osceola lay in exhaustion on his pallet while the women prepared the last meal of the day. His mind was rolling with the situations he faced. The calendar year was soon coming to an end, and the portents for the future were ominous. The information Sloan had given him about this new commander, General Jessup, had been enlightening, but it was Osceola himself who was more clearly apprised of the general's actions. Immediately after taking command, Jessup had ordered the building of several small forts in the heart of Indian territory. The new white commander of the Florida army must have left New Orleans shortly after Sloan because word had reached Osceola that his arrival was anticipated within days. And Jessup didn't come alone. There was word that he had recruited a unit of no less than four hundred Tennessee volunteers, experienced Indian fighters, to accompany him. It had come to his ears that these little forts were to be manned by navy marines and sailors, and were calculated to surround the Withlachoochee area and provide readily available supplies.

Turning over, eyes closing in sleep, Osceola smiled. Jessup's bringing the supplies directly into the area was encouraging. The winter would not be a hungry one after all. The Seminole would not have to travel far to find meat for their fires.

It was expected that the Withlachoochee area would be the target of concentrated attacks. In conference with the chiefs, Osceola had suggested that the bands spread out and gradually move southward. These chiefs, Arpeika, Alligator and Micanopy would shift toward the headquarters of the Oklawaha River. Alligator would operate in the vicinity of Lake Apopka. The oldest and most wily of all the Seminole leaders, King Phillip, was to maintain his position south of St.

Augustine, where his periodic attacks on the city terrified its occupants.

For now, Thlacko Osceola was content with his decision to move to the negro village in the Panasoffke Swamp. The sickness was coming fast upon him, and he believed he and his family would be more comfortable with the Indian-blacks who virtually worshipped him. And Arpeika was expected to be in the area, possibly staying in the Panasoffke village, and Osceola desperately needed his medicine.

Sleep came at last, giving the harried Indian peace, even if it was momentary.

# Chapter Five

In the black night, trees overhanging like a canopy to hide them from the stars, Chala walked beside Sloan, leaving the cook fire of Ina and Che-cho-ter behind. The moon was high in the sky as it peeped down at them through the branches. The rustling of brush and the silent whoosh of an owl's wing fell on their ears.

They had left the camp while Che-cho-ter tried to get the children to sleep. This was an exciting adventure for them, traveling with their father, sleeping out. Sleep would be long coming to them this night. Sloan was aware of Chala beside him, the scent of her hair, so remembered from the night before, came pleasantly to his nostrils.

Chala, herself, was silent, absorbed in her own thoughts. When she wasn't railing against him, she could be a quiet, peaceful woman. The Seminole ways had been well learned and practiced. He wondered if he had succeeded in taming her somewhat, if she was beginning to accept the fact that she now belonged to him. Or was it the presence of the warrior, Mico, that gentled her? Back at the camp the young brave's eyes had never left Chala as she moved about the fire, and he wasn't mistaken about the fury he'd witnessed in the Indian's eyes when Chala had brought Sloan his dinner.

Sloan's own eyes had followed Chala, knowing there was something astoundingly familiar about her, yet unable to place where he had seen her before arriving at Osceola's village. This evening, she had taken the time after their long walk through the forest to brush her wild, honey-colored hair back from her face, pulling it into a single, thick braid that trailed down her back. Wayward strands escaped and curled around her face, creating a nimbus of gold that softened her features and accentuated her wide, luminous eyes. Eyes as green as the waters of the Withlacoochee fringed with startlingly black lashes. Eyes he knew he had looked into once before. Her long, arching neck was set gently above sloping shoulders. Her body slim and lithe and delicate in proportion, offset by high, proud breasts and tiny waist. But it was the face, well defined, open and beautiful, that strained his memory. Now, in the shadows of the moon, he could look at her, even touch her, but recognition eluded him.

"Why do MacAllister's eyes constantly search me?" she demanded, breaking the silence they had shared. She turned to face him, her eyes seeming to ignite with sudden anger. Her full lips were drawn into a pout, yet were appealingly curved, as if able to erupt into a beatific smile at the slightest provocation.

"You remind me of someone, and yet I can't quite place who. And it must have been fairly recent. Galveston, New Orleans, perhaps I saw a face in a crowd, in a passing carriage . . ." It suddenly dawned on him. Jessup. The portrait over the mantle. The same honey blonde hair, the curving mouth, the insolent green eyes. Jessup's sister who had been killed by the Indians in Alabama. Memory flooded back. What had Jessup said? A child? A daughter? Savannah. Savannah James. The sister's name was Caroline. . . .

Abruptly, he caught her arm, swinging her around so the moonlight could fall on her face. Fingertips held her chin, turning her face into a portrait-like pose.

"What do you see, MacAllister?" Chala demanded.

"Tell me, Chala, what do you know of your beginnings?"

Her eyes dropped, refusing to look at him, as though she were ashamed to admit that her heritage was white instead of Indian.

"You must tell me. I must know! It may be of the most vital importance to Osceola."

This last statement seemed to prompt her to answer. "I only know what the old ones have told me. Nothing more."

"You're lying. You do remember something, and for some reason you don't want to admit it." His voice was urgent, sharp and insistent. "Whatever it is, no matter how small or how painful, you must tell me. You may be the only living soul who can help the Seminole. You claim them for your people; don't you think you owe them something?"

Still, Chala's face was set, her eyes downcast, lips pressed firmly into a thin, grim line.

"Let me tell you what I know about you," Sloan said gently, leading her over to a low hummock that bulged from the soft, fresh earth. She was watching him intently, her eyes expressionless, listening to his voice.

"You were a little child when your parents were killed by Indians, most likely the Creeks in Alabama. I'd venture a guess that you were taken by them back to their camp. Being warriors on the move, they probably brought you into Florida with the intention of selling you as a slave to the Seminoles. How close am I to the truth, Chala?"

Her eyes fell away from him; he imagined he could hear her heart beating a tattoo in her breast. "To the Seminole beginnings are the least important. It is only the person you become that matters. I was six summers old when Osceola and his old wife Ina took me to their chikkee."

"Do you remember your mother's name?" he asked her, his voice quiet, in a tone he would use to gentle a skittish colt.

"No." A long pause sent his hopes crashing. Then, "I only called her Mama." There was such a deep sadness in her, setting her lower lip to quivering.

"And what did your father call her?"

The question seemed to astound her; she had never

thought of it before this. The syllables came hesitantly; they were nearly a sob. "C . . . Caro . . . line. Caro-line."

"And she called you Savannah. Isn't that so? Savan-nah." He repeated the name Jessup had uttered with such drunken harshness.

She seemed to roll the name over her tongue as dagger sharp shafts of memory pierced her. A lone, silent tear trickled down her cheek, but she didn't seem to be aware of it.

"Savannah James," she told him at last. "They killed my mother. I saw them. Papa wasn't in the house, but they killed him too. They . . . they took me. Carried me with them. I was afraid of them and I screamed and cried, but they didn't listen; they didn't care. They had paint on their cheeks and feathers in their hair. The horses they rode were big, and wild, and I had to be carried across their laps. . . ." It seemed impossible for her to continue. She had told him enough. This was the girl General Jessup thought dead. The man wouldn't need any more proof that Savannah was indeed his niece. The comparison between Savannah and the portrait would convince him.

Chala's shattered cry broke the stillness, her low, tormented moans filling the forest with the sadness, terror and grief she hadn't been able to express as a child.

When he took her into his arms and held her, she continued to sway and issue low, tormented sounds. But there were no tears. They had been expressed through a lifetime of abandonment.

Her grief had exhausted her. She lay there weak and pale, unable to move. Sympathy and tenderness welled up in Sloan and with great care he lifted her in his arms, carrying her as easily as Redeemer carried him. She cradled there, resting her head against his shoulder, accepting this show of concern with relief.

The way back to the camp was a short distance, the overhead moon gave enough illumination to see the path clearly. Following the light from the camp fire, Sloan broke into the clearing, carrying Chala, and ran straight into Mico, dark and smoldering with hostility. The man's burning eyes followed Sloan, to where Savannah had laid their pallets. Dropping to one knee, Sloan gently placed her on the blankets, pulling the covers high under her chin to protect her from the chill night air. When at last he stood, it was to find Mico standing directly behind him, his face a mask of controlled rage.

"If the white-eyes was not called brother by my chief, I would have the pleasure of fighting you for her!" He spoke in guttural tones, not caring if Sloan knew his disgust. "I, Mico, Mikasuki Seminole, have looked upon the squaw with the honey hair."

Sloan knew that for a Seminole brave to "look at" a woman was the first step in claiming her for his own. But any regret for the upheaval he had brought into Chala's life and for the disappointment he had brought to one of Osceola's finest warriors, was immediately erased by Mico's brash threat. "You will never take her from this land," he told Sloan, so forcefully that spittle formed on his lips. His black eyes boiled menacingly.

Drawing himself up to his full height, Sloan peered down into the warrior's eyes. "Chala will do what she must for her people. Just as you must fight at my brother's side. You will not approach me again, Mico, or threaten me. Not because I am your chief's brother, but because I am not a man to be threatened." Authority rang in his voice.

Unconsciously, Mico's hand went to the knife he wore in his belt. "This will be settled at another time, white-eyes, when my chief no longer has use for you. Chala will belong to me, and the wild dogs will dig beneath the forest floor to consume your flesh."

For a long moment Sloan stared unswervingly into the warrior's eyes. Then he turned his back on the man and slid down into the pallet beside Chala. He half expected to feel Mico's knife plunged between his ribs.

After a moment he heard the Indian's footsteps take him away. Mico, passing the fire, in unrelenting frustration, kicked the shallow pile of embers in Sloan's direction, showering glowing sparks onto the blanket he shared with Chala. The pungent stink of singed wool filled Sloan's nostrils, but he pretended not to notice what the man had done. It would be difficult for Osceola to place himself impartially between his brother from so long ago and his most valuable warrior.

He touched Chala's shoulder and she turned toward him, sliding into his embrace and placing her head on his shoulder. She was sleeping, he knew, yet she had instinctively sought his comfort. A tenderness welled within him that was the most overpowering emotion he had ever felt.

Raucous calls erupted in the forest as brightly plumed birds greeted the dawn. A fox was skulking through the trees, pausing to sniff the smoking vapors from the campsite's banked fires. The forest was awakening to a new day, and Chala nestled into the warmth of Sloan's body, instinctively pushing her slim back and sloping haunches against him. His arms had wrapped around her during the night; his face was buried in her hair and she could feel his breath warm and soft against the nape of her neck.

Suddenly her green eyes flew open, instantly aware of her position. Scenes from the evening before assaulted her, bringing new pain. It had been years since she had allowed herself to remember her parents and the circumstances that led her into Osceola's guardianship. And MacAllister had forced her to remember, had stripped her naked of all her defenses, leaving her weak and frightened as though she were a child of six again.

Her life had become hellish since this man had come to her village. She had been chastised and humiliated before the entire village, forced to fetch and carry for a man she detested and constantly reminded by his mere presence that she was not a Seminole, but a white woman. He forced her to speak a language she had thought she had long forgotten, and to add to her misery, she must now share a pallet with him, allow him to intrude upon her, even in sleep.

Chala lay perfectly still, suddenly noticing a change in the rhythm of MacAllister's breathing. His arms that moments ago had been heavy and lifeless were now tightening around her, imperceptibly drawing her closer into his body's embrace.

Sloan had woken, driven by a shrill cry of birds praising the new day. Chala's weight lay warm and soft against him, the fresh woodsy scent of her hair was in his nostrils and the tender feel of her body was yielding in his arms. His first thought was of the misery he had caused her the night before when he dug into her past. She had been exhausted and near collapse when he'd carried her back to the campsite and placed her on their pallet. Throughout the night he had felt her tremblings and heard the tormented sounds she made in her sleep, both of which had made him curse himself for his cruelty and insensitivity. He wanted to hold her and protect her, even from himself. Like a kitten she had crawled against him, seeking his warmth, placing herself in his total care.

Fully awake now, Sloan's embrace deepened, his lips tenderly nuzzling the graceful sweet curve of her neck.

Wrenching herself from his arms, Chala jumped from the warmth of the pallet. Her cheeks were flaming, her eyes blazing with unbridled hostility. Her golden hair fell across her face in wild abandon. Still on her knees she turned to face him, her anger ripping through her, making her voice a lethal hiss. "MacAllister takes too much upon himself!" Her face was only inches from his, her tone low so as not to awaken the others, but strong and so intense he was taken aback. "I must cook for you. I must speak your language. I must fetch and carry for you like a slave without importance. I must even warm your pallet. These I will do because my chief says I must. Osceola does not say I *must* like it! And he does not say I must comfort MacAllister's nights and offer my body!"

Sloan was astounded. *She* had turned to him these nights, pressing her body against him. *She* had nestled her head on his shoulder, throwing her arm across his belly! *She* was offering a temptation any other man would have already taken to his own advantage! And to think he had pitied her, actually accused himself of cruelty!

Chala read the accusations in MacAllister's flinty gray eyes, and the color in her cheeks deepened. She knew what he was thinking and it was all true. Frustration bubbled in her breast and boiled to the surface, seeming to choke off her air. Her fingers curled into claws, itching to dig his eyes from his head.

Seeing her intent, Sloan seized her wrist in a bone crushing grip, and pulled her forward, sending her sprawling onto his chest. The fingers of his left hand tangled in her hair, snapping her head around to face him. "You little savage!" He gave her hair a terrible yank, making her wince with pain. "I've heard about the Spirit who walks the forest looking for defenseless children to eat them up in one bite!" He spoke of the Seminole version of the bogeyman. "What I didn't know was that the Okeepapa had honeyed hair and green eyes!"

Despite his grip on her, Chala was moved to action by this insult. Twisting, she dug her elbow into his groin, enjoying the pain flashing across his face and the sudden intake of his breath. "Be careful, MacAllister. This is one Okeepapa who has a taste for white flesh and grown men."

Bringing up his knees to protect himself, he released her. Instantly, Chala was on her feet looking down at him. "I will bring MacAllister his Koonti bread. He will need his strength to fight the Okeepapa again this night." Her tone was sarcastic and her lip curled into a malicious smile.

Sloan glared up at her, deciding if he should drag her

to the ground and beat her or wait and take her by
surprise. His decision was made for him by the appearance of Osceola's daughters who were looking for their
morning meal.

It was early the next day when Osceola's party
entered the negro village in the Panasoffke Swamp.
Nearly four hundred blacks lived here in abject poverty
since the army had made farming and raising cattle
impossible. Sloan walked beside Redeemer who carried Osceola into the compound. Just outside the
perimeters of the camp Sloan noticed how his brother,
greatly weakened by the rising tide of his malarial
attack, had willed himself to straighten in the saddle.
Back straight, head proud and high, he determined to
face his black compatriots a strong man, strengthening
their confidence in him.

The compound's leader, a heavily muscled black
named Artemus Woods, greeted them. At a glance
Sloan knew the runaway slave instantly saw Osceola's
feverish condition. Raising one heavily muscled arm,
he hailed the Seminole chief. "Our friend, Osceola, has
come to share with us." His dark, fathomless eyes
settled questioningly on Sloan.

"This is my brother, MacAllister," Osceola's voice
was strong and unwavering at a great price to himself.
"Behind us follow pack mules with supplies we have
brought as gifts."

Women and children stood around the perimeters of
the encampment. Men, armed with rifles, stood watching warily, their eyes never leaving MacAllister. Bare
chested, the sun glinting off their ebony bodies, they
appeared a formidable troop. Osceola had told him
they were fearless fighters, worthy allies to fight beside
the Seminole.

The largest thatched hut was assigned to Osceola and
Che-cho-ter, and Ina immediately took the children
inside to rest after their long morning's walk. Watching
his brother slide heavily down from Redeemer's saddle,

Sloan was aware of what this display of strength was costing him. Beads of sweat streaked down Osceola's face, and even in the warmth of the day, the blanket wrapped around his shoulders was pulled high to his chin. Soon now, he knew, the racking chills would begin, rendering the Indian a helpless victim to the fever.

Seeing to Redeemer's needs himself, Sloan led the animal to a watering trough, leaving him to drink while he went to the pack mules to rescue Redeemer's sack of oats before it found its way into the negroes' storehouse. Chala had joined the women in the hut assigned to her chief, leaving Mico and the two other warriors to stand guard outside the hanging blanket which served as a door.

Sloan rejoined Osceola as he was speaking to a council of blacks. They were seated in the shade of an ash tree, and their faces were grave and contemplative. The Seminole chief's voice was strong and rang with timbre. It was important that the blacks not desert the opposition against the United States Army now, especially not now when there was so little to be gained.

"The Seminole policy toward the negro is as clear as the water in the Silver Spring," he told them, watching their faces for signs of argument. *"No negro should ever be surrendered to the whites!"* His voice thundered: his eyes blazed with conviction. "The dilemma is a clear one. If the Seminoles abandon their resistance and move to the west as the government decrees, our negro allies here in the Floridas will either perish or will be captured once more for slavery beneath the lash of the white man. If the negro walks with us to the far side of the Great River, it will be with the same results. All of us then would fall prey to the slave catcher's rifle. Do not depend upon those dog cousins of the Seminoles, the Creeks, to raise a hand in defense of the black man."

Osceola's eyes read the black faces uplifted toward him. He pointed to Sloan, introducing him to the others as his white brother, a champion of their causes. "How do you see it, MacAllister? Speak and let your voice count among us!"

Sloan did not hesitate to bring forward his views. He affirmed the possibilities Osceola had already mentioned to the negroes, who, he was certain, were already doomfully aware of them. "Your only hope," he told them, "is to fight the army. Stand beside your Seminole brother when he takes the warpath. Stand beside Osceola! He fights not only for the Seminole and his rights, but also for you!"

"This white-eyes with the hair of the lion's mane, speaks the truth!" a voice rose above the others. It belonged to the medicine man, Arpeika, Osceola's mentor. He was a cantankerous, lean old man with dirty white hair and the skin of an ancient turtle. From everything Osceola had told Sloan, the man seemed to be as brusque and ill-tempered as ever. Standing beside the wizened medicine man were two Mikasuki, an exclusive rank of warriors.

Exercising his authority, Arpeika drew Osceola away from the gathering. With a backward glance, Osceola signaled for Sloan to follow. When they were out of hearing distance, the old man said, "I have a plan."

If Arpeika's wrinkled eyes took in Osceola's sick and weakened appearance, he gave no sign. Brushing aside the customary greeting, the medicine man said, "I am going to lead warriors. I expect many Mikasukis will follow me."

"That is as you wish," Osceola said in a weak voice.

"As you wish, as you wish," Arpeika mimicked furiously. "I can still fight better than most of the young fools."

"Then it is good. Does that mean you haven't changed your mind about moving west among the Creeks?"

"Never!" the old medicine man cackled shrilly. "If I am to die, then I will die on my own soil."

"Well spoken. I also will die on my own soil," Osceola said gravely.

"No," the old man and prophet exclaimed. He stared at Osceola through glassy, red-veined eyes. "I don't think you will die on this soil. And I don't think you die beyond the Great River Mississippi. But you die."

"A story!" Osceola said bitterly. "You spin white man's fairy tales. If you don't do something for me, I will die' at your feet, and how will you explain that to my people."

"Yes. I will do something now for you. I have waited all the morning hours." Following Osceola into his assigned hut, Arpeika then sent Ina, Morning Dew and the children from him. He then pointed to Chala. "You, too, leave us." He ignored Sloan as if he didn't exist.

Alone with Osceola, the old man administered some boiled herbs and began a ritual chanting that was the most important part of every medicine man's business.

Arpeika was not only a warrior-priest but he also practiced curative medicine. Herbs, such as snakeroot and sassafras, were used along with many others. Medicine men were more interested in the words of the chants believing that ritual drove out the disease: the herbs were only of minor significance.

When the old Indian left, Osceola slept and dreamed he raced after a deer, running at full speed, until he reached a lake where snags probed from the water like black, broken fingers. The deer swam between them, spreading ripples on the dark water, and Osceola plunged in to follow. On the far shore, he pursued the deer to a strange place where a cave gaped in the side of a hill. When the deer entered the cave, Osceola shuddered at the idea of following. But he entered the cave where, suddenly, in the blackness, there was a loud, popping sound.

Osceola wakened to find Sloan and his two wives bending over him. Three warriors stood behind them.

The popping sound continued, rifle shots, still at a distance, but approaching fast. His two wives were scooping up blankets and cookwear, the children clinging to their skirts.

"Soldiers!" Sloan barked. "Can you move?"

"I will walk," Osceola said hoarsely. To the three Mikasuki he ordered, "One of you ahead, the other behind me, the third behind my family. Sloan at my side if I falter."

They did as ordered. Debilitated or not, he was their thlacko. To Sloan, he whispered, "Tell me."

"It was quick. Too quick. It's my guess the attack was ordered by Jessup, probably one of his probing battalions. We can do nothing here."

"We must move on," Osceola affirmed Sloan's decision. "I know a hiding place on the Withlacoochee. Ready everything, brother, time is everything. I want as few casualties as possible. More Seminoles will come to help if I can reach the cove and send word."

Later, Sloan would learn that Jessup's battalion made a successful sweep of the village. More than fifty blacks would be taken prisoner with the rest escaping into the forest. If Osceola had been captured at that time, future victories in the Seminole cause would have been impossible.

Rushing across the clearing that was surrounded by low thatch huts, Sloan kept a firm grip on Osceola's arm, half carrying him, half dragging him, in the opposite direction of the gun shots to the shelter of the forest. The main fighting was still a good distance away, having been discovered by sentries guarding the village. Glancing back over his shoulder, he saw Ina pulling Osceola's daughter Mic-canna along, the little girl's toes dragging in the dust, fear widening her eyes. Che-cho-ter carried Hola, and Chala balanced the baby Lilka. The children were silent, their faces pale and sallow against the dark cloud of ebony hair. Che-cho-ter's face reflected her fear for her husband as she searched ahead to where Sloan assisted him.

They had almost reached the forest behind the huts when Sloan heard a woman's scream. Pushing Osceola into the arms of the lead Mikasuki, he ran back in time to see Chala thrust the baby she was carrying into its mother's arms.

With lightning velocity and seemingly without second thought, she pulled the knife from its sheath on her belt and rushed back toward the huts. Hair flying, teeth bared, she ran, knife raised in menace. Looking ahead of her, Sloan saw a black woman had been knocked to the ground, a bare-legged Indian straddling her. The scream hadn't been Chala's; it had been the negress's.

Before thought could become action, Chala came up behind the attacking Indian and stabbed her knife through the back of his neck. He seemed to crumpled forward into a lifeless heap, an expression of total surprise contorting his face.

Standing beside Sloan was Mico, a look of satisfied approval on his face. "It was a Creek," the young warrior said, spitting on the ground as if to be rid of a bad taste. "Chala is a brave one," he said, "a true Seminole!" This last was said as a reminder to Sloan that whatever he may think, Mico thought of Chala as a woman of her people, and although Osceola may have given her to MacAllister, Mico had not abandoned the possibility of claiming her for his own.

Ignoring Mico's veiled meaning, Sloan questioned. "A Creek? What's he doing here?"

"The army is using them as scouts. They fight beside the white soldiers. Like the fox, they mean to be the first at the chicken house. All blacks and Seminoles they capture the soldiers allow them to keep."

After seeing that the negress who was being attacked was able to fend for herself, Chala ran back to join the women, sheathing her knife as she ran. Sloan had already returned to Osceola's side after giving orders that the Mikasukis should help the women with the children. As they entered the depths of the swamp, the vision of Chala plunging her knife into the Creek's neck

haunted him. Like Mico, he admired her. Her commit-
ment to the Seminoles was total. She was a hellcat, a
tigress defending her cubs. A slow smile worked over
his mouth as he thought of how at night, thoroughly
feline, she could become a kitten, warm and soft in a
man's arms.

Had it not been for Redeemer carrying Osceola,
Sloan doubted they would have been able to escape and
make the long, hurried trek through the swamp, following paths that were ventured only by the Indians.
Several times the Seminole chief motioned for one of
the children to be placed across his lap, relieving their
fatigue and silencing their tears.

Sloan led the way, recalling all the things his brother
had taught him in the woods surrounding their farm
back in Alabama. Time was of the essence. Osceola
was desperately weakened. The medicinal herbs Arpeika had administered seemed to have quelled the fever
for the time being at least, but there was the man's
dreadfully weakened condition to consider. By the
evening, Sloan knew, the racking chills and fever would
again have him in their grip.

The night birds were chirping their last song of the
day. Mico and the two other warriors quickly set about
making a low fire. Their faces were set in grim lines.
Tonight the fire would be fresh; there had been no time
to collect embers from the fire they had brought from
their village. There would be no protecting Spirits
watching over them.

The children complained of hunger, and Che-cho-ter
looked at them balefully. Tonight her little ones would
go to sleep hungry. There had been no time to gather
supplies. The pack mules and foodstuffs they had
brought with them to the negro village were now in the
hands of the army.

Chala laid out a sleeping pallet, using one of the
hastily rescued blankets to cover a hummock of soft
pine boughs that would separate their bodies from the

cold, hard ground. The cove Osceola had led them to was sheltered by a ring of thick forest which broke out onto the banks of the Withlacoochee River. Here the waters narrowed and a man could throw a stone from one side to the other. It was a natural place for game to come out of the forest to drink. Tomorrow, when it was light, they would fish for their morning meal and set traps. Mico would hunt the squirrel and the coon and they would feast. The women would find wild potatoes and celery for the cook pot. Tomorrow the children would not be hungry.

Thought of preparations for survival thrummed through Chala's head. She could not allow herself to think of how her knife point had sunk into the Creek's neck and the sound he had made as he choked on his blood. The vision kept reappearing despite her determination to put it from her mind. It left her shaking, her trembling fingers unable to complete the simplest task. Even now, as she prepared MacAllister's pallet, there was a shuddering inside her, making the blankets quiver and the pine boughs rustle.

She had killed a man. That he was her enemy did not comfort her. That he would have killed her without compunction did not soothe her. Often, as a child, she had regretted being a female, sentenced by her sex to the care of children and a household. She would have liked to join the young braves who were learning to hunt and fish and fight. Now, contrary to those longings, she was grateful she could leave the killing to the men. Looking at Che-cho-ter and Ina as they rocked and sang the children to sleep, she realized that the Great Spirits had designed that women be the caretakers, the healers. Now she understood why strong warriors would return to the village weary and sick, looking to their women with haunted, questioning eyes for warmth and comfort. Being a wife and mother was as necessary as being a warrior. It was more difficult. The blood that stained a woman's hands belonged not

to an enemy but to a loved one. She tended their
wounds, choking back tears, praising and chanting the
bravery of her husband who would be revived to
challenge the enemy another day.

Chala's eyes drifted to MacAllister. He was sitting
near Osceola's pallet speaking to his brother in low,
gruff tones. She had listened while he spoke to the
black men, telling them their only hope was to continue
fighting with the Seminole against Jessup's army. A
pride had filled her that this strong, intelligent man was
her master.

Doffing her moccasins, she slid onto the pallet, her
thoughts a maelstrom of confusion. Only this morning
she had wanted to dig his eyes from his head. Yet this
afternoon she had stood and listened to him with
admiration. And she had killed a man. A terrible
quaking overtook her and she tried to still her traitor-
ous body with little success.

Minutes later MacAllister crawled onto the pallet
beside her. At that moment she wanted nothing more
than to turn to him and lie in his arms and have his
nearness chase away the devils that were pursuing her.
In his arms she had found peace, but after this morning
she must even deny herself that small respite. Pride was
a cold companion here in the night and offered no
shelter from the misery of her thoughts.

"Are you cold, little one?" he murmured, mistaking
her shuddering emotions for a night chill. Her silence
piqued his curiosity and he lightly touched her chin,
turning her face toward him. Her misery was marked in
her eyes and he seemed to understand. "Poor little
kitten," he said softly, opening his arms for her,
drawing her close against him. "You've discovered the
secret of all men. Killing freezes the soul. Even the
blood of an enemy stains the spirit. There is no greater
sin and those who must kill know the doom of their own
damnation."

MacAllister's sympathy and compassion choked

Chala with tears. For a long time she lay in his arms, accepting his comfort, allowing the cleansing tears to flow. At last he whispered, "Sleep now, kitten. Tomorrow is another day and I will be here if you need me."

Exhausted, Chala nestled in his embrace. He had chased away the night devils and promised her a brighter day. It was good to sleep in this man's arms, she told herself. It was good to share his warmth.

For the first time since putting eyes on him, Chala wondered what it would be like to share a chikkee with him and feel his body enter hers for the pleasure of the flesh and a meeting of the souls. MacAllister must have a beautiful soul. She had never known a man that way but she had heard other women speak of it. Again, she shivered, feeling him hold her closer still. She smiled and pressed her face into his shoulder, wrapping her arm around his midsection, enjoying the closeness, hearing his breaths fall and rise evenly, knowing he slept.

An unknown tenderness welled in Chala's heart for this man who seemed to read her thoughts. Little did she know he was formulating a plan that would have her wishing she had never placed eyes on him.

It was midmorning when Morning Dew finally acknowledged Sloan and allowed him to approach her husband. He left Chala behind, whose tender thoughts of the night before had been replaced by a smoldering rage.

When Osceola struggled to a sitting position to greet him, Sloan failed to mask the alarm in his eyes at his brother's weakened condition. He held up his hand to show that no formality was required on his brother's part. "Stay comfortable, I came only to talk and then will leave quickly. I have much to say and want to hear what you think of a plan I have devised." Osceola nodded and leaned back onto his pallet.

"Tell me what manner of secret you have been hiding

from me." It was a feeble attempt at humor on the Indian chief's part, but Sloan appreciated the effort it cost him.

"It concerns Chala. Her face has haunted me from the moment I first saw her, but I could not place it. A few days ago it finally dawned on me where I had seen her before. I saw a picture of her mother in General Jessup's home. You recall how I told you I played poker at his home in the hopes of picking up some valuable information to help you? Well, in his library there was a picture over the mantle of a woman who looks just like Chala. It can't be anyone but her mother." Quickly, he recounted the story Jessup had told him. He saw the Indian tiring before his eyes. "It's my plan to take Chala to New Orleans and let Jessup find her by accident. I'll make sure that she has some brief training from a friend of mine to make her into a lady. I've spoken briefly to Chala of this and, of course, she is fighting me. I need you to tell her there is no other way that I can think of to get you the information you need. She'll be in the perfect position to find out any military maneuvers. I'll concoct a cover story that will hold water; have no fear. I don't know what else to do for you, Osceola. I think it's our only hope at the moment."

"Send the girl to me. At this moment in time I must rely on your judgment. What you say sounds feasible to me. Please, brother, wipe the concern from your eyes. This disease you call malaria has laid me low before. I'll recover as I have in the past, but it takes time. Today, I feel stronger. Each day after will be better. Ah, I see the doubt in your eyes. Have I ever lied to you, son of our mother? Speak with Ina and Morning Dew. They will tell you I am on the mend."

"Your word is good enough for me. What kind of brother would I be if I wasn't concerned about your health? Chala and I will sail the *Polly Copinger*. Mico tells me this river leads to the keys where she is anchored. Send a few of your men with me as far as the ship so that they can bring you the rest of the stores from my hold. Somehow, I'll get word to you of our progress. Hopefully, when we lock eyes again, you will be hale and hearty."

There was such pain and sorrow in Osceola's eyes, Sloan felt a lump rise in his throat. "It is decided then. As soon as you speak with the girl, we will leave." There was no need for further words. Osceola knew sure as the sun would set this day that Sloan would be back with the promised aid of one kind or another.

Sloan motioned for Chala to approach her chief. She shot him a baleful look but did as she was told, quite different from the way she had railed and protested when he had first presented the plan to her.

Chala scuffed at the dust as she approached her thlacko's pallet. How could she have fooled herself into thinking that MacAllister understood her? Read her heart. Bah! He understood nothing. He thought she had softened toward him and, for a time, she had. Becoming aware of a man and wondering what it would be like to share his chikkee was one thing, being told she must leave her people was quite another. However much she had protested to MacAllister, Osceola was her thlacko and she must be obedient to him.

Twenty minutes later when Chala left Osceola she was more subdued than Sloan had ever seen her. She spoke quietly, careful to avoid his eyes. Her terse, "Chala will travel with you," was all he needed to hear. And now was as good a time as any to broach the next hurdle.

"From this moment on you are Savannah James. Chala is a Seminole. Savannah is a white lady." He stressed the word "lady" and wondered how in hell Annemarie would make a silk purse from this sow's ear.

Dappled sunlight penetrated the thick, overhead branches as Sloan and Chala, astride Redeemer, picked their quiet and cautious way through the woods toward

the west coast of the Floridas. Mico and the two other
warriors, whose names Sloan had never learned, followed at an easy pace behind them. Once reaching the
coast where the forest thinned to give way to sandy
beaches, the traveling would be easier northward to
Cedar Key, where the *Polly Copinger* and Captain
Culpepper waited. He hoped. It was quite possible that
marauding Creeks or a chance regiment of cavalry had
happened upon the *Polly* sending Culpepper out to sea
in order to save his ship. There would be no explaining
to the United States Army what the *Polly* was doing
berthed in the center of Indian territory stocked to the
hatches with supplies. About the only worry Culpepper
wouldn't have was the possibility of his crew jumping
ship. With nothing but miles and miles of dense forest
ahead of them, the crew would wisely stay with the
*Polly*.

Chala's multibanded skirt of bright colors rode high
on her tanned legs, exposing their lightly muscled
roundness. Ordinarily the sight of a well-turned limb
would have pleased Sloan, but he only frowned when
he noticed. Due to her dress and exposure to the sun,
Chala's body was probably patches of white and brown.
No lady ever exposed herself to the sun, and the latest
fashions revealed wide expanses of shoulder and breast
as well as upper arms, fashions that Chala would soon
be wearing. Worried creases formed between Sloan's
brows. Something was going to have to be done! And
her hands! No lady of quality ever had hands as work
worn as Chala's. As Savannah James she would need
soft, manicured fingers, buffed to a pampered gleam.

He couldn't bleach her skin, but he *could* even her
out so she was one color! He hoped. But where? Their
voyage across the Gulf would only take two days, three
at the most, if the *Polly* met head winds. There
wouldn't be enough time to solve the problem, even if
he hung her nude from the halyards. And the beaches
were no good, too much danger of being discovered.

The coastlines were always under surveillance. . . . The outer islands of Cedar Key. It would be perfect! MacAllister smiled to himself. How many men, he wondered, had dreamed of spending time on a deserted island with a woman only *half* as beautiful as Chala?

Redeemer carried both Sloan and Savannah effortlessly. It had been more than three hours since they'd reached the coast, and Sloan took the animal down near the water's edge where the hard-packed sand made for easier footing. Savannah laughed as Redeemer sometimes ventured too close to the surf and skidded crazily sideways to avoid soaking both himself and his master. Her laugh was light and musical, and Sloan realized that it was the first time he'd ever heard it. Even the two braves, jogging behind them, seemed to find something humorous in Redeemer's antics. Only Mico, his face like a dark cloud before a storm, soundlessly kept pace.

In the distance, less than a mile away, Sloan spotted the foremasts of the *Polly*. He raised his arm and pointed, calling it to the attention of the Indians. His knees dug into Redeemer's flanks, and he flew ahead of the following Indians along the curving coast to where the *Polly* waited. He was relieved that she hadn't found the need to put out for sea to save herself from Indians or the calvary.

The sea was deep, azure blue rippling along the edge of a narrow strip of sand. Here the trees were different, palms with tall, graceful trunks and full heads of long, spikey green leaves, swaying gently in the wind.

"Ahoy, Laddie!" Enwright Culpepper called from the bridge of the *Polly*. Sloan noticed that several of the crew were standing ready and armed with rifles. The *Polly* rode her berth nicely, moored remarkably close to the beach. A larger ship would have had to lay out at least three times that distance.

While they watched, Captain Culpepper was lowered in the *Polly's* dinghy to come ashore. Chala's eyes were

wide with fright as she studied the *Polly*. She'd never
seen so large a ship before and the thought of boarding
and sailing it across the blue waters of the Gulf was
almost more than she could comprehend. More familiar with the Seminole dugout canoes and rafts, the
*Polly* was an awesome sight.

Mico and his two companions seemed to share
Savannah's feelings. They stood on the beach, water
lapping at their moccasins, arms raised to cut the glare
of the sun, staring out at the *Polly*. Quickly, to put
them at their ease, Sloan explained how the stores were
to be unloaded and stashed at a place of their choice
until everything could be transported back to the
Seminoles.

Culpepper eyed Mico and the braves with wary
glances. He'd never been this close to an Indian before,
and for all intents and purposes, he didn't like it now. If
he was surprised when MacAllister told him he wanted
a week's supply of food for two, blankets and various
other necessities, he didn't let it show.

Sand, sun, sky and sea . . . as far as the eye could
stretch. Sloan had taken the *Polly's* second dinghy and
loaded her with supplies, taking Chala across the inlet
to the out island, last in the chain of Cedar Key.

If she knew what he had in mind for her, she didn't
say. She had followed his directives to the letter. If she
was frightened about crossing such an expanse of water
in a little boat, she was silent. They had hauled onto the
flat beach ringed by low growing trees that withstood
the constant buffetting winds. Sloan had dropped anchor, burying it deep into the sand.

The first order of the day had been to set about
creating a makeshift shelter to spend the nights, safe
from rain and winds. At this, Chala was most adept,
showing Sloan which branches and palm fronds she
wanted to fall beneath the blows of his hand axe. Two
hours later a flat roofed shelter had been created, and
although it stood no more than four feet off the ground

and demanded that one double over almost in half to enter, it would provide shelter from the elements.

Their evening meal had consisted of prepared food brought along from the *Polly*. Simple fare, it had been sufficient to satisfy their hunger. Exhausted after their long, hard day, they silently crept into the lean-to, falling asleep almost instantly. Sometime during the night, Chala realized that she was again sleeping with her head tucked away on Sloan's shoulder, and listening to the comforting sound of his deep, even breaths as he slept, gave her a sense of welcome security.

When Chala awakened it was to the aroma of fresh brewed coffee and the sizzle of eggs in the heavy black pan. Fresh corn cakes baked on smooth, flat stones near the edge of the cook fire. Rubbing the sleep from her eyes, Chala watched in amazement. Even on the trail, Seminole men only ate food brought from the village and occasionally a rabbit or fish caught in the wilds. Never did they bake bread or make eggs, especially if there was a woman about who would do the cooking for them. She smiled at this unusual treat and momentary respite from her chores. If all white men were as good to women as MacAllister, perhaps the future wasn't so bleak after all.

"C'mon out, sleepy head. Your breakfast is waiting!" He smiled at her, seeing her surprise that he had manned the cook fire this morning.

The coffee, something Chala never remembered drinking in her life, was bitter until MacAllister added several spoonsful of a white, grainy substance he called sugar to sweeten it. One sip told her she liked the black brew that was so fragrant in the chill of early morning.

As she wiped the last of the egg yolk from her dull, tin plate with the last bit of corn cake and popped it into her mouth, she sighed in contentment. Her forest green eyes found his. "What does MacAllister need on this island?" she questioned, turning her face up toward the sun, liking the feel of it on her skin.

Sloan wasn't quite certain how to approach the real

reason he'd brought her out here to this desolate place. Now she gave him the perfect opportunity. "I'm glad to see you like the sun, Savannah."

She looked at him questioningly.

Sloan began to stammer and then decided the best way to approach it was directly. But how did he begin? "It's the color of your skin, Savannah . . ."

Immediately, like all women, she bristled, indignantly insulted to be told there was something about her which displeased him. "And what is wrong with the color of my skin? I'm as white as you are! Whiter even! See?" she pulled down the neck of her blouse to display her creamy white shoulder.

"I see. And that's the problem," he tried to keep his voice clinical like a school teacher's or a doctor's, but he had seen the swell of her breast and the sweet cleft between its firm roundness and her arm. "In New Orleans, wherever, a lady, a lady of breeding and quality, that is, never exposes herself to the sun. We won't be able to take your tan away, but we can even you out a little, so when you wear fancy ball gowns, your shoulders won't be white and your neck and arms brown. It just won't do, do you understand?"

Chala stood, knocking her plate to the ground with a resolute clatter. "MacAllister is right; it *won't* do. If the white man thinks he can sit me out in the sun to cook my hide, he's wrong. Wrong, wrong, wrong!" She stamped her foot on the ground, punctuating her defiance.

"That's exactly what you're going to do," he told her, his voice holding a thinly veiled menace. Damn, how could one woman be so sweet one minute and so damned ornery the next?

"MacAllister is wrong!" She spit forcefully at his feet. "So much for roasting me like a chicken!" Crossing her arms over her breasts she glared at him, smoky green eyes staring levelly into his.

"No, MacAllister is right!" he told her, judging the distance between them, fully expecting her to run into the patch of woods directly behind them. "Another thing, Savannah, ladies don't spit! No matter what, ladies *never* spit!" In one swift moment he reached out his arm, intending to capture her and bring her to heel. Anticipating his action, Chala jumped backward, nearly tripping. She was just out of his reach and she intended to stay that way. Sloan saw the determination in her eyes, saw the way she brought her lower lip between her teeth and knew, if he didn't get his hands on her right now, he'd have to chase her around the island. He extended his arms, holding them wide apart, shoulders hunched, every muscle ready. He began to circle her, his flinty eyes never leaving hers, making her feel like a trapped rabbit.

Chala was more than his match. She backed up, feeling her way with the heel of her foot. Finding the path clear behind her, she turned and broke off into a run. The trees were just ahead of her. Hair flying, arms pumping, she ran as fast as she could. The loose sand beneath her feet impeded her progress, and she imagined she could almost feel his hot breath on the back of her neck. She had to get away from this crazy white man whom Osceola called brother. If her chief had known what a lunatic he was, he never would have given her to MacAllister. Everyone knew it was death to lie out in the sun! Anybody with half a mind. She had nearly reached the safety of the woods when she felt him grab hold of her skirt, pulling her backward, ripping the fabric from her waist. Backward, Chala sprawled, fingers curled, ready to fight him off. But before she could prepare herself, he was upon her, seizing her wrists in both hands and dragging her out to the beach.

"No, no!" she screamed, pulling against him, trying to use her weight to an advantage. But he was strong, stronger than she would have imagined. A fleeting memory of her wielding the whip against him, hurting him, bringing him to the ground with pain, flew through her thoughts. It would be good to whip him again, and this time she wouldn't stop. She would like to whip him to a bleeding pulp. "No! No!"

"Yes! If I have to strip you naked myself, you're going to go out there and sit in the sun! We're going to even you out if it's the last thing we ever do!"

"MacAllister is crazy! Crazy!"

"Crazier than you know for asking Osceola for you in the first place. If I'd known what I was taking on, I never would have opened my stupid mouth!"

Chala struggled against him, attempting to win her freedom. Her feet kicked out, her body writhed, anything to escape his grip. She wanted to shriek, to cry, to scream, but there was no one to hear her. How could this man, who had held her so gently in the chill of the night, who had comforted her tears, do this to her?

He held her fast against him, feeling her great, heaving breaths shudder throughout her entire body. "Are you going to come willingly, or do I have to drag you out and tie you down? Remember, I'm quite capable of tying you up."

She raised her head, allowing her golden curtain of hair to reveal her face. Her eyes were dark, almost black, with hatred. Her nostrils flared and her lips were drawn into a thin, mean line. Suddenly, she spit, spraying his face with spittle.

Too late he moved to stop her. His fingers gripped her under the chin in a steely, painful hold. "I told you, ladies *never* spit. Only men and spoiled brats!" For the first time since he had tethered her for all the village to jeer, she was frightened of him, truly frightened. He seized her arm, dragging her with him, oblivious to her struggles. Chala gulped. She had gone too far. Enraged him beyond reason. And now he was going to kill her!

Her shrieks were heard only by the birds overhead and by the man dragging her across the sand, back to the cook fire where sat a twenty pound barrel of flour. Sitting on the barrel, he pulled her over his lap in one terrifying show of strength. On her way down she caught a glimpse of his face. Stern, square features set in granite line; lips drawn back over his white strong teeth, hair glinting gold, falling rakishly over his sun-darkened forehead. Sinewy cords stood out in his neck like twisted hanks of rope. He was mad, crazy, and he was going to kill her!

Her rump was face up, leaving her helpless. Her fists pounded blows anywhere she could reach: his thighs, his legs, his haunches. At the first slap her eyes widened in surprise. He was hitting her! Spanking her like a child, repeatedly landing his blows to her backside, hurting her.

Her indignant screams resounded in his ears, piercing and shrill. He was ashamed of what he was doing, what she had driven him to, but before she could learn to be a lady, she had to relinquish the ways of a savage. Like a naughty child, this was one lesson she'd learn well.

Disgusted with himself and her, he landed one last healthy smack to her backside and abruptly stood up, toppling her to the ground. Stepping over her, he walked down to the water's edge, not caring if she ran away into the woods, wishing she would. Later, he would send Mico to look for her. Let her belong to Mico; let her stay with him; let her poison him with her cooking!

The Gulf waters lapped against the beach in a soothing, steady rhythm. Sloan stared into the distance, wondering how he had ever come to this: beating a woman! Regardless of how angry she made him, he was ashamed of his actions. Not that he'd ever admit it to her, the little savage. He almost chuckled aloud. Look who was calling whom a savage!

The sound of his name came to him over his right shoulder. There were tears in her voice and he dreaded facing her. After a long moment, after he heard her call him a second time, he steeled himself to look at her. What he saw made his eyes widen in astonishment. She stood there on the sandy beach, hair flying in the gentle breeze, face tear streaked, full mouth quivering in fright, eyes swollen from crying . . . naked.

"If MacAllister says I am to sit in the sun, then I will sit." Slowly, without any shame or coyness, she spread a blanket over the sand, and placing herself on top of it, stretched full out to catch the golden rays.

Her body was beautiful. The nights she had fallen asleep in his arms and he had felt her warm body pressed close against his had only been a hint of her womanly charms. Breasts, high and full and creamy white, tapered to a slender waist and round, full hips. Her legs were straight, lightly muscled and gracefully turned. Her body was totally feminine and yet athletic with none of the bony angles he had seen on women heavier than she.

Stretched out to full length, she propped herself up on both elbows, studying him, "Is this how MacAllister wants me to roast?"

In spite of himself, he laughed. "Exactly. Not too long now, it's got to be done over a period of days."

"Days?"

"Of course, the sun didn't make your arms and face brown in one day, did it? At least you've had time to pale from last summer and that's in our favor." He fought to keep his eyes away from her body. He mustn't allow himself to be aroused by this little hellcat, he warned himself. He was too involved as it was.

"Stay here, I'll be right back."

Leaving her at the water's edge, he went back to the campsite under the trees. He had to get control of himself! He had to keep reminding himself that he liked to travel light, and Chala, Savannah James, was certainly anything but light. But he couldn't seem to get the vision of her out of his mind. He took the shovel into the woods beyond the rim of trees and began to dig, placing shovelfuls of loamy, black earth into a bucket, and still he thought of her. Right now he was thinking of how he was going to make mud from this dirt and wondering how he was going to smooth it over her brown face, arms, throat and legs without falling completely to pieces. He could imagine how soft and silky her skin would feel and of the gentle curves and hidden delights he would discover as he applied the mud.

Backbreaking work, pulling aside the weeds and underbrush, digging between the tree roots, and still he thought of her. And he still had to go back there!

Passing through camp again, he stopped to pick up one of his extra shirts. One way or another Savannah James was going to drive him completely crazy.

She was positioned on the blanket in the sun just as he had left her. "Here," he threw her the shirt, "drape this over your . . . er . . . cover yourself with this."

"Why? MacAllister said I must sit in the sun. I am sitting."

"Yes, that's right . . . you don't want to burn, do you?"

"That is what I am telling MacAllister! To sit in the sun is to die! Creeks torture their enemies by staking them down in the sun. Soon the mouth is thirsty, the skin burns. . . . Why is MacAllister trying to kill me?" Her temper flared, words fired at him in rapid succession, green eyes blazing.

"MacAllister . . . I mean, I'm not trying to kill you Savannah, just, er . . . just even you out a little. Here, put this over your breasts and stomach. The skin is so white and tender, I don't want you blistering on me."

She took his shirt, touching the unfamiliar fabric, liking its texture. "What kind of cloth is this, MacAllister? Who weaves this?" Her fingers stroked the shirt in admiration.

"Worms," came the short reply. He was mixing the loamy earth he had dug with sea water.

"Worms?" she laughed, light and melodious and totally different from her shrieking tirades. "Who can make looms so little for worms?" She laughed again, indicating a small space between her fingers.

"No, no," a chuckle escaped him, there was so much Savannah didn't know. So much he could teach her. "Worms spin the thread, like the caterpillar spins his cocoon. Then it is gathered and spun into cloth called silk. If you like it, all of your new clothes when we get to Galveston will be made of silk."

A troubled expression muffled her laugh. "Galveston? Where is this?"

"Out there," he pointed westward with his hand. "It's an island off the coast of Texas."

"Texas, I know," she told him. "An island? Like this?"

"No, no, much bigger." He had mixed the dirt into a thick, sticky mud. As he applied it to her lower arms and neck, he explained that he didn't want these areas to become more tanned than they already were. During this intimacy, he kept up a steady stream of chatter, answering her questions about the ship, *Polly Copinger*, telling her it was the name of Osceola's mother which seemed to please her greatly. He told her about Annemarie Duval and her house in Galveston, about New Orleans and the lovely dresses she would wear. And the entire time he was sweating profusely, each agonized little droplet reminding him that this woman had him babbling like a school boy when all he wanted to do was tell her how beautiful she was. How smooth and soft her skin was, and how he wanted to touch her, really touch her, the way a man touches a woman when he's making love to her. The sun burned into his back, on the top of his head.

"MacAllister is burning . . . do you have a fever?" she asked quietly, and when he lifted his gaze to meet hers, he saw the invitation in her eyes.

She couldn't . . . he told himself. He was imagining it. It was what he *wanted* to see there. . . . "You stay here and in a little while, turn over. But be sure to keep that shirt over that sweet little behind of yours, or you won't be able to sit down for a week!"

"Already, I can't sit for a week," she told him,

pouting, turning over briefly to show him the red marks his spanking had left there.

"Just sit!" he hollered, running away as though a bee had stung him.

"MacAllister! Where do you go?"

"Fishing! For our dinner!"

He followed his own footsteps back to the camp, irritated by the pounding of his heart that had nothing to do with the short sprint.

Keeping a careful count of the time, he went back down to the water's edge, staying just within shouting distance. Out of the corner of his eye, he saw her turn over, obeying his directions and dropping the shirt over her derriere. Sloan shook his head to clear it. The Seminole believed the body was a beautiful gift of the Spirits and false modesty was definitely frowned upon. Savannah was an example of her upbringing, and she was completely enchanting.

Three fish later, he decided she had had enough sun. Loping over to her blanket, he told her to wash the mud off in the sea while he brought the fish back to the campsite. He missed the sudden dismay in her eyes.

Ten minutes later, she still hadn't returned. Looking down to the beach, he saw her, feet just touching the edge of the lapping surf. She was almost comical with her bare arms and lower legs caked with mud, the exposed portions, except for her torso, pink from the sun. She turned and saw him looking and waved, beckoning him.

"MacAllister, MacAllister!"

"Hell fire!" he swore, not wanting to go near her until she was fully dressed. She called again, waving furiously.

It wasn't until he was almost abreast of her that he saw the fear in her eyes. "What's wrong?" he asked sharply, disliking more and more the effect she was having on him. Mud and all.

"MacAllister wants me to go in the sea? No, no! You want to kill me?"

"You know I don't want to kill you, stop saying that! What's wrong with the sea? Too cold for you? You've been swimming in the Withlacoochee River, haven't you?" His tone was impatient, bordering on hostility.

"The Withlacoochee is a river, so deep," she placed her hand at hip level, drawing his eye to her slender haunches and the triangle of golden fleece only slightly darker than her hair.

"And the sea is only 'so deep,'" he mocked, "if you only go in so far."

"No. MacAllister goes with me or I do not go! I will share his pallet just as I am." Stubbornly, and with a gesture he was becoming more than familiar with, she crossed her arms over her chest.

"All right, I'll go with you. Damn, woman. You're going to drive me crazy yet! I wasn't counting on a cold bath today." He was already barefoot, so he stripped his shirt off leaving his buckskins.

Savannah cocked an eyebrow. "Everything," she toned authoritatively, wagging a finger at his buckskin breeches. "If it is good enough for me, it is *more* than good enough for MacAllister!"

"Fool woman," he muttered to himself as his britches dropped to the sandy shore. He felt insulted for some reason at her clinical inspection of his naked body. What had she expected, he wondered sourly. He raced to the water and made a headline dive. He came up snorting and sputtering. Christ, it was cold! "All right, get in here and wash off," he muttered.

Tentatively, Savannah waded out till the water was at mid calf. She hung back, obviously reluctant to go any further. Sloan swam closer, and before she knew what was happening, she was under the water. She came up whooping and hollering as if she had been shot. "For God's sake, will you shut that mouth of yours. Every Creek from here to Arkansas will hear you. Now, wash!" he ordered.

Savannah's shrieks continued to pierce his ears as she splashed and floundered in the water. "Are you telling

me you can't swim?" he asked in horror as he grabbed
her hair and pulled her up for the third time.

"That is what I'm telling you, MacAllister. I cannot
swim. I do not like water. If my feet do not touch
bottom, I do not go in. It is simple. I will hold on to
your shoulders and you wash me."

"Oh, no, none of that." He pulled her slightly in
front of him. "Now your feet touch the ground. Wash!"

"Why? Do you think I am ugly? My sisters in
Osceola's camp think I am ugly with my green eyes and
yellow hair. I look like you, MacAllister."

Sloan groaned. "All right, come here." He clenched
his teeth as he briskly washed the caked mud from her
body. Christ, a minute ago he was worrying about
freezing to death, and now he was hot as one of
Che-cho-ter's cook fires. She didn't feel cold either.
Why should she, he thought, she had sixty pounds of
mud caked on her. But, why were her eyes burning the
way they were. Like hell it was from the mud. The same
thing that was running through his veins was running
through hers. Jesus, even Beaunell's eyes had never
been this hot.

"C'mon, we have to get out of this water before we
freeze to death," he said, dragging her from the water's
edge.

Savannah sighed. White men had many problems.
She followed him docilely and waited for him to toss a
blanket over her shoulders. She wasn't cold. She wig-
gled a bit on the sand and threw her arms behind her to
flex her muscles. Sloan's groan made her frown. Now
what was wrong with him?

The night fell, and a spectacular galaxy of stars
appeared overhead, so close they thought they could
almost reach out to touch them. Dinner had been good,
more than good, delicious. Savannah had surprised
Sloan with her culinary efforts. After cleaning and
scaling his fish, she had impaled them on sticks and
roasted them over the fire, cooking them slowly until

the flesh was white and delicate, flaking easily. Sloan had brewed the coffee she liked so well while she cooked a skillet of fresh greens she had searched for in the woods. Recognizing sheep's sorrel as one of the vegetables, he made a face but found it delicious.

All through dinner she quizzed him about life amidst "civilization," she called it, with a sour expression on her face that made him laugh.

"You'll soon spoil, little one. And then Lord knows what I'll do with you!" The words he had thoughtlessly uttered brought a scowl to his face. What *would* he do with her? She was his now; Osceola had said that under no circumstances would he accept her back. "Mico!" he uttered aloud. He would give her to Mico, and they could build a chikkee together and have children and grow old together. . . . The thought made him angry, so angry he spilled hot coffee on his hand. "Clumsy . . ."

"What did MacAllister say?" she asked looking up from her fire.

"I said I was clumsy . . . I spilled coffee on my hand . . ."

Immediately, she was beside him, turning his hand over to see what damage he had done and proclaiming it insignificant. "What did you say about Mico?" she asked, questions forming in her eyes that were now lit by the fire and seemed to glow with a life of their own.

"Nothing. Nothing!" he denied too loudly even for his own ears. "Get back to your cooking. That corn bread smells like it's burning."

Obediently, she turned back to her work, looking up from time to time, trying to puzzle him out.

Later, after a nearly silent meal, Sloan said, "Savannah, you'd better get some sleep. It's been a long day. Tomorrow, you sit in the sun again."

Standing just at the edge of the pallet she expected they would both share, she casually dropped her clothes into a heap near her feet. The indigo-blue blouse and brightly banded skirt was a riot of color against the dull green carpet of wild grass. Slowly, she slipped into the silk shirt he had given her earlier that day. "MacAllister does not mind," she said softly, her eyes meeting his in a statement he dare not interpret. She was his charge; she was in his care. By Seminole law she belonged to him, but that didn't mean he could take advantage of her and then toss her back to Mico as used goods.

"Get to bed, Savannah. I'm going for a walk on the beach." Even as he said it, he realized it was going to be a long night. Every blanket they had was layered on the pallet to keep them warm through the night. The little leanto they had built was little protection from the too cool night. And he also realized that, more than anything else, he wanted to crawl between the covers with her, feeling the warmth of her nestled softly in his arms. But he couldn't. Not tonight or any other night, it would seem. Not ever. He just couldn't trust himself! Not after the effect she had had on him while they were swimming, when he had experienced the wet smoothness of her skin and felt her soft gentle curves slide against his nakedness. She had almost driven him crazy, and he was crazy now for not just taking her, gruff and hard, long and sweet, all through the night, every night until he had had his fill of her. Some niggling thought plagued him, and he feared that once tasting the delights she had to offer he would *never* have enough of her!

"Where does MacAllister go?" she demanded cruelly, freezing him in her icy cold accusations.

"I told you. Down to the beach." His voice was more intense than he would have liked. Gruff and angry.

"Among my people," she told him snidely, "we cast aside those warriors who will not look upon a woman and share a cnikkee with her. MacAllister is man enough to beat a woman but not to lay between her legs!" Her tone was derisive, insulting. "Poor, poor MacAllister. He does not have the juices of a real man!" She stood before him, incongruous in his silk shirt that only covered half her thighs. Her hair was tossed back, her sneer was in full evidence.

Rage and indignation coursed through him. In two steps he was beside her, looking down into her insolent face lit by the fire's flames. "You stupid woman! Can't you see that I'm protecting you?" He savagely seized her shoulders, shaking her with his terrible rage, rocking her head back and forth on the slim column of her neck.

Gaining control of himself, he went to push her away, only to find that she was holding onto his arms, pressing closer to him. Her eyes looked into his and what he read there sent his pulses throbbing, echoing through him. With a sound that resembled a groan and a plea, he brought her to him, crushing his mouth against hers, tasting her, feeling her lips yield to his. When he broke away he saw the flush in her cheeks, the way her lips parted, lifting once again for his kiss.

"What are you doing to me?" he demanded harshly.

"What has MacAllister done to me?" she asked, breathless, husky. "What is this when you put your mouth to mine?"

"A kiss, damn you. A show of affection, of liking you!"

"MacAllister likes me? Seminole do not kiss. Kiss again, damn you," she mimicked him, "I think I like white men's ways. What else do white men do to show aff . . . affection?"

Throaty, deep, her voice resounded in his head. She knew what she was doing to him and he was powerless against her.

"Kiss again, damn you," she repeated, lifting her face to his.

Helpless, hating himself, Sloan brought her closer, aware of the sea's scent in her hair. Her skin smelled of sunshine and delicious womanly scent that was hers alone. Her arms wrapped around his neck, tighter, pulling him with her down to the pallet. She was seducing him! Seducing *him!*

Something inside him rebelled, some part of his manhood and his pride. *He* wanted to the aggressor; *he* wanted to be the one to show her how it could be between a man and a woman. Mico, be damned!

She lay in his arms, fragile as the first flower of spring. He buried his face in her hair, luxuriating in its lushness, surrounding himself in her warmth.

As Sloan gazed at her form in the starlight, all of his pent up yearnings, feelings he hadn't realized existed until this day, rose to the surface, and he slid down beside her. The feel of her satiny skin, the voluptuous curves beneath the silk shirt she wore, exhilarated him.

Once again his lips clung to hers, and Savannah's head spun as she felt her body come to life beneath his touch. He was gentle, his hands unhurried as he intimately explored her body. His mouth moved against hers and her senses reeled as she strained against him trying to be closer to him, trying to make them one.

With infinite tenderness, Sloan loved her, realizing that in spite of her wantonness, she was inexperienced. He put a guarded check on the growing feverishness in his loins, waiting for her, patiently arousing her until her passions were as demanding and greedy as his own.

His hands burned her flesh as they traveled the length of her, stopping to caress a pouting breast, a yielding, welcoming thigh. The silken shirt she had put on with such delight was now an irritant and she wished to be rid of it. Hasty hands found the buttons, opening them, exposing her skin to his touch.

His lips left the sweet moistness of her mouth to find the tender place where her throat pulsed and curved into her shoulder. Down, down, his mouth traveled, turning her in his arms, finding and teasing places that brought consummate pleasure and sent waves of desire through her veins. The ivory luster of her breasts beckoned him, their pink rosy crests standing erect and tempting. Her slim waist was a perfect fit for his hands, her firm, velvet haunches accommodating the pressure of his thigh. He placed a long, sensual kiss on the golden triangle her nudity offered, and Savannah gave herself in panting surrender.

As the stars twinkled overhead, his lips touched her body, satisfying his thirst for her, and yet creating in him a hunger deep and raw. The intricate details of her body intoxicated him with their perfection. The supple curve of her thigh, the flatness of her belly, the dimples in her haunches, the lightly muscled length of her legs. But it was always to the warm shadows between her breasts that he returned, imagining that they beckoned him in a silent, provocative appeal.

Savannah's body cried out for him. She offered herself completely to his seeking hands and lips. And Sloan, sensing her passion, furthered his advances, hungry for her boundless beauty and placing his lips on those secret places that held such fascination for him. He indulged in her lusty passion that met and equalled his own.

Beneath his touch her skin glistened with a sheen of desire. She slid her hands down the flat of his belly, eager to know him and satisfy her yearning need. She strove to learn every detail of his flesh, touching his rippling muscular smoothness, feeling the strength beneath. She kissed the hollow near the base of his throat, tasting the saltiness left by the sea. And when she cried his name, it tore from her throat, painful and husky, demanding he put an end to her torment and satisfy the cravings he had instilled in her.

The galaxy of stars overhead became one world, fused together by the white hot heat they created. Together they spun out beyond the moon reveling in the beauty each brought to the other, seeing in each other a small part of themselves. Two golden-haired spirits, one pale as starlight and the other spun honey, came together in their passion, creating an aura of sunlight in the dark, endless night.

# Chapter Six

On the first day of the New Year, the *Polly Copinger* set sail for Galveston. If he lived to be a hundred and ninety, he would never forget the expression of fear on Savannah's face when she climbed aboard. Sloan knew she feared this journey. On the out island of the key she had grilled him, often, about sailing out of sight of land, how it felt, things that could go wrong . . . among the Seminoles, she had never sailed anything larger than a canoe or raft and the grassy treelined banks were always in sight.

The sun had achieved the required effect on Savannah's skin. She was still a trifle pink, instead of the deep, golden brown needed to even out her skin tone, but there were still at least three days to Galveston and the weather promised to be fair. Inwardly, he groaned. He'd probably have a fight on his hands when he tried to explain that she must not strip down to the buff in front of the crew.

The memories of the past five days flooded back at him like a raging, storm tide. Five days in paradise with a sun goddess. Loving her on the coarse yellow sand where he could see the passion rising in her sultry, green eyes; loving her in the night; feeling the heat emanating from her body as if it had captured the golden warmth from the sun and burned with a light of its own.

Enwright Culpepper found himself more than a little curious about his new passenger. Snapping blue eyes peered at the girl from beneath bushy, white brows. He'd seen scared rabbits with more nerve than this scrap of a girl in her indigo blouse and wide, multicolored skirt. Her beads and trinkets were obviously Indian in origin, and despite her honey-colored hair and golden skin, he knew she must belong to a tribe of savages. It would be interesting to see if a whole tribe of Indian braves came charging through the woods to rescue this pretty young thing. It never occurred to him that Sloan had done anything less than kidnap her and manage to get away by the skin of his teeth. Or, he had paid for her with the shipload of stores he had brought from New Orleans. Lord amighty, he was getting the best of the bargain, but then Sloan MacAllister always came out on top.

"Does she cook?" Culpepper asked thoughtfully. Anything prepared by a hand other than the one in the galley would be an improvement. Culpepper's one weakness, aside from the liniment he rubbed on his game leg, was food. A man had to be strong, true, but there were certain comforts he owed himself.

"Christ, yes," MacAllister snapped. He shouldn't be taking his annoyance out on his captain, but he was disappointed that he hadn't won Savannah's complete trust, despite the intimacies they'd shared. Didn't she know he wasn't going to allow anything to happen to her? Why, in the name of all that was holy, did she have to look as though she'd just been whipped?

Rubbing his palms together in gleeful expectation of a decent meal, Culpepper pressed, "If it isn't too much to ask, do you think you could get the little lady to rustle up something for the crew? I'm fearing we'll have a mutiny on our hands if they don't get something more to eat than dried beans and fat back. That's all that dog in the galley seems to know. Dried beans and fat back. Enough to make a good man turn mean! Not as if there's no fresh supplies, but the man doesn't seem to know what to do with a chicken or a potato. Pretty little thing like her ought to be able to cook like an angel."

Sloan grinned. "Something like that."

Savannah sat on the hatch of the rope locker, her

eyes riveted on the shore. It was true. She was leaving
with this strange man Osceola called brother. In spite
of the growing feelings between herself and Mac-
Allister, she was frightened, feeling torn away from all
she knew and held dear. Even Osceola's promise that
she could return when MacAllister's mission was complete, did not cheer her. To what and where would she
return? Would there even be Seminole people left to
walk and hunt in the Floridas or would they all fall
before the soldiers' bullets? She wanted to help her
Indian brothers and sisters, but to live among white
people, to look like them, talk like them, forget the
ways of the Seminole . . . and to pretend to love a
strange man she was going to call "uncle," the very
man the Indians feared and hated—General Jessup . . .
she couldn't do it! It was too much to ask! There was so
much she didn't know . . . she would make a grave
mistake, she knew it, disappointing Osceola who had
been her protector, father, brother. She must remind
herself it was for Osceola and her people that she was
making this terrible sacrifice.

Her life had changed irrevocably, the day Mac-
Allister appeared in the village. She had been humiliated by him, had suffered the jeers and insults
from her people for insulting the chief's brother. Yet he
was a white man and weren't white men the enemy?
Why was one better than the others? She hadn't
understood. And then to have him see her cry. A
stupid, silly mistake. More than the color of her skin
and the lightness of her hair, this, most of all, set her
apart from her Indian sisters. That, to this day, after all
the years of living in the chikkee with Osceola and his
family, she could still shed tears. No tear ever stained
the dark, soulful eyes of a Seminole woman.

Now she belonged to MacAllister, and she would
never make a chikkee with Mico who had wanted to
defy their chief and protest. She had convinced the
young, handsome brave that it would be useless. The
thlacko's word was law.

A slow, crimson flush settled in her honey-colored cheeks as she recalled the days and the nights on the island where he toasted her in the sun. Her skin tingled with the memory of late night hours and afternoons when the sun would kiss their hot passionate bodies. She had always wondered what it would be like to make a chikkee with a man, and now she knew. Many times she had heard some of the Indian women laugh and whisper behind cupped hands, but they would not answer when she questioned them, telling her she would know soon enough when she and Mico made their own chikkee.

MacAllister's touch had been soft, gentle, making her come alive beneath his fingers and his lips. In her heart, she knew Mico would never have been such a lover. Mico was a warrior, and there was no place in his life for gentleness and softness. Nor would Mico have whispered the tender words that could send her pulses racing and create the warm, hungry stirring deep inside her. Now she belonged to MacAllister; she was his woman. A shudder of excitement and apprehension rippled down her spine. She belonged to a white man, but no matter what she had agreed to do, no matter how many nights she lay with him, she would never be a white woman in her mind or her heart. She was a Seminole. To her death she would remain a Seminole.

Through narrowed eyes, she watched MacAllister approach.

"Savannah, the captain would like you to go below and prepare the food. We're all hungry. Come with me and I'll take you to the galley."

"Don't call me that name! Don't ever call me that name again!" she hissed through clenched teeth, suddenly frightened that she was losing something; that things would never be the same for her again. So many years she had strived to be one of her people, an Indian, despite the fact she was white. He wasn't going to take it all away from her now. Not now!

Sloan was staggered by this sudden change in her. For five days on the island, he had called her Savannah, and she had never complained. Angry, he growled through clenched teeth. "It's your name and you'd better get used to hearing it. As soon as we make port in Galveston, it's the only name you're going to hear. I'm not asking you; I'm telling you." For an instant he pitied her. How lonely and frightened she must be with the changes in her life. "Now come with me and prepare some food."

"I'm not hungry. MacAllister said nothing about cooking on this ship. Do it yourself!" she spat.

"I didn't ask if *you* were hungry. I said I was and so are the crew." Sloan took a deep breath. "I'm responsible for this ship and the men on it. I pay their wages and they expect to be fed. I don't want to hear another word out of you. If you persist in defying me, I'll turn you over my knee and whack the bejesus out of your backside. I can do it, remember?"

"You wouldn't!" Savannah said, steadily and evenly. "MacAllister is supposed to be civilized and I'm supposed to be the savage!"

Sloan was taken back momentarily. "Oh, wouldn't I? Don't try me, Savannah. Come to the galley with me. I meant it about paddling you, and I won't tell you something twice!" He reached out a long arm and the moment he grasped her wrist, she tightened it, pulling forward. Sloan had expected some resistance, but not this display of strength. She was tough as rawhide and twice as rigid. He lost his balance on the pitching deck and literally sailed past her. Squeals of delighted laughter sounded in his ears.

Enwright Culpepper's deep bellied guffaw made Sloan's breathing difficult. Bitch! Little she-lion!

"Madame," Enwright Culpepper addressed Savannah, bowing from the waist. "It is a pure pleasure to have your beauty aboard this clumsy ship. Excuse my employer for his rudeness; he's not experienced when ladies are involved. Insensitive, if you know what I mean. Surly and crude, not to mention crass and unrefined. A lady such as yourself deserves much more. Allow me to escort you to the galley where we do our cooking. While I'm certain you're not used to cooking for the scurvy likes of us, as a special favor to me, I wonder if you mightn't prepare a little something just to take the edge off our appetites? You don't necessarily have to make enough for Mr. MacAllister. After the way he's insulted you, you needn't be generous."

Sloan watched in stunned amazement as Savannah smiled serenely and allowed her hand to be kissed. He swallowed, not believing his eyes when she fluttered her long lashes and then lowered them coquettishly. Beaunell wasn't as adept at flirting, nor Annemarie. As the twosome walked away leaving him dumbfounded, he heard Culpepper say in his soft, Scottish burr, "Dear lady, you're quite the most lovely creature I've seen in a long time. But I'm afraid I haven't learned your name. What is it?"

"Savannah James," she told him. She heard, rather than saw, MacAllister's fist hit the *Polly's* rail.

It was early twilight three days later when Captain Enwright Culpepper ordered the anchor dropped in the Galveston Harbor. He liked Galveston and a certain widow lady who had a mind of her own. A man needed a woman and Maeve Carpenter was one hell of a woman. Hell, when she got done with him, even his game leg had a new spring to its step. Now, if MacAllister would take Miss Savannah James and move on into town, Culpepper could see to his own needs. The captain was always the last to leave the ship. Tonight, he wished he could change the rules a little. He felt an urgency he hadn't felt in months.

MacAllister didn't disappoint him. The minute the dark curtain of night dropped completely, he was standing waiting for the ship's plank to be lowered. He was as antsy as Culpepper and a little apprehensive about the reception he would receive from Annemarie. Beaunell, he refused to think about altogether. Together they waited on the wharf for Redeemer to be led down by one of the hands. They would ride directly to Annemarie's, and he would stable the horse after he made the final arrangements. He was leaving nothing to chance. With Redeemer tied to the hitching post out front he could make a speedy exit if Annemarie took it in her head to show the pair of them the door, refusing to have anything to do with his plan.

Aunt Jenny herself opened the door. Her squeal of delight was quickly stifled when she set dark, liquid eyes on Savannah. For the first time in her life she was at a loss for words. A new working girl? Sloan's woman? God have mercy on us, she prayed silently. Should she let them in the front door or order them around the back? MacAllister was a favorite customer and he tipped heavily. On top of that he was Miss Annemarie's very special friend. Better to invite them in and ask questions later. The door opened wider. Sloan pushed a stiff-backed Savannah into the bright glare of the foyer. He was amused as she looked around the colorful room. There was awe in the bottle-green eyes. Jesus, if the foyer awed her, wait till she saw Annemarie's ruffles and bows in her private quarters.

He admitted to himself that he would rather take a trip into a lion's den than go through with the upcoming interview with Annemarie and Savannah's unpredictable behavior. He danced nervously behind Aunt Jenny, shoving and pushing Savannah every step of the way.

Annemarie laid down her newspaper, a smile of pleasure on her features as she rose to greet the tall, fair-haired man who had been a good friend all these years. Her smile froze as Savannah skidded to a stop just inches from her. Annemarie's milk-white hands flew to her throat to stifle a gasp. Her eyes questioned Sloan.

"I was in the neighborhood," he said flippantly. "Annemarie, I need some help and you're the only one I could think of to help me." Quickly, he introduced Savannah and explained what he wanted, ending with, "A month, sooner if you can do it. What do you think, Annemarie?"

"A month!" Annemarie's voice was almost shrill, but she caught it just in time and lowered her tone. No lady ever raised her voice except perhaps in the bedroom. "Try a year, maybe two," she said crisply. "Just how savage is she?"

"You'll know soon enough. Look, I don't want a miracle. Polish her up, smooth over the rough edges, teach her how to eat and how to talk. She speaks English, almost perfectly, but it has to be smoothed out so it sounds natural."

"Just like that? I thought you said you didn't expect a miracle."

"You can do it, Annemarie. All you're going to need is a lot of patience and a strong whip. You have to let her know you're the boss," he said mockingly, knowing Savannah was listening with rapt attention to every word.

"And while I'm doing all this, where are you going to be?" Annemarie asked sourly.

"I'm going to register at the hotel. I'll be around to check on her progress. I don't want to interfere by stopping in all the time, and besides I'm not quite certain how she feels about me."

"If you want to know, just ask me," Annemarie said grimly as she stared into green, hate-filled eyes.

"Then it's settled, you'll do it?"

"I'll try, Sloan. You'll owe me for this one."

"I wouldn't have it any other way. You take care of her and I'll go upstairs and have a bath myself." Turning to Savannah, his voice was deliberately cold and hard, "You're to do as Annemarie says. Remember your promise to Osceola, so don't think about running away because there's nowhere for you to go.

Do you understand? There's no way to get back to Florida unless I take you." In the face of her blank expression, he pressed further. "One word of warning. It's frowned upon for a white woman to live with Indians. If you so much as make a move without Annemarie's approval, you could be thrown into prison. You'll never see the Seminoles again." He knew he was exaggerating the situation but could not think of anything else that would force Savannah's obedience.

He bent down with the intention of kissing her lightly on the cheek. She lunged with both hands trying to bring her nails down his face and neck. A high-pitched shriek split the serenity of Annemarie's sitting room. One moccasined foot lashed out, hitting him squarely in the midsection. Every nerve in Savannah's body was stretched taut and screaming. How could he? How could he treat her this way, especially after what they'd shared on the island? He was making a fool of her in front of this woman! Tears of rage filled her eyes and she willed them not to spill onto her cheeks. She half suspected this was retribution for the way she had behaved aboard the *Polly Copinger,* but it wasn't fair. It just wasn't fair! He wouldn't get away with this, not if she could help it.

"She has a bit of a temper," Sloan said gasping for breath. "I know I can depend on you to control it. I think you should call Aunt Jenny or some of the servants to help you. Sometimes you have to tie her up. Bath time is probably one of those times," he smirked mockingly in the face of Savannah's fury. "Do it now, Annemarie, before I leave." He whispered softly, "If she really gets bad, threaten to pull her teeth, every one of them. Sometimes that works."

Annemarie looked doubtful, almost fearful. "Sloan, I don't know if this is such a good idea. What I mean is, I can't keep this child tied up all the time."

"Why not?" Sloan barked, carefully keeping his eye on Savannah. "The first chance she gets she'll tie you and slit your throat, and, Annemarie, if there's one thing I've always admired about you, it's your lily white throat."

Casually, he dropped a sheaf of bills on the end table. "Be sure you get her some proper clothing. She doesn't even wear bloomers," he said in an amused tone. "A parasol too, but make sure she understands it isn't to be used as a weapon." Seeing the doubtful eyes, Sloan went on. "Annemarie, look upon this as the ultimate challenge. I'm depending on you. You have to do this for me. I'll be forever in your debt."

"All right," Annemarie said firmly. She tinkled a small bell and three husky looking negresses came into the room. Within minutes Savannah had her hands tied behind her back and her ankles neatly bound. Sloan saw the shriek that was about to erupt and stuffed his handkerchief into her mouth. "I'll check on you later," he said breathlessly as he sprinted from the room.

Once the door to Annemarie's quarters closed, Sloan heaved a mighty sigh of relief. He took the circular staircase two steps at a time, stopping by the foyer to pick up his roll of fresh clothing. He was anxious for a warm, soothing bath and a clean shave. Aunt Jenny met him, bath sheet in hand and a fresh bar of soap. "I been waitin' for you, Mastah Sloan. Now you shuck those evil smelling clothes and hop right in this tub."

"Jenny, go downstairs and help Annemarie. She needs you. I can see to my bath myself."

Jenny grinned toothily. "No, siree, my place is here with you to scrub you down. Now you'll get in that water and hush. Miz Beaunell don' want a no account, smelly man 'tween her pretty sheets."

"Annemarie needs you, Aunt Jenny. If you don't go, I'm going to drag you back down the hall and show you what us no account white men do to women who don't mind their manners." He advanced a step and then two, leering seductively at Jenny. Frightened that he might mean what he said, the old woman turned and fled the room muttering that all she ever got was promises and more promises.

Sloan grinned as he stepped out of the deerskin boots and buckskin britches. His shirt fell in a heap. He stepped into the round tub and immediately relaxed in the steamy wetness. A man could fall asleep in this comfort he told himself. As he sank lower and lower into the soapy water, he realized how tense he was. Was he waiting for a crash, a scream? The sound of a bullet meaning Annemarie couldn't cope and had shot Savannah? The thought brought perspiration to his brow.

He had hated tying her up, hated the betrayed look he read in her eyes, but she had given him no other choice. Osceola came first. If she wouldn't voluntarily help, then it would be involuntarily. Circumstances being what they were, he had to make the decisions for both of them. The first time he had tied her it was different. She had been nothing to him, just a girl with exceptionally bad manners. Now it was different. He knew her, had been intimate with her, had loved her body and touched her soul. He also knew if he hadn't tied her, Savannah would have run from Annemarie and that gracious lady would not have allowed her to return for any reason, any bribe. Still, his conscience pricked him because of his cruelty. Annemarie, with her soft manner and soothing voice, might be able to make it right for the frightened Savannah. And it was more fright than hostility, Sloan was certain of it.

As the tenseness began to drain from his body, Sloan allowed his mind to wander to the nights on the island and how Savannah had felt in his arms. She had trusted him, for a short while at least. Even on the ship her behavior had been above reproach, thanks to Captain Culpepper. She had been frightened then also, on the strange ship, crossing vast waters, traveling to a strange place. She was out of her element. Little wonder she had fought back. He would have done the same thing if the Creeks had managed to get hold of him. Old Jeb MacAllister had always warned him never to push a dog against a wall, because when the dog's done looking at you, he wasn't going to just stand there, he was going to get himself away from that wall somehow. Now, this evening, he had pushed Savannah against a stone wall. One way or another she was going to get away. It might take her a while, but somehow she would manage to get back to the Seminole.

He was feeling worse by the minute for his shoddy treatment of the frightened girl when the door opened a crack and then widened. Beaunell, in a rich creation of feathers and lace and incredibly high-heeled slippers, pranced into the room. "I knew you were here," she breathed sultrily.

Sloan groaned silently. The last thing he needed was Beaunell. It had been his intention to spend the night aboard his ship and set up temporary headquarters at the hotel the following morning. Beaunell had not been in his plans at all!

"Here, let me wash your back," she said reaching for the brush Aunt Jenny had laid on the side of the tub. "I've thought of nothing else but you since you left my bed on your last visit."

"I already used the brush," Sloan lied. "Listen, Beaunell, I can't . . ." The sounds of a crash and a high-pitched shriek exploded through the open door. "What the hell was that?" He was about to stand up and then thought better of the idea.

Beaunell was frowning. If there was one thing Annemarie insisted upon, it was quiet. Peace and quiet. Every sound was muffled, even the clink and clatter of silver had a muted sound. Again, the high-pitched wail ricocheted up the stairs. Sloan's mind raced. He didn't want Beaunell to go downstairs to see what was going on. If Beaunell and Savannah locked eyes and tongues, it would be a more violent confrontation than the war between Jessup and the Seminoles. When at last they did meet, which was inevitable, he didn't mean to be within shouting distance. He smirked, knowing he was the prize for the winner. "Pay no attention, Beau. I think Annemarie hired a new cook who breaks crystal.

Tell me," he said speaking louder than usual, "where is that beautiful dressing gown you wore the last time I was here? What pretties did you buy yourself with the money I left you?"

Beaunell answered automatically, her ears trained on the doorway. Something was going on. Something Sloan didn't want her to know about. "I didn't hear anything about a new cook. What happened to Dulcie? She's been with Annemarie forever."

Sloan shrugged. "I don't keep track of women's business. I'd like to keep talking to you, honey, but I have to get back to the ship."

Beaunell's eyes widened and her jaw dropped. "Back to the ship? You mean you aren't coming to my room, to my bed?" she asked stupidly, hardly believing her ears.

"Business, Beau, strictly business. I'll be back when I have time."

"You'll be back when you have time!" she parroted his words.

"Do you mind leaving and closing the door? It's not that I'm modest, but there are some things a man likes to do in private. I'll look in on you soon. Nice of you to stop by." He was babbling like an idiot. Time to get out of here before she went downstairs. He had to beat her to Annemarie. How in the hell had he managed to disregard Beaunell's jealousy?

"If that's how you feel about it, then I'll leave," Beaunell pouted haughtily, her delicate nostrils flaring angrily.

Now he'd gone and done it! He didn't know which was worse—Savannah's screeching or this one's pique. Whatever, he wasn't going to stay around long enough to find out.

Sloan grimaced. He thought his teeth shook loose with the slamming of the bathroom door.

Within minutes he was dried and dressed in fresh clothes and racing down the stairs to Annemarie's apartments. He rapped quietly. Annemarie herself let him in. "Shhh," she said laying a finger to her lips. "We got her to sleep. I gave her a mild sleeping draught, but the poor thing was exhausted, half scared out of her wits. We bathed her and washed her hair and gave her something pretty to wear. Come see for yourself." Sloan's eyes widened. Sleeping in Annemarie's high tester bed was a tiny figure dressed in a dimity nightdress with a delicate ruffle around the neck. Golden hair fanned the pillow. His eyes traveled downward to her bound wrists and ankles. The sight tore at his heart.

"She's beautiful, Sloan. Quite the most beautiful creature I've ever seen. I just hope this works and I can help you."

"Keep Beaunell out of here and don't let her find out about Savannah if you can help it. She came into the bathroom and heard the noise and the screams. She's a mite put out with me now and could cause a lot of trouble if she had a mind to. I'm going back to the ship and will check in tomorrow. Try to keep it a secret at least for a few days. Beau's jealous rages are something neither of us needs at the moment."

Annemarie's eyes rolled back in her head as she envisioned the forthcoming days. "I'll do my best," she whispered fearfully. Lord, all she had ever wanted, all she had ever asked for, was peace and quiet. Sloan was doing his best to see she didn't get it.

The *Polly Copinger* pitched to and fro in the gentle swell of the harbor water, lulling Sloan into a fitful sleep. He dreamed and then woke throughout the night. Toward dawn he fell into an agonized sleep, dreaming he was chasing Osceola through the woods back on the old farm. At the end of the dim tunnel created by the dense hickory trees stood Chala, Wild Honey. There was a winsome, dutiful smile on her lovely face as she watched Osceola take a slight lead in the boyhood chase. But it was to Sloan that she held out her arms, and when both boys crossed the invisible boundary at the same split second, she laughed, a rich, wonderful sound of happiness that seemed to blend and melt with the golden sunshine of late afternoon.

Sloan thrashed about on the narrow bunk as his dreams continued to torment him. The dream was the past, the present and the future. Chala was spitting and snarling, refusing to board the *Polly Copinger*. Thomas Jessup was racing along the shoreline atop a sure-footed steed, shouting obscenities, his Winchester rifle aimed at Sloan's midsection. Annemarie, her parasol in front of her, was standing next to Osceola who was braving the situation out with a stony look and his own rifle at his side. It wasn't till Jessup got within close eye range that Savannah pointed for Sloan to see what she was shrieking about. Seated behind Jessup and clinging to him for dear life was Beaunell in her scarlet wrapper, bare legs swinging wildly against the horse's flanks. "Help me, MacAllister," Savannah begged, clinging to him. "Help me and I'll do anything you want! Anything . . . anything . . . anything!"

Sloan woke, his body drenched in perspiration. The dream had been so real he could almost feel Beaunell next to him, breathing fire. He had heard, no doubt from Annemarie, that there was no hell like that of a woman scorned. And in his dream Beaunell was definitely scorned. Christ Almighty, how could he have forgotten Beaunell? Something was going to have to be done. Maybe Annemarie could send her away. A bogus trip, anything to get her out of Galveston. His gut churned. He knew it was too late. He also knew by the time he got to Annemarie's house Beaunell would be fully apprised of the situation through no fault of Annemarie's. Beaunell was an industrious young woman. One way or another she would have found Savannah by now and was probably plotting some dastardly act of jealous revenge, not only for the poor, unsuspecting Savannah, but for himself as well.

The sun was directly overhead when Enwright Culpepper tottered up the gangplank. Sloan suppressed a grin. Wherever he had been, the old salt had had a time for himself. "My head feels like a bloody powder keg," the captain complained. "I'll be no good to ye this day, Laddie. Perhaps if some of the hair of the dog that bit me were available, I might be able to see your handsome features," he said slyly.

"That I can arrange," Sloan grinned as he fetched a bottle from the cabin. As he handed over the bottle, he watched the captain closely. The damage he was suffering wasn't from the drink. "She must be one hell of a woman," he chortled.

Bleary red eyes blinked. "That she is, Laddie. The good Lord don't make them like Maeve any more. She's the only woman I've thought of taking for a bride. She loves me," he ended stupidly. "Can ye be believing that, Laddie?"

"I've led a precarious life, Enwright, as you well know. I don't think anyone or anything can surprise me. However, you've come this far without taking a bride, so why don't you give it some more serious thought. I want to talk to you about something that might put a crimp in your plans, so listen to me," Sloan said taking a second breath. If there was one thing Enwright Culpepper enjoyed it was danger and adventure, and not necessarily in that order.

"Speak up, Laddie, there's nothing wrong with my hearing. It's my nether regions that are feeling pain."

"This is serious business. My brother, Osceola, needs help. I want you to take the *Polly Copinger* back to Cedar Key with as many supplies as we can load aboard. You'll have to wait till one of his men spots the ship though. You cannot allow anyone other than Osceola's men to take possession. It's dangerous; you may be fired upon by the Creeks or Jessup's men. Do you think you can handle it?"

"Aye, Laddie, I kin handle it, but there's one small problem. One Indian looks like another. How will I know your brother's men from those ornery bastards, the Creeks."

"Christ, Culpepper, where the hell have you been?

The Seminole wears yellow and red war paint, the same colors as Osceola's standard. I'm going into town now to order supplies. You're to take mules just the way you did the last time. I'll be back late this afternoon, and I want you to set sail with the tide. Will you do it?" Sloan hoped his voice wasn't as anxious as he felt. Of late, he had been putting all of his eggs in one basket, something he usually avoided doing.

Culpepper shrugged. "Dying never bothered me, Laddie, it's the way of dying that gets to my innards. If I had my druthers, I'd just as soon go by an Indian's hand than a woman's if ye know what I mean."

Sloan suddenly developed a sensitive spot between his shoulder blades. He knew exactly what Culpepper was talking about. Without another word Sloan was down the gangplank and swinging himself onto Redeemer's saddle. Culpepper watched the young man with a mixture of envy and tiredness. Two more swigs from the brandy bottle made his spirits rise considerably. He set about to tidy his ship much the way an old woman with no one left to care for would do. It was spit and polish from stem to stern, but that didn't stop him from spitting on his handkerchief and rubbing at some of the brass here and there. He was home. He belonged, along with his sixty-four years, aboard ship. Just the thought of making the change to a landlubber set his nerve ends to twanging. A brief moment of insanity. Thank heaven he had the good sense to head back for the ship before Maeve worked more of her seductive magic on him. Thank heaven for young MacAllister and his Indians. A man, by God, needed a purpose in life. Lollygagging around with the voluptuous likes of Maeve couldn't be taken seriously. Not today any way. A week from today, a month from today, might tell a different story. There was a decided spring to his step as he made his way to the helm.

Annemarie walked softly down the carpeted hall to the room she had assigned to Savannah. It wasn't even nine o'clock in the morning and already she was up and dressed. Muttering beneath her breath, she swore she should have told Sloan to take his "little problem" elsewhere. As a rule, Annemarie kept late hours because of the business, and her clients expected to see her cheerful and entertaining. If she kept these hours, all they would see was a woman with dark circles under her eyes who found it difficult not to yawn with exhaustion.

Aunt Jenny was already with Savannah when Annemarie entered the femininely decorated bedroom. The morning light, with which Annemarie was so unfamiliar, was streaming in the lace curtained window illuminating the cherry wood furniture and rose-colored hangings. Savannah was seated in front of the dressing table quietly allowing Aunt Jenny to brush her hair. The girl did not acknowledge her hostess' presence but merely stared toward the window with a trapped look in her eyes.

"Sure is a pretty child," Aunt Jenny said enthusiastically. Not for the first time Annemarie wondered where the old woman got her energy. She kept hours almost as late as her employer and always seemed to be up and about at the crack of dawn.

"Aunt Jenny, I don't know how you do it," Annemarie said.

Mistaking her meaning, Aunt Jenny smiled a toothy grin. "I jus' take dis brush and pull it through like this. This gal's got some head o' hair. Jes look how long and silky it is and watch the way it wants to curl around my fingers."

Scrutinizing Aunt Jenny's demonstration, Annemarie said, "Yes. Lovely. Now put it up for her. Our job is to make her into a lady, and we might as well start with making her look like one. Something simple, Aunt Jenny, something she can learn to do for herself." Turning to the clothes press, Annemarie withdrew a morning wrapper of pale blue trimmed with ecru lace and satin bows. Sighing she remembered the girl hadn't even come equipped with her own underwear. She sized her up and thought that some of Beaunell's things might fit her until some could be made for her.

"Aunt Jenny, do you think you can get hold of some of Beaunell's lingerie without going into her room to explain why you want it?"

"Yes, ma'am. There's a whole stack of Miz Beau's laundry downstairs. I wuz gonna bring it to her after she woke up."

"Beau's a flighty thing. She won't miss a few garments. Go and get them for me, please. I'll finish dressing Miss Savannah's hair."

As Aunt Jenny left the room, Annemarie picked up the brush, finding that the old negress hadn't overstated the luxuriousness of Savannah's hair. "Lovely," Annemarie complimented. Still there was no reaction from the girl whose sullen eyes were focused on the window. It was a rare woman who could sit in front of a mirror and look at anything besides herself. Trying another tack to get Savannah's attention, she said offhandedly, "I'll bet Sloan loves to run his fingers through your hair. Has he told you how beautiful it is?"

Immediately, Savannah glanced into the mirror looking back at Annemarie. Her green eyes had come to life at the mention of Sloan's name and a fragile pink blush brightened her cheeks. "He tells me I have captured the sunlight." After a moment, "Where is MacAllister? Why does he not come? How long will he leave me here?"

There was something pitiful about the child that wrung Annemarie's heart. That blasted rogue, Mac-Allister, had no right to leave her with this frightened child whose very act of bravado was pathetic.

"Sloan had business in town. I've no doubt he'll come to see you soon. He was very worried about you, Savannah. He wants you to be happy, but he also needs your help. You will help him, won't you. You will help Osceola?"

Savannah turned to look up at Annemarie. "I promised I would help. Am I fighting? Are my hands tied? Am I gagged?" Quick tears glistened on her dark thick fringe of lashes.

Putting down the brush, Annemarie sat beside Savannah on the dressing bench. Instinctively, her arms went around the child, holding her and giving comfort and reassurance. "Poor kitten," Annemarie crooned, "thrown out in this big cruel world. I want to be your friend, Savannah. I want to help you learn to behave like a white woman. You have a very important task ahead of you, and Sloan wants you to be prepared. For your sake. For your safety. Did you know he came into your room last night after you fell asleep? He wanted to be certain you were all right. He wouldn't have brought you here to me if he didn't think I would take care of you."

Savannah stiffened, refusing to yield to the gentle pressure of Annemarie's embrace. "You know my MacAllister too much. Too . . ."

"Too 'well,' is the word you're looking for, child. Yes, I've known him for several years now, and he's always proved himself to be my friend. Friends help one another. That's why I'm helping him now. But rest your heart, child. MacAllister does not sleep in my bed, if that's what's peeving you, and he never has. A man and a woman can be friends."

Savannah instantly relaxed. Even though she had lived in a society where polygamy was the rule rather than the exception, she couldn't bear the thought of sharing MacAllister with another woman. Any other woman, even a Seminole woman! Annemarie's tone was soft, reassuring, and Savannah believed she really wanted to be her friend.

"Now, little one, if you'll try to learn quickly, you'll be back with Sloan in no time. And think of how proud you'll make him. Watch me while I dress your hair, so you can do it for yourself. Something simple and elegant," Annemarie told her, already standing behind

Savannah with the brush in her hand. Perhaps if she could keep up a steady chatter, Savannah would be too preoccupied to think about her fears. Even as she spoke, Annemarie thought about Beaunell Gentry and how she was going to accept Sloan's interest in this girl. Sighing, Annemarie stroked the bristles through the long golden hair. That was something Sloan himself was going to have to worry about. For now, she had the education of Savannah James to accomplish.

In the space of one short hour Savannah had made long strides in her education to be a lady. To Annemarie's delight, Savannah remembered many things her mother had taught her and what she was not taught she had seen Caroline do herself. This, added to the fact that Savannah was totally female and enjoyed being pampered, made the lessons go surprisingly well.

Savannah learned the easy method of bringing her thick, honeyed hair to the top of her head and winding it into a smooth coronet. She liked the scented water Aunt Jenny had brought in a basin and she washed with the perfumed soap from Annemarie's own supply sent from Paris. Savannah already appreciated the feel of silk against her skin, and with no difficulty, Aunt Jenny and Annemarie taught her how to carefully roll expensive silk stockings up her long, pretty legs and fasten them with frilly garters. Shoes were going to be a problem, Annemarie realized, but they would jump that hurdle later. Perhaps Dolores, another of Annemarie's girls, would have a pair to fit her. The first resistance displayed by Savannah was when Aunt Jenny produced a lightly boned corset that would squeeze Savannah's figure into the fashionable style of the day which demanded an incredibly tiny waist, rounded hips and a high, voluptuous bosom.

Dressed in chemisette and ruffled pantalettes, Savannah stood while Aunt Jenny placed the white satin corset with its long laces under her breasts and tied it at the back. It was only as she began to tighten the laces that were crisscrossed through a long series of eyelets that Savannah complained. "No!" she gasped. "What are you doing, Aunt Jenny? You're killing me!"

"Not too tight, Jenny," Annemarie snapped the order, realizing that Savannah's ribs were unused to being constricted in corsets and would offer resistance. "We don't want to crack her ribs, Jenny. She's not used to being strapped into one of these things like the rest of us. Thank heavens she has a naturally small waist, and we can camouflage it by making her skirts wider and adding a little more width in the shoulders. Besides, no one is going to look at her waistline once they see that spectacular face of hers."

"Yes, Ma'am," Aunt Jenny intoned, mentally disagreeing with her employer and biting her lower lip as she strained at the laces. "We gots to make it as tight as she can stand it, otherwise she ain't gonna walk and sit like the rest o' you white ladies." Jenny had a point, Annemarie conceded and sympathized with Savannah whose complexion was turning a decided shade of blue from lack of air.

"Loosen it, Jenny. She'll need time to get used to it."

"Why do I need this . . . this . . . thing? MacAllister likes to touch *me,* not a lot of clothes!" Savannah gasped with relief as Jenny loosened the corset.

"The idea is not for him to touch you, Savannah, but to make him *want* to touch you," Annemarie instructed. She could see that her logic was completely lost on her protege. Savannah's hands were braced on the bed post, and Annemarie noticed the rough skin and unkempt nails. Sighing, she told Jenny that a manicure was in order and said it should be accomplished while she gave the girl a few lessons in behavior. Manners were most important at the dinner table and she decided that's where she would start. "Jenny, ring for Odile in the kitchen and have her bring my breakfast in here."

"You nevah eats breakfast before two in the aftah-noon. . . ."

"Just do as I say, Jenny. If I'm going to keep these hours, I'll also need to keep up my strength."

Seated across a narrow table from Aunt Jenny, who clicked her tongue in dismay as she performed a manicure, Savannah devoted her attention to Annemarie who had assembled a small table and a chair nearby and was demonstrating proper table manners. Enjoying this demonstration immensely, Savannah listened carefully to what her tutor was saying.

"The way a woman comports herself at the dining table must be as pleasant and agreeable to her companions as the meal itself. A lady sits with her back perpendicular to the seat and never rests back against it. Instead, her back must be slightly at a distance from the back of the chair. Her feet are placed so," Annemarie lifted her skirts and petticoats for Savannah's benefit. "Flat on the floor and touching lightly at the ankles. One hand in the lap, so, the other gracefully on the table."

Savannah nodded, knowing this was something she could easily accomplish. Being a lady seemed to be filled with silly rules and all she needed to do was remember them. MacAllister would sing her praises!

"Now, pay attention, Savannah, I'm going to show you how to unfold your napkin." At Savannah's quizzical glance, she sighed. "This!" she said, holding a square of linen. "It is used to delicately wipe the mouth when eating." Savannah glanced at the back of her own hand which, until now, had served the purpose just as well and was easier to wash.

"The unfolding of the napkin," Annemarie told her, "should be in a manner which reflects breeding and taste. A woman who picks up the napkin between her thumb and forefinger and then shakes it open shows she lacks principle and a certain looseness of character."

Aunt Jenny shook her head and laughed. "Miz Annemarie is saying you don't wanna act like no whore and go wavin' your napkin around."

"What's a whore . . . ?"

"Ahem!" Annemarie cleared her throat to caution Aunt Jenny. "A woman of breeding and taste," she raised her tone to override Savannah's question, "discreetly removes the folded napkin to her lap where she unfolds it and leaves it doubled lengthwise across her lap."

"But my mouth is up here," Savannah pointed, "not between my knees."

"Just watch and listen and learn," annoyance riddled Annemarie's voice. "Most of these things are only common sense, and the rest make no sense at all. Nevertheless, it will be expected of you if you're to become a lady."

Chastised, Savannah gave her full attention.

"Now, when eating. A lady cuts all pieces of food into tiny morsels which she decorously raises to her mouth. She never bites, chews or crunches her food but nibbles noiselessly and daintily." Cutting into her already cold egg, Annemarie put the morsel into her mouth and demonstrated.

"I sure am glad I ain't never had to be no lady," Aunt Jenny said giving special attention to buffing Savannah's nails with a grainy pink paste. "Gals like me always goes on picnics."

"Picnics! Good thought, Jenny," Annemarie exclaimed, thoroughly entrenched in her lessons. "Now, Savannah, it's possible that you may be invited to a picnic. That's where food is packed and taken outside to be eaten. Usually, you'll be required to sit on a blanket . . ."

"This I know how to do!" Savannah said confidently.

Annemarie looked doubtful. "Well, I'd better show you anyway." Snatching a cover from the bed. Annemarie spread it on the carpet. "When you sit on a blanket for a picnic, it's very important that you behave modestly. Do you know what modesty is?" Savannah gazed at her blankly. "No. It's not calling attention to yourself, especially not to your body. Here, I'll show you. First, you accept the support of your escort, that's the gentleman you'll be with. Aunt Jenny, come here. Let's do this right."

"No siree, Miz Annemarie, you is on your own! When I goes to a picnic, it's ta enjoy myself. Ain't none of them fancy modesties gonna spoil my good time."

Exasperated, Annemarie continued. "Let's pretend there's a gentleman here with me, and he's going to help me get down to the blanket. See?"

Chewing on the inside of her lip, Savannah remarked, "Only old women need help. Are you old, Annemarie? I am not old! I can get down to the blanket myself."

"That's because you ain't tried it while you're wearin' that corset," Aunt Jenny interjected. "Just wait till I pull them laces another inch or two. You're gonna need all the help you can get!"

"Quiet. Both of you. Now watch. First, you accept the support of your escort by lightly laying your hand upon his arm and slowly bend your knees. See? It should be light and graceful, like a leaf falling from a tree. Now, once you're down here, you must turn your legs to the side and, above all, keep them under your skirts. Sit with your back straight and keep your hands in your lap. Never, never, never should you lean or slouch. And never, ever raise your arms above your head!" Annemarie lifted her arms to show what a lady must never, ever do. Her heel caught in the hem of her skirt and, losing her balance, she toppled backward.

Savannah and Aunt Jenny broke into a shrieking laughter as Annemarie shot them lethal looks.

"An' nevah, nevah, child, sprawl with your legs open and your back flat on the ground. *That's* the difference between a lady and a whore!"

Comprehension dawned on Savannah's face as she broke into peals of laughter.

Savannah lay across her high four-poster bed, the light from the oil lamp falling across the covers. Though it was only a few hours past dark, Annemarie had sent her to her room, telling her that it had been a very long day and she needed her rest. Savannah was exhilarated rather than exhausted. So many things a lady had to know. So much yet to learn. And all of it, Annemarie had promised, she *would* learn.

Trying to turn the page of an illustrated fashion book Annemarie had given her to look at, Savannah was again irritated by the gloves Aunt Jenny had insisted she wear to bed. First, a greasy cream had been rubbed into the chafed skin on her hands and the gloves were then pulled on. She must leave them until morning and as her reward she was promised prettier hands. Every night, Aunt Jenny had cautioned, she must perform this ritual. Perhaps for now, Savannah frowned, but not when she again was with MacAllister. He would not like the gloves. He would want to have her touch him with her hands, and in the dark he would not care if they were pretty or not.

Several minutes ago there was the sound of a piano coming from downstairs. She knew it was a piano because a vague memory of her mother's playing had come back to her. There were also the sounds of voices, men's and women's, and she harbored a bare hope that MacAllister had come to see her.

She would have liked to go to the top of the stairs and peek down, but Aunt Jenny had locked her door saying it was to keep other people out. What other people? She wondered when would she meet the other girls whom she knew also lived here at Annemarie's house. Was her hostess also teaching them to become ladies? Everything was so secret. Why had she been kept in this room all day? Didn't ladies ever go out in the sunshine?

Still straining to hear the familiar timbre of MacAllister's voice, she closed her eyes and found sleep.

Annemarie sat quietly on the edge of the sapphire-blue settee pretending to listen to the conversation of Mr. Lionel Bradshaw, an elderly gentleman of Galveston who liked to frequent Annemarie's establishment mostly for the companionship.

As she nodded her head from time to time, Annemarie kept her eyes fastened on Beaunell Gentry who was draped across the lap of one of her clients. Catching Aunt Jenny's eye, Annemarie gave a signal that Beaunell wasn't to be given any more wine. Her voice was too loud and her words thick. Ever since the other night when Sloan had deposited Savannah and had refused Beau's companionship, she had been imbibing too freely of alcohol. While Annemarie could understand Beau's disappointment, she couldn't forgive her actions. Her business had never been managed as a common bawdy house, and she would not allow it now. Beaunell Gentry would have to be sent somewhere, at least until Sloan could come to take Savannah away. "Oh, Sloan," Annemarie sighed to herself, "you've cost me my sleep, my peace of mind, and now you're going to cost me my percentage of Beaunell's earnings."

Deciding that Beaunell must leave Galveston for a while, Annemarie's mind searched for the method. What was Mr. Bradshaw saying? "Did you hear me, Anne? I said I would be leaving tomorrow for Mobile. I'm restocking my store, and I can't trust the job to that idiot who works for me. Last time he brought back a dozen banjos. Banjos! I can't even give them away! I will certainly miss my evenings here for the next three weeks. Er . . . perhaps you can suggest somewhere I can spend my off hours in Mobile? It's been some time since I was in that city and you know how discriminating my tastes are."

Annemarie's eyes swung from Beaunell to Mr. Bradshaw and back again. It was an answer from heaven. Beau was too dangerous to have around for the next few weeks; there would be no telling what she would do if she ever learned of Sloan's little scheme. One thing Annemarie did know about Beau was that she was vindictive and dangerous when crossed.

"Mr. Bradshaw," Annemarie said sweetly, smiling and openly flirting. "I, myself, have need of several things from Mobile, and I was thinking of sending one of my girls to get them. It would mean so much to me if you would volunteer to be protector and guardian to her while she was away. She would be no trouble, I assure you, and she would be a ready companion for the wonderful restaurants and theatres I'm certain you would want to attend. A refined gentleman, such as yourself, would find little to satisfy himself in the establishments I've heard of in Mobile. It's a wicked city, Mr. Bradshaw. Wicked!"

The old man's eyes showed immediate interest. Loneliness was the plight of the aged, and he wasn't looking forward to being alone and friendless in a strange city. "Whom were you sending to Mobile?" he asked, struggling to keep the excitement from his voice.

"Why, Beaunell. She's the only one I would trust to do my business." She watched as Bradshaw's eyes turned to Beau. She saw him lick his lips and smiled. Was it possible that Mr. Bradshaw would find himself with renewed passions in Beau's company? Playing her hunch, she leaned forward, lightly placing her hand on his arm. "Of course, dear Mr. Bradshaw, Beaunell would be expected to be remunerated for the pleasure of her company. You understand, don't you? A girl must prepare for her future."

"Of course, of course," Bradshaw agreed, already thinking of the pleasure Beaunell had to offer. Perhaps he wasn't as old as he thought.

Now, all Annemarie had to do was inform Beau. That would be no problem, she assured herself. Mr. Bradshaw was one of the richest men in Galveston, and Beau was expert at parting a man from his money.

It was mid-afternoon when Sloan let himself in through Annemarie's kitchen door. Silence pervaded. A small worm of agitation crawled around in his belly

as he tried to imagine the reason for such silence. Why
was the kitchen empty? Where was everyone? Usually,
at this time of day dinner preparations were in progress
and tantalizing aromas wafted about. Tentatively, he
inched his way across the kitchen on tip-toe. It occured
to him that he might appear ridiculous to anyone who
might be watching. Worry lines creased his brow as he
entered Annemarie's formal dining room. But a loud
sigh of relief escaped him as he saw Savannah bring a
delicate bone china cup to her lips. She seemed to be
doing fine. Fine, that is, until he looked into her eyes.
She met his gaze. Daintily, she set the cup down on the
saucer and folded her hands primly in her lap. She said
nothing.

He stood there returning her gaze. He would rather
have taken a beating than see the recriminations in her
eyes. Guiltily, he counted the days since he had left her
at Annemarie's. Nine days. Nine. From the expression
on Annemarie's face, the thought that he had deserted
Savannah seemed to be the general consensus. Shifting
his weight from one foot to the other, while fidgeting
with his hat like a schoolboy, he began to explain that
business had kept him away. He realized how ridiculous
that would sound to Annemarie and decided he would
have to brave this one through. That he was afraid to
face Savannah and had had to force himself to check on
her progress today was something he didn't want to
admit aloud.

"There you are," Annemarie kept her tone light and
friendly, not wanting Savannah to know she thought
Sloan's neglect deplorable. "Savannah has been worried that you might have forsaken her. I tried to assure
her that wasn't the case. You are her reward. I thought
a buggy ride around town might help. She's doing
marvelously, Sloan. She learns very quickly. You can
be proud of her."

Sloan had trouble with his breathing. He had known
Savannah was beautiful, but this breathtaking creature

dressed in bright yellow, the color of new daffodils, was more than he had ever imagined. She was a vision. Honey gold hair piled smoothly atop her head revealed the elegant curves of her throat and shoulders. Her breasts rose high and firm, their supple roundness making his hands ache to caress them. Her skin had evened to the color of ripe peaches, and he knew it would be smooth and yielding beneath his touch. He had missed her, had longed for her beside him at night, and seeing her here like this sent a stab of remembered passions through his loins. His heart started to pound in his chest as other thoughts raced through his mind. It was all he could do to nod and still remain on his feet.

"Good afternoon, MacAllister," Savannah said in an exaggerated sing-song voice. He knew she was deliberately baiting him, poking fun at her lessons. Annemarie knew it too, but said nothing, preferring to have Sloan handle his charge's mocking behavior.

"Is that the best you can do?" he said tersely.

"Because I am your woman does not mean I must do everything you say. I àm being obedient, am I not?" she questioned Annemarie who nodded her head. "You can see that I am not bound nor am I gagged." The sing-song voice grated on Sloan's nerves. "I am doing what you asked because I belong to you. If the way I do it does not please you then send me back to my people." Sloan could see the pulse working at the base of her throat. Aha, so that was what she was up to. She would go through with everything and stop just short of success. Then when she returned to Osceola she could truthfully say she had been obedient and done what she was told.

Sloan schooled his face to sternness. "Savannah, half measures do not count. You must give one hundred percent for this trick to work for Osceola's benefit. Even if I were to send you back for whatever reason, do you think Osceola would be proud of you? No. If you fail, you'll shame him among his people. He's counting on you, depending on you. This is no game. You're not a child any longer playing with grownups. You're a woman now, and Annemarie wants only to help you. I am not proud of you this day. I expected more." He turned as if to leave but not before he added one last thing. "You have made me lose face among my friends."

This was something Savannah understood completely. The emerald eyes filled with tears as she looked around at Aunt Jenny, Annemarie and the three handsome negresses from the kitchen. As if on cue, all the women lowered their heads. Sloan could see a satisfied smile play around Annemarie's generous mouth.

"Good afternoon, MacAllister. It is a lovely day, is it not? Please join us in some tea," Savannah said in perfect English. A gentle, winsome smile lit her features as she waited to see Sloan's reaction.

Sloan laughed. "You see, I knew you could do it! I told Annemarie you're smart." Then more formally, "I would love to join you for tea, Miss James, but I thought we might take a ride around town so you can see what it looks like in daylight."

"Aunt Jenny, fetch Miss Savannah the yellow ruffled parasol," Annemarie said with amusement in her voice. "Sloan, you'll stay for dinner." It wasn't a question but a statement. "You'll get firsthand knowledge of what Savannah has learned in the short time we've had so far."

"Depends on what time you plan to serve dinner. I have a meeting with a man who is selling me flour and cured beef. I'm storing it at the docks until Captain Culpepper can take the *Polly Copinger* back to Cedar Key with another full load for Osceola. I want to see that he gets underway with no problems." This was said to Annemarie, but his eyes were on Savannah making sure she understood he was keeping his bargain to his brother and she could do no less. He could see that she understood by the way her eyes thanked him.

"It's no problem, Sloan. We'll plan on a late dinner. We don't have to worry about interruptions. If you had come around sooner, I would have told you that a certain friend of ours," her eyes lifted to indicate the room Beaunell usually occupied, "is traveling in Mobile. Did you take a room at the hotel."

"I've heard you speak of a hotel. What is it?" Savannah asked out of the blue.

"A place where you sleep and you pay for the privilege. It's a temporary room while visiting or a resting place between stops if a person is tired," Annemarie volunteered.

Savannah's green eyes turned murky. "But I'm your woman. Why don't you take me to the hotel? I belong to you," she told Sloan. "When we were on the island, you said we were one. One in this house, one in a hotel. I don't understand. Am I your woman or not?"

"Savannah," Annemarie interrupted, "go upstairs with Aunt Jenny and she'll give you a parasol to match your dress." In the habit of obeying her hostess, Savannah left the room behind the negress, stopping only to throw Sloan a questioning glance.

Annemarie struggled to hide a wicked grin. "Let me see you wiggle out of that one, oh mighty MacAllister. This young lady is not going to be fooled for one minute. And I think you're going to have a rough time of it if that certain friend of ours discovers what's going on around here. It must be wonderful to be so in demand by two beautiful women. I hope you have the good sense not to make a mistake you'll regret later."

"So do I, Annemarie. So do I," he told her fervently. "You say our friend is out of town?"

"Only until Mr. Bradshaw's heart or money give out. I'm betting on his money. My quarters are off limits to the girls, as you know. But Savannah has met Dolores and Lina and a few of the others. They think she's perfectly charming. Women will talk, Sloan. You know that. I don't anticipate any problem for the time being, but if that certain someone should return sooner than expected, we could be faced with one. Which," Annemarie said quietly, "will be turned over for you to handle."

Sloan enjoyed seeing the sights of Galveston, seeing them through Savannah's wide eyes as if it were the first time. From time to time she asked a shy question or two and then settled back. He watched in amusement when she would turn in the carriage to look after a strolling woman. He knew she was cataloging her entire wardrobe. Savannah was a woman. And, she appeared to be liking her new role. There were moments when she let her guard down, and her shining eyes would light at something that pleased her. Then, seconds later, a curtain would drop over the green eyes making her remember who she was and what she was doing. If she did make the decision in the end to go back to the Seminoles, she would be hard pressed to forget the white man's luxuries. The thought that she might really and truly want to return bothered him, tore at his insides and made him jittery. It would be difficult to explain to her why he couldn't join her and make a chikkee, as she called it. What did he feel for this beautiful young woman sitting beside him. Desire? Certainly. But he couldn't be falling in love with her. MacAllister frowned. Annemarie would have picked up on it immediately. He wasn't the marrying kind. He had things to do and places to go, and this time was merely an interlude devoted to helping the Seminoles. Savannah just happened to be caught in the middle. He couldn't help it if one went with the other. He'd be like Enwright Culpepper, a man unto himself. The thought made him grimace.

Savannah watched Sloan out of the corner of her eye. She had preened under his compliments and admiring glances. Being a lady had its rewards, she admitted. She had progressed much further than he had expected.

Her English was nearly faultless, and she had learned her manners well. It was only when she was upset that she groped between the two languages, making her English seem stilted.

Was this plan of MacAllister's going to work? If she did what was expected of her, it would. It wasn't at all difficult to sleep in a soft bed with sweet-smelling linens. The food was delicious and sitting at a table, eating with a fork, was second nature to her. Unconsciously, she allowed her fingers to play over the soft fabric of her dress. It was luxurious. She admitted she still didn't like being confined in a corset, and MacAllister wasn't going to like it either. It took a long time to dress in underwear, and it took almost as long to take it off. She wondered if he would let her sleep in his hotel. She liked sleeping with him. He was hard and warm. Comforting. Most of all she liked their lovemaking. She turned in the seat to face Sloan. "When will you make love with me again?" she asked bluntly.

Sloan was taken off guard. He had been busy watching some workmen lay a new foundation for still another church. "Soon," was all he could manage to say.

"When? How many nights?" she demanded.

Sloan shrugged.

"What does that mean?" she imitated his gesture.

"It means when I'm ready. Ladies don't ask questions like that."

"Why?" Savannah asked nonplussed. "I liked it."

"I know you did," Sloan blustered as he remembered the way she had responded to his touch and how she had given herself to him.

"Did I not give you pleasure with my body? I am your woman. Tell me when?"

Goddamn it. "Of course you gave me pleasure, but I can't give you a calendar date. It doesn't work like that. I have to feel . . . I have to be in the . . . what I mean is, it isn't time," he faltered lamely.

Savannah shook her head sagely. She had heard of such things with the older men in the tribe. "How many summers are you?" she asked anxiously.

Sloan didn't like the turn the conversation had taken. "Not summers, years. Thirty-two years." He hated the way the girl's eyes widened. He wasn't *that* old. Blast! How had he let this conversation develop to this point?

"The twilight of your life is running on swift moccasins to catch up with you, MacAllister."

By God, there was a touch of smugness to her voice. "Now, listen, Savannah, there's nothing wrong with me! While you live in Annemarie's house, we cannot . . . you can't . . . it isn't done. Now, that's all there is to it. I don't want to hear another word."

"You will not take me to the hotel when it is dark? You will not wrap your body about mine and make me love you? Not this night. Not in four or five nights. Maybe one month. Too much time!" she said emphatically.

"Maybe I can work out something. Right now, it's time to get you back to Annemarie's, and I have to keep an appointment. We'll talk about this some other time. Hold on," he said, slapping the rump of the horse lightly with his buggy whip. The obedient animal did a complete about turn and headed back toward the stable.

Savannah smiled at the tiny beading of perspiration that dotted MacAllister's forehead. She liked the slight twitch that played around his eye, but, most of all, she liked the sight of his muscular thigh in his tight britches. She was his woman. MacAllister better remember that or the twilight she was speaking of would creep up at an alarming rate of speed to end in the final sleep. She *was* his woman!

A week passed and then two and then three. When the last, lingering days of winter came to Galveston, Savannah developed an acute case of cabin fever. She became sharp-tongued and belligerent, refusing to obey Annemarie, saying she had had enough of fancy white ladies' ways. She wanted to race through a wild meadow filled with flowers.

Annemarie sympathized. She knew what was really troubling Savannah was Sloan's neglect. He had come by two weeks ago to explain he had business in Florida. He would accompany Captain Culpepper with the latest hold of supplies for Osceola and then sail around the tip of the southernmost territory up to Atlanta. Blankets, cookware and mules were more readily available there. She remembered how Savannah's lower lip had trembled with Sloan's news, and she had entreated him to take her with him. She was feeling alone and was homesick for her people. If only she could see them, talk to them. . . . No! Sloan had roared at the mention of her idea. She hadn't accomplished her lessons yet, and there was no time to bring her back to Galveston before sailing on to Atlanta.

Savannah lay atop her bed listening to the music coming from below. She had met Rufus, the black man who came to play in the evenings, one afternoon when he had come to tune the piano. He was a small man with a gold tooth in the front of his mouth. And when he played, he bounced on his stool in rhythm with his music. She could imagine him now, smiling broadly to show off his tooth, his dark fingers dancing across the keys.

The door to her room hadn't been locked since a few days after arriving at Annemarie's, and often she had crept to the top of the stairs and hid behind a large chest of drawers that Annemarie called an armoire to watch the people below. At first, she hadn't understood what she had witnessed until she confronted Odile, the black kitchen maid.

"Why, honey, them gentlemen come here for a little entertainment. Miz Annemarie has the most entertainin' girls in the Texas territory. Men like to see them in their underwear, watch them smile and be invited to their rooms."

"Why?" Savannah had persisted. Perhaps if she behaved like one of Annemarie's girls, MacAllister would think she was entertaining and would come to see her more often. Perhaps there were things about being a white woman Annemarie wasn't teaching her.

Odile had laughed as she took away Savannah's breakfast dishes. "Why? Because they like to sleep with the girls. 'Specially Miz Beaunell. Why she's the most popular girl here! Yes siree! Miz Beaunell flashes them eyes and takes 'em upstairs for her good lovin' and them gentlemen can't stay away! Yes siree!"

"Who is Miss Beaunell?" Savannah demanded.

Odile turned with a blank look. "That's right! You nevah met our star boarder. She's travelin' in Mobile right now with Mistah Bradshaw and havin' a time for herself! Yes siree! She's havin' a fine time for herself."

After that conversation Savannah was more curious than ever to see how the girls conducted themselves downstairs while Rufus played the piano. She had seen Dolores flash her huge dark eyes and smile enchantingly at a man who seemed to have difficulty keeping his eyes off her bosom which was carelessly concealed by a thin, gauzy dressing gown. Lina's bright red hair hung seductively over one pale and creamy shoulder as she sat on a man's lap tickling his ear with her tongue. He seemed to be enjoying it from the way he kept laughing and kissing her and fondly rubbing her little bottom. Suzann flashed her blue eyes at a man in a soldier's uniform, and he had carried her up the stairs at a dead run, heading for her room. Blossom was the girl who interested Savannah the most. She had even practiced some of Blossom's expressions in the mirror when she was alone and found she could imitate the girl surprisingly well. First, she would tuck her chin down to her chest and look up with a hot, sultry expression in her eyes. Lips parted in a wet, sensuous pout, she would run her tongue over them from time to time. Blossom liked to dress in black stockings with red garters and very little else. The silky petticoats and chemise she wore left very little of her anatomy to the imagination.

She had already learned that the girls made several trips to their rooms each night and often with a different man each time. There was only one man she wanted to take up to her room, and that was MacAllister. She was constantly reminded by her surroundings how much she missed the delicious feel of his arms around her and the touch of his mouth upon hers. All around her people were making love, and it was having a strange effect on her. There was an emptiness in the center of her that only MacAllister could fill. There was a hunger for him, a yearning that went deeper and sharper than any she had ever known.

Once, when she had been spying on the group below, she had been discovered. Lina was bringing a man up the stairs when he saw her hiding behind the armoire.

"And what have we here?" he had asked, coming toward her, reaching out a hand to touch her.

Savannah had shivered at the way he had looked at her, undressing her with his eyes. It was the way he had been looking at Lina downstairs, and it sent a tiny thrill through Savannah. This was the way she wanted MacAllister to look at her.

"Leave her alone," Lina had said, pulling him by the arm. "She's not one of us. She's Annemarie's special guest."

"What's your name?" the man asked, ignoring Lina. "I'll ask for you the next time I come in."

"Leave her be, I told you!" Lina warned. "Annemarie won't like it."

"Oh, I get it! She's a virgin and Annemarie's saving her for a good price! Well, I'll never have more in my pocket than I do right now. Where's your boss?"

Lina was angry as she looked from the man to

Savannah. "Get out of here," she told Savannah, her eyes snapping. "You know you're not supposed to be here. Now, git!"

Running back to her room and slamming the door shut behind her, Savannah gasped for breath. She hadn't liked the man, and she was worried that Lina would stay angry with her and tell Annemarie.

Lina hadn't said anything to Annemarie, but Savannah hadn't dared to hide at the top of the stairs again. The man had frightened her and she couldn't risk Annemarie's anger. She would have to content herself with listening to Rufus' music and dreaming of MacAllister.

Several nights later Savannah paced her room. Boredom was a curse, and she whispered every Seminole oath she knew, and each one was directed at the absent MacAllister. Ladies' fashion books held no interest for her. She was sick of practicing how to write her name on the slate Annemarie had given her. Her days were spent in abject misery as she practiced her table manners and her English. Lately, a seamstress, commissioned by Annemarie, was fitting her with a new wardrobe. She had to stand for hours on end being stuck with pins and hung with fabrics. She wanted to rail and scream. She wanted to kick and cry and tear the room apart. Where was MacAllister and why had he forgotten her?

She prepared for bed, thinking that at least sleep would bring relief from the empty, endless hours. She pulled the pins from her hair and brushed it to a gleaming softness the way she had been taught. Odile had filled the copper tub with hot water, and she had bathed, hoping the ritual would relax her. After donning a white silk wrapper, she sat on the edge of her bed and buffed her nails the way Aunt Jenny had instructed. Always her thoughts turned to MacAllister. When she heard a familiar voice, she thought her mind was playing tricks on her. Only by looking outside her window and seeing Redeemer tied to the hitching post did she realize it wasn't a dream. He was here! He was here!

Her first thought was to leap from the bed to her dressing table to do up her hair. Mentally sorting through her dresses, she wondered which one she should wear for him. She wanted to make a good impression. She didn't want him to forget her again!

Halfway between the bed and the dressing table she stopped, frozen by a sudden thought. The hairstyle and dresses and her manners hadn't stopped MacAllister from forgetting her before; why should now be any different? This time she would be certain he would never forget her. Never!

Sloan was ushered into Annemarie's as usual by Aunt Jenny who manned the door in the evenings. If nothing else, Aunt Jenny's bulk and handy iron skillet deterred the clientele from becoming too rambunctious. Stepping into the parlor, his eyes scanned the room for Annemarie. The girls were in their usual state of disarray and the men were panting after them. Aunt Jenny told him her boss was in her private quarters but would see him. Picking his way through half-naked women and men with salacious expressions in their eyes, Rufus' music bounced off his ears. God, he'd be glad to get Savannah out of this environment. Even if Annemarie's was a distinguished establishment, it was still a bawdy house. Before he knocked on the door to the private quarters, he laughed at himself. Since when had his sensibilities become so delicate? It wasn't too long ago since he was one of the customers with a hot look blazing in his eyes. Of one thing he could be grateful. Beaunell didn't seem to be in evidence. Unless of course she was upstairs in her room with someone. Beads of perspiration broke out on his upper lip. Talk about walking into a lion's den. Only these felines had soft breasts and willing hips. But they had claws, he reminded himself. And hungry mouths!

"Come in," Annemarie's voice answered his knock.

She was lying on her sofa, a cloth pressed over her brow.

"Headache, Anne?" he asked consolingly.

"Have I ever. And it's all of your making. When, Sloan? When are you going to take her out of here? And how dare you go off and leave me to answer for you. She doesn't believe for one minute that you're coming back. Now, at least, she can see I wasn't lying to her."

"Aren't you going to offer me a cognac?" he asked, avoiding her questions.

"Over there," Annemarie pointed. "You know where it is. As a matter of fact, pour one for me. I need it."

Handing her the glass, he settled himself opposite her. "I'll take her out of here as soon as Culpepper gets back from Florida."

"What?" she cried, sitting up and throwing the wet cloth at him. "How can your ship be off to Florida? When did you get back to Galveston?"

"Only hours ago. Listen to me, Anne. I would have stopped in Florida on the way back only I wanted to see how Savannah was doing. The crew jumped ship in Atlanta, and it wasn't easy finding another we could trust. We couldn't take that chance on them leaving us here, so Culpepper dropped me off and set sail again. I could have stayed away another week."

"You are too kind, Sloan, too kind. When do you expect him back? You've got to get that girl out of here. Beaunell will be getting back soon, and I don't want her tearing this place to pieces. Besides, although it's never been said between us, the less she knows about what you're doing, the better. She can be vicious when she wants to, and whether you want to face it or not, you are committing treason by helping Osceola."

"Damn it! Don't you think I know that?" He smacked one fist into the palm of the other. "Even with the help I've been giving, things aren't much better for the Seminoles. Jessup's raiding parties have been taking their toll. Do you think Savannah is ready to meet her uncle? She'd better be. We can't wait any longer."

"She's as ready as she'll ever be, Sloan. If she still wants to cooperate, that is. You know, that girl needs you, and you've made her feel abandoned. You don't know what I've been through with her. She's hardly better than the savage you dragged through my door the first time you brought her here. She doesn't obey; she won't listen. She's spending more and more time with the girls and learning things that you couldn't imagine."

"Spending time . . ." Sloan was speechless. "Why didn't you keep her locked in her room? I depended on you. . . . I thought you'd take care of her. . . ."

"Calm down, Sloan. Nothing's happened yet. I can't keep the girl chained in her room. She's got a raging case of cabin fever. I've even allowed her to go into town with Aunt Jenny or Odile. Unfortunately, several of my clients happened to see her and made inquiries. I hedged, but only tonight someone asked me who my new girl was. It's time to take her away from here, Sloan, or I may find myself with a new employee. You know, sweet, it's quite difficult to live in this environment and resist all these earthly temptations. I must admit, even I get sorely tempted."

Sloan's eyes widened. Annemarie had never spoken to him this way before, never revealed her womanly drives and passions.

"Oh, spare me, don't look so surprised. No, I haven't taken to sharing my bed for a profit, but I do have a certain friend who comes to see me whenever he's in town. It's been some time since he's been here, and I can understand what Savannah is going through. She still thinks you're the only man she wants to share her bed with; don't let her find out differently, Sloan. Now, get out of here and leave me alone with my headache and my cognac."

Sloan's thoughts spiraled. Annemarie had had

enough of Savannah James. What in hell had the girl been up to, and why was Annemarie trying to warn him that he'd regret it if he didn't take Savannah away soon? Did she know something he didn't?

Backtracking through the parlor, he anticipated picking his way through much the same scene as he had witnessed before seeing Annemarie. Only this time, something was different. Lina and Dolores were standing in the doorway with their hands on their hips, their lips curled into snarls. Rufus was playing the piano and hitting a few off notes because his attention was riveted to the far side of the room. Suzann was sitting on a sofa, a sulky expression pouting her mouth. Something was going on. Their clients were packed in a circle around the love seat, and it wasn't until he heard a soft, familiar laugh that he skidded to a halt. It wasn't! It couldn't be!

Elbowing his way between manly shoulders, he saw her, laughing and smiling at someone's inane joke. The sight of her nearly took his breath away. This wanton couldn't be Savannah!

She was perched on the love seat, one black-stockinged leg propped up on the arm of the chair. She wore nothing, save a white silk wrapper and lip rouge. Her hair fell in a heavy cascade around her shoulders, curling around one barely concealed breast. She held a drink in her hand and a slim black cheroot between her fingers. When she looked up and saw him, she offered him the most sexually inviting smile he had ever seen. Her green eyes looked up at him through the thick, dark fringe of her lashes and her mouth was parted and glistening from being constantly moistened by her tongue. Speechless, he stared down at her, muscling his way through the circle of her admirers until he stood before her.

Instead of lowering her eyes in shame and at least trying to appease him that way, she pouted her rouged lips and traced a line from her throat to a place between her breasts, the motion of her fingers opening the gap in her dressing gown still wider. The flash of black silk against her honeyed thighs distracted him and he reached down to cover them with the hem of her gown.

"What do you think you're doing?" he roared, a lion ready for the kill.

"What is it I'm doing?" she taunted, batting her lashes at him.

"I know what it's called! I've seen whores before!"

"A whore lays on her back with her legs open; Aunt Jenny told me," she volunteered. Her voice was not as confident as she wanted it to be. The rage in his eyes was deadly, making goose bumps break out on her arms and legs. Why was he looking at her this way? What had she done? The other men seemed to approve; why not Sloan? What was the matter with these crazy white people? Wasn't this the way a woman could keep a man from forgetting her?

Shock froze MacAllister's features into a mask of fury. She couldn't have just said what he'd thought she'd said! Where had she learned what a whore did? Something in Sloan cracked. His hands doubled into fists and he wanted to beat her, wipe that sultry, knowing look off her face. He should beat her, he told himself. Then he should have himself beaten. This was all his fault. He never should have neglected her the way he had.

"Get upstairs," he commanded through clenched teeth.

Seeing this order as a way to rid himself of her, Savannah rebelled. "No. I think I like it down here," she trailed her fingers along the flesh of her thigh, watching for his reaction. "I don't want to go upstairs. I want to drink and dance and listen to Rufus play the piano!"

Sloan's eyes widened until she could see the whites. Just like Redeemer's eyes before he threw a strange rider. Fury was unleashed. Before she had a chance to blink, he had her in his arms and slung over his shoulder. Raucous calls issued from the men who protested this interloper escaping with their latest entertainment. Hardly aware of her weight, Sloan ran up the stairs two at a time before he was forced to fight over her. If he had to fight, he'd end up killing someone.

Down the hall to her room, he carried her. She could hear his labored breathing, like the panting of a huge animal just before it devours its prey. He wasn't panting from exertion, she knew, it was anger, white and hot. Never had she seen such anger! Her fists beat at his back, her legs kicked, aiming for his tender parts; she screamed and hollered and swore in Seminole. Nothing would stop him. Instead, he slapped her elevated bottom and told her to shut up.

Reaching her room, Sloan kicked open her door and threw her on the bed. Never taking his eyes from her, he went back to the door and turned the key. The lamplight struck his face, and she saw the raw emotion contorting his features.

"If it's a whore you want to be, maybe you'd better get some firsthand knowledge of that timely profession." His eyes never left her, and they hardened to silver as his hands worked at his belt.

Savannah was thunderstruck. Why was he so angry? Why couldn't he like her the way the men downstairs seemed to like her? She only wanted him to desire her, to love her, not to forget her again. The other girls were never treated this way? Why did he hate her so much?

MacAllister crossed the room, the golden hairs on his body seemed to glow in the yellow light. His flat belly and lean hips tapered down to strong, muscular legs. His upper body was powerful and sinewy, deceivingly slim and lithe beneath his clothes. Savannah already knew the power in his arms. She had felt his strength and had been the object of his anger. And this time MacAllister was more angry than she knew a man could be. He stalked the bed with slow, deliberate steps. His broad chest heaved with each breath he took, his hands were doubled into fists.

Cringing, Savannah scuttled back across the covers. Her eyes flashed to the door and back again. There was no escape.

The slash of his mouth was set in a hard line. His flint-gray eyes never left hers. His hands were rough and cruel as he pulled her toward him; the bed sank beneath his weight. The white silk wrapper was torn open, exposing her vulnerable flesh to the onslaught of his hands and mouth. There was no tenderness, only rage. There was no pleasure, only anguish as he forced her legs open and held her arms above her head to save himself from her frantic, clawing fingers.

Savannah's heart stopped with fear. A silent cry for mercy swelled in her throat. *This* was not MacAllister. Not *her* MacAllister!

Suddenly, he fell on top of her, and she braced herself for his brutal entry. Instead, he wrapped his arms around her and buried his face in her neck. For long, long moments he held her, stilling her fears, murmuring indistinguishable words that only the heart could hear.

At last she spoke, softly, soothingly, following her womanly instincts, caressing the muscular expanse of his back, yielding her body to his. "I wanted only to belong to you, MacAllister. I thought if I was like the other girls you would like me better. I thought you wouldn't forget me again. The other men come back again and again. They never seem to forget Blossom and the others."

He heard the truth in her voice, the plea in her words. She was so innocent, so loving, and he had almost brutalized her because of his own guilt at having left her for so long. She had felt abandoned and he was responsible. "Savannah, you are my woman. I could never forget you. Never. You should hate me for what I almost did to you. I was an animal. I never want to touch you unless it's with tenderness."

She lifted his head from her shoulder and looked into his pain-filled eyes. There was a curious glistening there, and his voice was thick with emotion as though his heart was breaking. Cradling his head against her breast, she crooned to him, knowing how to heal the wounds as every woman since the beginning of time has known. "Touch me, MacAllister," she whispered. "Show me your tenderness. I am your woman."

His lips closed over hers in a gentle caress, softly, sweetly, as though he were drinking at a cool spring. Her arms closed around his neck, answering his embrace, her mouth tasting the bittersweet saltiness of their shared tears.

When Annemarie learned of Savannah's parody from Blossom the next morning, she hastily climbed the stairs to her pupil's room, expecting to find her bruised and beaten. Sloan had already left, she knew from Aunt Jenny, and she was steeling herself to comfort the poor child he had left behind.

Instead, upon entering the rose-colored room, she found Savannah dressed and sitting before her mirror, a dreamy, contented expression on her lovely face. She was humming one of the tunes Rufus liked to play on the piano.

"What happened?" she asked, breathless from her run up the stairs.

Savannah turned, questions in her eyes. "Happened? When?"

"Last night, you little fool. Haven't I told you to stay in your room in the evening? Do you realize Sloan might have killed you? And me too for that matter!" Annemarie's anger blazed. Her friendship with Sloan was too valuable to her to have this child destroy it.

"MacAllister is still your friend, Annemarie. He's not angry with you or with me." The dreamy, romantic expression returned, and she began to hum that silly tune again.

"Well, what happened? You look like the cat that ate the canary! Wasn't he angry when he found you downstairs behaving like one of the other girls?"

"Angry? Oh, yes, but I forgave him. It was wonderful!"

"You're not making any sense at all!" Annemarie scolded. "Why did you go downstairs?"

"Because I didn't want to be forgotten again. Blossom says men have a short memory and you have to give them something to think about."

"You certainly gave him something to think about from the account I heard," Annemarie said, her voice softening somewhat. "I hope you made him understand it was all your own idea and that I had nothing to do with it."

"Oh, yes. Sometimes my ideas are good, aren't they? *This* time MacAllister won't forget me. He told me I'm leaving with him day after tomorrow."

"That's a relief," Annemarie said, moving across the room to the window. Lord, she still hadn't become used to keeping these early hours since Savannah had been left in her charge. She never realized how strongly the sun shone through these lace curtains. Perhaps she should have new ones made that would filter out the morning light. It's a wonder that Dolores, whose room also faced the front of the house, hadn't complained seeing as how the girl never left her room before three in the afternoon.

"Day after tomorrow? We'll have to contact the dressmaker and rush her on the last of the gowns she's making for you. Where's Sloan now? Aunt Jenny said she heard him leave at the crack of dawn."

"No, it wasn't that early," Savannah told her off-handedly, her cheeks flushing slightly as she remembered their passionate lovemaking before he had left. "He told me he has business and not to worry, that he'd be back day after tomorrow."

Annemarie was barely listening. She was watching a carriage drive up to the top of the hill and park outside the door. A groan erupted in her throat as she dropped the curtain and peered through the lace. Beaunell Gentry was stepping lightly from the hired vehicle and was instructing the driver to carry her trunks to the house.

"Savannah, listen to me," Annemarie said hurriedly. "I want you to stay in your room. I don't want you to come out for any reason, do you understand? Not for any reason!" She heard the panic in her own voice. Calming, she said slowly and distinctly, "I don't want Sloan to be angry with you or with me. Later, when I send for you, you'll come downstairs and stay with me in my private quarters. Aunt Jenny will move your things. Now, remember, stay in your room and don't come out! I want you to lock your door after I leave and be quiet as a mouse. Don't open it or answer to anyone except Aunt Jenny or myself."

Savannah nodded her agreement, her green eyes wide with puzzlement over Annemarie's erratic behavior.

Downstairs, Beaunell was telling the driver where to put her baggage when she saw her employer at the top of the stairs. "Annemarie, what are you doing up so early? I never remember seeing you before noon. I had the most wonderful time in Mobile. I can't thank you enough for arranging everything with Lionel."

"Lionel, is it? When you left I recall you dreading the idea of spending a few weeks with a man old enough to be your grandfather," Annemarie said sarcastically.

Beaunell gave an elegant shrug. "It's Lionel now. How could I continue to call him Mr. Bradshaw after all the beautiful things he bought me? I swear, I haven't brought back a single rag I took with me. Everything is new. Everything! And very expensive. Where's Aunt Jenny? I need her to unpack for me. Do you want to come to my room and see what I bought?"

Annemarie rubbed her temples. She was fast developing another headache. Why couldn't Beaunell have stayed away for another two days? "Not now, Beau. I've got this headache coming on. I really must lay down."

"Annemarie, has anyone come looking for me while I was gone?" Beau asked brushing imaginary lint from the shoulders of her new burgundy cape, hoping the new sparkling ring she wore would be noticed. "I mean, has Sloan come here to see me?"

"No, he hasn't," Annemarie told her honestly, watching Beau's expression change from smugness to consternation.

"Has he left Galveston?" Consternation turned to disappointment.

"Yes, I think he has. Now you must excuse me, Beau. I really must get something for this headache." She couldn't get back to her rooms quickly enough. She knew she was being a coward. She should just tell Beau how things stood between Sloan and Savannah and let the devil take them. Beau really wasn't such a bad sort, and she'd been in Annemarie's employ for quite some time. Although Beau was given to put on airs and was a trifle trying at times, she still owed something to the girl. But she didn't want to be around when all hell broke loose.

Beau still had designs on Sloan and intended to marry him one day. It was hard enough to lose at love, and when a woman was approaching thirty, like Beau, it could be devastating. And Beau wasn't one to take things lying down. If she ever sniffed out what Sloan was up to, she'd see to it that he was hanged for treason. If she couldn't have him, she'd be damned certain no one else ever would either. Annemarie laughed. Had she just told herself that Beau wasn't such a bad sort? Lord, this headache was really clouding her thinking!

Shortly after the noon hour Savannah was installed in Annemarie's quarters. Aunt Jenny had assured her that Dolores, Lina and Blossom had agreed not to mention Savannah's presence to Beau as a special favor to Annemarie. Suzann was another matter entirely. She would love to break the news to her arch rival that Sloan had found himself a young, golden-haired girl who was everything Beau wasn't. At Annemarie's fearful look, Aunt Jenny soothed. "Don't you worry, Miz Annemarie. I told her if'n she breathed one single word about *anything* to Beaunell I was gonna scorch every stitch of her clothes with my flat iron. She don' want that pretty behind of hers stickin' out through her drawers. Don't you worry, that Suzann will keep her mouth shut good!"

Annemarie laughed in spite of herself at the picture Aunt Jenny made as she shook her stubby finger, her many chins quivering and her mammoth hips jouncing. "Sometimes, Aunt Jenny, I think *you're* the boss around here. Not me!"

Savannah spent the remainder of the day with Odile in the kitchen, an area of the house where Beaunell never set foot. If she wondered why she was being secluded from everyone else, she never mentioned it. She contented herself with learning from Odile the workings of the magical wood stove and memorizing the recipe for bread pudding. She took her dinner with Annemarie and, shortly afterward, a delivery was made to the kitchen door for her. Sloan had sent her a package from Bradshaw's store containing a gold tipped quill pen and lovely inlaid inkpot. Enclosed was a note saying simply, "Never forget. S."

Annemarie had to read the note for her. "I must learn to read," Savannah said, admiring the iridescent feather on the quill. "I have practiced signing my name and I know my letters. Now I must learn to read."

Seeing an opportunity to occupy her pupil until Sloan could come and take her away, Annemarie seized on the chance. "There's no time like the present to begin. You already know your letters and the way they sound. Now, all you have to do is learn to put them together. I think I have a book here . . ." Annemarie paused, looking at Savannah who was holding Sloan's note, her eyes closed. That the girl was in love there was no doubt. Something akin to pity struck a chord within her. Sloan hadn't expressed any thoughts for Savannah's future. It seemed he simply felt that once the girl's mission was completed she would be eager to return to her people in Florida. Men are fools, Annemarie thought sadly, and Sloan MacAllister, you're one of the biggest fools I know.

The next morning before lunch another package was delivered from Bradshaw's. This time a bottle of scent directly from Paris. Savannah was elated and begged Annemarie to read his note. "Tomorrow," it said. "Never forget. S." For the rest of the day Savannah struggled with her reading lessons, determined to learn in the quickest time possible.

That evening when Annemarie had completed dressing for the evening ahead of her, she was surprised to find Aunt Jenny leading Sloan into her apartment. Savannah was in the bedroom practicing her letters from a chart Annemarie had made for her.

"Sloan, I hadn't expected you until tomorrow. You don't know how glad I am to see you. Beaunell is back and she's getting frisky. If I had a dollar for every time she's knocked on my door, I could retire and live a life of leisure. She knows something is going on. What amazes me is she hasn't found out. And Savannah is starting to ask questions about why she hasn't met Beaunell and why she's being confined to my apartment. Where have you been?"

"I have a problem, Anne. Culpepper returned from another trip to Florida. Right now, with the provisions I've sent food isn't a problem for the Seminoles. But they desperately need ammunition and guns. According to Culpepper, Jessup is making inroads and there was a skirmish that lasted for six days. A band of Creeks were determined to take my ship. Culpepper and the crew had quite a fight on their hands, and the only way they were able to save the cargo was to pull out for sea and anchor at another spot. Finally, the Creeks lost interest and the *Polly* was able to go back to Cedar Key. Not only do I have to get artillery, but I also have to find another anchorage to rendezvous with Osceola's men. I hate to ask you this, Annemarie, but do you know someone who deals with munitions? Wasn't there a man I met here sometime ago? Was he from Cuba?"

Annemarie flushed. The sight stunned Sloan and he realized Annemarie herself was intimate with the man. He had simply thought he was a client of one of the girls. "I'm sorry, Annemarie, I didn't mean to embarrass you . . ."

"You seem to be doing that quite a lot lately. Forget it, Sloan, the day had to come when you had to realize I wasn't the epitome of virtue. It's just that I don't care to share my personal life. I'll write a letter. You take it to him and he'll help you. For a price, of course. A bonus wouldn't be out of order if you follow my thought. He'd be sticking his neck out."

"Where is he?"

"New Orleans. He keeps an office there. For the right price you might be able to convince him to arrange delivery of the cargo. It's risky, Sloan. If the government finds out what you're doing that handsome neck of yours might swing. Sending food and provisions are one thing, artillery is quite another."

"You let me worry about my neck. Write the letter; we'll set sail on the morning tide. We'll have to go back to Florida first to arrange a delivery point. No sense going on to see your man without knowing where he should deliver the goods. Savannah will enjoy seeing her people again, even if it's only for a few days. Do you think she's ready to go through with her part in this?"

"As ready as she'll ever be. If you can get her to keep her shoes on," Annemarie sighed. "Every chance she gets, off come the shoes."

"I'll see what I can do," Sloan promised. "Where is she?"

"In the bedroom with Aunt Jenny."

"Write the letter for me. I'll get Savannah. Are her things packed. Does she have everything she'll need?"

"For the most part. A shopping trip or two in New Orleans will take care of the rest. I've included a list in her baggage. . . ."

Savannah suddenly appeared in the doorway.

"MacAllister! It's you!" Savannah's face lit like a thousand lanterns.

Sloan opened his arms to her and she ran to him. "Savannah, are you ready to leave in the morning? Annemarie is pleased with your progress and says you're ready to be presented to society. How would you like to put on that blouse and skirt you're so fond of and come with me to Florida for a few days before we sail to New Orleans?"

Stepping backward, Savannah smoothed her hands over the pink striped silk gown she wore and frowned. Her frown deepened as she remembered the coarse fabric of her indigo blouse and the short, colorfully banded skirt. How could she have become accustomed to satins and silks in so short a time? After an instant's dismay, she realized that she was going to be with MacAllister again. Such happiness filled her that she would have worn sack cloth and ashes and not minded one bit.

In her joy, Savannah rushed toward Sloan, tripping over her shoes and falling headlong into his arms. Savannah was enthusiastically planting kisses on his mouth and cheeks when the parlor door opened. When Sloan glanced up and looked over Savannah's shoulder, he was staring directly into Beaunell's stormy, dark eyes.

"I knew it! I knew something was going on! Who is this person?" she demanded arrogantly. "I've known all along that something fishy was going on. It was a conspiracy, wasn't it?" Not bothering to wait for a reply, she rushed on, her anger hissing and sputtering like water droplets on hot coals. "Take advantage of me, will you? Use me when the mood strikes you! Take me when you need me? I'll be damned if I'll let you use and abuse me. Do you hear me, Sloan? Who is this woman?"

Sloan stepped back, unsure of his next move. "You're acting like a child, Beaunell. Behave yourself. I've been busy."

"I can see that," Beaunell said icily. "Liar! Cheat! You found someone younger, firmer, is that it? Well, I don't want to hear about it. All I want from you is payment for the hours I spent waiting for you. Hours that could have been put to more productive use. Who is she? Damn you, answer me!"

"My name is Savannah. I am MacAllister's woman," Savannah said sweetly.

"That's what you think. I've been his woman. I guess he didn't tell you about me, did he? Well, he didn't tell me about you either. You aren't getting any bargain, let me tell you."

"*I* belong to MacAllister," Savannah said more firmly.

"That's a line he hands all the women," Beaunell snarled. "Don't believe a word of what he tells you. Liar!" she shrieked in Sloan's direction.

"I *am* his woman," Savannah repeated. "You lie!" Suddenly a thought occurred to her. "Where do you sleep?"

Beaunell stopped to think before she answered. "Upstairs. Why?"

"MacAllister sleeps in the *hotel*. It is simple. You lie."

"What?" Beaunell exploded. "All men sleep in hotels. He comes here when he feels like taking a bath and climbing in my bed. He snores; what do you think of that? *And* he has three moles, here, here and here," Beaunell said pointing to her derriere.

Aunt Jenny rolled her eyes back in her head. This

was one place she didn't want to be. Wasn't Miss Annemarie going to stop this? Was she going to let the handsome Sloan stew in his own juice?

Savannah looked from Sloan to Beaunell. She was trying to make up her mind about something, some plan of action. Whatever it was going to be, Sloan knew he wasn't going to like it!"

"He promised to *marry* me," Beaunell said imperiously.

"Now just a damn minute, Beaunell. I did no such thing. You were the only one who talked of marriage. I never agreed, never consented, to anything."

Beaunell was so angry, saliva sprayed from her mouth as she tried for a fitting come-back. "I knew you were a liar, but I didn't think you would make a fool out of me in public."

"I'm not doing any such thing. You're doing it yourself."

"*I* will take care of this witch," Savannah said advancing on Beaunell.

Before Sloan could stop her, Savannah had her hands in Beaunell's hair and was pulling her forward. She slapped, kicked and pushed the screaming Beaunell without mercy. "You will apologize to MacAllister and to me for what you said," Savannah said gasping for breath.

"I should have known. You work as a team, is that it?" Beaunell said bringing her elbow up and hitting Savannah square in the neck. A string of bitter Seminole curses erupted from Savannah's throat as she grabbed both of Beaunell's ears and banged her head against the wall.

Sloan tried to pull the battling women apart only to find himself the object of several well-aimed kicks. "Annemarie! Annemarie, stop them!"

"Why?"

"Someone is going to get killed! You have to stop Beaunell. Send her upstairs, fire her. I don't care what you do, just do it?"

"Very well, but after all the fuss and bother you've caused me, why should I quibble over a little sitting room brawl? Beaunell, you will stop this unladylike behavior this instant." Annemarie clapped her hands imperiously.

If Beaunell heard, she gave no sign. She was busy pelting away at Savannah who was herself busy trying to rip the feathered wrapper from Beaunell's creamy white shoulders. In that instant, Annemarie pulled her free and literally threw her in Sloan's direction. "Go to your room, Beaunell, until I'm ready to talk to you about your disgraceful behavior. You know I deplore fighting of any kind. And as for you, Savannah, what has gotten into you? Ladies do not fight, scream or carry on like this. For shame!" To Sloan she added, "This is the very last time I pull your chestnuts out of the fire. You got yourself into this mess, and you're going to have to get yourself out. It's good that you're taking Savannah with you. Perhaps I can salvage my relationship with Beaunell. If I lose her because of this, the price is going to be heavy, Sloan. I'm a business woman you know."

Sloan didn't like Savannah's silence. For some reason he knew that up till now he hadn't truly known the meaning of trouble. He could have taken her shrilling screams, her fighting tirades, but her silence unnerved him, made him jittery. It had to be because of Beaunell. He had thought he was going to die on the spot when she had asked the enterprising Beaunell where she slept. That was it, he was sure of it. A good Indian always covered his trail one way or the other. He knew in his gut he better do the same thing and do it before Savannah had a chance to think too long and too hard.

# Chapter Seven

Lights rimmed the outline of Galveston harbor. Savannah sat beside Sloan in the borrowed carriage, her baggage stowed in the back. In his pocket was Annemarie's letter of introduction to the arms manufacturer from Cuba, Señor Rico Mendoza. She had cautioned Sloan to see to it that Savannah purchased a more extensive wardrobe in New Orleans. Even the prospect of frilly gowns and silken lingerie did not seem to lighten the dark shadows in the girl's eyes.

Captain Enwright Culpepper had come to Sloan with a problem. "It's the tiller bracings, sir. We must have damaged them when we were looking for a deepwater anchorage on that last trip to the Florida territory. I suspected it, but it didn't seem to be giving us trouble or I would have seen to it in Galveston. Seems to me we'll have to change course for New Orleans."

Sloan had been disappointed, for Savannah was eagerly looking forward to seeing Osceola and his family again. "We can't take a chance on being marooned, Culpepper. Change course for New Orleans. There's a gentleman there I must see."

Sloan was more than a little surprised when Savannah boarded the *Polly Copinger* and went straight to her cabin. There were no comments about sharing Sloan's cabin, no comments about making love. The fine hairs on the back of his neck stood at attention. Perhaps a little manly talk with Enwright Culpepper would be in order. He needed crystal clear thinking from here on out.

All night he lay in his narrow bunk, remembering, imagining he could taste the times he had shared with Savannah. Twice he swung his legs over the side of the bed only to groan and lie back down. As far as Savannah was concerned, Beaunell was bitter medicine, and while she had been forced to swallow it at the time, that didn't mean she had to like it. Perhaps there was a way to explain, a way to salve Savannah's womanly pride. He hadn't scorned her, hadn't cast her aside in favor of Beaunell. Beaunell was the past, and he had no intention of making her a part of the present or his nebulous future whatever it might be.

Sleep was out of the question. A walk around deck might settle his nerves. A couple of swallows of some good brandy should take the edge off his twanging nerves. This was the perfect place; it could be the perfect mood for making love to a willing Savannah. He grunted as he climbed the steps to the deck.

Warm, sultry breezes washed about him as millions of stars glittered, chasing one another across the boundless sky. Bright moonlight bathed the *Polly Copinger* in a silvery glow, the shiny brass and highly polished deck sparkling as they never did in bright, golden sunshine. A night for romance. A night for lovers to lie entwined in each other's arms. Was Savannah sleeping or was she lying in her narrow bunk as tormented as he was? Savannah was being stubborn. A woman's trait that he had run up against on more than one occasion. A trait he detested because it made him feel weak and ineffectual.

His gut churned and he wiped at perspiration on his brow that had nothing to do with the warm breezes wafting about him. Goddamn it, he wanted Savannah, wanted to feel her in his arms, wanted to know that she wanted him as much as he wanted her. The hell with it, a glib tongue had always been one of his major attributes. If he was careful, he might still be able to convince Savannah of . . . what?

If he kept prowling about like this, he would never

know, never be able to force himself to go back to his
narrow, hard bunk alone.

Once his mind was made up, his long legs raced down
the deck to the stairway and down the companionway.
Cautiously, he opened the door and quietly stepped
inside. Soft moonlight circled the room from the porthole. Deep, even breathing greeted his own labored,
uneven breaths. He forced himself to a calmness he
didn't feel. She couldn't be! But she was, sound asleep,
her breathing deep and regular. How could she sleep at
a time like this? Didn't she feel what he was feeling?
Didn't she want him as much as he wanted her?

He stood for a long time, undecided. Should he wake
her or not? Should he bend down and kiss her gently on
the mouth hoping to wake her? A frown worked its way
across his forehead. Indians were supposed to sleep
with one eye open and one ear ready for the slightest
sound. And he had thought she was as Indian as
Osceola. Disgust coursed through him. Annemarie, in
the space of a month, had wiped away one of the most
valuable skills an Indian has.

In the soft moonlight he noticed that Savannah still
slept in his shirt. The thought pleased him when he
remembered how Savannah had fought tooth and nail
to keep the shirt in place of one of Annemarie's soft
plisse gowns trimmed with ruffles and bows.

Savannah heard Sloan's footfalls the moment he hit
the last step on the ladder. She waited, her tears long
since dried. She forced her body into the relaxed pose
of sleep, making her breaths low and deep. She stirred
slightly, trying to afford herself a better view through
her heavily fringed lashes of the man who stood inside
her cabin. She should hate him, but her body ached for
him to hold her in his arms. The way he must have held
the woman adorned in feathers and ribbons. No, she
didn't hate MacAllister, but she did hate the beautiful
woman she had attacked with such vengeance. Was she
his woman or wasn't she? Osceola had two women.
MacAllister might need two women also. Her heart

pounded at the thought of sharing a chikkee with MacAllister's other woman. If he wouldn't take her to his hotel, she didn't want him. Didn't need him. Chikkees were from her other life. She knew now that she belonged more to the white man's world than the Seminole. Whatever she was supposed to share with MacAllister she would share alone, not with the woman in feathers and ribbons who wore cherry-red paint on her cheeks and mouth. To Savannah the bright glossy paint on Beaunell's cheeks and mouth meant the woman was prepared to go to war to have MacAllister for herself. Annemarie lied to her when she told her that ladies do not fight. Even MacAllister lied. The thought was like an arrow in her heart.

Savannah felt rather than saw Sloan approach the bunk, felt the slight movement of his body when he bent down on his knees. She stirred, the sooty, dark lashes opening slightly. The moment his lean, strong hands reached for her, she had both his wrists in a viselike grip. "Do not ever sneak up on an Indian, MacAllister, for you could be dead in seconds. I could kill you now without a weapon. Why have you invaded my cabin? What is it you want from me in the middle of the night?"

"To talk with you," Sloan said honestly. He realized the words he spoke so defensively were true. He did want to talk to her, to make things right between them. And he wanted the pressure on his wrists released. She had him in the worst of all positions. He was on his knees, and her grip on his arms was that of a warrior's. All she had to do was bring her knee up to his chin and snap his neck. He swallowed hard as he waited for her to make her decision. A white woman's decision.

"So you can tell me more lies? I have no wish to hear lies from your mouth, or from Annemarie's."

"I didn't lie to you. As far as I know, Annemarie didn't lie to you. You haven't been among us long enough to understand certain things, certain ways people resort to when they feel that . . . what I mean is, sometimes when a person feels cheated for no reason he retaliates in ways that are hard to understand."

"I understand better than you know, MacAllister. I believed you. I trusted you. All because you are Osceola's brother, and he said to trust him was to trust you. I believed those words, MacAllister. I was your woman. You left me in that house where your other woman sleeps. That is not trust. You refused to let me sleep in your hotel. I have no wish to hear your weasel words. You sound like the white man who makes treaties with Osceola's people. They make promises, and as soon as the words are on paper, they say it is not so. *All* white men lie!" The last was said so emphatically Sloan clenched his teeth.

"I am not like *all* white men. All I'm saying is you don't understand. I do not lie and I do not cheat. My brother would listen to me, why can't you do the same?"

Forgetting the hold she had on Sloan's wrists for a second, Savannah raised her hand and pounded her chest. "Because you have wounded me here," she cried dramatically.

That was all Sloan needed. He rose off his knees and threw Savannah back against the bunk, his lean, hard body on top of hers, intent only on saving himself from her scathing nails once she recovered herself. Her disappointment in him made him angry, implausibly so, he realized, but angry. He had done nothing to cause her this pain which she seemed to think he had deliberately inflicted. Manly pride, ego, stupidity, would not allow the comforting words to come to his lips.

"Let me go, MacAllister!" She seethed, heaving his weight, attempting to slide out from beneath him. "Go back to Galveston and your painted lady! Go back and take what you want from her! You won't find me so stupidly willing to share your bed again!" Glistening tears welled in her eyes. There was just enough light spilling through the porthole to see them sparkling on her lashes.

Sloan looked at her incredulously. This couldn't be the same woman who had seduced him for the first time on the Cedar Key island. He must have dreamed that the day he'd taken her for a buggy ride she had openly compromised herself, practically begging him to take her back to the hotel with him? Not possible, he thought irrationally, not this hellcat with curved claws and hair-raising screams!

A sly smile formed on his lips, and his eyes took on the gleam of a fox with a rabbit within its clutches. Savannah's blood ran cold at the sight of him advancing on her, reaching out for her. Like the rabbit, she stood frozen, unable to move, to breathe. She saw his outstretched hand come close, so close. She wanted to run, to escape, but still his hand came, touching her. His fingers were warm against her cheek, his palm burning where it came to rest near her lips. His touch was gentle, soothing, quenching some of the hurt and disappointment that was stabbing her heart.

"I touch you only with tenderness," he told her, his tone soft and intimate.

In the light spilling through the porthole he saw her and had never known her to be more beautiful. Her hair gleamed with silver that belonged to the stars alone; her skin smooth and glowing, softer and sleeker than the silk shirt she wore. At his touch on her cheek she leaned her face into his hand, eyes closing, lips parting. Wordlessly, he smoothed her golden curls, feeling the satiny strands between his fingers, thinking that her hair was like the moon itself, shining and sleek.

When she turned to him, it was to offer her lips to him, clinging softly with arms wrapped tightly around his middle, pressing herself against him. Her appetite for their lovemaking was as intense as his own, and the knowledge of this heightened his desire for her. She was the most exciting woman he had ever known: soft and lovely one moment, scrapping and feisty the next, but always, always beautiful.

Savannah's emotions found an answering response in Sloan as his mouth took hers hungrily, desperate to satisfy his need for her. Their hands reached for one another, softly touching, rediscovering each sweet caress.

Sloan brought her back to her bunk, stopping only to remove the shirt that guarded her most tender, sensitive spots from his greedy lips. He kissed her neck, tasting the sweetly perfumed skin of her ear lobe, the gently curving softness of the arch of her throat, that hollow between her breasts which constantly beckoned to him. The intricacies of her, the delightful differences invisible to the naked eye that made her different from all other women. His lips lingered, taking and giving pleasure.

Savannah's hands found the smoothness of his back beneath his shirt, luxuriating in his warmth and solid physique. He shrugged out of the confines of his shirt, freeing himself for her touch. Her mouth tenderly nipped at the place where muscular shoulder yielded to his neck, and she was aware of the quiver of delight that rippled through him.

MacAllister moved away from her, and when they touched again, he was naked. His hands slid down her body to worship her, adoring her, lifting her into a realm of passion and desire known only to lovers.

His arms encircled her, drawing her tightly against him, reveling in the length of her body pressed against his.

Her hands were woven in his hair, pulling it back from his forehead as she kissed him, opening her lips, bidding him enter. Straining against him, her body rose and fell rhythmically, desperately seeking to fill this sudden need that throbbed within her.

Seizing his shoulders, she pressed him backward against the bed. His breathing came in short, rapid rasps, and when she leaned over him, pressing the fullness of her breasts against the fine furring of hairs on his chest, she heard him emit a low, deep groan.

Beneath her fingers his skin glistened with a sheen of perspiration and the long, hard length of him heightened her lusty appetite and hungers. Learning her lessons well, lessons taught by him, she tasted every detail of his body, luxuriating in the rippling, muscular hardness of him.

Her legs tangled with his as she held herself above him, melting herself to him, rubbing against him, bringing him to the height of his desires. The contact between their bodies was as smooth as the silken fabrics she so admired. She crushed his face into the firm plentitude of her breasts, giving . . . wanting to give . . . only to give. In giving she was receiving and being filled with a sense of power that she could evoke these emotions in this strong, masculine man. Bringing him pleasure, pleasuring herself.

He was alive beneath her touch, and she felt his expectancy throb between them. His eyes were upon her, delving the darkness, perceiving her with more than his eyes. She was a goddess, golden and fair, bringing the warmth of the sun to his cold, hungry needs.

She mounted him and the flatness of her belly was hard against his, drawing the aches and the hunger from his loins. Her breasts were offered to his hands and her mouth was as greedy as his own, and he knew there was more between them than finding a momentary respite from the urgency of passion.

The moonlight smiled on the *Polly Copinger* as she braced the rolling tide toward the city of New Orleans. Below decks, Sloan lay beside Savannah, body curled around hers, hands lovingly stroking her arm, brushing her hair back from her face. The ship rolled gently, rocking them in their bunk.

Her skin was warm and smooth, smelling faintly of

himself. Placing his lips close to her ear, he held her gently, whispering low and soft, "Savannah, you *are* MacAllister's woman!"

Murmuring in her sleep, she fit herself closer into the curve of his body, never hearing the words that would have made her heart fly the path of the bumble bee whose nectar she was named for.

The *Polly Copinger* sailed into New Orleans' harbor, sails crisply catching the breezes. Her hull was high on the water, seeming to skip ahead of the rollers bringing her into land. Sloan and Savannah stood on the deck near the bow, the warm wind ruffling their hair and caressing their cheeks. Behind them, Captain Culpepper shouted orders to the crew to reef sail and lower the main jib. Anticipation and excitement danced through Savannah's veins. This was her first pleasure trip.

Sloan watched Savannah's face as she peered off into the distance, watching the busy harbor and the activity beyond. Her green eyes flashed with a sense of adventure; her skin glowed from the freshets of wind blowing across their faces. He was enjoying her excitement. She had already told him how many gowns she wanted to buy and petticoats and those naughty silk stockings Annemarie had told her every lady wears. When he mentioned suitable negligees and shoes, she frowned. She much preferred sleeping in his own silk shirt, she told him unabashed, and as for shoes, she could hardly bear to keep them on her feet!

He had roared with laughter, pleased that she liked his shirt so well and promptly rewarded her with another, his best, with his monogram embroidered over the left pocket.

Her only request before Sloan left the *Polly* to accomplish business ashore was a tub of hot water for her bath. Her lids lowered in sultry invitation, and it was with great reluctance that Sloan had to remind himself that business came before pleasure.

Hailing a hansom cab, he entertained himself all the

way to Rue du Belle Fleur with images of Savannah
lowering her naked sun-kissed body into the tub and
luxuriating in its fragrant water. He couldn't wait to get
back to her, all soft and sweet and so willing.

It was still early in the day when Sloan opened the
door to Rico Mendoza's offices. The lightly scented
letter of introduction from Annemarie rested next to
his heart. He didn't anticipate any trouble, a denial of
his wants for the Indian. Money was the only thing he
needed, and in his right breast pocket was enough
money to outfit the entire United States Government
with guns. The thought that he was being un-American
didn't enter his mind. Osceola's face, along with those
of hungry women and children, was all he needed to
remind him he was doing the right thing. If the United
States Government couldn't honor its commitments to
the Seminole, then he was justified in what he was
doing. He would never lose sleep over this transaction.

A scholarly looking individual accepted the letter
Sloan held out. "One moment, Señor, I will return.
Please, make yourself comfortable. There is a recent
newspaper on the table if you care to read it."

Sloan settled himself comfortably and had just
turned the page when Señor Rico Mendoza himself
came out to greet him. "Señor MacAllister," he said
holding out his hand, "it is a pleasure to make your
acquaintance. Come into my offices where we can talk
privately."

Sloan followed the tall, lean man and knew why
Annemarie felt as she did. He was a soft spoken,
handsome man with silvery hair that was almost white.
He guessed his age to be around fifty. Clear, unwrin-
kled skin the color of tanned leather complimented the
frosty hair. He poured brandy from a decanter, that
was as elegant as himself, into fine crystal glasses. A
heavy gold ring with a diamond the size of a pig's eye
winked at Sloan as strong, sun-darkened hands closed
over the fragile stem of the brandy snifter. The two
men leaned back comfortably in deep leather chairs.

They discussed the weather in New Orleans as opposed to that of Galveston. Annemarie's name did not come up in the course of the conversation. It was Mendoza who changed the conversation to the matter at hand.

Mendoza's voice was low, cultured and pleasant to Sloan's ear. He liked the man immediately. "As you are aware, we are talking about a very large transaction. For me it is no problem. I am a businessman and have no loyalties to either the American or the Seminole. I want to be certain you understand the matter. Miss Duval has explained your position in her letter to me."

"Can you help me?" Sloan asked carefully, not sure where Mendoza was leading the conversation. The packet of bills in his breast pocket felt very comfortable.

"But of course. Was there any doubt in your mind when you came here?"

Sloan shook his head. Money always spoke more eloquently than any words man could devise. "I'm not a soldier. I know that you shoot a rifle and it can kill. I can shoot and am quite accurate. That's the extent of my knowledge, Señor Mendoza."

"Then let me give you a brief lesson. The American infantryman relies on the shoulder arm. Generally speaking it is a flintlock muzzle loading musket of a standard .69 caliber. What that means is it is fired by a flint and steel mechanism, is loaded downward through the muzzle, and has no rifling and bore. Believe me when I tell you, it is not the latest in weapons. The army does have some rifles but the ratio is one to twenty-two muskets."

Sloan frowned. He didn't want a lesson in American weaponry. All he wanted was guns for Osceola. Still, he had to be polite and hear the man out. After all, according to Annemarie, he was an expert.

"Thanks to the expert craftsmanship of my people that is not and has not been the case with the Seminole. They use a small bore Spanish weapon manufactured in

Cuba. Unfortunately for the Seminole they use the weapons carelessly. After the first shot they seem to flounder. All the guns in the world won't help them if they don't use the weapons wisely. In short, Señor MacAllister, your Seminole needs to be trained in the use of the rifle. Many tales have filtered back to me. It's said that they take pains with the first shot, but after that, more often than not, shoot carelessly. The cavalry seems to be of the opinion that a Seminole shot is not dangerous beyond twenty feet. As much as this may cause you dismay, I must tell you that the Seminole shoot, not necessarily aim, whoop and then shoot again. They must be taught and reeducated."

"I didn't know this, Señor Mendoza," Sloan said briskly.

"I thought as much. I can sell you rifles from a small stockpile but no more than three hundred at this point in time. By early summer I can give you another two thousand. My plan would be to ship you the Hall rifle. It can strike hard at four hundred yards compared to the one hundred yards of the musket. Because of the breechloading, it can be fired four times as fast. I have to caution you on one factor. It's said that because of the mulelike kick oftentimes the stock breaks. We can fix that. We can work out the kinks for the right price. It's a superior weapon to what the Seminole is now using. It's your decision, Señor MacAllister."

"I'll take them providing you work out the kinks, as you say. What is the price?"

"Twenty-five thousand dollars now. Twenty-five thousand *American* dollars. Twenty-five thousand upon delivery. If I run into problems, the delivery price will rise. Acceptable?"

"Acceptable," Sloan said drawing the packet of money from his inside pocket. He counted out twenty-five crisp one-thousand-dollar bills and laid them in a neat pile in front of Mendoza. "Let us discuss the point of delivery. If possible, I would prefer it to be six or seven miles south of Cedar Key on the west coast. I'll have my captain, Enwright Culpepper, send you word of the exact location. He tells me it's a deepwater harbor."

"It's as good a place as any. General Jessup's troops have the shoreline well guarded. Gun running is not something I'm fond of doing. Let me think on the matter. If I need to get in touch with you, I'll get word to Miss Duval. Is that agreeable?" Sloan nodded. "The matter of the three hundred rifles for now is no problem. I can have them taken to wherever your ship is berthed. Or did you come by horseback?"

"Ship."

"In a few hours they will arrive at the harbor in barrels that resemble water barrels. My men know how to handle such things. It would be wise if your men do not split the containers. Once they leave my hands I deny all complicity. *Comprende?*"

Again Sloan nodded. He stood. The meeting was over. Mendoza made no move to pick up the money laying in front of him as though not wanting to dirty his hands. They shook hands; Mendoza's was firm and hard and confident. A slight smile played around the smooth mouth of the Spaniard. "We will meet again one day, I'm sure of it."

Sloan's eyes blazed into the coal black eyes of the man standing next to him. "I doubt it. Unless of course something goes wrong. Like the kinks not being worked out of your Hall rifle. I trust we understand one another."

"We understand each other perfectly, Señor MacAllister," Mendoza said coolly.

Redeemer galloped down the cobbled streets, intent on getting Sloan back to the *Polly Copinger* in record time. The warm, near spring breezes buffeted him as he gave the galloping horse his head. He couldn't wait to share his news with Savannah. She would be elated at the munitions deal he had made for Osceola. He felt so good, so pleased with himself for Osceola's sake, he decided to take Savannah on a shopping spree in downtown New Orleans and let her pick out anything that pleased her. A few bangles and beads, a new hat, a new parasol would do the young girl a world of good. He felt as though he were twenty years of age and about to court a young girl. It was a good feeling.

Culpepper shouted from the ship's railing. Savannah stood next to him dressed in a persimmon-colored dress. Her back was to the brilliant sunshine throwing her in shadow. It looked as though she was smiling as broadly as Culpepper. Was it just because they were happy to see him? The thought pleased him. He had been alone too long without anyone to care about what he did or where he went. Every man needed someone to care about him.

Quickly, he shared with them the results of the meeting with Mendoza. To Culpepper, he added, "Be on watch for the supply wagon. I'm taking Savannah shopping, and if we have time, we might stop for tea at a sidewalk cafe I know. Can we fetch anything for you, Captain Culpepper?"

"Not a thing, Laddie. You two go off and shop for Miss Savannah. I'll be keeping a sharp eye peeled for the wagon. Go along with you."

"It's a beautiful day, Savannah. Would you mind walking? The shopping district isn't far and we can hire a buggy for the ride back."

"I would like that, MacAllister. What will we buy?" she asked, her sea-green eyes sparkling with delight. It would be her first shopping trip. Annemarie had been afraid to take her to the shops in Galveston and had ordered dressmakers to the house. It would be exciting with Sloan voicing his opinion. She would purchase only things that he liked. Things that made his gray eyes soft and happy. She felt confident about using money. Annemarie had been most careful to make sure she understood how much each piece was worth and how to tell them apart. She even liked the feel of the money in her hand. While she had barely enough to buy a few ribbons, she still felt rich. If she was truly MacAllister's woman, he would give her more.

Savannah walked beside Sloan, feeling happier than she had felt in her entire life. There were times these past weeks when she had almost forgotten about Osceola and his people, and the life she had left behind. This was all so new and exciting.

When they reached the main shopping area, Sloan stopped and groped in his pockets. He handed her a sheaf of bills and assorted coins. He didn't bother to count it, but just handed it to her. "Buy what you want. Get whatever pleases you. See that cafe?" he said pointing down the street, "I'll wait for you there. Gentlemen do not shop with ladies."

"How will I know if I'm buying the right thing and that you will like it?" Savannah asked apprehensively.

"You must buy what pleases you. If you like it, then I'll like it. Take your time. I'll have a drink or two and smoke a cigar."

Savannah looked doubtful but accepted Sloan's orders. In the first shop she bought a reticule with a twisted braided drawstring and a peach-colored shawl with long silken fringe. When she held it to her cheek, she smiled. How good it would feel on bare shoulders. In the second shop she bought six pairs of gloves. Simply, she told herself, because she didn't like to wash them. One could never have too many gloves, Annemarie had cautioned. Shell combs, then a mirror with a shell back, were added to her spoils. A frothy, lacy petticoat that made her blush was next. MacAllister would like it, she was sure of it. The camisole with even more lace kept the flush on her cheek till she left the store. Her last stop along the avenue was the milliner's.

Sloan settled himself comfortably knowing he was going to have a long wait. He lit a fragrant cigar, propped his feet on another chair and defied the proprietor with his eyes to tell him to remove them. It was mid-afternoon with little business and the rotund man saw Sloan as a profitable hour or so. After all, he had ordered a whole bottle and he looked like a man who would tip well. He felt in a generous mood knowing the tip would be good. He handed a wrinkled week old newspaper to Sloan with a toothy grin. Sloan accepted it, but soon tired of reading old news. His attention wandered as he watched shoppers walk up and down the streets. A figure that looked familiar suddenly caught his eye. It was Brevet Major General Thomas Sidney Jessup. Dressed in full uniform in mid-afternoon. He seemed to be out for a stroll. There was nothing hurried about his saunter as he stopped to peer first into one window and then another.

Suddenly, he bolted upright in the cane chair. Savannah was in one of the shops Jessup was peering into. He knew that Jessup had spotted Savannah when he saw the general's back stiffen and the way his hand went nervously to his brow. He was even more convinced when he watched the general bend closer to the window and press against it. Of all the rotten damn luck. What to do? Wait for Savannah to come to the cafe or approach Jessup and try to sidetrack him? Blast it, she wasn't ready yet! Not for the likes of Jessup. She still didn't have the confidence needed to carry off the scheme.

Sloan's gut churned when he saw the general square his shoulders and enter the shop. It was too late now to do anything. He poured another drink with hands that were less than steady and waited.

Savannah was trying on a tantalizing creation with tiny scarlet ribbons. She turned this way and that admiring herself in the milliner's mirrors. She was aware of the tinkling bell over the door and assumed it was another customer.

A warning bell went off in Savannah's head when she noticed the man's intense stare. Her green eyes darkened as she took in his military uniform. This could be her first test. She deliberately averted her gaze from the man and looked into the mirror again. "I'll take this

one and the one with the blue ribbons," she said
quietly.

"Will there be anything else."

"No, thank you. Perhaps another time." Her breaths
were quickening as she sensed the man approaching
her. She widened her eyes at his obvious bad manners
in addressing a woman without formal introduction.
Annemarie had told her never to speak to a stranger!

"You must forgive me, but you remind me so much
of . . . of someone I used to know. Please, don't be
frightened." Savannah backed off a step and then two,
her hands going to her throat at the man's audacity. She
said nothing, looking beyond him, calculating escape.
He reached into his pocket and withdrew a card. He
extended it to Savannah who reached for it, knowing it
wouldn't help her since she couldn't read. She recognized the letters that Annemarie had begun to teach
her, but she couldn't remember them now. Reading
and writing were her next lessons.

Savannah let her eyes drop to the card. "Should this
mean something to me?" she questioned coolly.

"I was hoping it might," the general said in a
trembling voice. There couldn't be another woman in
the world who was an exact duplicate of his sister
Caroline. It had to be Savannah, her daughter and his
niece. "Might I ask you your name and what you're
doing in New Orleans?"

Savannah wanted desperately to make Sloan proud
of her. She had to remain calm and cool and be very
careful of how she answered this man. A pity she didn't
have a fan to hide behind. Annemarie said a woman
always flirted behind a fan. Well, she didn't have one,
so she would have to make do. "Yes, you might ask my
name," she said coyly. "Savannah James. I'm traveling
with friends. Why do you ask?"

Jessup's face paled, then reddened and then paled
again. "I knew it!" he exclaimed. "I knew it! My dear,
you are going to find this hard to believe, but I'm your
uncle, your mother's brother. I've searched for you for

years and years and finally gave up. And now this," he cried in agitation. "It's almost more than I can bear. Child, I'm your uncle, doesn't that mean anything to you?"

Savannah backed away another step. "I'm afraid not, sir. You see, my parents died when I was quite young. I barely remember them, and I have no memory of an uncle. I'm sorry. Perhaps you have me confused with someone else. If you'll excuse me, I must be leaving."

"No. No, you can't leave. You must let me explain how you became separated from your family, from me! It was because of those savages, the Indians. Please, I beg of you, meet me tomorrow afternoon at the cafe down the street and let me convince you. Bring your friends with you if that will make you feel better. I can prove that I'm your uncle. I have credentials. I have all of your parents' papers. I even have a picture of you when you were five years old."

Savannah allowed doubt to creep into her face and voice. MacAllister was going to be so excited at her news. "I'll speak to my friends about the matter. It's possible that I may join you, but I cannot make a promise. I barely know you. I can't promise you anything."

Savannah was astounded at how steady her hands were when she paid for her hats. The moment the door closed behind General Jessup her knees buckled. She grasped the edge of the ornate desk where the salesgirl was busily writing a receipt for her. "I think," Savannah said in a clear, high voice, "I will leave these parcels and pick them up later. Will that be all right?"

"Of course. It's almost closing time and I don't anticipate many more customers. I'll wait for you; it's no problem. I live behind my shop." Savannah thanked her and left. She stood outside a moment, staring up and down both sides of the street to see if the general was in sight. The moment she was certain the coast was clear she picked up her persimmon skirts and raced to the cafe. Her cheeks were flushed, and her eyes sparkled with her news when she sat down on the cane chair opposite Sloan.

"You will not guess who just approached me! You cannot guess what he said to me!" Her eyes widened till they were like round pools of green water. Tomorrow I am to meet him and bring my friends to this very cafe. MacAllister, can you hear me? Why aren't you saying something? Look, he gave me his card. I pretended to read it, and he didn't know I was fooling him. I cannot read, MacAllister." The thought seemed to bother her more than it should. A month ago learning letters would have seemed the most foolish thing in the world. Now it seemed like the most important.

Sloan took the card. "Brevet Major General Thomas S. Jessup."

"That's because you can read. I wanted you to guess." She was clearly disappointed. Sloan hated to spoil her fun but he had to. "I saw him while he was staring at you through the window. There was nothing I could do at the time but wait. Did you tell him your name?"

"But of course!" His face drained of all color. "I did not make any promises. I thought that best in case you might want to think this matter over. Did I do well, MacAllister?"

"Very well." Sloan smiled. He ordered her a cup of tea and forced his mind to think. This changed everything. He barely noticed Savannah as she poured a healthy jolt of the whiskey into her steaming tea. Now he had a problem. He continued to smile as Savannah sipped at her "tea."

An hour later Sloan stood up. "All right, now this is what we're going to do. We have to register you in the most respectable hotel here in New Orleans. Tomorrow you'll meet Jessup as planned. I want you to go to the meeting alone. Culpepper and myself will be here just in case anything goes wrong. You'll tell him that you have some business to attend to and you want to think about his offer to move into his house with him. That's the first thing he's going to suggest to you. You must not appear eager. I want you to demur, to stall him as long as possible."

"MacAllister, I cannot read or write. What if . . ."

"You'll just have to cover yourself the way you did with the general's business card. I'm sure he's going to arrive at the meeting with a picture of your mother to prove what he's told you this afternoon. He won't want to take no for an answer. You will be charming but firm in your refusal to go with him until you're ready."

"MacAllister, what of your plans to sail to Florida to deliver the guns to Osceola and train his warriors?"

"I can't leave you now. I won't leave you. I must stay in case anything goes wrong. We've come too far to have things go wrong now. At this moment Osceola is holding his own. He has foodstuffs to see him through till summer. Culpepper told me that he showed Mico the navigation charts and explained to him as best he could where to meet him the next time he lays the *Polly* at anchor."

"What of the new guns? Who'll train my chief's men?" Savannah was agitated. He knew she was frightened of the prospective move to her uncle's house. Frightened that she would do something wrong and that harm would come to Osceola through her mistakes. The Seminoles were again first and foremost in her mind and this he understood and admired. She loved her people and wanted to help them, just as he did. But he knew that one day, when all this was over, settled either to the Seminoles' advantage or the government's, he would resume his life in the world he knew. The world of the whites. And Savannah? Which world would she choose for herself? He had promised her she could return to the Seminoles. He hated the thought and refused to dwell on it.

"Culpepper can give them a brief instruction, for now," he told her, answering her question. "For now, this is more important. I didn't mean for Jessup to discover you this quickly, but what's done is done.

We'll arrange to meet here at this cafe from time to time so that you can keep me informed of what's happening. There's nothing for you to worry about now. Clear Osceola from your mind and concentrate on your uncle. Tomorrow you'll move into your hotel room. We'll spend this last night aboard the *Polly Copinger.*"

Savannah's eyes shimmered. It was right that her last night with him be spent aboard the ship where she had found such happiness.

It was early evening when Sloan guided Savannah up the narrow gangplank. Culpepper met them at the rail. "Ye be late for dinner, Laddie. Cook made a mess he calls rabbit stew. Fresh killed rabbit that he bought off a hunter early noon time. 'Tis nothing like the ambrosia ye made fer me, Miss Savannah," he added hastily. After the first and only day of Savannah's cooking, Captain Culpepper had never asked her to enter the galley again. Next to women, Maeve Carpenter in particular, the most important thing in Culpepper's life was good wholesome food and a bottle of whiskey.

Shortly before noon the following day Sloan and Savannah registered at New Orleans' finest hotel, the new Grand America. Sloan took a room down the hall from Savannah just to reassure her. The last thing Sloan had done before depositing Savannah's luggage in the spacious hotel lobby was to open a sizable bank account in her name at the Merchants' Bank of New Orleans, where she had oohed and aahed at the amount of money Sloan was entrusting to her.

Savannah sat on the bed in the hotel room and looked about. So this was what a hotel looked like. She wasn't impressed. There was too much floor space carpeted in a green and blue design that made her grimace. The flouncy coverlet on the bed felt soft and downy but appeared dirty to her eye. She bent down to smell it. Her nose wrinkled. A few hours in the bright sun with a strong wind would work wonders. The room smelled stale as if a thousand different bodies had shared it, and, now that she understood the meaning of the word hotel, she knew this to be true.

Savannah unpacked her belongings and hung them in the cedar closet. She liked the sweet, pungent smell of cedar that wafted about her from the depths of the closet. One long finger reached out to trace the knot hole in the rough wood. It was different, and she liked it. But did she like this hotel or not? With the door closed she had to remain inside and she liked more space. She needed more space. But it did have its advantages. She was finally in a hotel with MacAllister. She was truly his woman now that he had taken her to this hotel. The thought warmed her all over.

How weary she felt with this new life. How tangled her emotions were becoming. Sometimes it was difficult to bring Osceola's face and those of her people into sharp focus. It was easier to picture Sloan, Annemarie and Captain Culpepper. Tiredly, she fell back against the down pillows. MacAllister had told her that her uncle would bring a picture of her mother for her to see. How was she going to feel? Would long forgotten memories rise to the surface to torment her? Would she be able to accept long conversations about her parents and hear of shared memories between her uncle and mother?

She had been only six summers. No, six *years* old when she lost them both. The years with the Seminole had been good to her. She had been free to remember or not remember if she chose. Sometimes late at night, when the camp was asleep, she would remember her bed and the doll that had been a Christmas present. Christmas. How strange that she should remember that holiday and the word, Christmas. An evergreen with a candle. A festive dinner with . . . linen napkins and then a present. The china doll with green eyes and golden curls. As if a long locked door opened, memories came flooding back helter skelter. There was a spotted pony. A tall man with laughing blue eyes

picking her up and swinging her onto the animal's back.
And she remembered fear, when the tall man was out
of her range of vision. His arms had been strong and
protective. And the beautiful woman who looked just
as she did, with her hands crossed under her throat in
fear that her little girl would topple from the frisky
pony's back. So long ago.

Tears for all that was lost burned her eyes. The
thwack and thump of the loom while her mother sat
weaving cloth. It had been red. A cape, a red cape with
a blue lining. Rain pelting the windows. Apple muffins
baking in the oven. Did she wear the red cape or was it
her mother's cape? She wished she knew. She knew the
material would have been coarse, unlike the fine mate-
rials she now had. If only she had the cape to touch.
Just once. Just to be able to hold it to her cheek and
remember still more.

She was tired. Tired of memories that hurt her. Tired
of memories she could do nothing about. She didn't
want to cry. Only small children cried. Had she cried
when she was a child? Of course. When one of the arms
fell off the china doll, she cried. And she had whooped
and hollered with pain when she fell from the pony.
Memories, from the forgotten recesses of her mind,
came flooding back, haunting her, filling her with
stabbing pain. Through the long night, she remembered, smiling, laughing, crying, finally sleeping. Never
knowing that Sloan had crept into her room in the dark
of night to brush away the tears that lingered on her
cheeks.

An hour ahead of schedule Sloan and Enwright
Culpepper stationed themselves at a far table in the
outdoor cafe. Sloan held a newspaper in front of him.
Culpepper devoted himself to the bottle in front of him,
his eyes raking the nearby streets. At the first sign of a
military uniform he would kick Sloan under the table.
Savannah had been told to take a corner table at the
entrance and to be there fifteen minutes ahead of

schedule so Jessup would have to join her, not the other way around.

"What's going on, Culpepper?" Sloan asked two hours later.

"Not much. The general seems to be doing all the talking. Miss Savannah just handed back a miniature. I suppose it was the likeness of her mother ye told me about. She seems to be in control. She's sitting like a real lady, and she hasn't spit or snarled once in her uncle's direction. Miss Savannah's acting like a real lady."

"Why shouldn't she act like a real lady? She is one." He didn't realize how curt and terse his voice was when he answered the old sea salt. Culpepper smirked to himself.

"She's shaking her head 'no' over something. She's doing it again. Now she looks stern. Now she's reaching out her hand and touching the general on the arm. She's still shaking her head. Put down yer paper, Laddie, and look at the angel smile on the lass's face. That's a powerful beautiful woman ye been squiring around, Laddie. Tell me," he said, a slight slur to his words, "what will ye be doing when the general matches her up with some handsome cavalry officer. Women swoon over a uniform. Ye might be finding yourself adrift on the sea without a paddle. Ye can't count on a woman to remain faithful with all that handsome flesh culling about her. This man Jessup looks a might dandyish to me."

Sloan frowned behind the newspaper. Damn it, why hadn't he thought of the uniforms? What Culpepper said was true. For some strange reason women found themselves drawn to tailored, brass-buttoned uniforms and spit polished boots. A lump settled in his stomach. How would Savannah react to a bevy of handsome young men paying her court? He thought of all the young officers who hung about General Jessup, and his fists clenched till the knuckles showed white.

Culpepper found himself amused once more. It

would do the lad good to squirm a little. There were
other fish in the sea, as Maeve had pointed out to him
on more than one occasion.

Sloan rustled his newspaper in agitation. "I hope he's
buying Savannah's story that she was taken in by a
merchant and his family and that they took her with
them to Baton Rouge. I rehearsed it with her often
enough."

"Aye, Laddie. As I well know. The whole story is
plausible. Savannah was taken in by John Palmer and
his wife, Sophie, a dry goods merchant who only
recently settled in Baton Rouge. Don't worry, Maeve
Carpenter was a personal friend of theirs so Miss
Savannah is on safe ground if Jessup gets curious and
decides to check on her story. The Palmers both went
on to their reward a year or so ago, and Maeve would
back up anything I told her. But rest your mind,
Laddie. From the way Jessup is looking at Miss Savannah he's only too ready to believe she's lived on the
moon if that's what she tells him."

"I pray you're right, Captain. I'd hate to have put
Savannah through all this for nothing." Sloan was grim
and tight lipped. "I've learned not to count on anything, and where Jessup's concerned, that goes double.
The only thing I can be certain of is that Savannah will
follow my instructions and not appear too eager to
move in with Jessup. I told her she had to make him
convince her over a period of time. At least a week." A
sudden black thought crossed his mind. "Culpepper, do
you think he'll want to take her in? That's what we're
counting on. That when Jessup discovers Savannah is
all alone in the world he'll want to take her under his
protection."

"Easy, Laddie. Easy. Things will be just the way you
want them. Even that black-hearted Jessup couldn't
resist Miss Savannah. No doubt about it. He'll want to
take her in, all right. I've seen his kind before. All
arrogance and pride, thinking himself noble. After all,

Laddie, it would be the correct thing to do, and if he has aspirations to the Presidency, it wouldn't hurt to have someone as pretty as Miss Savannah to act as his official hostess."

"Looks like the meeting is breaking up, Laddie. The general is standing up, and Miss Savannah is batting her eyes at him and shaking her head again. The man is frowning but accepting it in good grace. He wants to touch her so bad he can almost taste it, Laddie. The look in his eyes is one I used to see in me old mum's eyes when I was but a tad. He's looking for family ties, and he's not about to let the lass get away from him. He's writing something on a card, and now he's handing it to her. Most likely his address. He's walking down the street now. All right, ye can lay down the paper now. Miss Savannah is leaving. Ye best help me polish off this bottle and be on yer way. I'll be taking the *Polly Copinger* out with the tide. By my best calculations I'll be returning in a week's time. Any messages for that surly Mico?"

"What?"

"Any messages for that Indian, Mico?" Culpepper repeated sourly. He hated to see a man so caught up in a woman's charms that he had to be spoken to twice. But he forgave Sloan because he was nothing more than a whippersnapper with too much money and in love with a woman who was turning him into a jealous man. Culpepper wondered if Sloan knew he was in love. Not likely. Men were always the last to know.

Savannah's spirits were in the doldrums. Nothing, it seemed, could move her or bring a smile to her face. For dinner Sloan took her to one of the finest New Orleans restaurants, ordering steamed crayfish, thinking the familiar food that she had eaten while living among the Seminoles would lift her spirits. She ate them only because he had practically ordered her to do so. A light white fish baked in a wine sauce, oysters, fresh vegetables, even the flaming crepe suzettes were viewed without an appetite. Knowing her to be a ravenous eater, Sloan's brows drew down into a scowl.

"It's delicious, MacAllister," she said softly, forcing a smile to her lips.

He knew she neither saw nor tasted anything. Her thoughts were preoccupied with General Jessup and the fact that she would see him the next day with the news that she would be glad to accept his offer to move into his household in order to get to know and love her mother's brother. It was a lie, a sham, and he had come to know Savannah disliked it intensely.

"You're thinking about Jessup," he told her, bringing the subject to the fore. "What's worrying you, Savannah?" he asked gently. "Whatever it is, tell me." A sudden thought occurred to him. "Are you troubled because you've finally met someone from your own family? Someone who is really connected to you and who knew and loved your mother? He did, you know, really love your mother. In spite of everything else the man is, his feelings for his family are noble."

Savannah's lips drew into a sneer, and he thought that if she hadn't been so well schooled by Annemarie, she would have spit.

"MacAllister wants to know if I can love that man like I should love my uncle. The answer is no. No, no, no! How could I? Not the way he hates the Indians. The very people who gave me my life! And for what he's doing to the Seminole . . . MacAllister, I have no doubt here," she said thumping her small fist against her heart, "that even if I told the general it was Osceola who saved me and made me a member of his tribe, it would not make any bit of difference. The man is half crazed when he speaks of those with red skin. I know what you said about him is true. He wants to win the war against the Seminole because he hates them, and because he can gain glory for himself. Do you know he even told me that if I were to come and live with him, some day we would go to the capital, Washington, where he would seek a political career. MacAllister, the man believes with luck he can become President like Andrew Jackson! I hate Jackson and I hate General Jessup!"

"Uncle Thomas, Savannah, you must remember. Uncle Thomas!"

At his correction, Savannah narrowed her eyes to mere slits, "And I can hate you too, MacAllister!" Tears sprang to her eyes, and drizzled down her cheeks.

Sloan painfully understood what the girl was suffering. There were confused loyalties churning inside of her. Whom to love? To whom to be faithful? Much as she claimed she hated Jessup, and she believed herself to be telling the truth, there was still a familial tie. Blood relations. Living among the Seminole she had learned how important family and blood ties were. How could she help but feel something toward the general? The trouble was she hated herself for it.

Walking back to the hotel from the restaurant, Savannah was still too quiet for Sloan's liking. Instead of enjoying the sights; the city streets lit with deeply glowing lanterns, the ornate carriages carrying handsome couples dressed in their finery to and from various parties and socials, she silently walked beside him, her hand on his arm quivering from time to time with the trembling she felt within. He led her back to the Grand America as though she were in a trance. He hated to leave her at the door and told her he would return shortly.

Savannah entered her room and lit the oil lamp on the bedside table. Try as she might, she couldn't seem to pull herself out of this depression. Soon, within days, she told herself, she would be moving into the enemy's camp. She was to spy for Osceola, gather information no matter how insignificant and pass it on to MacAllister.

Carelessly tossing her shawl and bonnet onto the chair, her gown and undergarments quickly followed. Usually so careful of the clothing Annemarie had given her, she left them in a pile, not caring if she ever wore them again, hoping she wouldn't. What she wanted was her indigo-blue blouse and colorful banded skirt. She wanted her moccasins and beads. She wanted to be back in Florida before MacAllister had come to help Osceola. It was safe then, even though the Seminole nation was at war, it had been safe. She knew who she was then and what life could promise her. Now, everything was upside down and inside out. She was Savannah James; she was Chala, Wild Honey. She had thought she might become Mico's woman and had ended being MacAllister's. Nothing was true any more, nothing was safe. Drawing Sloan's silk shirt over her nakedness, she pulled the covers back from the pillows and crawled in. It wasn't so long ago when she had slept on a layer of blankets in Osceola's chikkee. Now the blankets were comforters made of down and the sheets, something she had never known before, were smooth and white and ironed. Where had her life gone? What had she come to? As she laid her head against the plump, feather pillow, she faced the question she had been avoiding for longer than she wanted to remember. After being here in the world that was hers by birthright, could she ever go back to the Seminoles? Would she want to?

Leaving Savannah inside her door and slipping the key into his pocket, Sloan went downstairs to the lobby to check if Culpepper had left any messages for him. Finding nothing that would inhibit his quick return to Savannah, he strode into the dining room, requesting a bottle of fine wine and two glasses. She was going to sleep tonight and erase those dark circles from under her eyes if he had to get her drunk to do it!

"I would be happy to have someone bring the wine to your room, sir," the waiter told him obligingly.

"No, that's quite all right," Sloan told him, slipping a bill into the man's hand, "this is something I'd rather do myself." Realization dawned on him that when it came to Savannah, he'd rather do everything himself.

He didn't want anyone else to do for her, only him. A sad smile turned the corners of his mouth down as he thought of her pain and hoped he could lessen it just a little, to help her get through the night.

Opening her door, he was glad to see she was prepared for bed. Good, the wine would help. Putting the tray on a table in front of the windows, he inserted the corkscrew and uncapped the bottle. He filled her glass generously, and sat on the edge of the bed, encouraging her to drink.

At first she wrinkled her nose but then drank deeply, savoring the light, fruity wine and holding her glass out for more. "Sweetheart, you're not supposed to chug it down like a stevedore. Wine is to be sipped slowly; it is to be enjoyed."

"I am enjoying it, MacAllister," she told him solemnly, her face drawn into a pretty scowl. "More please."

By the third glass her eyes were growing heavy. Suddenly, her lower lip began to quiver and tears filled her eyes. Taking her glass from her, Sloan thought his heart would break in sympathy. She was a lost little girl who wasn't certain where she belonged or what lay ahead. He sat on the bed beside her, propping himself against the pillows and took her in his arms. She nestled against him, wrapping her arms around his midsection, holding, clinging, trying to chase away her fears.

"Tell me, Savannah," he whispered, his voice soft, gentle.

"I'm so afraid, I don't know where I belong," she answered.

He wanted to tell her that she belonged with him—always. But the words wouldn't come to his lips. She already had so much to contend with, so much to know and deal with, he couldn't add to her burden and confuse her still further. Now was not the time to ask her not to go back to the Seminole, to Osceola, but to stay with him forever and always be his woman—his wife.

Cradling her as though she were a little child, he offered her solace and protection from those night fears that steal sleep and seem to grow into monsters in the dark. Long, long into the night he held her, loving her.

Savannah whimpered, her face pressed in the hollow between his neck and shoulder. She felt the caring in his touch, in the way his lips rested against her hair. She knew he understood and no words were needed. He held her and asked for nothing in return, giving all he had to give. She was his woman, only his; she found comfort in the thought, not daring to ask herself the question: Was he her man?

# Chapter Eight

By the end of the week Sloan's nerves were stretched wire tight. Savannah alternated between fits of crying and outright sullenness. The day her personal belongings were brought down to the hotel lobby, Sloan found himself almost as sullen, almost as taciturn. Six trunks, twelve hat boxes, four portmanteaus, eight shoe cases, along with assorted cartons and boxes, littered the lobby of the new Grand America Hotel. The desk clerk with his beak nose and narrow eyes surveyed the assortment with a jaundiced look. His face changed quickly when Brevet Major General Jessup himself entered the lobby to see to the supervision of his niece's baggage. One had to keep on the right side of the military. You just never knew when the Indians would take it into their heads to invade New Orleans.

Savannah descended the wide staircase to the lobby in time to see the last shoe case being carried out to the carriage by one of Jessup's men. If only she could turn back the clock and calendar. She knew she had to go through with the charade. She was even accepting it, but that didn't mean she had to like it. She didn't like her uncle, Thomas Jessup, with his possessive eyes and his white hands. She had wondered on more than one occasion why she had no memory of her uncle, especially when he told her he had dandled her on his knee when he visited the farm where she lived with her parents. He spoke kindly, lovingly, possessively, of his sister, Caroline, but he rarely mentioned her father. Perhaps MacAllister was right, and Jessup resented

Alfred James for taking his sister from him. It made
sense to her. No matter what, she did not like him and
dreaded the move into his house. What would she do
with her time? How would she fill her hours? Reading
and doing needlepoint her uncle had said, like all ladies
amuse themselves. Behind her smile Savannah felt
disgust. She would have to pretend to stare at printed
words that held no meaning for her. Needlework was
something ladies learned from childhood, a skill she
could never accomplish, she knew, remembering
Annemarie's handiwork. Perhaps she could take long
walks. Jessup had said he owned a very old dog who
needed exercise. She wondered what had happened to
the mangy dog from the village. Had he starved to
death or had someone remembered to slip him scraps
from time to time? It was difficult now to visualize the
slat-ribbed dog with the soulful eyes.

Thomas Jessup held out his arm for his lovely niece, a
truly delighted smile widening his mouth. It was true!
At last he had found her, and she was so much like
Caroline it was almost like having his sister with him
again. She was lovely today in her green voile gown
with lace edgings and her pert little hat that perched so
coquettishly over her brow. Caroline's hair and skin
had been a trifle lighter, more golden than honey, but
her features were perfectly echoed in her daughter's
face. Savannah James. His own precious Caroline's
child. A quick frown appeared between his thick, white
brows. Perhaps, at a later date of course, Savannah
might agree to have her last name changed to Jessup. It
would please him most heartily. Alfred James had been
a milk livered sop in his opinion, and what Caroline had
ever seen in him had always been a wonder. Why
should Savannah want to carry the name of a man she
barely remembered? Jessup, he told himself, would
someday be an honored name in Washington, and she
would do her uncle honor and show her gratitude by
adopting it for her own.

Savannah tried to show some enthusiasm for her

uncle's home, but the brace of four soldiers standing outside the door and the aide-de-camp sitting at a desk just inside the foyer frightened her. Jessup, seeing the bleak look in her eyes, questioned, "What's wrong, dear? Are you disappointed in my home?"

"I hadn't expected to be under guard, Uncle . . ."

Jessup laughed, the first time she had ever heard him do so. "No, you mustn't think you're under guard. A man of my position requires assistance," he told her pompously. "Actually, the guard outside my door dignifies my rank, and the aide-de-camp merely sits there to carry out my orders and receive messages and such. In essence, they are there to protect us from outside invasion. There's a great many people who would like to approach me on matters of their own concern. Feel better now, Savannah?"

"Yes, Uncle," she told him; her eyes narrowed, thinking how difficult it would be to escape the general's notice when there were no less than six pairs of eyes ready to report her actions to him.

The interior of Jessup's house had a pleasing austerity, but the lack of a woman's touch was noticeable, so different from Annemarie's, where frills and ornaments abounded. The only concession to decoration was the carefully displayed military memorabilia consisting of medals and mounted maps and framed documents.

"Come over here, Savannah. I want to show you something." The general opened a door and led her inside a room obviously of masculine decor with its leather chairs and various tables. She immediately noticed a round table covered with a soft, green cloth around which six chairs were drawn. This must be the place where MacAllister played cards with the general, Savannah thought, feeling somehow a little closer to MacAllister and a bit less alone.

Jessup led her over to a fireplace and pointed above the mantle. "Look," he told her, "I've kept it all these years. It goes with me wherever I go," he said, emotion softening his voice.

Looking down at Savannah was the portrait of her mother, Caroline. For a moment, it could have been a portrait of Savannah herself. She drank in every detail, instinctively knowing the artist's rendering was accurate. Caroline's smooth, white hands were folded in the lap of a peach-colored gown. Her neck was long and graceful and her shoulders sweetly sloping and white. But it was her mother's eyes that struck Savannah. Turquoise and fringed with dark lashes and gentle, so gentle. Savannah remembered those eyes, looking down at her before she went to sleep; those hands, touching, smoothing her own curls. Those shoulders where she had nestled her head and listened to Caroline's soft croonings. Mother.

Tears sprang to Savannah's eyes, trickling down her cheeks. Jessup noticed immediately. "There, there, child," he clucked, reaching for his linen handkerchief to dry her tears. "She was lovely and she loved you dearly. She wouldn't like to see you cry. She was my baby sister and I thought the world of her. I still do. If only she hadn't run away with that no account Alfred James, her life would have been so different. . . ."

"She loved my father," Savannah said harshly, refusing to hear anything the general had to say about the man who had been the world for both her mother and herself.

Jessup immediately knew he had blundered. "Of course, child," he told her, not wanting to alienate her, wanting more than anything else that she should come to love him as her uncle and her mother's brother. Later, when they knew each other better, they could share memories about Caroline.

A tall, kindly looking woman with slate-gray hair stepped into the room. Her eyes flickered over Savannah in cursory inspection and apparently found the girl to her liking. "Savannah, this is Mrs. Bouvier, my housekeeper. So, you see, you won't be the only female in the household. Mrs. Bouvier, this is my niece, Savannah James, whom I've told you about. You will please see she has everything she needs to make her comfortable."

"Of course, sir. Miss James, would you like to see your room now?" The woman smiled, the gesture lifting the corners of her eyes, showing her amiable personality.

"Yes, I would," Savannah answered softly, glancing once again at the portrait on the wall. "Will you be joining me for dinner, Uncle?" Was that cultured, feminine voice really hers? She marveled at her own ability to carry off this charade. For a charade it was. She couldn't seem to find any feelings for the man regardless of his obvious affection. Perhaps her mother had also run away from her brother's possessiveness, wanting instead the love Alfred James offered, although he had little else he could claim. Now that she thought of it, there was a certain sadness in Caroline's gaze, a certain trapped look.

Jessup's eyes softened. She had forgiven his blunder in demeaning her father. "I will, my dear. I can think of nothing that would please me more than being your dinner companion."

Smiling sweetly, Savannah turned and followed the housekeeper into the hall.

Taking her up the curving staircase, Mrs. Bouvier carried on a running conversation. "I've already had your luggage brought to your room. If you like, I can help you unpack and put things away."

"Not right now, Mrs. Bouvier, thank you. I think I'd like to rest a while."

"That's what you will do, cherie. The general is so delighted you've agreed to come and live with him. I've only known him a short time since he's come to New Orleans, but you have made his step lighter and his eyes brighten with a smile. We are all happy you've come to New Orleans. Your resemblance to your mother is quite remarkable. Both of you beautiful women."

When Savannah entered her room she would have thought she was entering a garden. Bouquets of flowers

filled the room with their fragrance. Special pains had
been taken with the room in anticipation of her arrival.
In spite of herself, Savannah showed her delight,
touching the soft flower petals and inhaling their perfume.

"Your uncle arranged everything, Miss James. You
can see how happy he is to have you with him. Would
you like me to help you undress? If you like, I'll see to
hiring a personal maid for you. Or would you prefer to
do that for yourself?"

"Actually, Mrs. Bouvier, I'd . . . I'd rather do it
myself. You see . . ." she stammered with the erupting
lie, "I've sent for someone from home. It will be
several weeks before she can arrive and I'd rather
wait."

"Of course, Miss," Mrs. Bouvier eyed the young girl.
It was strange that a lady of Miss James' obvious quality
would consider doing for even a day without a personal
maid, much less for weeks. But it would be nice to have
a lady in the house. The all male household and the
limited occasions where Mrs. Bouvier could display her
talents were sometimes annoying. Now there would be
balls and dinner parties and teas and socials . . . the
thought suddenly struck her that she had no idea in
what condition the table linens were. It was something
she must see to immediately.

"If you will excuse me, Miss. I have duties to attend
to."

"Of course, Mrs. Bouvier. Would you please close
the door behind you?"

Alone at last, Savannah sat in the little boudoir chair
near the window looking down at the overgrown gardens. She sat there for a very long time, thinking of
nothing and thinking of everything. Mostly, she found
her thoughts returning again and again to MacAllister
and the night he had come into her room and held her
until the first light of day, soothing her, comforting her,
giving her the strength to do what she must.

And with the first light of day, when things were

clearer to her, he had turned her over in his arms and traced a delicate path of kisses from her ear to his most favorite of places between her breasts. And when, with the impatience of desire, he had ripped his shirt from her to expose her body for his lovemaking, he had swept her away with him to a place far beyond the stars where time has no meaning and being MacAllister's woman filled her world.

Two days later Savannah's uncle informed her that a dinner party was being planned in her honor. Savannah found her throat muscles tightening at the thought. Upon learning that the dinner party was for twenty-four, she almost succumbed to a fainting spell. Annemarie's wise words of, "If you find yourself suddenly in the midst of something you can't handle, plead a headache or smile and flirt. Never open your mouth unless you're sure of what's going to come out!" were suddenly recalled to her. She wondered if the advice included being able to swallow. She was terrified. Officers and their wives, adjutants and their wives and a few close friends would make up the dinner party.

"Savannah, what do you think would be suitable for dinner? It makes little difference to me. That's one of your duties from now on. You'll be overseeing the kitchen. I do like Creole shrimp and am partial to gumbo, but don't let me influence you. You arrange whatever pleases you. Every eye will be upon you, my dear, and no one will notice what is being put in their mouths. I don't want to be overbearing, so you just make your plans accordingly. I realize that this is all new to you. I must even seem like a stranger to you after all these years, but I hope the feeling deserts you quite soon. I want us to have a full, wonderful life now that we've found one another. We're the last of my side of the family."

"What of my father's family, Uncle, do you have any knowledge of them?"

Jessup's face closed. "Not in recent years. I believe

there was a brother in the Dakotas, but my memory isn't what it used to be."

Savannah stared at her uncle, recognizing his defensive tone. She knew he was lying. Evidently, he wanted her all to himself and wasn't about to share her with her father's people. The thought saddened her. Her father's people. Not her people, the Seminole. Not Osceola and his people, but *her* people, her father's people. She smiled. Her uncle seeing her warm smile laughed. "You see, I knew you would like it here in our house."

Savannah pretended not to hear the word "our." It would never be her house no matter how long she lived in it. She didn't like the stiff, ugly furniture with the polished tables that smelled like wax. Everything was spartan and unattractive. The house needed a woman's touch, one that a housekeeper could never give it. But not her touch. She would never dare tamper with this austere dwelling. Hopefully she wouldn't be here long enough to develop more than an acute dislike for the unattractive house.

The fat dog followed her around on his short, stubby legs, wheezing and breathing hard. She detested it thinking Jessup had ordered the ugly animal to guard her. She knew the thought was silly but she couldn't shake it. Even when she slept, the animal was outside her door, sniffling and trying to catch its breath. Why her uncle didn't put it out of its misery eluded her.

A week passed and then another. With each day she missed MacAllister more and more. Several times a week she made a pretense of going shopping and she would meet him in the Vieux Carré and escape with him to his hotel room. The added secrecy and danger gave a new flavor to their loving especially since Jessup had insisted that his niece not go shopping alone and had appointed his aide-de-camp as her escort. After purchasing a few trifles in the shops Savannah would insist the aide go and find some refreshment for himself while she kept an appointment with the dressmaker, fitter, milliner. She giggled when she thought of the way the aide-de-camp would look with disdain at the few boxes she carried more than likely thinking her a very vain woman. If he only knew, she giggled, that while he was waiting for me, I was wrapped snugly in MacAllister's arms, feeling him touch me, kiss me . . . she must stop this line of thought. She could feel the heat burning in her cheeks!

It was the day of her first dinner party, and her uncle seemed keyed up, anxious about something. That afternoon Savannah had told Sloan she had an idea that it had nothing to do with the dinner party but rather it was some sort of military business. When she had tried to draw Jessup out, he had turned taciturn and told her she wouldn't be interested in hearing about savages. How wrong he was! Savannah decided not to press the issue but hoped that something would come of his remark over dinner conversation with other army officers.

Savannah's elaborate toilette preparations took close to three hours. Time and again she cursed herself for not allowing Mrs. Bouvier to hire a personal maid for her. At the time she didn't want to complicate her personal life with still another pair of eyes watching her. But now, nervous about the coming evening, she was all thumbs. First she was dissatisfied with her hair and then her dress, changing her choices not fewer than seven times. Her petticoats didn't seem to lay right, and her silk stockings itched; the camisole was too confining. Out came the hair pins and combs and another hairdo was arranged. In the end she simply brushed it back and tied it with a lavender velvet ribbon that matched her gown. She added another around her throat with a cameo Jessup had given her, saying it had once belonged to her mother. She had no idea how he came to have it in his possession, but had accepted it gratefully. She didn't like the man, uncle or no. She had come to believe her dislike had nothing to do with his antipathy toward the Indians.

Savannah stood beside her Uncle Thomas to greet the guests as they arrived. Introductions were made and cordials were served in the little-used front parlor. Mrs. Bouvier had hired a staff of servants for this evening to help serve the guests. Through it all, Savannah smiled and made pleasantries. She knew Annemarie and MacAllister would have been proud of her.

The women examined one another's gowns, complimented each other and generally lied with straight faces. Of the ten women present, Savannah felt the best dressed and the prettiest, certainly the youngest. She smiled till she thought her face would crack with the effort. Not one of the women so far had mentioned the Indians. Savannah herself was about to bring up the subject when Mrs. Bouvier announced dinner.

Thomas Jessup walked proudly over to his niece and held out his arm. Daintily, she placed her hand on his wrist and walked with him to the elaborately prepared table. For a second she panicked as she tried to recall the place setting at Annemarie's table. Her sigh of relief when it came into focus amused the general. "I grant you this is a rather big dinner party for your first introduction. But as you can see, these are my favorite people, and I wanted you to meet them all at one sitting. It's time that you and the ladies became acquainted. You can't spend all of your time reading and sewing. A casual luncheon, a walk in town or along the waterfront is an excellent means of ridding oneself of boredom."

Dinner conversation was casual. There was talk of the weather, how nice spring was going to be this year. Several of the women couldn't seem to make up their minds if they should plant flowers or not since they didn't know if their husbands would be relocated by early summer. A vegetable garden was a necessity, one stout lady said loudly and literally defied Jessup to comment. A needle-thin woman with a beak of a nose asked if anyone at the table was going to see the outrageously wicked play at the newly renovated theatre on Rue de la Paix. All the women blushed and shook their heads. "I plan to go," Savannah said brightly. "Just as soon as I can get a ticket."

"My dear, is that wise?" her uncle demanded in a tart voice.

"But of course. It was all the rage when I was in Baton Rouge. I wanted to see it then, but my plans were changed suddenly. Perhaps you would join me, Uncle." Jessup smirked and allowed as how he would.

A woman named Clarisse said her old mare had passed on and now what was she going to do. Savannah again came to her aid by telling her to buy another one. One must be able to get about, she said in her best and haughtiest voice. Again, her uncle agreed with her. At that point she felt she had contributed enough to the conversation and left the talk up to the other women. All of them suddenly became tongue-tied. Jessup started small talk on a variety of subjects. This was getting her nowhere, Savannah thought sourly. It was time to do something.

"Tell me, Uncle Thomas, how do you fare with the Indians? Now," she said, wagging a playful finger in the air, "don't tell me that the Seminole problem is not fit dinner conversation. I just know that all of us are fascinated with what you men are doing to secure our safe futures." She smiled such a charming smile that Jessup melted and smiled in return.

"You're right, my dear, we are making all the states safe and secure from the savages. I have no objection to telling you now that in two days' time we'll be signing a treaty with the Seminoles." He waited for gasps from the women. He wasn't disappointed. Encouraged, he continued. "We've been negotiating for over a month now at Camp Dade. We've decided to stop fighting. Osceola and his people have promised to go to Tampa Bay by April 10th and board ships for the west. They'll travel to the Texas coast and from there we'll march them north into Arkansas where they'll assimilate

themselves among those other savages, the Creeks."
Smiling and bowing slightly, Jessup addressed his female companions. "The original plans were to take them through Louisiana, but I've convinced Washington that this fair city, with its lovely occupants, were not to be threatened or exposed in any way to their disagreeable presence. Texas is wild, a fitting place for the likes of them.

"Our government plans to support them for a year. We had to make concessions, I can tell you that. The Seminoles have insisted that they be secure in their lives and property from the Creeks especially, and the negroes whom they consider to be their property shall accompany them west. We're calling it the Capitulation of the Seminole Nation."

Savannah was stunned at her uncle's words. What should she say? How should she act? This was no flirting, laughing matter. She had to manage to get in touch with MacAllister. Did this change things? Was it a trick, a lie, on her uncle's part? She schooled her face to impassiveness as Jessup continued. "It's important that the Seminoles feel secure. If they become alarmed and hold out, the war will be renewed. That's one of the main reasons the treaty specifically mentions the word 'allies,' the free blacks who were assured their life and property. It also guarantees that those blacks who are the property of the Indians would go west with their masters. There's a Seminole black named Abraham who wanted that assurance, and so did the army. If the runaway blacks are assured their safety from white slaveholders, they will not be a barrier to Seminole migration. What we don't know and can't anticipate at this point is how the Florida settlers and the white slaveholders are going to react. It could become a sticky mess if we aren't careful."

Savannah's heart dropped to her stomach. At what price had Osceola agreed to this treaty? She knew instinctively that it was her thlacko who had insisted that provisions be made for the blacks in this agreement. He, above all men, treasured life and freedom. But to give up his homeland! To leave the Floridas for a precarious life within the Creek nation! To save lives, to share peace, she told herself, wanting to cry in sympathy for Osceola's pain. MacAllister. She needed MacAllister to grieve with her, to share their sorrow for Osceola.

Savannah could sense that her uncle didn't like this treaty. He would just as soon kill every Seminole in Florida. MacAllister had told her of his meeting with Jessup before he came to Osceola's camp and how Jessup hated Osceola and his people. No, it had to be some trick, some sleight of hand to force Osceola and his people to move and keep moving. How could he have agreed? Abraham, she could understand, but not Osceola. Did he understand? Did he fully understand? Did he sit in the treaty negotiations? Could it be possible that he believed these white eyes? There she was thinking like an Indian again. Damnation. She had to think like these people seated at the table. And it was time she said something; they were all looking at her. Since she was the one who invited her uncle's confidences, it was up to her to reply. "How wonderful," she cooed. "Ladies, isn't it wonderful what my uncle and all your husbands are doing? How proud we are that the United States Government brought the Indians to their knees." There was a chorus of agreement. Jessup positively basked in her praise.

"I am humble in your praise, my dear," he smiled thinly. "I have always maintained the belief that this great country was civilized by white men and therefore should belong to our race." The smile turned to smugness as he made his speech and more than one person at his dinner table thought he was already campaigning for the White House.

"The papers say there is a good deal of hostility between the Seminoles and the Creeks, General. Do you think this settlement will incur further outbreaks of Indian hostilities on our western frontiers?" This was asked by the wife of an officer. From the way she spoke, Savannah knew this had been thoroughly discussed between the woman and her husband.

"Hostility, yes. And that would seem to be their problem, wouldn't it? Also, it is good military strategy to have the red man located in one territory. Perhaps we'll be lucky and they'll massacre one another, saving us the trouble."

Savannah thought she would choke. She could feel the blood draining from her face leaving her white and shaken.

"Dear one," Jessup immediately rose from his chair and was swiftly at her side, supporting her with his arm before she collapsed onto the floor. "Forgive me, please. It was unthinkable of me to allow this turn of conversation. I've injured your sensibilities."

Savannah was regaining her composure. She wanted to shrink away from her uncle's touch. Smiling bravely, she murmured that she was quite herself again and please not to mind her. Reassuring himself that she was sincere, Jessup once again took his place at the table, eyes full of concern continually returning to her, making her feel like a fish in a bowl.

After dinner the women once more separated from the men. Savannah watched her uncle herd the men out to the verandah after offering fat Havana cigars all around. She didn't fail to notice the smug, self-satisfied look on his face. She was instantly suspicious. She excused herself prettily, promising to be right back to join the chattering ladies. She moved on silent feet to stand within inches of the open doorway leading to the wide verandah. She listened unashamedly.

Brigadier General Davis slapped Jessup on the back. "That was a pretty fairy tale you spun for your niece at the dinner table. For a minute you almost had me believing we were going to honor that asinine agreement."

"What I say and what I do are two different things,"

Jessup said smugly. "Women only want to hear the fair, nice things. They don't want to think about the hard trading and the blood and gore that goes with any deal made with those goddamn savages. I expect to be under great pressure from southern slave owners as well as Florida landowners. If I must," he said casually, as though his decision had nothing to do with human life, "I will draw the line between those blacks who have lived with the Seminoles *before* the war and those who have run off to them or who have been picked up by them *during* the war. I will do all I can to urge the Seminoles to accept this distinction and hand over all the wartime runaway slaves."

Savannah thought she would choke on her own saliva. She did indeed have a headache now. Osceola was going to sign a false document. He had to be stopped! Her mind swiftly calculated the distance between New Orleans and Cedar Key and then the overland ride to Camp Dade. She had to reach MacAllister as soon as possible. When was this damnable evening going to end? How soon could she sneak away? Thirty minutes was all she was going to give Jessup and then she would faint dead away from excitement.

Thirty minutes turned into sixty and then ninety. By the time the last guest was through the door Savannah thought she would go out of her mind. She couldn't bear to look at her uncle, couldn't bear to have him kiss her cheek. Her hand went to her head just as a grimace slashed across her face. He would have to walk the fat dog himself. There were a lot of things he was going to have to do by himself from now on. Filthy, lying white man, she spat as she flounced into her room. The door slammed shut with such force she thought the wood would come off the hinges.

The minute her uncle's door closed, she had hers open. Silently, she crept down the stairs and let herself out quietly. Before racing down the verandah steps she slipped off the kid slippers and placed them neatly under a wicker chair. Gathering her skirts in her hand, she fled down the street on winged feet.

Once she reached the Grand America Hotel she skidded to a stop. She had no shoes. What would the desk clerk think? Who cared what the desk clerk thought. Within seconds she was up the wide, circular hotel stairway and down the hall to MacAllister's room. She let her eyes rake the numbers on the doors. The upside down six, just the opposite of her own room number when she stayed at the hotel. She banged on the door with clenched fists. Sloan opened the door and stepped backward. "What happened?" was all he could manage. The words tumbled out as tears cascaded down Savannah's cheeks. "We can do nothing for Osceola now. It is too late. MacAllister, what are we to do? My chief is signing a false document. Your people have tricked us again. My uncle," she made the title sound obscene as her lip curled back in anger, "leaves for Camp Dade tomorrow. He goes overland. If you took the *Polly Copinger* by water, could you get there first?" Her grass green eyes pleaded with him to say yes.

"I can try." He was already pulling on his boots as Savannah continued her tirade against the white man. Without answering her, he pulled a wrinkled shirt over his head, and then stuffed his personal belongings into a small case. "Come with me, I'll walk you back to the house."

"I refuse to go back there. I'm going with you," Savannah said adamantly.

"You have to go back. I can't take you with me now. I'll do my best and then I'll return. This is something I didn't expect, didn't foresee. You must stay, Savannah. In truth, what could you do? Be honest with me now. There is every possibility that you will be more help here. You can sit in the cafe where the military gathers and possibly pick up some more information. At luncheon with some of the ladies who are married to those closest to the general. Pick their brains. I'm counting on you, depending on you. The general will be gone and you'll be alone. You won't have to look at him. Promise me, Savannah, that you'll stay here. I don't want to have to worry about you."

If he hadn't said he was depending on her, counting on her, she would have fought to go with him. He was right, what could she do?

"Come," Sloan said taking her by the arm. He bent to kiss her, thinking to reassure her, and noticed her missing shoes. He said nothing, knowing she had run the distance from her uncle's house to the hotel.

"This is no time for kisses, MacAllister. You must hurry. I can find my way back to the house alone. You must take Redeemer from the stable and ride to the harbor. I will do as you ask. Sail on safe waters, MacAllister, for my heart is with you."

"I'll be back as soon as possible. Remember, Savannah, I can make no promises, there isn't much time." In the darkness outside the hotel he stared deeply into her eyes for a minute. "On my return I'll arrange to meet you at the cafe, or else I'll send Culpepper. Go now."

Without another word, Savannah turned and fled down the darkened tree lined street. Tears of betrayal coursed down her cheek. Her very own uncle, her very own flesh and blood. Osceola would never understand.

Eleven uneventful days passed before Thomas Jessup returned to his house on Mulberry Street. Savannah was sitting on a white wicker chair on the verandah, the fat old dog close by. She had been staring at him for what seemed like a long time. There was something different about the animal. She stared a moment longer. Of course, he wasn't breathing. He was dead. The thought pleased her, knowing Jessup would grieve over the dead dog. She was trying to make up her mind what she should do about the animal when Jessup rode up in a swirl of dry dust. Her decision was made. How she hated this man she was forced to call uncle. She felt a momentary pang for the dog lying on the floor. It was a dumb animal and couldn't fend for itself. The slat-ribbed dog from camp could at least move. Hunger always kept one on the move and on the alert. Jessup's dog ate better than the Indians. His food for one day could have fed three braves. No, she felt no pity for the man or his dog.

Jessup tied his horse to a small hitching post next to a giant hickory tree. He rubbed the dust from his blue sleeves with gloved hands and literally bounded up the steps. Exuberantly, he pecked Savannah on the cheek. "I can't tell you how good it is to come home to someone. My dear, I've missed your presence and your beautiful face. Up to now the only welcome I've received is from my dog and the housekeeper."

Savannah allowed her eyes to go to the dog. Jessup followed her gaze. "Oh, no," he breathed sadly. "Not old Henry. When did this happen?"

"I have no idea. I thought there was something strange about the way he was lying. He's been there since last evening." She hoped the viciousness didn't sound in her voice. On second thought, she really didn't care. Now perhaps was the time to talk to him when he was overcome with grief for the dog. "Did you sign the treaty, Uncle? Did everything go according to plan?"

"What? Oh, yes, my dear. All the chiefs were there. You know, of course, that the treaty was ready in early February but we had to wait for all the chiefs. They arrived on schedule. I didn't anticipate any problems. The Seminole trust their white brothers. A pity we can't trust them in the same way."

Bitter gall rose in Savannah's throat. It was all she could do to remain quiet. If things went the way her uncle had wanted, it meant MacAllister had been too late. Her heart soared momentarily at the thought that he would be returning soon. She didn't need details of the treaty signing, didn't want to hear Jessup gloat. It was enough to know that Osceola and the other chiefs had been tricked.

"Child, why don't you go for a walk while I take care of old Henry. I'd like to be alone with my old friend." Savannah stared at her uncle for a moment. How sad that he could feel so much for an old dog and nothing for the lives of human beings. Perhaps he personally wasn't responsible for this particular treaty signing, but he had helped. He was elated by the fact that the Indians had been duped again. She wouldn't allow herself to feel anything but hatred for Thomas Jessup.

Gathering her skirts in her hand, she descended the stairs and walked slowly down the street. Her heart would sing if she saw MacAllister or Culpepper in the cafe.

It took Sloan three days more before Culpepper docked the *Polly Copinger*. It was mid-afternoon when Savannah set her lemonade glass down on the glass-topped table and spotted MacAllister. She wanted to leap from the chair and run to him. How sad and disheartened he appeared. He had failed, it was obvious.

Both men sat at the next table and ordered a bottle of whiskey.

Savannah waited till both men were settled then she spoke. "My uncle returned three days ago and said things went well. Osceola signed the treaty along with the other chiefs." She hated the sound of reproach in her tone, but she couldn't help it.

"We couldn't dock the goddamn ship, much less take to the ground. The Creeks were thick as flies over rotten fruit. At one point Redeemer and I took to the water and got to shore, only to be turned back by soldiers. We tried everything. It was a mistake and one I should have recognized. The military planned this for a long time. Every footpath, every trail, every waterway was guarded. A stray dog would have had a hard time going through the guards undetected. I had no bona fide business there. We were forced to return. I'm sorry, Savannah, we tried but it was fruitless."

Savannah left, followed by Culpepper who said Maeve was granting him an all-night audience. Sloan sat for a long time. He didn't ever remember feeling so alone, so cut off from everyone and everything. He was well into a second bottle of whiskey when he felt a presence next to him. "Beaunell!" was all he could manage.

Beaunell Gentry approached Sloan's table, the little cockade feather on her fashionable hat bobbing with each diminutive step she took. She wore a sapphire silk gown trimmed with military style braid and tiny brass buttons. Her dark hair was piled into fat curls at the back of her head, and her pink glistening lips parted in a demure smile. Beaunell appeared every inch a lady; her bedroom profession completely hidden.

"Sloan, I thought it was you, but I wasn't sure. What are you doing in New Orleans?"

Sloan hedged. "What are you doing here? Has something happened at Annemarie's?"

Beaunell gurgled with laughter. "Something is always happening at Annemarie's house as you know. We parted company. It was time for me to move on. A dashing major invited me to New Orleans and being at loose ends I decided to accompany him. He's very handsome and most generous," Beaunell said quietly, hoping to make Sloan jealous.

"I'm happy for you, Beau. I'm glad you found someone who pleases you. Do you plan to stay here or move on with the major?"

"What do you mean you're happy for me? What did you expect me to do, sit and twiddle my thumbs waiting for you? That's not my style, Sloan. How could you cast me aside the way you did after all we had, after all we shared. You led me to believe . . ."

"Beau, stop right there. I never made any promises. I paid for everything you gave me and may I say I was also more than generous. If you chose to misinterpret, that is not my fault. I'm fond of you; I have always been fond of you. In my own way I care for you, Beau, but I'm not in love with you. I have no intention of marrying you. We had some good years and a lot of pleasant memories. Why can't we let it go at that? If you need money . . ."

Rage suffused Beaunell's face. "I don't want your money. I don't need your money. You aren't fooling me for one minute. It's that damn savage, isn't it? The one who attacked me in Annemarie's sitting room. Don't worry, your precious Annemarie didn't spill the secrets but Jenny did. Fat old Jenny couldn't wait to tell me all there was to tell. I knew you were up to something, and whatever it is, it isn't finished, is it? I'll fix you, Sloan, one way or the other. I won't let you get away with what you've done to me," she snarled hatefully.

"Jesus, Beau, will you shut up before everyone in New Orleans hears you. When are you going to get it through your head that we couldn't make a go of it? So we were good in bed, but there are other things in life besides rolling between the covers."

"Like making whoopee with the Indians, right?" Beaunell snapped. "I'll find out what it is you're up to and then you'll regret the way you've treated me."

"Go find your major and marry him if he's so inclined. Have some kids and settle down. That's what life is all about. Forget about me, make a new life for yourself."

"I could make a new life if it were you I was marrying, Sloan. You know I've always loved you. I thought you loved me. When I spoke of marriage, you didn't say no. You let me assume, let me think . . ."

Sloan hated the whine in her voice, detested the tears that were filling her round eyes. They meant nothing. He had more money than the major; it was as simple as that. Still, he had to be gentle with her, convince her that he wasn't for her before she set eyes on Savannah and made trouble. His gut churned at the thought of what Beaunell was capable of doing.

Several days later Savannah opened the door to her room and was walking past her uncle's room when she noticed the door was wide open. Stealing a peek inside, she found him packing his personal belongings into a case. He was going away. Her heart thumped in her chest. She said nothing, but her eyes questioned these strange actions. After all, he had just returned. Something must be wrong.

"My dear Savannah. How pretty you look. I'll be leaving in the morning. I have to go to the front and wipe out those damn savages. It's an all-out attack. We're going to squelch any resistance right from the beginning."

Savannah's mind raced. "But you just signed the treaty. You said . . ."

"I know what I said, and I know what I'm saying now. Every last one of those savages is going to be wiped out. I'll see to it personally. I thought we would dine at Antoine's tonight. I want to remember you in a pleasant setting and Antoine's is the perfect place. The service is impeccable and the food is wonderful. I must leave before sunup to be at the rail depot to see my troops assemble. It's my duty. There's no reason for you to rise so early. We'll have dinner, some wine, and say our good-bye's this evening. I've arranged everything. I've added additional monies to your bank account. Mrs. Bouvier will continue to run the household. Your every comfort will be seen to. I know you're going to be lonely, but my officers' wives will visit with you. I'll try to get back as often as possible to see you. Now that I've found Caroline's daughter, I don't ever plan to lose her again. I can't tell you how happy you've made me. Having you here in my home is like having my beloved Caroline again."

Savannah was thunderstruck. Another shoeless trip

to MacAllister's hotel room was all she could think of, but first she would have to go to dinner with her uncle. What would MacAllister say to all of this news?

"Will an hour be enough time for you to change for dinner?" Savannah nodded. She could change in five minutes if she had to. Five minutes to change her gown and fifty minutes to think, or was it forty minutes in an hour. She couldn't remember. Not that it made a great deal of difference. Her uncle would wait for her if she were two hours late. He might chastise her, but he would smile and tell her how much he loved Caroline's daughter.

Savannah changed into a gown elegant in its simplicity. The color matched her eyes perfectly. The velvet ribbon with the cameo was tied around her neck. She debated over changing her shoes. She hated shoes of any kind, and once the miserable things were on her feet she preferred to keep them on till she was ready to retire for the evening. It was torture to take them off, rummage for a pair to match the gown. But she did it. Quickly, she brushed her hair, letting it fall in loose waves about her shoulders. MacAllister said he liked her hair when it fell about her shoulders, telling her she looked like an angel. Perhaps she would see Mac-Allister in the dining room and she could flirt with him. Annemarie had been right; it was very easy to flirt. She even enjoyed the look of discomfort on MacAllister's face when she batted her lashes at him. She loved it when his eyes took on a sleepy look and he squirmed in his chair as though ants had crawled into his pants.

Thomas Jessup looked over the tables in the dining room, finally selecting one where he felt Savannah and himself would be shown off to the best advantage. It was a small, intimate table surrounded by potted plants. To the left was a gilded cage with a pair of lovebirds sitting together on a perch. Anyone entering the room would immediately notice the decor first and

then the patrons at the table. Anyone sitting would find
their eyes drawn to the gilded cage and Caroline's
daughter.

Jessup ordered for both of them: roast lamb, pars-
leyed potatoes, a crisp green salad, along with fingertip
carrots. Soft, mouth-watering rolls, along with thick,
yellow butter ended the meal. The wine, he ordered
firmly, was to be properly chilled. Coffee and fresh
strawberries would be the perfect dessert. She was
having trouble with the mint jelly. Annemarie had
overlooked lamb with jelly. When in doubt, play with
the food, stirring it about on your plate till someone
came to take it away. Savannah stirred and stirred.

"Aren't you hungry, my dear?" Jessup asked, concern in his voice.

Startled, Savannah looked at her uncle. "No, I was
thinking about you leaving in the morning."

"That's exactly what I thought. Now, you must not
worry. I'll be back as soon as I can. Nothing is going to
go wrong." His voice was gentle with what Savannah
thought was concern for her. She stirred some more,
the mint jelly melting around the meat on her plate.
The small, white potatoes, with their flecks of parsley,
were long since mashed and soaking in the jelly. Her
stomach turned at the mess on her plate.

"This is quite good, but Mrs. Bouvier makes a better
roast, I think. It's probably in the spices she uses. No
two cooks cook alike," Jessup said in a knowledgeable
voice.

"I'm sure you're right, Uncle."

A small stir was being created at the entrance to the
dining room. Savannah gasped. The woman who had
attacked her in Annemarie's sitting room. Mac-
Allister's old woman! She bit down on her tongue and
felt the salty taste of her own blood. What was she
doing here? Would she come over to the table? For the
first time in her young life Savannah knew gut fear.
There was no place she could hide, no place she could
go. All she could do was brazen the situation out.

Beaunell, on the arm of a handsome man in uniform, sailed down the center aisle, her head held high, paying no attention to anyone. That was good. Savannah sighed as she attacked the luscious red strawberries in front of her. She wished she could pick them up in her fingers and pop them in her mouth. It was so hard to cut a strawberry with a spoon the way her uncle was doing.

Where was MacAllister's former woman sitting? Would she see her and her uncle when they rose to leave? She wished she had paid more attention to the seating arrangements in the dining room when they entered. She couldn't do anything about it. Now she had two things to tell MacAllister. They lingered over coffee and the remainder of the wine. Savannah made small talk about inconsequential things, such as her latest needlepoint pattern and the color of thread she was using opposed to what the pattern called for. She could tell her uncle was not excited with her boring habits. Nor was she.

"If you're finished, my dear, I think we can be on our way. I would like to retire early. The train leaves at seven, and I must be there a good hour ahead of time. Let me say, I enjoyed this precious time we've had this evening. It's almost the same as having Caroline next to me. Come along, my dear," he said rising to hold out her chair.

Savannah tried to wiggle out of the chair without turning so that the woman from Annemarie's wouldn't notice her. She failed miserably. Even from where she stood, she could hear the woman's gasp. She turned deliberately and stared straight at Beaunell, defying her to make a scene.

"Who is that?" Beaunell demanded of her companion, Major Steven Foxe.

"That's Miss Savannah James. Do you know her? If so, I would like an introduction."

"I just wager you would. Not her, the man she's with. Who is he?"

Foxe stared at Beaunell. "That's Brevet Major General Thomas Jessup, my commanding officer. Do you wish to make his acquaintance? Miss James is his niece. Every officer serving under Jessup is waiting anxiously for a dinner invitation to the general's home."

Beaunell seethed and fumed. So, that was the way it was. Her agile mind clicked away trying to make sense out of what was going on. Toward the end of the meal she thought she knew. Foxe's words startled her, shaking her from her deep thoughts. "Jessup is leaving by railroad in the morning. He's heading for the front. I'm staying behind to clean up a few details. Then I'll join him in a week's time. If he needs me, I'll be leaving sooner."

"In the morning you say?" At his nod, Beaunell bit into a bloody red piece of meat. She chewed viciously, her eyes narrowed with what the major thought was lust.

Savannah settled herself in a highbacked windsor chair in the sitting room. When was her uncle going to go to bed? Why did he persist in prowling around as he was doing? His bags were packed and resting near the front door. Perhaps he was anxious, uncertain about how he was going to slaughter Osceola's people. Perhaps he was conscious of his own safety too.

It was midnight when Savannah finally climbed the stairs to her room. She couldn't go to Sloan now. The morning would be soon enough. Just as soon as her uncle left for the rail depot.

She slept badly, tossing and turning. She woke while it was still dark, bathed in perspiration. She washed and donned a fresh gown. She quietly crept below stairs and entered the kitchen. Mrs. Bouvier was already about. Coffee was bubbling on the stove. The ingredients were on the table top for a hearty breakfast, something Jessup always insisted upon. The thought of food gagged her, but she knew she would have to join her uncle at the breakfast table and wish him a safe trip as he swilled down his coffee and ate his way through a half-dozen eggs and a stack of wheatcakes.

Savannah was already seated at her place at the table when Jessup entered the dining room. Surprise and pleasure lit his features. She was her mother's daughter. How kind of her to rise so early to see him off. Caroline would have done the same thing. "Good morning, my dear. May I say it is a pleasure to see you this morning. The sight of you will make my departure that much more bearable. I can't tell you how pleased I am. I just wish I could sit and converse with you, but my men are waiting for me." He dabbed at his lips and rose from the table. Savannah rose, too, and followed him to the front door. Standing outside at attention was his aide-de-camp. He immediately gathered up the general's bags and loaded them in a buckboard. He saluted smartly and drove off. Jessup embraced Savannah and smiled down into her eyes. "You are truly a likeness of Caroline." Without another word he was gone.

The minute the door was closed Savannah raced up the stairs to her room for a shawl. At the last minute she splashed on some cologne and brushed out her hair. She was arranging a pretty lavender shawl about her shoulders when a knock sounded on the front door. Her eyes widened as she peeped over the upstairs railing. Mrs. Bouvier answered the door and invited a young woman inside. Savannah's hand flew to her mouth—the woman from Annemarie's.

"I'd like to see General Jessup please before he leaves," Beaunell said quietly in what Savannah later called a very ladylike voice.

"The general's gone, Miss. But you should be able to catch him at the depot. His train leaves at seven."

Beaunell digested the information. "And the general's niece, Savannah, is she at home?"

"Yes, Miss, she is. Would you like me to call her? She just retired to her room when the general left. I expect she's feeling quite alone now and saddened at the general's departure."

"I'm sure you're right. We won't disturb her. I can

call again when she's more up to things. I'll just
go along to the depot and see General Jessup off."
Beaunell turned and left, her bearing regal, as though
she paid visiting calls at six in the morning every day of
the week.

Savannah's knees trembled so badly she could barely
stand. Her breathing was harsh and labored as she
fought to bring herself under control. She had to get
out of here before the woman got to the depot. She had
no idea where the depot was, much less how long it
would take to get there. She raced to the window in
time to see the woman's carriage turn the corner. Off
came the shoes and on went her moccasins. No one
would notice them beneath the gown. From the looks
of things outside her window not too many people were
stirring at this time in the morning.

Quietly she crept down the stairs and let herself out.
Once she was on the street in the cool morning air she
ran like the wind. When she reached the hotel, she was
breathing heavily. She paid no mind to the disgruntled
desk clerk but raced up the stairs. She didn't bother to
knock. Frantically she threw open the door. Obviously,
he had been asleep. How could he sleep at a time like
this?

"What the hell!" Sloan sputtered alarmed at seeing
her at his door at such an ungodly hour. "Savannah!"

"Listen to me, MacAllister." Quickly she recounted
Jessup's words of the previous day leaving nothing out,
not even the death of the dog. She finished up with
Beaunell and her trip to the depot.

Sloan ripped off his nightshirt and pulled on his
trousers and boots. "Beaunell," he muttered, giving
the woman from Annemarie's a name. "Little bitch. I
should have known to expect trouble from her. No time
to pack. There's nothing here I really need." He fished
for money in his wallet and drew out a sheaf of notes.

The desk clerk looked at the pile of money fluttering
on the counter. His eyes widened as he stared at
Savannah and Sloan's backs. Such an odd couple, he

mused to himself. But his mother liked to hear about all
the strange customers the hotel drew in. She was going
to like the fifty dollar tip the anxious man had left even
better than the story.

Sloan dragged Savannah to the stable, threw another
sheaf of bills at the stable hand and then saddled
Redeemer. Even the huge beast seemed to know it was
time to move on.

The first thing Jessup would do, Sloan knew, after
Beaunell told him what she knew about Savannah,
would be to streak back to the house to confront his
niece. After pondering the question of why Savannah
had lied to him about where she'd been all these years
and why she had suddenly decided to turn up when he
was involved in the most heated war with the Seminoles, he would have his answer. Savannah, living
among the Seminoles, had placed herself back into
Jessup's life to spy on him for the Indians. Beyond that,
he would neither know nor care. Quite possibly, he
would have murder on his mind. After what Savannah
had told him, MacAllister knew that Jessup's devotion
toward her was only because of his sister, Caroline.
Savannah was only a replacement.

Down through the Vieux Carré to the wharf. The
*Polly Copinger* sat neatly in her berth. Hopefully,
Culpepper wouldn't have much difficulty in rounding
up the crew. At least, MacAllister told himself, Beaunell knew nothing about his ship. That was one little
piece of information she couldn't impart to Jessup.
They would be safe enough for the time being. But
feeling as though the hounds of hell were on his heels,
Sloan wanted to pull out of New Orleans. Soon.

The hour was late, the lights from the harbor fell
onto Savannah's face, lighting it to his tender gaze.
"We should be going below," he told her, touching her
arm in soothing little caresses. "We've done all we can
here. Culpepper has rounded up the crew and he plans

to sail on the next tide. Less than five hours from now. We'd better get some sleep."

"MacAllister, I keep thinking that it was all for nothing. All of it. I would have been more help to Osceola if I'd stayed with my people and cared for the wounded. Nothing. All for nothing."

"That's not true," Sloan scolded. "You did everything you could, all anyone could. All of the information you gathered was valuable; it was my own blundering that made it impossible for me to deliver it to Osceola." His fist hit the rail with such force that Savannah winced.

Tender emotions rushed within her. No, she corrected herself, it was not all for nothing. If she had stayed behind with the Seminoles she would never have known who Thomas Jessup was. Never would have learned enough to find her father's family some day. There were things she learned about her mother that she never would have known. She would have spent the rest of her life wondering, missing a piece of herself.

Their cabin was softly lit by an oil lamp. Savannah changed into a silk shirt that MacAllister had left behind. She felt his eyes watching her, drinking her in. This was where she was meant to be, here with MacAllister, preparing for bed and the passion they would share. But tonight it would be different. Tonight they would solace one another and soothe their disappointment.

Sloan's arms reached out for her, drawing her close to stand between his knees. "You always wear one of my shirts; it pleases me."

Her hand ruffled his hair, liking the thickness and feeling the golden strands slip through her fingers. Even if he didn't say it, she was his woman. Only his.

Arms wrapped around her hips, he pressed his face against the flatness of her belly. He held her this way for a moment before pulling her down on the bed beside him. His lips made delightful excursions along her jaw, down over her throat to his favorite place between her breasts.

Savannah yielded to him, offering herself, anticipating the pleasure he would bring her. Pleasure that would help to heal the sorrow, pleasure that would make her forget, for a little while, at least, her fears.

Sloan had told her that they were going to Florida. Back among the Seminoles. Together. At last, she told herself, as his hands found the smoothness of her thighs and the center of her desires, she would be with MacAllister and together they would build a chikkee.

# Chapter Nine

It was the end of March; balmy breezes blew off the Gulf of Mexico across Osceola's land. The hardwood trees were green and in bud. Spring had touched the earth and new life was born. Young fox pups nuzzled their mothers' bellies in hungry anticipation; birds were busily finding food for their nestlings, and wild flowers praised the sun with their radiant colors.

The *Polly Copinger* had made anchor at the mouth of a secondary river which emptied into the Gulf, far enough north of the Fort Dade area to remain undiscovered by the army.

Making contact with a band of blacks who had been instructed to be on the lookout for the *Polly*, Sloan and Savannah were led to a temporary camp inland, grateful that the crew could remain aboard with Culpepper. Each negro would carry a crate of rifles on his strong back.

Savannah quickly re-adapted to the rigors of the forest and made the day's walk easily. It was just approaching nightfall when they entered the Seminole camp.

There was much embracing from Osceola and many words passed across the camp fire. "What went wrong?" Osceola demanded.

"General Jessup is not a man of his word. I tried to reach you earlier when I sailed here and could not get near the shore line. The Creeks and Jessup's men were patrolling every strip of beach. I was forced to return to New Orleans. I have brought three hundred Hall rifles with me. A promise of two thousand more will arrive by the end of May, the latest the first week in June. You and the other chiefs signed a false document. By now, you must know this. Jessup was behind it, as you might have guessed. Bring me up to date; tell me what has been going on. How can we help?"

Osceola pondered Sloan's questions for several moments before he answered. "Only to you, my brother, would I admit my worry. My nation, my people, are losing strength. My best warriors are the blacks, and soon they will walk from me. They think for themselves. I am proud of my black brothers. There is an ugly rumor that Coa Hadjo, a chief who has many under him and makes his camps to the south of us near Lake Okeechobee, has been parleying with General Jessup. Just yesterday, word came to me that a band of blacks defied Coa Hadjo to send them back to the whites. They said Coa Hadjo had not captured them, so it was not up to him to return them. I am inclined to believe the story. We are now a divided people, and one does not know who speaks true words and who speaks false words. I, myself, had sharp words to say to Coa Hadjo last week in council. He wanted the runaways returned. I spoke out in anger against this change in policy. As long as I am in the nation, it will never be done. What more can I say, brother?"

"It is my intention to train your men with the new rifle, to show them the discipline they need to fight the white man. Without discipline and organization you cannot hope for victory. Our success will depend largely on your men's cooperation. I'll start with your lieutenants and they can train others. Jessup will bring all of this to a head by late summer. Your people must be ready." He quickly recounted his and Savannah's time spent in New Orleans. "We wouldn't be here now if it wasn't for Savannah. She feels, my brother, that she was of little help to you. She wanted to return tall and proud for your eyes. A kind word, perhaps, by you would not go unnoticed."

"It will be done. I am grateful to both of you. Your foodstuffs are almost gone, but we will survive. And if we are to die as the great God in the sky predicts then our spirits will live on. You, brother, are in danger as long as you stay with us. An unauthorized white man caught in these parts is dead. You will have to dress as one of us. Your ship, the *Polly Copinger*, where is it? I worry for your safety, brother."

"Don't. I've heard this all before from a friend in Galveston. I assure you, brother, I have long before this weighed the odds. I am an American. A white man. But I cannot live with the trickery and deceit I see being staged here. I don't think of my actions as treason. I am merely attempting to even the odds, if only in a small way. If most Americans understood what was being done to the Seminoles, they would not find me guilty. Enough said." The gravity in Sloan's voice subsided and in a lighter tone he added, "As for the *Polly*, she's in a deepwater inlet with a sharp-eyed sea salt who will shoot at the first sign of trouble. My crew is well paid and will do as ordered. Our mother's namesake will not sink to bottom, and she may be just the vessel to get us out of a tight spot."

"One day I must see this ship you named after our mother." A smile played around the corners of his mouth as he stared into the flames, remembering long ago days when he grew under his mother's watchful eye.

The silence was not uncomfortable. When Osceola spoke again, it was in a gentle tone. "And the girl, has she come to mean something to you? You will make a chikkee when the time is right or has this been done?"

Sloan laughed. Right to the core. "You always did want to know the answer before the question was asked. Yes," was all he said.

Amusement glittered in the coal black eyes. "You tamed the wildcat!"

"More like she tamed me," Sloan grinned.

"The hour grows late, brother. I'll dispatch a runner

to have my lieutenants here by first light. We will talk again tomorrow. My children were promised a story before sleep, and they wait for me. What do you think, Sloan, should this story be about two brothers who grew only to love one another more?"

"If I had such lovely daughters as you do, it is the story I would tell them. Sleep well, brother. Tomorrow is the start of a new day. For all of us. We'll work together to build something no man can take from you." Both men stood at the same time. Jet black eyes stared deeply into silvery gray ones. Simultaneously, their arms reached out, and each touched the other's shoulders gently. It was right that they were united again.

Sloan was tired and he went in search of Savannah. She stood at a distance talking quietly to one of the women. When she noticed Sloan, she moved toward him. He noticed in the flickering light of the fire that she had shed her silk dress and donned a sky blue cotton skirt with yellow overblouse. A gift, she told him later, from Morning Dew, for what she had tried to do for her husband. Sloan watched her as she spread the blankets in a secluded spot near the fire, but far enough away to afford them some privacy.

Mico had night guard. When he saw Savannah spread the blankets, his teeth clamped shut. His dark eyes swallowed the two forms as Sloan took Savannah in his arms.

For two weeks Sloan drilled Osceola's men till they pleaded with their chief for mercy. Osceola turned a deaf ear to all such pleadings, calling his braves sick women. "My brother wants only to secure your life and the lives of our women and children. Any further mewlings will be punished." Dark eyes snapped and crackled as the young lieutenants loaded, aimed and fired. Again and again, they worked with the new Hall rifle till their shoulders ached with the strain.

One day Sloan announced that the men were ready

and he promised an exhibition for Osceola and the rest
of the camp. The braves donned their war paint and
their best dress.

Osceola sat crosslegged near his chikkee. Both little
girls sat next to him, their mother behind. "You must
be the one to order your lieutenants to train the others
as they have been trained. If they don't follow proce-
dure and work the men mercilessly, it will be for
naught. Now that they have mastered the art, they must
continue the way I've trained them. It is not my place to
issue orders."

"It will be done. I see the confidence, the exuber-
ance, that you have instilled in them, shine from their
eyes. They are proud men, my braves, and I can count
on each of them. We will have no problem. Rest easy,
brother."

"They can shoot better than any front line army
soldier, Osceola. Discipline was all that was needed.
I'm only glad I could make this deal for the guns."

"You have done much for our people. It will never be
forgotten."

The exhibition lasted well over two hours. The
braves lined up, shot at targets for starters. Then they
fired in unison at another target. Each time Sloan
raised his arm or lowered it, they would crouch and
shoot or run and aim and then fire. They were expert at
dropping to the ground, rolling to the right, and firing,
and then rolling to the left to reload. They never fired
from the same position twice. At the end of the
exhibition the braves lined up, their guns at attention.
They waited. Sloan stood and then walked in front of
the men the way an inspecting general might do. To
each he had a personal word. To Mico, the last in line,
he said quietly, "You are by far the best shot in this
camp. I'm proud of you." Jet black eyes revealed
nothing as Mico returned his level gaze.

Sloan turned to the camp. "Completely acceptable!"
he shouted. There were whistles and shouts of approval
from the camp.

Osceola himself stood, one of his small daughters perched on his shoulder. "You have made me proud this day. We owe my brother thanks. Thanks that can never be paid by words alone. He is truly your brother from this day on." A wicked grin stretched across his generous mouth. "Dismissed!" he shouted loudly. Aside, he whispered to Sloan, "Did I do that right?"

Sloan matched his grin. "Better than any general could have done."

Osceola sat near the council fire, listening, holding his tongue, until it was time for him to speak. His rage burned inside him, making the flickering flames from the fire cool by comparison. When would it be his turn to speak? To turn the heads of his brothers to face in one direction? Sloan, sitting behind his brother, could sense the Indian's outrage and admired his control in keeping his tongue until his time came. Sam Jones, Arpeika, sat across the fire from Osceola, his hooded, ancient eyes never leaving the tormented chief's face.

Osceola brooded, furious with what he was hearing. Micanopy, Holacoochee, Alligator, Jumper . . . all voiced their intention to assemble at the detention center at Tampa Bay with their people to ready themselves for the trip westward aboard the ships the Government was to supply. And in so doing, they were surrendering the negroes taken during the war, delivering them to the commanding officers of the posts on the St. Johns.

Already Sloan and Osceola had witnessed the hardships imposed on their black brothers. None of them willingly accompanied the Seminole chiefs to the stations on the St. Johns River. Being warriors, they resisted. When at last they were overcome by their Indian brothers, they were brought in bound and tethered. Never, Osceola told himself, did he ever expect to live to see the day when the Seminole would betray the negro. Yet, it had come. Perhaps he had lived too long.

The time had come, he told himself, when he must assert himself again and seize control. Over at Fort Mellon, Coa Hadjo, King Phillip and Coacoochee had already turned in their negroes.

Prior to the council, during which each thlacko would have his turn to speak, Arpeika and Osceola had discussed the expected outcome. Both were puzzled and aggrieved as to what should be their next move. The idea of turning in runaway slaves was inconceivable, even worse than any agreement about going west. Now they were being isolated from the rest of the Seminole Nation.

"We have one choice," Osceola had told the old medicine man. "Phillip and Coacoochee have gone to Fort Mellon. I think they will agree with us to resist the whites. They can't come out to join us without causing a great deal of trouble, but *we can go in* to join them!"

When Micanopy finished speaking, encouraging his equals to put an end to this war, it was at last Osceola's turn to speak. So involved was he with his own thoughts that Sloan had to prod a finger into his brother's back to remind him. Standing before the council fire, Osceola lifted his voice, bringing strength into its timbre, placing the facts before the War Council.

Savannah, sitting among the women, listened with rapt attention, hated tears springing to her eyes at the emotion her chief brought to his words.

"We are brothers together here in the Floridas beneath the watchful eyes of the Great Spirits. We are brothers to the blacks who have been our friends and have served us well. It is to profane the eyes of the Spirits to turn the blacks over to the white soldiers who will give our brothers back to the slavers." Here Osceola reminded the chiefs of how many Seminoles had taken black women in marriage and of the children whose blood was Seminole and negro mixed. "Phillip and Coa Hadjo have committed themselves to turning in the blacks. It is because *we* were not strong enough to unite and give strength to their decisions. But if we group at Fort Mellon and go in to join them, I know they will fight beside us." For nearly two hours Osceola spoke, recounting past victories and past defeats, returning always to the belief that by displaying unity King Phillip and Coa Hadjo would reverse their decision to surrender.

Hope was reborn amidst the council. Osceola had said the words they wanted to hear. Instead of living with defeat, the Seminole might claim victory for his own.

Sloan was overcome with emotion and pride. Glancing past the now low-burning fire, his eyes met with Savannah's and he saw her smile. Arpeika nodded his dirty gray head and he thumped his breast with a gnarled, old hand. The Seminole would be men again. They would release the prisoners from the detention center. He had heard rumors that the nation of Seminoles would be loaded and crammed into the twenty-six ships waiting in Tampa Bay and drowned at sea before reaching Texas en route to the Arkansas Territory.

Why, why, Arpeika asked himself, wouldn't the white-eyes allow the Indian and their allies to go south where the land was swamp and the game was plentiful? There, living on land that no one else would ever want, they could live in peace. The land called the Everglades would provide subsistence for his people. Shaking his head with sorrow, Arpeika thought that he was getting much too old to lead Mikasukis, warriors, into battle. His weary gray head filled more and more with thoughts of peaceful hunting and fishing instead of the fiercesome war cry of his braves.

Following Osceola's orders, Sloan had stayed behind to lead the Indians when the thlacko sent for them. Together with Arpeika, Osceola arrived at Fort Mellon and reported to Lieutenant William Harney, telling him they were prepared to emigrate.

Osceola was thin and weary, another recent bout of malaria had laid him low and his spirits were sagging, but he was determined to follow the plan. He would release his people from the white soldiers or he would die trying. Standing tall, displaying strength and conviction, he reported to Lieutenant Harney that more than twenty-five hundred Seminoles were expected to arrive at Fort Mellon shortly.

News traveled quickly to General Jessup, and he prepared to journey to Fort Mellon, at last to witness the infamous Osceola's defeat. Jessup had been irritated by the outbreak of measles in the detention camp further south at Tampa Bay. The Indians were frightened, rumors of small pox were reported, further delaying the emigration.

Osceola was prepared for the visit from his esteemed enemy, General Jessup. The day was warm, too warm for late May, and his leggings of scarlet and decorated turban felt hot and clinging.

Demonstrating his annoyance over the slow progress of the Seminoles into the detention camp, Jessup unceremoniously strode up to the waiting chief; his complexion was flushed with anger. "Osceola," he began perfunctorily, his antipathy for the Indian bringing his mouth down into a scowl, "your people are delaying in assembling at Tampa Bay!"

Although Osceola understood and spoke perfect English, his dark, haunted eyes swung to the Indian interpreter Jessup had brought with him.

Answering the interpreter, he said, "My people are fearful of the white man's disease, small pox. Is it necessary to kill them even before they leave on the boats the army provides? Is not their sorrow heavy enough because they must leave this land they have called home long before the white man came with his rifles and hatred?"

Jessup sputtered when he listened to the interpreter's message. "You tell this savage I'll brook no more delays!" he roared. "Tell him that I intend to send exploring parties to every part of the country throughout the summer, and that I shall take all negroes who belong to the white people. Tell him to be careful not to allow Indians to mix with the runaways because they'll be taken also." Pausing for a moment, Jessup's small, shifty eyes glittered with frustration. "And tell this savage that I am sending to Cuba for bloodhounds to trail his people, and I intend to hang every one of them who does not come in of his own volition!"

Osceola listened to the interpreter with his full and solemn attention. He had understood the general implicitly. He also understood, to his amusement, that General Jessup was almost at the end of his rope. He wanted this war done with, and he expected to step out of it with full honors. If only the Seminoles wouldn't keep delaying the outcome. Osceola suppressed a smile. He could almost smell the general's desperation oozing out of his pores.

Osceola and Arpeika had left for Fort Mellon, and by this time would have made contact with Coa Hadjo and King Phillip who had defected from the Seminole viewpoint to accede to the demands of the government. Sloan knew Osceola would not be able to convince his fellow chiefs of the wisdom to resist the army's demands without many long nights before the council fire. Once having committed themselves publicly to turn over the blacks under them and to migrate to Arkansas, it would appear to be a loss of face to withdraw from the treaty.

Most of Sloan's time was spent with Osceola's lieutenants training the warriors in the use of the rifle. Mendoza's shipment had arrived from Cuba, and the weapons were being dispensed. Now would be the most difficult assignment; waiting for the signal from Osceola to take action to free those Indians and blacks who had followed their chiefs into the army's hands.

MacAllister was anxious to make the move, to set into action the training he had provided, to share in the success the Seminoles so desperately needed. He knew that until now Jessup had been raiding the Indians mostly for a show of strength to force them into agreeing to the Dade Treaty. The man had his public image to protect. Knowing the general as he did, Sloan felt Jessup wouldn't satisfy himself with moving the Indians and returning the blacks to the slave market. He was out for much bigger game; the annihilation of the Seminoles, and if it couldn't be accomplished here in Florida, then it would be done in Arkansas where he could also destroy the Creek nation. It was Sloan's opinion that Jessup would wait until he had migrated the Florida Indians; it would be a matter of two birds with one stone. Both the Seminole and the Creek would fall under the concentrated blows of his Army.

In the hours before dawn, long after the council fire had burned low, Arpeika and Osceola sat beneath a willow tree on the shore of Lake Munroe and watched the fish snap at hovering insects. The Indians had been given the freedom of the area because it was realized that it was impossible to confine the Seminoles behind the stockade fences. The chiefs would not wander far, the Army reasoned, not with their people being held hostage at the fort. The two men sat in silence, each intent on his own thoughts. It had been many days since turning themselves into the fort to make contact with King Phillip and Coa Hadjo, but tonight had been their reward. At last, the two chiefs had capitulated and agreed to join forces with Osceola and resist the migration.

A bugle sounded from the fort to signal reveille, and Osceola felt a stirring of excitement as he always did before a battle. All that needed to be done was to decide when Sloan should organize the attack.

"So, the great thlacko closes his eyes in sleep," Arpeika taunted, spitting into the still, black waters of the lake.

"Not sleep," Osceola defended, "I dream."

"Yes, with one eye open, like the alligator stalking

the bird. Tell me your dream," the cantankerous old man grunted.

"I dream that this time tomorrow night I take my warriors to Tampa Bay." Osceola voiced his intention to send Sloan the signal for the next night. "When all are asleep, we free Micanopy and our people. A word to Coacoochee and his people scatter also. I dream that Micanopy, a traitor to his people, will no longer be a chief. I dream there will be a new chief, elected to lead all the Seminoles under one heart, one brain."

"Phillip?" Arpeika growled, spitting again to show his disapproval.

"No, not Phillip. This great chief must be a great warrior with great wisdom. He must be a Mikasuki. His name is Arpeika."

"Hieah," the old warrior-medicine man grunted. "If the Spirits allow me to live so long. And what of yourself? You are younger, stronger. You should be chief of all the Seminole."

"Not I, old man. I have another dream. It is as you once told me. I do not die here on Seminole land. I do not die in Arkansas beyond the Great River. But I die."

Arpeika was silent, listening to the chirping of crickets in the tall grasses. What Osceola said was true. He had read it in the signs and in the sand. Only his own stubbornness prevented him from laying a comforting arm on the younger man's shoulder.

Sloan watched the women of the camp through narrowed eyes as they gathered together their few belongings. It was a hard life at best. They were always moving, always on the run just to stay alive. How hungry they looked. But how proud as they herded their children near them. They would move as often as necessary, go hungry as often as necessary. They were used to this gypsy life that Sloan hated.

He dreaded the forthcoming scene with Savannah

more than he would admit. What was he going to say to her to make the parting easier? Of late, the words failed to sail past his lips. He found himself thinking more and speaking less. Events were moving too fast for him to comprehend what was happening. The day Culpepper was dragged into camp by three blacks, screaming that he was Osceola's uncle, would be a day he would never forget. By the time Sloan had the sea salt's bonds cut, he knew that Maeve was closing in for the big wedding, and Culpepper had gotten away by the skin of his teeth. He was demanding to fight alongside Sloan for something he had believed in thanks to Sloan and all of his brothers. "If it's me time, Laddie, I want to go to me Maker doing something I believe in. And I do believe in your cause. So, hand me a rifle and I'll be next to ye fer whatever good I'll be."

Sloan was delighted with the old man. He proved himself invaluable as they set about storing what provisions he had brought along with the two thousand rifles. "The price was high, Laddie. Yer man charged $35,000. I paid up as ye said without a word."

"There is no price on life, Enwright," Sloan said using the captain's Christian name to show he was serious. "For my brother's life and the lives of his people, it is a cheap price. The dozen horses will save our lives. Don't tell me where you got them, I don't want to know."

"Ye wouldn't be believing me anyway. They were a wedding present from Maeve. I just took them and skedaddled," he said sourly. "Appaloosas," he said proudly.

"Christ!" was all Sloan could say. "Enwright, you have style. There aren't many men who would do what you did. I'm proud of you," he said, slapping the old man on the back. Culpepper grinned sheepishly as he set about carrying rifles into the forest.

Inside of an hour the camp was dismantled. The women were ready for their long journey. Something tugged at Sloan. How alone Savannah looked, how frightened. He hated good-bye's of any kind, but this was unlike anything he had ever felt before. He walked over to her slowly. Gently, he drew her close to him. "Go now. Make as much progress in daylight as you can. Take good care of the children. My brother and I are depending on you."

Tears gathered in Savannah's eyes. "Why can't I go with you? I know these forests better than you. I do not want to go with the women and play nursemaid to children. I want to be at your side."

"We've talked this over before, Savannah. Captain Culpepper said there is an outbreak of measles. We both know that the Indian cannot resist that disease. You must go deep into the forest. I gave you the map. Follow it the way I showed you and I'll join you as soon as possible."

Savannah wiped at her eyes with the back of her hand, but took her place behind Ina and Yahi. Sloan knew he had never seen anything sadder, more heart-breaking, in his life. A lump settled in his throat, making it hard to swallow. Culpepper patted him on the shoulder in a friendly manner. Together they joined the others and headed in the opposite direction. There was nothing more he could do.

All two hundred of the men assigned to Sloan by Osceola filed into the dense forest. Sloan and Culpepper were the last to leave the camp. Sloan cast a long, angry look around before he turned to Culpepper. Just then, a Seminole runner appeared. Sloan waited as he spat out his information. "It is said General Jessup is considering unleashing bloodhounds from Cuba if the holdouts continue. Those Indians in the detention camp would be hanged if the delay continues." Sloan considered the statement.

"Let it be known that the Indians are on the way. When stomachs are empty, moccasins move slowly." The runner departed, not liking the message he would let filter back to one General Jessup.

The trek to join Osceola was a long and arduous one.

Only Culpepper lagged at times. Feeling sorry for the
sea captain, Sloan ordered him atop one of the Appaloosas. Culpepper protested bitterly at this undignified
betrayal on Sloan's part, saying he felt like a woman.

"I'm concerned with your lame leg. I want you in
fighting condition when we join Osceola." Culpepper
grimaced, relieved secretly that he could ride and see
over the heads of the Indians and the blacks.

The moon rode high in the heavens, majestic in its
shimmering brightness, when Sloan reached the rendezvous point. His men settled themselves comfortably
to await their chief. Tampa Bay was but a stone's throw
from where they were quartered.

Osceola was the first to arrive. Within minutes the
men behind him joined Sloan's men. Whispered words
passed in the stillness of the forest surrounding them.

"Mico, Yahoola, Culpepper, come with me." Seeing
that his brother was about to object, Sloan spoke to
him in English. "No, I will go. If something should
happen to me, you will be safe. Your people need you.
I am expendable. We go only to survey the guards and
the garrison. Have no fear, brother, I have become
attached to my skin. I have no wish to die in Tampa
Bay. I plan to live to a ripe old age with many
grandchildren at my feet. How do you think they would
like it if the story I tell them does not include some
foolhardy bravery." Without another word he fell in
behind Mico; Yahoola and Culpepper at his heels.

An hour later they returned to the temporary camp.
It was to Osceola that Sloan addressed himself. "A
mounted company and more than a hundred Creeks
surround the camp. The number is closer to one
hundred fifty. We can outnumber them and overtake
them without too much trouble." Osceola nodded to
show that he would agree to anything Sloan said. In the
bright moonlight Sloan broke off a stout branch and
proceeded to draw a rough map, in the loamy earth, of
the detention camp. Osceola's lieutenants were given

their positions. There were nods; no words spoken among the assembled men.

Sloan raised his arm and the men broke apart, their moccasins making no sound as they surrounded the camp.

It was a silent, bloody battle. The Creeks, angry at their white employers because of abuse to their families by the whites in Alabama, had no desire to fight to the death and the expertise of Osceola's warriors quickly overpowered them. They fled into the bay, wading out into the water. When Osceola raised his arm high overhead fifty minutes later to show the battle was over, Sloan dropped to the ground. He had taken a bullet alongside his neck that stunned him. Next to him, he saw Mico with a vicious chest wound. His head reeled and then he knew no more.

Osceola strode into the detention camp and searched the long, barrackslike room for Micanopy. He was disgusted with the looks of the fat chief. Evidently, he had been fed well with white man's rations. Anger that he had slept through the attack further disgusted him. Osceola yanked on his plump leg. Micanopy sat up, snorting and bellowing, and was pulled into the dim lights at the far end of the room. "As you can see, we have you surrounded. You will come with us."

"I cannot go with you. I promised, gave my word to go west," Micanopy protested fearfully.

Hatred fanned Arpeika's features. "Either you come or you die."

"Then kill me now," Micanopy blustered.

"Put the old fool on a horse," Arpeika snarled, turning to the warriors behind him. "He'll change his mind tomorrow."

Osceola let his eyes go to Alligator and Jumper. His gaze locked with Jumper's. "Where's your horse?"

"I sold it," Jumper bleated.

"Then you walk. We'll talk later."

"I only obeyed Micanopy," he said fearfully.

"Later. I said we would talk later," Osceola said sharply, dismissing the whining Jumper from his thoughts. He must find his brother. Spotting Culpepper, he raced toward him. "My brother? Have you seen him?" Culpepper was astounded at the dread he saw in the Indian's eyes. Dread and concern that something had happened to Sloan.

Culpepper forced a jovial note into his tone. "He took a bullet alongside the neck, but he'll live. I meself treated the lad and he's resting easy over there out of sight. Your men are making litters for the wounded. We only have three dead and seventeen wounded. Mico is among them and even with expert doctoring, he will not live. There is hope for the others." The relief in Osceola's jet eyes made Culpepper feel good. He wished he had a brother, someone to share feelings with, someone to care if he lived or died. Sloan was the closest thing to a son he had ever had. His hand had shook when he tended the wound and then it had gentled more than any woman's hand. He loved this strange breed of man who fought an Indian battle alongside an Indian he called brother.

Sloan sat with his back to a gnarled, deformed sea-grape tree. His grin was lopsided as he stared up at Osceola. "On many occasions you have made me proud to call you brother," Osceola said softly. "Today you have made me proud once more. I am only sorry that you were wounded." He dropped to his knees, his face within inches of Sloan's. "There are no words in your language or mine to convey my deep feeling for you and what you have been doing for my people. Sloan," his voice rose slightly, "did I tell you that my people have bestowed a title upon you. It is truly an honor, one to tell those grandchildren some day. They call you the Swamp Fox. Truly you are."

Sloan heard the words, but the only thing he locked in on was Osceola's use of his Christian name. It warmed him greatly and his pain seemed to ease. He smiled weakly. "Now when I tell that story when I'm old and gray, I can add a little blood, embellish my wounds and add my title. I shall hold them spell-bound."

Osceola laughed, a deep, rich sound. "I trust you will make the story brilliant with your golden tongue. I must bid you farewell now."

Sloan hated to see his brother leave, but he knew there was no other way. His people needed him. "Brother," he said softly, "I plan to take our mother's namesake to Galveston as soon as Culpepper thinks we can travel. I'll bring back what supplies I can. I'll do my best to fill the *Polly's* hold. Horses, foodstuffs, mules and some trinkets for the children."

Osceola's voice was suddenly shy. "I would like to make a very large request of my brother. Would it be possible for you to buy presents that would be seemly to give my family. I know nothing of such things, but I did see Morning Dew's eyes brighten over Chala's dress and the adornment she had around her neck. Something beautiful."

Whatever it was that burned his eyes moments ago had come back making it almost impossible to see. "I think I can arrange that for you. Culpepper has exqui-site taste when it comes to women." He held out his hand and Osceola's shot out to grip it. His clasp was firm and hard. "I think our mother would be proud of both of us this day," Sloan said softly.

"You only think," Osceola smiled. "I know she would. Good luck, Sloan." Before Sloan could reply, Osceola was off and running into the forest to join his men.

The women and children followed their chief's or-ders, breaking into camps of small numbers to await their men in the forest. Many more women with their children in tow were beginning to drift in after being released from the detention camp at Tampa Bay. This, Savannah told herself, was proof that Osceola's and MacAllister's raid on the camp had been successful.

The newly arrived women talked of guns being fired and some wounded. Many soldiers, they told the eager ears, were killed, falling down dead in their tracks. They elaborated on the strength and bravery of their own warriors, but their eyes were pained and anxious. Would it be their own men who were being killed? And what of the men, lying wounded in this dampness that seemed to make injuries fester and suppurate? Even the strongest medicine sometimes failed.

Savannah realized Osceola's wisdom in ordering that the women were not to gather in a single large encampment. It would have been too easy for the soldiers to capture them. This way, while some may be captured, many more would find the opportunity to escape.

Che-cho-ter and Ina, along with the children, were camped to the north, awaiting word of their husband and father, Osceola. Only Yahi, the widow woman she had battled for the privilege of whipping MacAllister, elected to come with Savannah here to the camp closest to Tampa Bay. It seemed a lifetime ago that Savannah had first set eyes on MacAllister, and she dreaded that it might be still another lifetime until she saw him again.

Stoic and silent, except for a small group chanting prayers in unison, their light voices lifting softly to the tree tops, the women went about preparing medicines and putting children to bed. Secunna, a white-haired old woman, whom many believed talked with the Spirits, padded around the camp on her moccasined feet, shaking a string of bones and chanting in her aged voice to keep the bad spirits away from the camp.

Because this camp was closest to the fighting, the wounded and dead would be brought here. Silently, Savannah prayed a mixture of prayers learned from the Seminole and taught by her mother. Feverishly, her eyes pierced the darkness beyond the torches for signs of the first runner.

Since having returned to Florida with MacAllister nearly two moons . . . eight weeks ago, she corrected, they had not been apart for a single day or night. Now she was bereft without him. This was long past the time of night when they would be asleep in their chik-kee, the thick, thatch walls separating them, isolating them from everyone and every thing. There, together, they would renew the wonder they had found in one another, touching, kissing. . . . She was his woman. MacAllister's woman. And when passion was reborn with an urgency of its own, they would satisfy it, feed it, nurture it like the Spirits fed the fish in the streams and the birds in the woods, with a loving touch. The words he would whisper in her ear were soft, appealing, and could excite her beyond the plains of the earth to a place behind the moon where nothing else existed, only the two of them. He would tell her how beautiful he thought her, how soft to his touch, how exciting . . . "Please, please," she stared upward to the heavens where MacAllister's God looked down, "please bring him back to me!"

She saw her fears reflected in the eyes of every woman who had a loved one, husband or son, out there beyond the darkness at Tampa Bay. Tonight could be the turning point of the war. Tonight the Seminole must put the white soldier down and make his voice heard above the tallest trees in the forest. Tonight. Tonight.

Every moment they had shared together became most precious to her. The days when she had watched him drill Osceola's lieutenants, the nights when he would fall exhausted onto their pallet, but never too exhausted to take her in his arms and crush her against his chest and hold her until she fell asleep. The afternoons at the river where they would bathe, wash-ing one another with gentle, exploring fingers and never seemed to tire of one another. Afternoons when the sun would beat down upon them, warming their skin, stirring their blood. Closing her eyes, she could see him, water glistening on his magnificent body, the sun lighting his hair to a shade between silver and gold. And his eyes, always his eyes, flinty gray, deepening to ash when he looked at her, wanting her, smoldering embers burning in their depths.

"Please . . . please . . ." she prayed.

The night was hushed, crackling with expectancy. Most of the children seemed to be asleep; only the women sat waiting, eyes peering the darkness, ears anxiously awaiting their men's return.

Beyond the rim of light from the camp were sounds, running feet, panting breaths. Savannah steeled herself. This was not the sound of soldiers' approach. This was too quiet, too expert. She braced herself, hand reaching out, feeling the rough bark of the southern pine under her palm. "Please . . . please . . ." seemed to sound with every heart beat.

Chakika, a young brave of seventeen summers, led the forward movement. His face dripped with perspiration from his long run, but his eyes were glowing with victory. The women converged on the youth demanding answers to their questions. Only Savannah held back, waiting news of the Swamp Fox.

Speaking rapidly, Chakika recounted the events of the night, reporting many wounded. Unable to give them news of their men, the women asked about their chief. "Thlacko Osceola is well. I saw this with my own eyes. He is going ahead to the camp where Che-cho-ter and Ina await him. Arpeika is also safe and well. He joins our chief to plan the next move." Chakika was full of news, reporting the escape from the detention camp. Suddenly, he was silent, feeling Savannah's eyes boring into his back. The youth turned, meeting her eyes levelly, "I have no news of Swamp Fox. The last I saw him he was with Mico and Yahoola. The old uncle, Culpepper, was with him also. I know no more of him."

Breath strangled in Savannah's throat. Please . . . please . . .

As she had expected, the wounded were brought into this camp, it being closer than the others. Her eyes searched for the bright head of MacAllister as she went about her duties of fetching water and binding injuries.

Every woman whose man had not yet returned watched the edge of the darkness, eyes straining, searching faces and asking the returning warriors of news of their men. Secunna visited each wounded, laying her gnarled, old hands upon their heads, chanting medicine words and peering with clinical interest at their various wounds, clicking her tongue and issuing orders for their treatment.

The night air was filled with the joyous sounds of reunions and the piercing shrill cries of grief. Savannah stood helplessly by as a woman she was working with heard news of her husband's death. Raising her fists to the sky, the woman called her husband's name, the sound stabbing icy fingers into the heart of every woman whose husband had not yet returned.

Savannah attended her duties, still listening, still searching. Many more wounded were being brought in now. Faces she knew and recognized. Faces from her own village. Yet, she could not bring herself to ask about MacAllister, as if postponing the dreaded inevitable.

"Chala, Chala!" an anguished cry called her name. The sound was guttural like a drowning man beneath the water. She turned, bracing herself. Mico!

Someone had already laid him upon a pallet and bound his chest with strips of cloth. The blood was seeping through the bandages, trickling down his side onto the blankets. The light from the fire illuminated his strong, hawklike features, and he was pale, dark shadows forming beneath his eyes.

She went to him, going down on her knees at his side, her tentative fingers reaching out to touch him. Death was upon him, taking his life in deep, greedy swallows. His breathing was labored, the excruciating pain he was experiencing evident in his ebony eyes.

Savannah took his hand, pressing it against her breast. This man whom she had known from childhood was dying. This man, whose woman she had once thought she would become, was leaving this world of sorrow to ride beyond the earth on the wings of the Spirits. Deep loss and grief filled her for an old friend.

"Chala," he breathed, contented now that she was beside him, a costly smile turning up the corners of his mouth as he lifted a trembling hand to touch her honeyed curls.

"Mico," she whispered, "you must not talk, you must save your strength."

"Women, always telling a dying man to save his strength. Always wanting the last word, never allowing a man to speak his heart."

Savannah was quiet, waiting for him to catch his breath. The hand she held in her own momentarily tightened as a wave of pain engulfed him. She must not cry, she told herself. For once she must be the stoic Seminole woman Mico expected her to be.

"I have wanted to build a chikkee with you, Chala, to claim you for my own . . ." his eyes closed with the effort of speaking through his vale of pain. "I was not quick enough . . . I waited . . . too long. When MacAllister took you . . . I wanted to kill him, feel my knife plunge between his ribs . . ."

Mico's head fell back in exhaustion, but his eyes flickered open again, determined to speak his heart. "My thoughts have always been with you, Chala. Even though you sailed the great sea with the white man, I knew you would return." A sob erupted in Savannah's throat. This man was telling her he loved her, something pride would never allow him to say until now.

"I hated MacAllister. I was wrong. He was a brave man, true to his brother. And when I saw him fall beneath the soldier's bullet, I knew how wrong I had been to be jealous of the love you found in his chikkee." Mico winced with pain, his back arching up from the pallet.

What was he saying? MacAllister fall? Dead? No, no!

"Chala," Mico breathed, the sound softer than the owl's wing beating the air. He tried to raise himself, to touch her. Savannah leaned closer, taking his head into her arms, holding him, comforting him, her heart breaking. She must think of Mico now, make his last moments peaceful. There would be time to cry later. Pressing her lips against his brow, a tear fell down onto his face.

An eternity later, someone took Mico out of her arms, leading her away. There was no feeling, no tears. Without MacAllister there was no life.

The "abduction," as General Jessup preferred to call the escape from the detention camp, brought his peace plans crashing down, and with them his quest for glory. Fiercefully bitter, the general blamed various factors: the Creek spies who were supposed to give warning; Captain Graham who had been in charge of the detention camp; and the greedy slaveholders who had pressed too hard for the return of their property. In contrast, antislavery advocates blamed Jessup himself. Had he scrupulously adhered to the agreements in the March 6 Treaty and not gone back on his word concerning the runaway slaves, there would have been no foray at the Tampa Bay detention camp.

The impact of the "abduction" on General Jessup was inescapable. At first, he was thrown into a deep depression. "This campaign for the Indian migration," he wrote the Adjutant General, "has entirely failed." Now the only way to eliminate the Seminoles from Florida was to exterminate them. Knowing the stain such an action would leave on his record, he had to abandon this plan.

Ever since learning of Savannah's duplicity, the general had little heart for campaigning. It was as though he had lost his precious sister for a second time. That Savannah could have been raised among those savages seemed entirely implausible until, after leaving Miss Gentry at the depot and rushing home, he had found Savannah gone. Throughout the day he had waited for her, dispatching his officers to comb the city

for her. She had escaped, disappeared without a trace,
and he had no word of her since.

Jessup had been personally wounded by the Indians.
First, his sister and then his niece. Growing more and
more cynical by the day, he was willing to employ
treachery to carry out his orders to quell the Seminole,
despite the sour press he was receiving in the tabloids.

He had no confidence whatsoever in the promises
made by the Seminoles, and he felt little compunction
about violating his promises to them. The war was
entering a new phase where all was fair, and winning
was its own reward.

His new strategy in this campaign was one that he
had the most confidence in: divide and conquer. His
first effort was to split the milder Alachua bands away
from the Seminole nation. He would promise the
Alachua that if they fought against the others, he would
secure permission for them to remain in Florida. The
policy worked poorly. If a few Alachuas came over to
the white cause, it only stiffened the resistance of the
Seminoles. Micanopy was degraded and Arpeika became chief of all the Seminoles, fulfilling Osceola's
dream. The scrawny, old warmonger and his warriors
fought with renewed vigor, successfully eluding capture.

The divide and conquer plan could still work, Jessup
told his officers. Now they would try to separate the
blacks from the reds. What had given Jessup this idea
was the news that some of the runaway slaves were
slipping away from the Seminole and going back to the
plantations. It would do Jessup service for rumors of
privation and mistreatment to reach the ears of the
antislavists who had become the general's most severe
critics. No one seemed to consider that after twenty
months of hardship in combat only fifty of the black
fugitives from the St. Johns region decided to trade
freedom for food. Among them was John Phillip, a
slave of Chief Phillip.

Another reason for the black defeatism which the

general refused to consider was the great loss in their leadership, suffered when several of their outstanding men were taken into custody.

Jessup seized his chance. He put out offers of freedom and safety to blacks if they would leave the Seminole. More and more blacks took his offer and came in, most of them reported to be starving. The general knew he had no legal power to grant them the freedom he had promised, and those who could be proved to be the property of whites would be reclaimed as slaves.

This was exactly what the slaveholders wanted to hear; they were certain the blacks were better off in slavery than in any other condition. They propagated tales of extreme hardships and torture their blacks had suffered at the hands of the Seminoles.

General Jessup paced his sparsely appointed office. Tales of starvation were true for the scattered blacks who could not find their way back to Seminole camps. Damn! He pounded a heavy fist on his desk. Where were those savages getting their supplies? At first he had doubted the reports he had heard concerning a mystical man known among the Seminoles as the Swamp Fox, who was running supplies and foodstuffs in to the Seminole. And those blasted rifles! Where did the Indians get them? They were Cuban made, he knew, but what surprised him and his officers more was the fact that somewhere the Seminole had learned to use them! No longer did they fire off a volley and then whoop, missing their target with greater frequency than hitting it! Where had they learned? Who had taught them? Some of the blacks spoke of a golden-haired white man the Indians called Swamp Fox who was the benefactor of the Seminole. Who was he? Where did he come from? Did he actually exist?

Rubbing his hand over his chin, Jessup collapsed into his chair. With the Indians so well supplied, the army would need a new consignment of goods to see them through the forthcoming campaign. The list he was composing for these supplies lay beneath his hand. He scrutinized it, looking for something he had overlooked.

Dearborn wagons. Most important items were listed first. Valuable because they had large wheels and could travel through boggy swamps. They could even be used as boats when needed.

Horses, mules and wagons. Pack saddles, steamers for the rivers and hundreds of small hand tools. The general was even willing to try new firearms, such as Colt's revolvers and Cochran's repeater. Shotguns were needed for use by the light companies. More Mackinaw boats were useful, flat bottomed with a double set of oars, each capable of carrying twenty men.

Haversacks, wall tents, common tents, hospital tents, camp kettles, mess kits, canteens, axes, spades, hatchets, all must arrive in time. Large sheets of lumber, sheepskins for saddle blankets, halters, hobbles, wagon harnesses, whips, saddler's tools and several thousand horseshoes must be on hand for the mounted men. And of course, food.

Jessup smiled bleakly as he once again perused the letter he had received from the Secretary of War in Washington. The government would supply any and all requisitions made by Jessup if he would agree to delay the start of his operations until November. The summers were intolerable, the Secretary of War stated, and it would be impossible to gather a large supply of commissioned goods until that time.

Stuffing the list for commissioned supplies into an envelope and sealing it, he smiled wryly. That his list was complete, he was certain. Now it would be in the hands of the Secretary of War. His would be the most completely outfitted army in the history of the United States. Not even the Swamp Fox could boast bringing such supplies to the Indians!

# Chapter Ten

Arriving in Galveston, Sloan registered for himself and Culpepper at a hotel close to Annemarie's house. Both men treated themselves to long baths, close shaves and clean clothes. Sloan departed for Annemarie's, his intention to get the latest newspaper and devour it while drinking some of her best cognac.

Annemarie greeted him with open arms, all her aggravation over past encounters forgotten. She wanted details of Savannah's life in New Orleans, news of Rico Mendoza and Sloan's own adventures. "I want to know everything," she cried excitedly, "don't leave out a single detail."

Quickly, he filled Annemarie in on recent occurrences, expressing his hopes that he had had a hand in the turning point of the war between the Seminoles and the United States.

"How awful for Savannah to be separated from you. The poor child must be beside herself. You should have brought her back with you. She could have stayed with me. I know, I know, she feels she can be of some use to the Seminoles. But I also know, Sloan, that she considers herself a part of your world now. If it came to a choice, she would choose this side of the fence." Annemarie's certainty pleased Sloan. He knew the day was going to come when Savannah would be forced to a choice.

The newspaper Annemarie offered was read from front to back.

"What's this?" Sloan chortled gleefully. "Brevet

General Thomas Jessup has written Washington asking to be relieved of his command unless he was given full sanction and support by the government to deal with the Seminoles with expediency." Sloan's smile became a glower and his flinty gray eyes held shadows of disgust. "For a minute there I was hopeful. But any fool can see that Jessup is holding up the government by threatening to leave his command because he knows that assigning a new commander would only drag this business on indefinitely. If the government refuses Jessup's resignation, in essence Washington is giving its permission for Jessup to slaughter the Seminoles without regard to humanity or to policy." The news correspondent went on to say that in his own opinion Jessup had only one goal in mind: stop the war by stopping Osceola whose influence over the Seminoles was almost spiritual. While other chiefs were important, all were shadows compared to the determined Osceola.

"The correspondent is right you know, Annemarie. When I first went to Florida, Osceola was a chief of minor importance. True, he held a large section of Seminoles under him and he had gained some influence, but nothing like he has now. The fires of justice burn brightly in my brother; he seems to glow from within. I swear, there's something saintly about him and his people see it. He is the only one, aside from the old man, Arpeika, who has never turned his sights. The others, Phillip, Coa Hadjo, Micanopy and all the others have all vacillated. With my brother there is only one way. He demands justice for his people and he will fight until he has it."

Annemarie listened with rapt attention. "It would seem that same fire burns in you, Sloan MacAllister. I've never known a man more committed to an ideal. You've risked a lot to help the Seminole, and you're still risking your neck. Be careful, Sloan, from what you tell me of Jessup, he'll put the rope around your neck himself!"

"Truer words were never spoken, Anne. He's been thwarted one turn after another. He still can't claim any major success in this war and, God willing, he never will. I see here in the newspaper that Jessup describes the battle at the Tampa detention camp as a 'mere abduction.' No mention that we cleared the camp out and 'freed' the emigres."

Time dragged for Sloan while gathering supplies. It was most difficult. The United States Army was paying top dollar to supply the southern army and they bought in huge quantities, creating a shortage in the marketplace. Sloan and Culpepper rode up and down the coast, stopping at each town for a sack of this, a bag of that, a few pounds of something else. Annemarie and the girls in her employ did their share by helping to accumulate as much as they could. But it was not nearly the load Sloan and Culpepper had taken out on previous trips.

Word reached Sloan in early August that some of the Indians were arriving at some of the posts, particularly Fort King. Jessup, whose resignation Washington rejected as Sloan had expected, agreed to a conference with Coa Hadjo, Tuckose Emathla and Tuskeneho. It was also said that Osceola and Arpeika would send representatives but not attend themselves.

Several days after the conference Sloan read in a newspaper that Jessup had said he would never agree to recognizing Arpeika as chief, and that the general was extending the time of emigration to October. It went on to conclude that he threatened to execute Seminole prisioners the moment fresh depredations were committed. Jessup was quoted as saying he had "a thousand Creek warriors ready to kill the Seminole."

Sloan knew Osceola must be in a turmoil trying to decide what his next move should be. Up to this point, Osceola's war had been a defensive one, and Sloan knew he wanted to keep it that way. If attacked, he would fight. Sloan also knew his brother would never stay in the boundaries Jessup devised. Nor would Arpeika, Phillip and Coacoochee, who was Phillip's son.

It was the first week in September the the *Polly Copinger* set sail once more with supplies, horses and mules. In Sloan's cabin, in gaily beribboned boxes, were the gifts that Annemarie had bought for Osceola's family.

For Morning Dew there was a delicate lace shawl the color of the sky on a summer day. A string of matching beads lay next to the gossamer wrap. For Ina, a flowered skirt trimmed with bright fringe. For Yahi, who now resided in Osceola's chikkee, a pair of scarlet slippers lined with lamb's wool. For the children, a doll in Indian dress, harmonicas, several colored bracelets and pretty yellow shell combs. In a closed canister some candy sticks of assorted colors and flavors. For the baby, a Golliwog, a soft, rag doll popular with English children, and a box of brightly colored wooden building blocks.

The *Polly Copinger* dropped anchor in a deepwater inlet off the Halifax River. Sloan and Culpepper waited for two days before the Seminoles arrived. Sloan was anxious, barely able to contain himself with his forced inactivity. "Something is wrong, I can feel it here," he said pounding at his stomach.

A little past noon on the second day an Indian named Hola Alto crept aboard the *Polly Copinger*. Sloan's heart lurched at what he read in the Indian's eyes. "Tell me," he croaked.

"Four days ago King Phillip was captured by an underling of Jessup, General Hernandez. As far as we can tell, he was camped at a ruined plantation thirty miles south of St. Augustine. They surrounded Phillip's camp sometime near midnight and attacked at first light. No guard was posted. No horse neighed; no dog barked. There were no injuries. Tomoka John, a negro, was captured also. They say he offered to guide the troops to a Yuchis' camp six miles away and again they circled the camp during the night and attacked at first light. They captured Yuchi Billy and his brother, Jack." There was disgust on Hola Alto's face. The soldiers could never have reached the camp, for it is a pine barren placed like an island in the middle of the swamp. Only one familiar with the trails could get there. "Tomoka John betrayed the Seminole."

Sloan wasn't surprised. To Culpepper he said, "I feared something like this would happen. It makes for a serious breach in Seminole leadership."

Sloan knew there was more to come from the Indian standing in front of him. "Give me the rest of it."

"General Jessup ordered Chief Phillip to send out a runner to call in his sons, Coacoochee and Bluesnake. When they came in with the white flag, the general detained them, ignoring one of the most respected rules of war. My people are angry," he said stony faced.

"They have a right to be angry. What happened to Bluesnake and Coacoochee?"

"The general liberated Coacoochee and sent him out to bring in more of his followers, knowing that Phillip, his father, was being held as hostage."

Sloan stared at Culpepper a moment, dreading the next question he had to ask. "What of Osceola? Where are his people?" He couldn't ask about Savannah.

The Indian's eyes were defiant when he replied. "Osceola and Coa Hadjo sent word to General Jessup that they would parley. It is to take place near Fort Peyton near Moultrie Creek. They have erected a log work and they have a garrison with a detachment from the Second Dragoons."

"When is Osceola due to parley?" he demanded in a harsh voice.

Hola Alto shrugged. "Nothing is for certain. A few days time, a week, a moon. Swamp Fox knows that my

chief will not parley, he will be captured in the same
manner as King Phillip and Tomoka John. Your brother
flies the white flag over his camp."

"What?" Sloan exploded. "What of the yellow and
red standard?"

"Your brother flies a white flag," Hola Alto said
stubbornly.

"How many days' ride to the camp?"

"On horseback, on that monster you ride, perhaps a
day and one half. I will have to lead you. I have no
horse. Our time will be slow."

"On our ride to Osceoloa's camp will we pass any of
his smaller camps?"

"One, maybe two, but only women and children.
They cannot help you."

"Culpepper, bring Redeemer topside along with
horses for yourself and Hola Alto. Once we get to land
you will signal for your people to meet me, here,"
Sloan said pointing a finger at a spot on his map. "A
three-hour ride at top speed. We can make our presence felt, if nothing else. I can't sit here and do nothing.
We'll rendezvous along Moultrie Creek and attack in
darkness."

"The Swamp Fox has the eye of the eagle in darkness?" There was amusement in the Indian's tone.

"Hell, no. We're just going to fight them by their
own dastardly ways. While they sleep. That's the way
they attack the Indian. We'll turn their own strategy
around and do the same. They won't be expecting us.
Jessup is probably sitting in some soft, easy chair
swilling brandy and smoking cigars while some other
bastard does his dirty work."

Sloan followed behind Hola Alto with the wind at his
back. The Indian rode the horse like demons were on
his heels. Sloan looked behind him once to see
Culpepper hanging on to his mount for dear life, his
watery eyes squeezed closed.

The three men rode for six hours before reaching the

arranged meeting place which Hola Alto had ordered. Darkness was complete when the first Seminole reached the temporary camp. The others followed swiftly until they numbered sixty-seven. Sloan was pleased. He recognized some of the men from his training program. All of them looked at him with respect.

"I don't like this," Yahoola said sharply. "Why is your brother, our chief, flying a white flag over his camp?" His voice was bold and full of anger.

Sloan stared at the man in front of him. He was an expert marksman, better than himself as a matter of fact. "Osceola has not spoken with me. Perhaps he thinks it is time to make peace. I have no answers for you."

"Peace. It is impossible with the white men! They lie, cheat, steal and kill our women and children. You talk to me of peace. Save your breath, for it will not work. My people who stand here before you, ready to fight, think as I do. Do you believe your white generals will parley with Osceola? If you do, you're wrong. It is one more white-eyes trick to capture all of our chiefs. Mark my word, Swamp Fox, for I speak true. A runner is on his way to Osceola to advise him of this foray we plan. Also to advise him of the general's troops that are headed in his direction. The *wrong* direction. If the intention was to parley as Osceola thinks, then why are Ashby and Hernandez heading for his camp?"

"Goddamn it, I didn't say you were wrong. I'm not even saying that Osceola is wrong. I don't know what's going on. I've just arrived yesterday. My brother never does anything without a reason. We must all trust to his good judgment. It is just possible that he and his men are planning an ambush on their own. Did you consider that?"

"Of course it has been considered." Yahoola spat into the ground to show what he thought of Osceola's methods.

"Then why are you here? Why are these men here? If there's no hope, why are we planning a raid on the white camp?"

"Because it is my time to die, and before my spirit leaves my body, I want to take my enemies with me. The others feel the same way. When the troops descend on Osceola's camp, there will be that many less white-eyes for our chief to look upon."

Sloan grimaced understanding perfectly Yahoola's logic. "We are not women; let us not think like women. Whatever we accomplish will be better than doing nothing. Are we all agreed?" There were loud mutterings and much shuffling of feet as the men stared at him.

"Agreed," Yahoola said firmly.

"Good. Now show me the way we travel. How many hours before midnight will we be close enough to make our plans work?"

Yahoola squatted down on his haunches and proceeded to draw a rough map for Sloan in the dirt. "We do not have many horses among us. My brothers can outrun that monster you ride, so have no fear. We do not travel as one. We scatter and meet when the moon is high, here," he said pointing to a spot he drew in the dry ground. One by one the men filed past the crude map, and Yahoola spoke to each. They scattered silently till there was just Culpepper and MacAllister left.

"Do you get the feeling, Laddie, that those brothers of yours aren't too keen on being seen with the likes of us? Do ye think we be tainted or something?"

Sloan laughed. "Never! An Indian travels best alone. Even on horseback we'll be hard pressed to keep up with them. You're forgetting that we can't arrive in numbers and horses make noise. A good scout can pick up a horse's hoof beats as much as a mile away."

There was a vicious ache between Sloan's shoulder blades when he rode into dense undergrowth to meet Yahoola and his men. Culpepper looked done in.

Twelve hours on horseback was something the old man wasn't used to. Nor was he, Sloan admitted to himself.

"How far?" he demanded of Yahoola.

"An hour by foot."

An hour by foot. Leave the horses or take them? Sloan pondered. Perhaps it would be best to go up the creek, wade through the water and attack from the rear. If there were Indian scouts in the white camp, he would have to use every trick, every wile he knew, to attack under cover of surprise.

"We'll ford the creek. Tether the horses on a marshy bank for a quick exit once we depart. Any objections?" It was clear from the surprised looks on the Indians' faces they never would have thought of the creek. The Swamp Fox was a good man to join in battle. Sloan demonstrated how the men were to carry the guns once they were immersed into waist-high water. The ammunition belts hung from their necks. They knew what would happen if they got wet.

The moon was slipping behind thick cloud cover, and the water was cold, making Sloan's teeth chatter.

Culpepper prayed that the moon would stay hidden as he floundered in the dark, murky water. He liked the water as long as he was in a ship on top of it. This evil smelling swampy water was enough to make a man want to toss up his innards. Once he slipped and would have gone under but for the help of a giant Indian with no teeth. He grinned as he hauled Culpepper up by the scruff of the neck and set him upright. "Mighty obliged," the sea captain managed. The Indian grunted and forged ahead.

"Problems, Culpepper?" Sloan asked.

"None I can't handle," the captain lied.

The quarter moon played hide and seek for the next thirty minutes, finally settling behind a dark black cloud. It was good. They would be on their way back before daylight.

Up ahead, Yahoola lifted his arm to show they had

arrived within what the Indian called spitting distance
of the soldiers' camp. Word came back to Sloan: dogs,
first with a knife; sentries with a garotte, and from that
point on anything goes.

Sloan leaped to the creek bank, shaking the water
from his body and shivering in the cool night air.
Culpepper was right behind him waiting for an order.
So far, so good. No sound of barking dogs which, in
itself, was unusual, unless of course they were Indian
dogs to begin with who recognized the invaders from
previous camps. The horses were quiet, something else
that surprised Sloan. Either the white men felt safe or
somehow they were expecting an ambush. He preferred
to go with the former thought rather than the latter. It
was an eerie kind of quiet and Sloan didn't like it.
Culpepper's teeth were chattering so loud, Sloan was
sure the entire camp would wake from the harsh
clickety-clack. He pulled the red bandanna he had tied
around his head to keep the hair from his eyes and
handed it to the captain. "Bite down on this," he
whispered. "You're making enough noise to wake the
dead."

Culpepper bit down and immediately felt better.
There were times when he regretted the decisions he
had made. But if he had to do it all over again, he
wouldn't change a thing. A man had to do what he had
to do.

Sloan and Culpepper crept closer to the camp. He
could almost feel the warmth from a low-burning fire.
A sentry was walking slowly around the fire in a sleepy
manner, his rifle held sloppily at his side. As his eyes
became accustomed to the darkness, he picked out a
sleeping dog at the outer edge of the fire. He watched
as both sentry and dog went to their eternal rewards.
Another guard at the outer perimeter fell, and then
another. A third was bringing his rifle to his shoulder
when a knife slashed across his throat. Sloan imagined
he could hear the rush of blood flowing from the man's

throat. Culpepper gagged behind him. For fifteen minutes the silent slaughter continued. Suddenly, lanterns were flaring up and gunshots sounded. Wild, frenzied war whoops echoed as Yahoola and his men attacked savagely. Sloan had just fired off three shots in quick order. Three men fell, one screaming obscenities about Sloan's origins. Another volley went off, this time from Culpepper's rifle. A man with a captain's insignia dropped at Sloan's back. "I didn't think ye noticed him, Lad," Culpepper grinned. Sloan grinned, enjoying the old man's success with the rifle. Under normal conditions, he couldn't hit the broad side of a barn. "You saved my life, Enwright. I owe you another one."

"I'll let ye know when it's time to collect," Culpepper said firing off another shot and getting his man in the middle of his chest. He blanched slightly, but recovered quickly and reloaded.

Sloan swiveled like a dancer, firing and reloading, hitting his target each time he fired. At a signal from Yahoola he danced his way to the outer confines of the camp. "We are victorious. To stay longer will endanger our men. We leave now while they are still stunned. They must report to their superiors that it was our battle. We lost none and none were wounded. They have no liking for night fighting, unless it is to capture women and children and knifing my brothers while they sleep. We fight as they do. We are victorious!" A blood curdling war whoop sounded. Sloan shivered.

"Culpepper, where the hell are you? We're making tracks. Culpepper, get your ass over here before someone shoots you. Now!" Sloan ordered.

"I'm coming, Laddie, but slow it is. I picked up a shot in me foot. Some damn fool corporal thought I didn't need a foot. Well, the bastard was wrong. I shot his guts right out of his body."

A look of relief washed over Sloan's face. He was trying to decide what to do with Culpepper when the tall, toothless Indian who had fished him out of the

creek approached. His dark eyes took in Culpepper's
bleeding foot. Without a word he bent over and slung
the captain over his shoulder. He loped ahead following Yahoola and the others.

"This is a disgrace," Culpepper shouted to Sloan.
"Make him put me down. It's indecent, I tell you!"

"Shut up, Culpepper. You'll slow us up if you walk.
You want to see Maeve again to tell her how brave you
were. Women love wounded war heroes." He fired off
two more shots, getting one man smack in the kneecap
and the other at the base of the throat. He felt nothing
as the men fell, one to his death, the other moaning
that he would never walk again. He had chosen his
side, and he wasn't about to back out now no matter
how white the man's skin was.


Sunlight dappled through the trees, falling softly
upon Che-cho-ter's face. This was the way he always
wanted to remember her, Osceola told himself. Fresh
from the waters of the river where she bathed, preening
beneath his eye. She had given him children, this
woman with the dusky skin and thick sweep of black
hair. Soon, he told himself, before the moon makes
another arc in the night sky, he would leave her.

"My husband's eyes grow dark with sorrow," Morning Dew said softly, touching his cheek.

Osceola turned his head, burying his face in the palm
of her hand. "My eyes are filled with looking at you,
Che-cho-ter, breath of my soul. I have never looked at
another woman such as I have looked upon you." It
was important to say these things to her, to tell her
what she had always known. But it brought comfort to
have them said aloud. He drew her into his arms for an
instant, loving the feel of her body against his. How
long would he be able to hold her this way? Forever, he
scolded himself. As long as there is memory, as long as
I draw breath.

Che-cho-ter rested against him, her heart heavy and

thoughts troubled. There was little need for words between them; then why was he saying these things to her? Did he think they had just looked upon one another and were about to build their first chikkee? These words were for the very young who had not learned the faith and trust that comes with loving.

Taking her hands in his, he led her to the bank of the river where they sat down, gazing at their own reflections. "I can see us as we once were, not so many summers ago. You were heavy with our first daughter. I put my hand against your belly, so, and felt the life within you," he smiled remembering. "Such a man as you should have sons, you told me. What will we do if it is a girl child? I told you that a child from the womb of Che-cho-ter was a child given in love, a blessed child who would find the Spirits of the forest smiling. And so it was." He nodded his head, smiling with the bitter-sweet reverie.

"And so it was, my husband," Che-cho-ter told him. "And so it will be again. There is time for more children, for the seed of my husband to spawn in my body and grow into life."

"No, wife of my soul, there is no more time." His voice quaked, his spirit breaking under the heavy burden of sorrow and regret.

Che-cho-ter tried to break him out of his misery. "You only speak this way because your efforts go unrewarded. Soon, my husband, the other chiefs will find their courage and stand behind you."

"Yes, soon they will. But only at great sacrifice made both by my wife and myself. I know this is so and Arpeika has seen it in his dreams."

A shadow passed over Che-cho-ter's face. She, too, had dreams, but the mornings had always come and she found her husband at her side. When her soul talked with the Spirits at night, they lied to her. They must have lied! Unless . . . unless . . . her eyes searched Osceola's face, finding there the truth. It was to be. She

must hold each precious moment and keep it close to
her always. When she was an old woman, she would tell
her daughters' sons of their grandfather who fought the
white soldiers to keep their home in Florida. Her tales
would be peopled with heroes.

The forest was suddenly still, only the shrill cry of a
bird fell on her ears. There was already an emptiness in
her heart, and the spark within her soul that united
all living things with the Great Spirit was somehow
dimmer. Yes, my husband, she wept silently. You
will reunite the Seminole but it will cost us your
life.

"When?" was all she asked and he loved her for
knowing him so well.

"Soon. When the time is right. I will allow myself to
fall into the white general's hands. I will allow him to
trick me like the fox tricks the rabbit. And there will be
an outcry among my people and they will see that
Jessup is never to be trusted. That his words fall
without meaning like clouds brushing the treetops.
Shed your tears now, Che-cho-ter, for when the time
comes you must be brave. You must speak my heart to
our people and let them never forget the Seminole
belong in the Floridas."

Che-cho-ter was struck by his impassioned statement. His tone was bitter, his dark eyes sharp and
suspicious. She wrapped her arms around him, burying
his face into her breast, willing the hate to drain from
his heart, leaving him pure again, receptive to her
love.

Her fingers traced the planes of his face, committing
it to memory. She wished, more than anything, never
to forget the way he looked and the warmth of his arms
when he held her. Death was a sorrowful parting for
the one left behind with only memories to comfort the
long nights. Lovingly, she took his beloved face in her
hands and pressed her cheek against his. "My husband,
my chief," she told him softly, "as long as there is

breath in your wife's body, you will never be forgotten."

Osceola stood beside Coa Hadjo beneath the shade of the trees. The weather continued to be unseasonably warm for late October and the Seminoles took it as a good sign. The wild winds would come again, whipping from the east, churning the oceans into a froth, whistling through the forests and bringing torrential rains. Just the sort of weather to immobilize the white soldiers, giving the Seminole time to re-group.

For a fleeting moment, Osceola thought about Checho-ter and the children. Believing he had said his last farewells to them, he was now prepared for anything General Jessup might throw his way. Stiff-backed, rigid, he appeared the essence of the strong Seminole warrior. Word had been sent to the army command post that both he and Coa Hadjo were ready to parley.

Osceola narrowed his eyes, engrossed in thought. By now General Jessup had made his decision, and if it was the one Osceola expected, the general was well on the road to disgracing himself. Counting upon Jessup's quest for glory and knowing his hatred of the Indian, Osceola planned to use the general's weaknesses to reunite the Seminole nation. When word was spread of the general's deed, the Seminoles would rise again, fighting for their land, knowing they could have no faith in this white leader's promises. Glancing upward, Osceola focused on the white flag of truce flying over the camp. "Now, Jessup," he swore under his breath, using a white man's profanity, "now you come, you bastard!"

Spies had already informed Osceola that orders were sent out to General Hernandez to reconnoiter to Fort Peyton and commandeer a detachment of Dragoons. Fort Peyton was only a mile from Osceola's camp, and the chief expected them to arrive at any moment.

Listening intently, he could hear the sounds of mounted men approaching the camp, and Osceola expected their numbers to be great. A runner came flying into camp, reporting to his chief, Coa Hadjo.

Breathlessly, he reported, "Dragoons, like mosquitos, over the swamp. So many horses you can smell them from where you stand!" The runner's eyes were wide with alarm. He was only a young boy, inexperienced on the battleground. But today there would be no battle.

Osceola offered the boy an inscrutable smile. So, Jessup had taken the bait! The general could not resist capturing the two most important chiefs in the Seminole nation. Only Sam Jones, Arpeika, was more important to the Indians for leadership.

"We are ready," Coa Hadjo intoned solemnly.

"But we fly the white flag!" the young runner exclaimed. "Under the rules of war the flag is a sign of truce! No injury should be done!"

"So it would mean to a man of justice," Osceola told him. "Stand straight and look upon your enemy when he comes. Know that these lands in the Floridas belong to the Seminole and never forget what you are about to witness."

Osceola swallowed hard, his mouth feeling dry and parched. He had recently fought off another bout of the fever and he still did not feel his usual strength. "When they come, Coa Hadjo, you must speak for the Seminole. Let there be no slip of my tongue. Let all the words belong to the white soldiers. A man cannot be condemned for what he does not say."

Coa Hadjo looked at his old friend sadly. He knew what Osceola expected of Jessup and it lay heavy on his heart.

In a thunder of hooves, the Dragoons rode into camp, a gold-braided leader at their head who introduced himself as General Hernandez. So, thought Osceola, Jessup could not bring himself to do his own dirty work.

Dismounting, General Hernandez approached the two chiefs, two aides-de-camp flanking him on either side. Raising his hand in greeting, Hernandez made the first overture. "I have come as a friend," he began, his dour glance instinctively measuring the men before him. "As a friend, I have a question to ask. What prompted you to seek this parley?"

Osceola remained silent, listening. Coa Hadjo spoke. "We have come for the good of our people."

Not considering this an answer to his question, Hernandez asked, "At whose request did you come?"

"A message was brought from Coacoochee from his father, King Phillip."

"And what do you expect from me?" Hernandez persisted. "Have you come to give yourself up to me?"

"No," Coa Hadjo said quietly. "We want to make peace."

Quirking a heavy black brow, Hernandez said, "And are you also ready to surrender all the property you have captured?"

Pretending innocence, Coa Hadjo shrugged his shoulders. "We have no property that is not ours. We have only a few negroes . . ."

Not allowing him to complete his statement, Hernandez glowered. "Why haven't you brought your negroes in before as you promised at Fort King? Why did not Micanopy, Jumper and Cloud come instead of sending a messenger?"

Calmly, coolly, Coa Hadjo stated, "They all have the measles." His glance was accusatory. Until the arrival of the white man, measles and small pox were unheard of among the Indians. Their effects had been devastating on the Seminole population.

Seeing Coa Hadjo's anger, Hernandez cooled, saying smoothly, "I am an old friend of Phillip's and I wish you all well, but we have been deceived so often that it is necessary for you to come with me. You will all see the good treatment you receive. You will be glad that you fell into my hands."

"We will see about it," Coa Hadjo said sternly, knowing that Osceola's heart was lifted in victory. This

was exactly what his friend had expected and wanted.
Now Jessup would lose face. It would be reported that
Coa Hadjo and Osceola and their small band of people
that did not number seventy were taken prisoner by
two hundred and fifty Dragoons under orders of treachery given by General Thomas Jessup himself. The
Indians had agreed to parley and the white general had
seized the opportunity to capture them! Under the flag
of truce!

Hernandez issued a prearranged signal and the Dragoons moved in, their lances pointed at their prisoners.
Although the Seminoles carried guns, there was no
resistance.

Before being herded out of camp, Osceola took the
white flag from its place in camp. He carried it bravely
for all to see. Never had there been a single instance of
a failure on the part of the Seminoles to respect the flag
of truce. In all civilized parts of the world it was held to
be inviolable, and yet Jessup had made a mockery of it.
As he mounted the horse given to him by MacAllister,
Osceola told himself, soon the Seminoles will reunite
when they see what sin has been committed.


Word began to spread throughout the country that
Osceola, the famous Seminole leader, had been seized
while attending a conference under a flag of truce. The
public reaction was one of outrage: Jessup had performed a dishonorable deed, staining the honor of his
country. Papers throughout the nation editorialized
about the disgraceful means by which Osceola was
captured. The English were shocked by the dishonorable performance of an American general. One English
writer said there was "never a more disgraceful piece of
villainy perpetrated in a civilized land." The writer was
Andrew Welch and he pointed out with consternation
that the Americans had recognized the Seminoles as a
nation by making treaties with them. They were not
rebels. To seize a Seminole leader under a flag of truce

was as much an act of infamy as it would be for an English general to seize an American general under similar circumstances.

Fort Marion, where Osceola and Coa Hadjo were brought, was an old building formerly known as Castillo de San Marco. It had been started by the Spanish in 1672 and was the oldest fort in the United States. It had been used once before as a prison, and in 1821 a dungeon was found beneath the high turret with human bones and other indications of cruel imprisonment.

The prisoners held by the army were allowed visitors. Indeed, so much had been made of the dishonorable way the Indians had been brought into the camp that the army was setting aside many of its regulations to accommodate them.

Sloan gained admittance to the Fort early in the afternoon. All that was required of him was that he sign his name to a registry and that he be welcomed by the Indians.

He found Osceola sitting on a bed of straw, his cell door wide open to the fresh air and sunshine of the courtyard that was guarded by blue-coated sentries. It was obvious that for all intents and purposes, the prisoners were allowed to go about their business undisturbed.

Sloan stood in the entry to his brother's cell. Osceola's suffering resembled that of a captive eagle. He knew he had been betrayed, and he resented it fiercely, but his resentment was tinged with elation. Word had come to him that the chiefs who still enjoyed their freedom in the Florida swamps were pledging to fight for their rights and property.

"My brother," Sloan said softly, great sorrow creeping into his voice. "It sickens me to see you this way. Captive in your own land."

"Lift your heart, MacAllister, my brother. I have nothing to be ashamed of. My soul is free to fly with the

Spirits of the air and the forest. It is for those who entrapped me to feel shame." Osceola looked at Sloan with a calm and steady gaze. He knew he was looking into the eyes of a brave and honorable man. A man who had made sacrifices for his people.

"You planned this, didn't you, old fox? To bring shame upon your enemy and make his words false to all Seminoles?" MacAllister spoke in the Seminole tongue, abiding by his brother's wishes, bringing him a taste of home.

"I am fulfilling Arpeika's prophecy. He told me I was not to die in my home, nor was I to die beyond the Mississippi. But I was to die. For this, brother, I am prepared. But my people are not. Jessup has already begun his campaign, and his storehouses are full to the rafters. But the Seminoles are ready to fight, and their storehouses will never be empty because of the generosity of the Swamp Fox." Osceola smiled sadly, his eyes showing gratitude.

"My brother's people are also mine. Can I do anything for you? Send word to someone?"

"Yes," Osceola's answer was quick. "Go to the camp where Che-cho-ter and Ina and my children are staying. Bring them here to me. It is allowed."

"Why haven't they been brought to you before this?" Sloan demanded, knowing Osceola's need to have his family surrounding him at this time.

"There was no one to trust. I could not chance that the army would take them and hold them hostage, keeping me from them. But now," he shrugged elegantly, "there is so much hostility against Jessup he would not dare to commit another act of treachery against me. Until now, I did not have you to depend upon. Bring them to me, brother. Quickly. Each day I awaken to see the sun I know not whether I am blessed or cursed. To live behind the walls of a prison breaks the spirit of a man."

For a long time they sat together, silently. No words

were needed, none were said. Their camaraderie was complete.

It was mid-November with the bitter hurricanes long gone. Savannah sat before the fire with Osceola's daughters at her feet. The cruel weather and the hardships the women and children had endured, had frozen Chala's heart, making it difficult to face even one more day. The children played quietly with pieces of twigs and stones, smiling up at Savannah from time to time. Mic-canna spoke softly. "You must not look so sad, Chala. My father does not like to look upon tormented eyes."

"I am not sad for your father, little one, but for something else."

"What is that?"

"Your father's brother, he is lost to me. My heart no longer sings for he is not here to listen. My eyes can no longer weep. I have only my memories now."

"My mother is sad, also. My sisters are sad. We are a sad people, is it not so, Chala?"

"It is so," Savannah replied with a catch in her voice.

"Will we be forced to leave this land?" the little girl questioned.

Would they? She didn't know. The days seemed endless and without hope. How was she to answer this child? "Perhaps, one day," she said vaguely, praying the child would be satisfied with her answer.

Idly, she poked at the ground near her with a spindly twig. How frail it was. It would crack if she exerted too much pressure. Angrily, she tossed the stick into the fire and watched it burst into flame. That was what had happened to her. She had taken life from Sloan MacAllister; she had broken into flames when he was near. But he was gone and she was nothing, a cold shell.

Sloan went in search of his brother's family. Because of the gravity of their situation, Osceola's people were

scattered throughout the forests, and only by vigilant
inquiry was he able to find out where Che-cho-ter and
her daughters were camped. Despite the fact that he
knew Savannah would stay with Che-cho-ter, Sloan's
eyes would comb each encampment, searching for her
bright golden head and gypsy green eyes. Only yesterday had he learned where he might find them.

Redeemer responded to the pressure of his knees,
following a stream bed, watching the slow trickle of
crystal water run swifter and become broader in its
rush to join the sea. It had been more than a week since
he had left to find Che-cho-ter—at first traveling southward and then to the west, thinking they would still be
camped somewhere near Lake Okeechobee. Coming
almost full circle, Sloan realized they had kept moving
northeast, their migration taking them within a two
days' walk of St. Augustine where Osceola was being
held captive.

It had occurred to Sloan time and again that Savannah must feel abandoned by him. Annemarie had been
right; he should have taken her with him to Galveston.
He hadn't known a minute's peace since he had last
been with her. Even now, with the bright sun filtering
through the trees, there was a coldness in the center of
him, an emptiness that only Savannah could fill. He had
never thought a woman could come to mean so much to
him. Had never dreamed that his heart could be held so
softly in a woman's hands. She had surrounded him
with love and he needed her beside him. Always.

His thoughts of Savannah were so intense that he
thought he was dreaming when Redeemer brought him
through the trees and he recognized a slim, feminine
form kneeling at the stream, her golden mane of hair
reflecting the sun's brightness. He watched silently as
Savannah glided the tortoiseshell comb she had
brought from Galveston through her silky, long hair.
Her arms were raised above her head, back arched in
delicate symmetry, accentuating the rise of her breasts,

the sleekness of her haunches. She must have just
finished bathing; a precious bar of perfumed soap and a
towel were resting nearby. Her thin blouse clung to her
damply, the wide neckline revealing a creamy, graceful
shoulder.

Sloan drank in the sight of her, nourished by her
presence, feeling once again the peace she brought to
him. He wished he had arrived earlier to watch her
bathe, remembering those halcyon days on the island,
feeling the quiver of excitement only Savannah could
stir within him. Her lovely face was raised to the sun,
the delicate patrician nose, the sweet curve of her chin,
the purity of her brow were illuminated, and she
became a goddess of femininity. It was only when she
turned her head that he saw the dark shadows in her
eyes.

Redeemer issued a friendly snort, recognizing the
slim girl who had ridden with his master atop his back.
Savannah was startled by the sound, her eyes immediately turning toward him, peering into the shadows.
Within the space of a heartbeat, Sloan was out of the
saddle and crossing the distance between them with
long, quick strides. Savannah swayed, the earth rocking
beneath her. She would have fallen if Sloan hadn't
captured her in his arms, holding her against him, filling
her world and dragging her back from the world of the
dead into a place where his love was warmer and
brighter than the sun.

His hands were in her hair, his lips covered her face,
tasting her, devouring her. How much he had missed
her. There was a sudden relief flooding through him, as
though all these long weeks he had held his breath and
could now at last draw fresh, sweet air. He inhaled her
freshness, recognized the scent of the soap mingled
with the smoky fragrance of the woods. Having her in
his arms, it was impossible to release her, to explain, to
tell her where he had been and why he hadn't come to
find her before this. These things would keep until

later, until he had had his fill of her, if that would ever be possible.

Savannah clung to him, reveling in the feel of his arms around her, the pressure of his mouth upon hers. She could not spoil this moment with questions. Perhaps he was a ghost after all, conjured up by her dreadful longing for him, sent to her by the Spirits to help heal her lonely heart. And if he was a ghost, then she must not break the spell; she must close her eyes and welcome his embrace. And if a cry escaped her lips and she moaned his name, she would be forgiven. The sound of her name filled her ears, his touch filled her senses. There was only MacAllister and all else was a void, an emptiness where only the pain of separation penetrated the nightmare. The delicious weight of him pushed her backward to the ground, falling upon her, pressing his length upon her. She understood his sudden hunger and responded with an appetite of her own, tangling her legs with his, impatient with the scraps of cloth that separated her from him. She wanted to be naked with MacAllister, just the way they had been on the island, with the sun searing their bodies, with the salt sea breezes cooling their passions.

As though listening to her thoughts, Sloan sat up, freeing himself from her arms, his fingers working at the laces of his buckskin tunic and his belt. Savannah stood and slipped her colorful skirt from around her waist, her blouse quickly followed. Golden skin and golden hair, sultry green eyes and moist parted lips. . . . She was a goddess, made for loving, designed by the muses to spark a man's desire and fill his heart with passion's song.

They clung to each other, seeking that which the other could give, wanting to end the torment their need for each other had created. With each touch something of themselves was restored. Each caress, each kiss carried with it the power to heal, to broach the time they had been separated and melt the ice that had sprung in Savannah's heart. He loved her, had come back for her, and now he was whispering soft words against the hollow of her throat, telling her of his love.

The words were sweeter than wild honey, and she gathered them into her soul. She offered herself to him, pressing his palm over her breast, lifting her mouth to kiss his ear, opening her eyes to see him; at last believing he really was here with her.

The sunlight kissed his hair, glinted off the smooth, muscular expanse of his shoulders. His eyes locked with hers, seeming to draw her into him, and she learned there all she would ever need to know; she was MacAllister's woman and he loved her.

It was twilight before Sloan and Savannah left their haven near the stream to go back to camp. They walked with their arms around each other; Redeemer following in their steps.

The women were gathered around their cook fires preparing the evening meal while the children hovered nearby. Che-cho-ter stepped out of her chikkee, carrying her youngest daughter, and when she noticed her husband's brother she froze.

Savannah dropped her arm from around Sloan's waist, feeling a sudden guilt that she should have her love back with her while Che-cho-ter's husband was held prisoner by the white soldiers.

After a moment, Che-cho-ter seemed to regain herself, her soft, dark eyes searching Savannah's, silently telling her that she was happy MacAllister had found his way back to her. With her natural grace and dignity, Che-cho-ter walked toward Sloan, head high, bearing proud. It was only as she came closer that Sloan could see the single, heartbreaking tear that glistened on her cheek. "Tell me of my husband," she entreated.

"He wants you with him, and I've come to take you. He needs his family. We'll leave at dawn. It is a long trip for the little ones, but their father wants them."

"He is well." It wasn't really a question, but a positive statement.

He couldn't lie to her. "No, he is not well. I don't

know how much time he has left. There is nothing more
I can do. It was your chief's choice to put himself into
Jessup's hands and both of us must accept this."

"I do accept it, but it does not stop my heart from
breaking, Sloan MacAllister. He is my husband. He is
my children's father. What will become of our people?"
Her voice broke on her last words.

"There is no need for worry. I will see to you and the
children and the rest of your people. As long as there is
breath in my body, you will never want. That is the only
promise I can make you."

"It is enough, more than enough. Does Osceola
know of this promise you make to me?"

"There is no need for such words between Osceola
and myself. He knows, without asking, that I would
protect you. It has been understood since we were
small boys. If I could breathe life into my brother, I
would do it at the cost of my own. If I could bleed for
him, I would. If I can make his last burdens easier, I
will do it. We are brothers."

"No man has ever had a brother such as you,"
Che-cho-ter said quietly as she placed a grateful hand
on Sloan's arm.

Damp, clammy fog swirled about Sloan's feet as he
crept from Savannah's chikkee. It was almost light but
the women were already at the fire. Their breakfast
finished, they waited for him. Surely, they wouldn't
. . . they weren't all planning . . . he shook his head.
He should have known. He was going to have to take
the whole damn camp. His heart broke a little when he
saw Che-cho-ter in the clammy air with nothing but the
flimsy blue shawl and blue beads around her even
thinner blouse. Yahi had on the red sheep-lined slippers, and Ina was dressed in the brilliant skirt. The
children clutched their dolls to their chests, their dark
eyes solemn and wide. Even the baby held on to the
Golliwog. Gifts from their father.

Everyone was dressed in her best for the trip. The

single file parade from the camp reminded Sloan of a rainbow. He smiled to himself. He wouldn't have this any other way either. If Osceola got five minutes of joy out of seeing his people, it was worth it. Savannah was the last to join the long column of people. She wore her black ribbon with the cameo around her neck. It was her only concession to her heritage.

Sloan pushed hard to lead the camp through the forest, in a northeasterly direction. He was determined to arrive at St. Augustine by noon of the following day. Grim-faced and silent, Osceola's people followed; the women, the children, the aged. There were no young braves or fiercesome warriors to protect them and scout the way. All those who were capable of fighting were with Arpeika in central Florida.

Savannah walked beside Che-cho-ter, helping her with the children, offering a silent companionship. A great sadness was heavy on her heart as she recalled the kindness Che-cho-ter had always shown her. Savannah had been almost twelve summers when Osceola had brought his second wife to live in his chikkee with Ina and herself. From the moment the dusky-skinned maiden smiled at them with her soft, dark eyes, they were a family. Osceola was always proud of his women. There were no squabbling or jealousies between them as there sometimes were in other chikkees where two wives resided. Ina, whose marriage to Osceola had been of a mutual convenience, had stepped into the role of a mother to them all, and Che-cho-ter, always respectful, had come to love Ina in a very special way.

And now this special sister was taking her children to a prison to be near their father. Che-cho-ter's eyes were always on the horizon, measuring each step that would take her closer to the man she loved.

As the sun dipped behind the trees, Sloan gave the order to camp for the night. Provisions, prepared the night before, were brought out. Tonight, all would sleep under the stars. Tomorrow, they would arrive in St. Augustine. Savannah slept on a pallet beside Sloan.

Through the night they reached for one another, touching, holding, comforting. There was no joy to be shared, only anxiety. A baby cried during the night, its mother soothing it with hushed, crooning words. Savannah nestled her head on Sloan's shoulder and listened to the sound of his heartbeat. Tomorrow. Tomorrow.

As they neared St. Augustine, the salty sea air blowing off the Atlantic was fresh and pungent to their nostrils. But there was another scent also, harsh and fetid, rotten. Sloan and Savannah recognized it instantly. It was the smell of civilization. People, crowded into the confines of a city, garbage and human offal.

The column of Seminole Indians led by a flaxen-haired white man riding a huge black horse brought immediate attention. People lined the cobblestoned streets in unabashed curiosity. Small boys, taught the sins of prejudice and hatred, hurled stones and trash until they were chastised. There was a dignity to these Indians that brooked no insult.

The Castillo, or Fort Marion as the soldiers now called it, rose above the city, the yellow cochina, from which it was constructed, shining dully in the sun. Sloan led his brother's people up the long hill to the gates. He had dismounted and Savannah walked beside him at the head of the column. Uniformed soldiers opened the draw gate allowing the Seminoles to gather in the central court, hemmed in by the tall battlements.

"You will come with us, MacAllister?" Savannah asked hopefully.

"I brought you this far; I won't desert you now. Come, we must first ask permission to see Osceola. It is a formality and the request will be granted."

Osceola entered the compound where his family and the rest of his camp stood. He walked slowly to his wife and drew her into his arms. He kissed the children and smiled down at them. His eyes saw "his gifts" and he lifted grateful eyes to his brother.

Sloan stood to the side not wishing to intrude in his

brother's private moments. He felt Osceola's eyes upon him. Nothing more than a slight nod of his head was evident to Sloan. Words weren't necessary.

"General, general, what am I supposed to be doing with all these people, sir?" a young sergeant shouted to be heard over the chattering Indians.

"Feed them. We're not barbarians," a harsh voice replied. He could be generous now that he had Osceola, Jessup thought arrogantly. It would look good in the history books in later years. Brevet General Thomas Jessup fed and bedded the Indians from Osceola's camp when they visited their chief at Fort Marion. He preened, liking the pictures his mind was weaving.

"General, sir? Are these people moving in or are they visiting?"

"They're moving in, thanks to my generosity. See to their comfort."

"What about the white man and woman?"

Jessup frowned. "What white man and woman?"

"The white man and the white woman who brought Osceola's people here."

The young sergeant noticed something strange happen to Jessup's eyes. He looked as though he had just been handed his death sentence. "Where are they?"

"Right outside your window."

Jessup felt a pain in his chest as he walked to the window. He knew what he was going to see and he wasn't wrong. But the man standing next to his niece looked familiar. By God, it was the gambler named MacAllister from New Orleans. Sloan MacAllister. Sloan MacAllister and Savannah. He should have known. How hard it had been that day to pretend disinterest to save his face when Beaunell Gentry called on him at the rail depot. It was easier to delude himself. Easier to not think about it. Easier to think only of his sister, Caroline. Caroline would never betray him. Once she had, but he had forgiven her. She had only been a young girl, mistaking his protectiveness for possessiveness.

Jessup straightened his military jacket, touched the braid reverently and then smoothed down his hair. He would behave like the general he was and take his cues from the couple standing outside, waiting for him.

His mind raced as he took in MacAllister's attire. A sudden insight told him this was the Swamp Fox, that the myth was indeed a reality. Savannah stared at him insolently. How dare she wear Caroline's cameo! Saying nothing, he reached out and tore the cameo from Savannah's neck. Sloan immediately stiffened, forcing his hands to remain at his sides. He wanted to pound his fists into the general's face, wanted to hear his cries for mercy, but better judgment prevented him. He couldn't chance a fight that would cause a retaliation against Osceola and his family.

"You have no right to wear my sister's cameo," Jessup was hissing. "I gave it to her. You've disgraced my sister's memory, taken up with the savages who murdered her! You're a traitor to her and to your race, and I will never forgive you!"

"I don't want your forgiveness," Savannah said calmly, as the general's face bloomed red with rage. "I know why my mother left it behind when she went with my father to the farm. She wanted to be away from you, from your disapproval and interference. You're an evil man, Uncle, and my mother knew it."

Something in the general seemed to crumble. Savannah was repeating the very accusation Caroline made before she left his life forever. "I loved your mother. Caroline was my life! There was nothing I wouldn't have done for her," Jessup protested, his voice suddenly husky and brimmed with emotion.

"You would have done anything except to see her happy. And she was happy. A child knows these things. The very fact that it was my father who could make her so happy and not you is what you've hated the most. You were a fool, Jessup."

The general seemed to have difficulty catching his

breath. Savannah stood there accusingly, the same look in her eye as in Caroline's before she left him. "I loved her," his voice was a whisper now, "I only wanted . . ."

"You only wanted to own her, to possess her. You needed her gratitude, her obligation to love you in return, the same things you wanted from me when I lived with you in New Orleans. It wasn't the Indians who killed my mother. It was you! You drove her out to that isolated farm . . . you drove her away from yourself. It is this you can't live with, so you choose to blame the Indians. It was Creeks who murdered my family. The Seminoles took me in and made me one of them. Ironic, isn't it? The Seminoles saved me and you want to throw them into the hands of their sworn enemies, the very ones who murdered my parents." Savannah's lip curled into a sneer. "I could hate you, Jessup, but I only pity you."

Desperately, Jessup's hand reached out to touch Savannah's arm. "I am your mother's brother, your uncle. In time, things can change between us. Savannah, I'm asking you not to throw away all we could have . . ."

"Don't touch me!" Savannah bridled. "Look down there in the compound. That is my family. They're the ones who looked after me, loved me, helped me, and never asked for anything in return. You can't order someone to love you, General. That's something you have to earn. All you've earned is my pity."

Jessup stared as Savannah and Sloan turned and left him. He wanted to strike out, to hurt her. It would be so easy to have MacAllister arrested and held under suspicion of treason. If he was the Swamp Fox, and Jessup instinctively knew he was, MacAllister could face a firing squad. He was about to call the sergeant-at-arms but he thought better of the idea. If it were common knowledge that his own niece paid her allegiance to the Seminoles, and that the man known as

Swamp Fox had been entertained in the general's own library, he would never find a political career in Washington. He would do nothing. Prove nothing. They could leave here and he wouldn't stop them. But he had the last laugh, Jessup consoled himself. He had Osceola!

Savannah rode behind Sloan on Redeemer's back. She was leaving a part of her life behind. Osceola was being held prisoner within the fort, but at least he had his wives and children with him. Her uncle, a link with the past and her heritage, was also there, in his own way more a prisoner than Osceola.

Burying her face into Sloan's broad back, Savannah wept. Her arms gripped him around the middle, holding fast. Here was her future, she told herself. This man with the flinty gray eyes and the heart of a lion. It seemed a lifetime ago that she had given herself into his keeping and found him a gentle master. A soft smile broke through her tears.

Coa Hadjo approached Osceola in the courtyard of Fort Marion shortly before the end of the year. They had been imprisoned for nearly seven weeks, and during that time Osceola had found himself gripped in a severe relapse of fevers. But the sun felt good today, warming the bones and erasing some of the pain. Word had been received of fighting taking place far to the south of St. Augustine, miles away from Fort Marion. The Seminoles were winning small victories. Every Indian in the prison wished they too could raise their weapons against the enemy.

"I have heard rumor," Coa Hadjo said abruptly. "General Jessup does not consider this a fitting prison for such a dangerous enemy. He fears our people will come to rescue us. We are to be moved to South Carolina to a place called Fort Moultrie. Prepare your family, Thlacko. We will leave by ship before the week is out."

Osceola said nothing, his face impassive, and retreated back into his cell.

Osceola stood on the deck of the gun boat taking him away from Florida to Charleston, South Carolina, and to the prison in Fort Moultrie. That his family was allowed to travel with him was a great consolation. His shawl was tightly pulled around his shoulders, and the fever sweat was cold on his face as he watched the shores of Florida disappear in the distance. The breeze blew off the land, and he could detect, faintly, the smell of earth and grass and trees. Morning light blazed off the gray turrets and battlements of Fort Marion while gulls wheeled above the ship. Behind him was the blue streak of the Gulf Stream.

Some had whispered that the fight was over now, that the dreams of freedom had been blown on the wind, but Osceola, chief of the Seminoles, knew otherwise. Freedom always had a price, but it was there, just over the horizon, just behind the moon.

A dark shadow crossed his eyes, blinding him. It was a portent of his death. Only in Florida had life found meaning and purpose. In leaving Florida he left behind his spirit that was linked to the very forests and earth he was walked. Leaving the spirit was to leave life—it was to die.

The *S.S. Poinsett* arrived at Fort Moultrie on January 1, 1838, and the prisoners, including Micanopy, Phillip, Coa Hadjo and Cloud, along with one hundred sixteen warriors and eighty-two women and children, were brought inside the enclosure. The quarters assigned Osceola were spacious enough to include his whole family and the women immediately set about housekeeping.

In the days that followed, Osceola spent a great deal of time reviewing the events of the war. Had he been wrong to fight? Had he committed a sin against nature to lead men into battle where they would suffer injury and death? Had the white man been right in wanting them to leave their forests and streams behind for a new life in Arkansas?

No. The white man had lied and cheated and allowed them to starve. Then he had stolen the bitter dignity of starvation from the Seminole and had tried to force them at gunpoint from the land of their birth. Resistance had been the only choice.

Che-cho-ter joined him one early morning as he stared out into the southern sky. "My husband is troubled," she stated softly. His arm came around her, holding her close. "You watch the southern sky with such longing, it wounds me here," she said thumping her breast with her fist.

"Once my brother, MacAllister, said much the same thing when we were boys. You keep your eyes on the eastern sky, he told me. And I said that was where I would find my destiny. And so I have."

A chill swept through Che-cho-ter. Not a chill of cold or ice but of death. She knew the time was fast approaching when she would be allowed to go back to Florida with their children. Only Osceola and the warriors were prisoners. The women could be released at any time.

The thought of filling her days without him brought a heaviness to her heart. He had been fighting the fever since arriving here in South Carolina, and was losing the battle. His will to live had evaporated, smothered by the mists that hung over the swamps and his hunting ground. There was nothing to be done, Che-cho-ter told herself, gasping back the cries that were swelling in her breast, but to wait with her husband for the end.

On January 28th, a night-long vigil was held inside Fort Moultrie. The soldiers of the fort had fallen under Osceola's spell, and fires burned long into the night in respect for the Seminole. A physician was called, Dr. Strobel, who was a professor of anatomy in the college of South Carolina. When the doctor, a man in his late fifties, stocky and well fed, entered Osceola's cell, he found the chief with his head in Che-cho-ter's lap while she bathed his throat with herb-soaked clothes.

"Bring me a candle," the doctor ordered, immediately seeing that the Indian's situation was grave. Peering down Osceola's throat, he saw swollen tonsils and a mucous membrane formed over his pharynx. Shaking his head, his many chins quivering, the man intoned, "He'll suffocate if we don't scarify those tonsils."

Immediately, Pa-hay-okee, the medicine man, jumped to his feet, shaking his magic bones that were strung on rawhide. His shadow on the stone walls created by the flickering fire trembled and shifted. "No," the conjurer said, meeting the doctor's level gaze.

"He'll suffocate, man!" the physician warned, looking quickly at the interpreter to deliver his message. Still, the answer was no. No!

Several other treatments were recommended. Each time Dr. Strobel received the same answer. No.

Osceola delivered himself into Che-cho-ter's hands knowing his life was over, wanting it to be. The dark shadow that had chased him these past moons was closer now. He thought of his family, of his children, and still the darkness that seemed to be just beyond the circle of light loomed threateningly. His throat pained him gravely; the fever was raging in his body. The end was near.

Unable to speak, he looked deeply into Che-cho-ter's eyes. With motions of his hands, he signified that he wished for the chiefs and officers of the post. Pointing to where his war dress was laying, he glanced once again at Che-cho-ter. He wanted to wear them when the end came. He wanted to leave this world dressed for battle, not wrapped in a blanket like a woman at birthing time. With the last bit of his strength, he sat up in bed, helping to dress himself in his shirt, his bright red leggings and his moccasins.

Ina, the old woman whom Osceola had married to

save her from the privations of widowhood, wrapped
his war belt around his narrow waist-and attached his
bullet pouch and powder horn. His hunting knife was
reverently placed beside him on the cold stone floor.

In a final gesture of defiance, Osceola signaled for a
looking glass and his red and yellow paints. He streaked
the vivid colors across his face and throat, a ceremony
denoting the irrevocable oath of war. Shaking hands
held his knife for the last time, placing it in its sheath
under his belt. Carefully, with the ease of long practice,
he arranged his turban on his head, aided by Che-cho-
ter who placed three feathered plumes which were an
insignia of his status among the Seminoles.

Fully prepared, he turned to his wives, sharing with
them a last moment of understanding. He made a signal
for them to lower him down onto his pallet. Slow,
unsteady hands grasped his knife and held it to his
chest. Despite the obvious pain, he smiled, giving up
his last breath without a struggle or a sound.


The *Polly Copinger* had been anchored in the port of
Charleston since the day Osceola had been led to Fort
Moultrie. Although Sloan and Savannah were not
permitted to see him, they were determined to remain
close by. Sometimes, Sloan secretly thought of their
vigil as a death watch; reports were frequent of Osceola's failing health.

On this day, Sloan felt a prickling at the nape of his
neck and his feet itched to touch dry land, but most of
all, he had a desperate need for word of his brother.

Savannah joined her husband on deck, the cold
Atlantic air ruffling the stray curls near her cheeks. She
was wearing a thick woolen shawl around her shoulders, and the somber brown of her gown seemed to
reflect her emotions. Gypsy green eyes searched the
horizon as her hands found warmth within Sloan's.
"Soon," she whispered, "his suffering will come to an
end."

Taking her into his embrace, Sloan was aware of her

thickening waistline and of the new life that grew within her. On the night she had told him she was with child, she had cried, great gulping sobs racking her body. Alarmed, he had held her against him, pleading with her to tell him why she was so unhappy. "I have everything a woman can want," she told him. "A man I love, a marriage, and now a child. Everything, and the Seminole have nothing. Not even a future."

Port Charleston was a barren harbor, all the leaves from the trees long gone since the onset of winter. Sloan felt depressed as he waved to Savannah from the dock. It was bitter cold and his teeth chattered. He didn't know if it was from apprehension or from the weather. The sooner he got a newspaper, the sooner he would know.

Inside the lobby of the closest hotel he asked for the latest paper. The banner headline shook him to his very toes. "Seminole Chief dies at Fort Moultrie." He laid a bill on the counter, but not before the startled desk clerk noticed the tears in the metallic eyes. They slipped down Sloan's cheeks and he made no move to wipe at them. The freezing cold air crystallized them and still they flowed. He walked blindly down the long, deserted street back toward the *Polly Copinger* and to Savannah. Always to Savannah. How was he to tell her?

His step lagged and he had to force himself to grasp the rope handrail to help him gain momentum. Once aboard, he sought her out. She asked no questions, correctly interpreting his news from the slump of his shoulders and his glistening eyes.

In the end it was Savannah who comforted Sloan. "Your brother's spirit lives on. It will never die as long as there is a Seminole to walk the earth. Already the chiefs are reuniting under one cause of action. Surely, you read that in your newspaper."

"How do you know this?" Sloan asked, bewildered by Savannah's calm acceptance of Osceola's death.

"Because he knew this is what would happen. You

forget, my husband, I lived among the Seminole for many years. Osceola was all things to me. One learns to read the signs. He wanted peace."

Savannah stood on the deck of the *Polly* for a very long time. She had realized Sloan's need to be alone and respected it. He had gone below to be alone with his grief and his memories. The gray sky had deepened to ash and the evening was calm and still; hardly a breeze rocked the *Polly* on her moorings. Gentle white flakes were falling onto Savannah's nose and shoulders. Snow. Soon it would blanket the earth with its purity, making everything seem bright and clean. She thought it symbolic that today of all days it should snow. Such a thing was a rarity in this region, and she herself had only witnessed it once before. Perhaps God and the Spirits had sent the snow to cover the dismal failures of the past and to bring hope to the future.

Gathering her skirts around her, Savannah crept below. It was time. He had been alone long enough. Soon now, his need for her would rise and she must be there for him.

Slipping into the cabin, she found him asleep on their bed. The gentle glow from the lamp revealed his grief ravaged face, the bitter line of his mouth. Silently, she unfastened her gown, stepping out of it, feeling a sudden chill against the flesh her petticoats and chemisette did not cover. Sliding into the bed alongside him, she pressed her body against his, offering warmth and consolation.

He stirred and reached out a muscular arm to bring her closer, bringing her head onto his chest and kissing the soft golden curls that lay so sweetly on the gentle curve of her neck. She heard him sigh, felt the sudden rise of his chest against her cheek. Instinctively, he tightened his embrace, whispering her name softly. "Savannah," he whispered huskily, "come closer. Let me love you." His mouth closed hungrily over hers, blazing a path to her throat. And always he whispered her name, beckoning to her, calling for her love.

Long afterward, he lay beside her, resting his head between her breasts, his hand lovingly caressing the gentle swell of her belly where their child slept. No words were wanted, none were needed. As long as they could be together like this and their love could reach out to one another, they could look to the future and live with the past.

# Epilogue

Osceola was never conquered, although he died in prison, a victim of treachery and deceit. The Seminoles never surrendered as a nation, and the United States Government was unsuccessful in its goal of removing the Indians from Florida. Despite white greed, despite dishonor, the Seminoles were the victors. Osceola's death did not end the Second Seminole War, instead his spirit inspired his people to continue their fight. In the end Osceola won his war. His people were never vanquished.